By the same author

Novels
Under the Rainbow
Family
Before Natasha
Smiles and the Millennium
Loving Mephistopheles (Peter Owen)
Nina in Utopia (first in the 'Bedlam Trilogy'; Peter Owen)

Short Stories
A Thousand and One Coffee Mornings (Peter Owen)

Non-fiction
Bed and Breakfast: Women and Homelessness Today

THE FAIRY VISIONS
of
RICHARD DADD

a novel by
MIRANDA MILLER

PETER OWEN
London and Chicago

PETER OWEN PUBLISHERS
81 Ridge Road, London N8 9NP

Peter Owen books are distributed in the USA and Canada by
Independent Publishers Group/Trafalgar Square
814 North Franklin Street, Chicago, IL 60610, USA

First published in Great Britain 2013 by
Peter Owen Publishers

ISBN 978-0-7206-1503-6

A catalogue record for this book is available from the British Library

Typeset by Octavo Smith Ltd in
Constantia 9.5/13.5 (text) and Engravers MT 18/13.5 (display)

Printed and bound in the UK by
CPI Group (UK) Ltd, Croydon, CR0 4YY

For Gordon

'Novels arise out of the shortcomings of history.'
– Novalis, *Fragmente und Studien*

AUTHOR'S NOTE

Richard Dadd's murder of his father in August 1843 caused a sensation. The 26-year-old artist had studied at the Royal Academy Schools and had many friends and admirers in the art world. Dadd was committed to the Criminal Lunatic Department of Bethlem Hospital, popularly known by generations of Londoners as Bedlam. He was later removed to Broadmoor, where he stayed until his death in 1886. Throughout those years of isolation and captivity Dadd continued to draw and paint, encouraged by his doctors, several of whom collected his work, and his reputation as an artist has soared as attitudes to mental illness have changed. His work can now be found in a number of major galleries including Tate Britain and the Louvre in Paris. In May 2013 the Metropolitan Museum in New York bought one of his watercolours.

I have known and admired Dadd's mysterious painting *The Fairy Feller's Master-Stroke* for many years. When I was writing my sixth novel, *Nina in Utopia*, the first in the 'Bedlam Trilogy', I felt a shock of recognition when I discovered that Dadd would have been in Bedlam at the same time as my fictional heroine. Nina is a young Victorian woman who, traumatized by the death of her daughter, finds herself in London in 2006. There she meets Jonathan and, as a tourist in our century, believes she is visiting a Utopia, free from poverty and violence. When she returns to 1853 Nina speaks of her experiences, and her husband, Charles, has her committed to Bedlam.

More on Richard Dadd and the background to this novel can be found in the Afterword.

I could not have written this novel without reading Patricia Allderidge's scholarly book *The Late Richard Dadd*, published to accompany the first ever exhibition of his work at the Tate Gallery in 1974, which she curated. Colin Gale at the Bethlem Royal Hospital Archives has been extremely helpful, and I would also like to thank Sylvia Hammond at Cobham Hall who kindly sent me a list of the paintings Dadd would have seen there. George Henry Haydon remained a shadowy figure until I was lucky enough to find *George Henry Haydon (1822–1891): An Anglo-Australian Life*, a 2008 thesis written by his descendant Katherine Haydon. Nicholas Tromans's excellent book *Richard Dadd: The Artist and the Asylum* (Tate Publishing, 2011) examines both Dadd's art and his mental illness in depth. Another invaluable source was William Powell Frith's *My Autobiography and Reminiscences*. This entertaining account of the nineteenth-century art world went into several editions, and in the 1888 edition, after Richard's death, there is a chapter about him. I have also referred to *Suggestions for the Future Provision of Criminal Lunatics* by William Charles Hood (1854), to the letters Richard wrote to friends from abroad and have quoted from his long rambling poem 'Elimination of a Picture and Its Subject – Called the Feller's Master Stroke'.

I would like to thank my son-in-law, Dr Jonathan Rohrer, for reading this Preface and my brother, Timothy Hyman, RA, for reading the manuscript. I am also grateful to Peter Owen, Antonia Owen, Simon Smith, Michael O'Connell and all at Peter Owen for their support of my work.

1
THE WONDER OF HIGH HARROGATE

He strides across the floor so confidently that at first I think he is a new member of our exclusive little community. Oxford, who is practising his violin, puts his instrument down to stare at him.

The stranger ignores Oxford and walks straight towards me. He carries a black leather bag, capacious enough to contain his clothes and possessions, but he is too buckishly dressed, too full of brio, to belong among us. The fellow is about my age; too old to be young. His hair clings to his pink scalp in two shrinking bushes above a long clean-shaven face with thin lips and shrewd, calculating eyes. A self-made businessman puffing on a fat cigar to flourish his money at us. His smoke precedes him like the steam around a frantic engine. Instinctively, I cover the painting on my easel.

'What brings you here? Have you killed anybody?'

'My dear old friend!'

Then I know him by his Yorkshire accent that has not been smoothed down with the rest of him.

'I have no friends.'

Neville, our chief attendant, rushes in through the door at the end of the long gallery and pauses to calm an altercation between Jonson and Eggars who have grown bored with hitting billiard balls and who are attacking one another's heads with their cues instead. Neville comes to stand in our smoky corner, and I feel his calm warmth behind my right shoulder. My hands, bereft of my paint-brush, dangle awkwardly. Powell grasps my right hand and crushes it with such force that I squirm and shake it free, afraid he will damage my fingers.

'Mr Frith has come to see you, Mr Dadd,' Neville says in his neutral way, drawing up a chair to chaperone us. 'It is not permitted to smoke in the hospital, sir,' he adds.

Powell is confused, stubbing out his cigar in a spittoon as he beams at me with a warmth I do not pretend to return. 'Do you know me now, my dear Richard?'

A useful man for you to know, says my father. *A fiery demon come to destroy you,* Osiris roars. I have learned to ignore them, but Powell's voice is more insistent.

'I've been intending for years to visit you in your chamber of horrors. Not such a bad place really. And I see you still amuse yourself by painting. Excellent! May I see?'

I shake my head.

He gazes around M4 with eyes hungry for sensation. 'Have you any subjects for me? They must be interesting and sympathetic. I pay thirty shillings for two sittings.'

Neville, Oxford and Rowlands, who are within hearing range, attempt to look interesting.

'Perhaps you could do a crowd scene – *A Day in Purgatory.*'

'I think not. Pictures with too many men and no pretty females are unsaleable.'

'But what a lot of morals could be drawn.'

'I'm inundated with commissions. Can't find the time to paint Dickens, although he has begged me to. Forster wants me to wait until he's clean-shaven; says he's far more handsome without his beard.'

Powell was always inclined to drop the name of anybody he had met for five minutes. I give him no encouragement, but he brags on, sits forward on his easy chair and breathes the Stilton and brandy fumes of a good lunch all over me as I withdraw on to my wooden chair, stroking the edge of my canvas through its cover. 'Egg sends his regards and hopes you are . . .'

I am obviously not, but Powell carries on anyway. Light come, light go. 'I often remember our discussions about art when we were boys. How you were all for the imagination, and I only wanted to paint the golden olden times, what Leech calls my mouldy costumes. I was afraid of modern life, of the general unpicturesqueness of trousers and hats and steam trains and cotton mills. Well, do you know, a few summers back I went on holiday to Ramsgate with my family and changed my mind.'

I do not give him the satisfaction of telling him that an engraving of his big daub *Life at the Seaside* hangs in our corridor.

'Of course, I never read my reviews.' He always did claim to be little taken with worldly applause while fishing vigorously for it. 'But it was a great hit, and as long as my paintings sell I don't care what people say about them. Sold it to a dealer for a hundred guineas and then to the Queen herself! She adores it, and I had a long chat with the Prince. Such a cultivated mind. Knows all about art and music and suchlike.'

I glance at Oxford, who is sitting a yard away studying German. 'Now that you are moving in royal circles you must meet Edward Oxford.'

'What did he do?' Powell leans forward, eager for horrid gossip.

'Tried to assassinate the Queen. Missed, though, didn't you, old chap?'

Oxford nods and returns to his German. Powell would like to ask more questions but is afraid that too much curiosity about attempted royal assassinations will lose him his knighthood.

'So, you've become a snob, Powell?'

'Not a bit of it. Can't bear aristocrats. They all think artists ought to live in a garret and dine off red herrings. They'd rather visit their dressmakers than me, always turning up late for sittings. Yesterday Lady Fitzwhatsit mistook my wife for a parlourmaid and told me I should dismiss her.'

'You are married. Have you any children?'

'Very much so. Nine I think it was at the last count – and a new baby on the way. Perhaps you do not know, your dear sister has been for some years a member of our household – your elder sister, that is. Miss Dadd is our governess.'

Poor Mary Ann. She always hated children and is doomed to spend her life among them. I suspect him of condescension and kindness. He must have employed her as some kind of favour to me. Rebecca never writes to me, but I have heard that she, too, never married and is sentenced to life as a governess.

13

'I did not know. My family . . .' What a ridiculous word. Of course, they cannot bear to visit me or George. They are ashamed. 'Have you any news of Maria?'

When we were students she was a beauty, and all my friends were a little in love with her. John Phillip carried her off, so I heard, but I have not seen her since she was twenty-two. She sends me parcels of brushes, paints, herrings and peppermints, enclosing notes that give very little information.

He looks pained. The news must be catastrophic.

'Have you seen my sister?' I ask again, remembering her vivid presence.

'Phillip is doing well. No longer Aberdeen Johnnie but Phillip of Spain. He visits Seville frequently and does a roaring trade in ladies in mantillas, duennas, matadors and so on.'

'And does my sister accompany him on these *vacaciones*?'

'I don't really know. I did hear she has been unwell.'

'Do you mean that she is ill?'

Powell lowers his eyes. Charming little Maria, so bright and loving. I remember now that there were danger signals: my sister believed she was being persecuted by the Jesuits and the clergy. I loved her because she had an imagination, unlike my other sisters. Phantasy, the Dadd curse. Perhaps she will join us here.

'I must say, Richard, you look awfully well.' He means to charm and please; he always did. Suddenly I see him as he was at eighteen. Thick eyebrows over clever eyes, dark-brown hair, a sensitive and slight figure. His appearance was considered homely, and I was thought handsome. Now it makes not the slightest difference.

He looks into my face as if he also glimpses the phantom of our boyhood. His voice softens. 'Do you remember when we were students and had adjoining painting-rooms in Charlotte Street? We were like brothers, brother artists, and saw each other every day. A tap on my wall would bring you with ready suggestions to relieve my pictorial difficulties. I was always in trouble, and you always knew what to do. Such talent and common sense you had, although you were always such a singular fish.'

We cannot bear to look at each other after that. Powell hums and stands up. I hope he is about to leave, but then I see he is going to do one of his acts and get ready not to laugh.

'Yes, art pays, Richard, that's one thing I've learned since we were boys. I've a splendid dealer now, Flatow, a good, fat, vulgar little Jew.' Powell becomes him, speaking in a nasal cockney, 'Lor' bless you, there ain't a dealer in town as knows 'ow to manipulate a customer better. You must walk around them, like a cooper walks around a tub. It's me and my money as will make the picture go.'

Powell was always a gifted mimic, and, unwillingly, I do laugh. A rusty sound.

'What sort of a view do you have from your windows? Can't see much of the city out here, can you?'

To me, when they first moved me up here a few months ago, it seemed a miracle to be able to see anything at all.

'Yes, London's the place. I'd never live anywhere else now. Do you remember when we first arrived here as boys? I was the wonder of High Harrogate, and my dear old father insisted I had to be an artist, although I'd just as soon have followed his trade.' I can just see him as a jolly inn-keeper. 'And you, Richard, were the Michelangelo of Chatham. How we longed to make a hit of our lives. There was never much of the sacred fire about me, but you were always of the high-aim school. These swells, you know, the ones as buys my paintings, all they want is something to impress their guests with. If it was the fashion to hang up a flitch of bacon in their drawing-room they'd do it. One fellow – made his money in biscuits, I think it was – bought my *Pope Makes Love to Lady Mary Wortley Montagu* and said to me, chuckling as he handed over the cheque, "Fancy that! The Pope having an affair with a married woman!"'

Encouraged by my laughter, Powell brags. You'd think he had bought London: *my* night watchman, *my* beggar girl, *my* crossing sweeper. On and on he goes. 'I walk the streets of London looking for my victims. Yes, you have to find just the right face. That pretty girl who posed for *The Sleeping Model* – found her on the Strand selling oranges – she was happy to sit for a month's wages, but she couldn't keep her eyes open. So I made the best of it. And when she woke up, do you know what she said? She said, "Gentlemen is much greater black-guards than what blackguards is."' Was that a guilty laugh? Powell was always lustful. 'I'd like to cram all that glorious life on the streets of London into a picture. Like Hogarth. I'd love to paint a street in London at every time of the night and day as he did and show absolutely everything.'

'You couldn't, Powell. Hogarth was strong meat, and your patrons wouldn't like that. They want sugared water and bread and butter with their tragedy – and a comfortable moral. Such scenes as Hogarth's would not be proper for the eyes of a British matron. She wants pictures to hang on the wall of her home.' From which I am for ever banished.

He looks surprised that I still have a voice, and he is no longer used to being criticized. 'I know I'm not a great painter, but I do adore watching crowds. I want to portray them – not caricatures as Leech does for *Punch* but as they really are; all sorts and conditions of men and women. Life itself. My photographer can do it. Last year we went to the Derby together, and in just a few hours he captured the whole splendid panorama: horses, pickpockets, swells, beggars, duchesses, gypsies. Ever been to the Derby?'

'No. The season rather passes us by up here. So you've become a racing man?'

'Oh, I'm not horsey. I go to see the bipeds not the quadrupeds. And I enjoy the hamper from Fortnum and Mason.' My mouth waters. 'But most of all it's watching the people, thousands of 'em sleeping in the open the night before. German bands, hurdy-gurdy players, organ grinders, gypsies, tramps, beggars, costermongers . . . You'll do, Richard.'

'Do for what?'

He fumbles in his large black-leather bag, brings out a sketch-book and some chalks. 'For the crowd in my Derby-day painting. My photographer caught the outlines, and I use them as an *aide-memoire*, but I'm putting flesh on them, colouring them in and bringing them to life. I shall do you in a fez. I need a spot of red up on the left there.' My criminal lunatic.

'I hope you're going to pay me.'

He puts his hand in his pocket and brings out fifteen shillings, which he hands to me. I have nothing whatsoever to spend it on, but I shall add it to the fifty-three pounds I have earned over the past fourteen years selling my work to the doctors here.

Powell and I used to sit like this for hours, drawing each other. It feels as if nobody has really looked at me since. My fingers twitch for a piece of chalk or a brush to explore his face with, but he would want to see my work, and I cannot bear to expose it to him.

'Phrenology, Richard, that's the science that unlocks the mysteries of the soul.' Mysteries of which he has never been aware. 'Fascinating. I've been going to craniological seances on Tuesday evenings when this scientist chap takes off someone's head.'

'I trust he puts it back on again.'

Powell laughs obligingly. The air between us quivers with dead intimacy.

'Most of what he says is miles high over my head, but I'm convinced there's a deal of truth in it. Face is a sure index of character. Why, just look around you at the low and villainous brows of the criminally inclined. Nature has written gentleman on some faces, criminal upon others.' He appears to think that my fellow inmates have lost their hearing as well as their freedom.

'I am of the opinion that there is a great deal secret in the matter. Faces hide far more than they reveal.'

Powell turns to Neville and discusses him as if he was an umbrella stand. 'This fellow, for example. The length from the ear to the eyebrows denotes intellectual grasp. A long, straight upper lip signifies moral purpose. But his snub nose is characteristic of children, savages and the uneducated. Such a nose indicates defective intellectual power and prevents him from rising in the world. Wellington could not have won Waterloo without his colossal fighting nasal organ. Good looks in a servant indicate good blood –'

'He is not a servant but the chief attendant here.' Neville has wiped my arse and fed me when I was unwell and listened to my childhood reminiscences for hours. He cannot very well defend himself but flushes with embarrassment. 'And what of your own face? I see you've lost most of your hair and eaten too many rich dinners. There's a great swilling of spirits and liquor evident in your nasal organ, and the domestic faculties are not well developed in your bumps. Sherry, sir?'

He is not offended but laughs at this reference to one of his early potboilers. Powell is so happy that nothing I say can wound him. 'Dear Richard, how good it is to sit with you like this again. So you have managed to go on painting for all these years. Will you show me your work?'

'No.'

'I ask only because I might be able to help you.' You ask only because you want to make quite sure that you have triumphed over me.

He draws me in silence for a while, and my voices, which have been crushed by the great blast of his self-love, resume their war inside my head. *You see what kind of life you could have had, my boy, if only you had listened to me.* My father was never a man to leave the obvious unsaid. Osiris snarls and gnashes his teeth, which makes my own teeth ache. *You should kill him now while you have the chance. He has a palette knife somewhere in that immense bag. Find it and stab him!*

I must speak, if only to reclaim my own head. 'I heard that poor old Turner died a few years back. Captain Crumble, bow-legged and with a nose like Punch. Do you remember what a figure of fun he was for us when we were at the Academy?'

'An opinion I have never revised – although I do owe him something, for I was elected to the Royal Academy to take his place when he died.' Powell smirks and waits for the congratulations I do not give him. 'I thought his late works as insane as the people who admire them. Well, they say his mother died in Bed . . .' A pause when he glances around him and looks abashed; but not for long. 'Those seascapes are so wild, altogether formless and eccentric. Painted with soapsuds, whitewash, currant jelly and excrement. That is to say, not painted at all.'

'No, Powell, you are wrong. He painted with the very elements, with rain and sun and mist and moonlight and cloud.'

'One can't expect the public to accept such ravings. When he died he left a whole leaking gallery of paintings he couldn't sell.'

'And yet he was a very great painter. I admire his late works.'

'Richard, that is ridiculous! Besides, you cannot have seen them.'

'Haydon, our steward, has shown me engravings and copies. They have a power and vision that will outlive banal representations of modern life.' I would give anything to see them in the flesh. If only I could lock Powell up in one of these cubicles, steal his clothes and walk around London for a day.

'Nonsense! People love modern art, and, of course, the best of it is British. I should not boast about my own work –'

'It is a little late, Powell, when you have been sitting here for the last hour boasting . . .'

'Egg, for example, shares my enthusiasm for pictures that tell a story about real people in the real world. He's working on a marvellous triptych that shows the tragic outcome of female adultery. How I wish you could see it. A woman falls from respectable married life to destitution. Most affecting. I do not always agree with Egg. I can't understand why he admires Holman Hunt and his namby-pamby Brotherhood –'

'Again, you are mistaken. Those young men are wonderful colourists, and their paintings are full of poetry. They are right to try to return to a purity that has long been lost and to reject the rigid laws of Sir Sloshua.'

'You're becoming overexcited, my dear fellow. I'm merely defending art that is pleasant and moral. Mark my words, the fools who are rushing to buy Rossetti and Hunt are making a very poor investment.'

'All you can talk about is money! They are young. Of course they want to do something new and idealistic. Have you forgotten how we felt when we were students at the Academy? How we hated Sir Sloshua and all he stood for and raged and vowed to invent a new kind of painting that would take the world by storm. All those evenings when we ate bread and cheese and drank beer and stayed up until dawn discussing art and God and love and . . .' I am on my feet now, waving my arms at Powell, furious with him for betraying our ideals.

Neville jumps up to restrain me, and my father says, *Sir Joshua was a great man, Richard. You must not mock him, or you will never get on in the world and provide dowries for your sisters.* Powell is packing up his bag and trying to escape when I knock the cloth that hides my painting, and it is revealed. My crowd scene.

Of course, Powell stares at it, and I turn my back on him, shut my eyes, try not to see him or hear his comments.

'Still in the fairy department, Richard?' He laughs, and I turn on him in a fury. He dances around my canvas, an expression of gleeful malice on his face as he sings in a hearty music-hall style, 'Oh, the fairies, whoa the fairies, / Nothing but splendour and feminine gender.'

He has insulted my painting, and I will never forgive him. No fairy would bother to visit him, for he stands in one world only. His voice fades as I hear their giggling, rustling, whispering, shameless, tormenting voices. They are refugees from his age of reason and progress. Like me, they seek asylum.

'Mawkish stuff, Richard. I would have hoped that your bitter experience might have taught you to see life with a straighter eye. Richard? You will not speak to me?'

I struggle with the rising vomit of my rage and hatred, but my words spew out in ugly confusion. I shout and rave. I am no better than the other imbeciles here, and the sharp knives in my head will not come out of my mouth.

Powell backs away nervously. 'Well, I must be off. Egg and I are going to the theatre tonight to see *A Midsummer-night's Dream* – more blasted fairies. Delightful actress playing Titania, such a pretty figure and altogether so paintable. Richard Ansdell's to come first thing in the morning to finish off the dogs – such a bore painting animals – so I must be up early. Richard? Sorry if I've offended you. I have a present for you. I will leave it here. You won't look at me? Well, I have enjoyed our meeting. Goodbye, my friend.'

I stand with my back to him, staring at the wall, which seethes with angry, buzzing, humming, hissing, spitting, venomous fairies. They do not like to be insulted either. My head is about to explode with pain, my heart thunders, my mouth is dry, and I'm so dizzy I think I will fall.

'Mr Dadd? He has gone now. Will you come and lie down in your cubicle? I will keep your supper for you, and you can have it later. Come and rest. Look, Mr Frith left this parcel for you.'

I feel Neville's strong hand gentle on my arm as he guides me to oblivion.

2
DR HOOD'S
NOCTURNAL

My lodge meeting finished at ten. When at last I passed through the door to our own little house in the portico of the hospital the children were in bed and Jane sat at the table in the dining-room, surrounded by letters and lists of statistics, compiling the weekly journal for the governors. She works as hard as I do, and I rely on her calm and powerful intelligence. When she looked up from her labours her face was haggard and her dark eyes bloodshot from too much reading. I went to her and felt her slender body in my arms, making me strong again. All day as I go about my business on the other side of the wall it comforts me to think of her.

'Have you eaten?'

'I think I forgot.'

'Really, Billy, you sound like one of your patients.' She brought me a chop with a glass of wine and a bowl of rice pudding.

'How are the children?'

'The boys rampage and are happy. Louisa sews and is not.'

'At her age it is natural for a girl to be sullen.'

'She says she wants to help you with your work.'

'She can hardly accompany me. Perhaps she could help you with our interminable paperwork when she has finished her sampler and piano practice.'

'She says she wants to be a doctor like you, Billy.'

'How absurd. Who has been putting such ideas into her head?'

'Ideas have a life of their own. And you might say that Louisa was born with such ideas.'

The subject of Louisa's birth is not one that I care to dwell on. We have told her that she is Jane's younger sister, orphaned when their parents died of the cholera. 'In the autumn we will send her back to school. We can't afford more than another year of education for her if we are to pay the boys' school fees. It is not healthy for her to spend all her time here. She needs to make friends of her own age and join in normal social activities.'

'You have no idea what they are, Billy, and neither have I.'

'Then we must find out. Girls go to dances, don't they? At-homes, tea parties, those sorts of things.'

'Louisa is never invited to anything. She is considered odd.'

'We must train her to be normal. Perhaps in a few years she will marry some young doctor and be a support to him – as you are to me.'

'She says she will never marry and tells me I am stupid to put your name to letters and articles I have written myself.'

'I always intended to give her a thorough and rational education – but not to make a monster of her.'

'She says she wants to do useful work and not make pies and babies.'

'Then she has had more than enough education, and we must watch her carefully.'

'Neville was here looking for you.'

'I meant to ask him about Frith's visit to Dadd, but I had no time.'

'He told me about it. He said, "If I hadn't played the duenna, madam, them two would of come to blows."' My Jane has a sharp ear and sounded just like the excellent head attendant with his slow West-Country vowels. '"I remembered them drawings the police found in Mr Dadd's rooms after it happened, every last one of his friends, Frith among them, with a slash of red across his throat. And that list they found, of them as was to die, with his pa's name at the top the list followed by all his friends and the Emperor of Austria. So I sat and I played the wise monkey, and I listened to every word, and that Mr Frith was very provoking. Teased him about his fairies and bragged about his grand friends and got poor Mr Dadd so excited I thought he was going to wallop Mr Frith."'

'I had such high hopes of their reunion. Frith has been writing to me for years, begging to be allowed to visit his old friend. I hear from Haydon that he has had great success as a painter, although his private life leaves much to be desired. He has nine children by his wife and five more by a mistress. He insisted on being allowed to visit the ward instead of meeting Dadd in the waiting-room like an ordinary mortal. These great men imagine they honour us with their presence when they only bring their anger and strife inside our fragile little community. How is Dadd now?'

'Neville says he slept all evening and had a fit of weeping when he woke up.'

'At least he wakes up in decent surroundings.'

Jane reached across the dining table and gripped my hand. More than rice pudding, I need her belief in me. 'Billy, it's wonderful what you've done for them. Compared with that dreadful Home Office dungeon, M4 is paradise.' Her eyes filled with tears because she knows, better than any of us on this side of the wall, what it is like to be a sensitive person in brutal surroundings.

'You are tired, my darling. I must write some letters. It is not enough to improve the lot of a handful of outcasts. We must change the way that all the insane are cared for. Go to bed, and I will join you soon.'

'Let me stay a while and watch you. For you know you won't sleep more than a couple of hours, and I shan't see you again until tomorrow night.'

'Sleep is a luxury.'

I turned up the lamp and worked on the draft of my pamphlet about the treatment of criminal lunatics. After a while I saw that Jane had fallen asleep where she sat, her head on her arms. Her brown hair had come down and flowed over the green tablecloth as if she was reaching out to me even in sleep. I stretched out my hand across the fruit bowl to touch a soft tentacle, put down my pen, went over to her and whispered, 'I'm going to put you to bed as if you were Donald.'

I lifted her out of her chair and half carried her to the bedroom. Every day I examine the bodies of men and women, seeing and touching what Donald calls their wicked places. Ever since I was a medical student human anatomy has been as much of a mystery as a tub of lard. Only Jane's slender, creamy body still moves me.

I unwrapped her as tenderly as I did that first night. She was too tired to be amorous but allowed me to undress her and lay her in our bed, where she smiled and blinked at me before falling asleep again. I sat beside her in the dark with her hand in mine, longing to lie beside her all night but knowing that I would not be able to sleep for the tables of figures dancing before my eyes. Our little house quivered and vibrated with the breath and dreams of my sleeping wife and children.

In my study I searched through the tables of statistics Jane has copied out for me. My vision of a magnificent building that is a hospital not a prison in the middle of the countryside, where criminal lunatics can be usefully employed and humanely understood, must be built on numbers and logic.

From the window of my study I could see the looming shadows of the male and female criminal blocks and drew the curtains against their reproach. The loss of liberty for life is a fearful doom. Those dark buildings, unhealthy and overcrowded, are our skeleton cupboards. The law that built them is an ass that must be whacked into the nineteenth century.

My new pamphlet deals with the issue of criminals who feign insanity and who are detained indefinitely at Her Majesty's pleasure and our exasperation. We all see through their pretended madness but have no powers to transfer them to the hulks or back to prison. Dadd told me they call our criminal block the Golden Bank, for compared with Newgate or Millbank it is comfortable. Freed from working and plentifully fed, the criminals live long at the expense of the nation.

In that dismal Home Office block sleeps John Ferguson, a worthless man who murdered a warder at Millbank Prison while awaiting transportation. He has spent the greater part of his life in prison, his moral character is infamous and debased, and he would gladly sacrifice the life of any fellow inmate or attendant to give colour to his pretended insanity. Here we wish to treat all the inmates with gentleness and kindness, but Ferguson is so depraved that he can only be controlled by stern discipline. He is no more insane than I am. Such men are given the useful label of insanity on the evidence of medical 'specialists', a modern and very undesirable sobriquet. After examining the accused for an hour or two the specialist is hurried into the witness-box to give his opinion before a learned judge, an astute and adverse counsel and a perplexed jury. Some of the most delicate questions of psychological science are thus decided in less time than one would devote to hiring a new housemaid.

Shouts and screams disrupted my writing, and I jumped up, terrified. In my recurring nightmare a screaming mob of lunatics breaks into our house to attack Jane and our sleeping children. Our hospital used to be known as England's Bastille, and although conditions are much improved 'The Storming of Bethlem' plays nightly in my sleep. I am ashamed of such fears, but they are fuelled by these reports of the rebellion in India, of innocent wives and of little ones slaughtered by devils.

I opened the front door of our house on to the vast lobby. A dreadful caterwauling was coming from the male galleries. For a moment I feared that Angus Mackay had returned and was filling the hospital with his barbarous pipes. Mackay was our dear Queen's First Piper, sent here soon after my arrival as superintendent. Under the influence of ardent spirits he insisted that he was married to our beloved monarch and that the royal children were really his, Prince Albert being an impostor who had defrauded Mackay of his marital rights. The man's brain was rotten with whisky and syphilis, and all night he would serenade our hospital with his hideous tune, 'The Laying of the Foundation Stone at Balmoral'. I managed to have him transferred to Crichton in Dumfries, arguing that he would be nearer to his actual wife and four children. The poor fellow escaped from the asylum one night and was drowned in the River Nith.

So this cannot be Mackay, I thought, as I galloped up the stairs to the men's galleries. There was some kind of instrument, not bagpipes, something high and screechy. I followed the trail of noise to M4 and opened the door upon uproar.

Jim, who is paid to watch the patients all night and make sure they do not commit suicide, had arrived just before me and was trying to prevent Oxford from playing his violin while Dadd howled with grief and the others, all wide awake, shouted, laughed, fought and roared. Jonson, who was a sea captain until he murdered all his crew, was dancing some kind of hornpipe, and Daniel McNaughton was yelling wild oaths and performing a Highland fling.

McNaughton is a crazed Glaswegian whose delusion that he was being persecuted by the Tories and followed by their spies led to his attempt to assassinate Peel. His actual victim was Edward Drummond, Peel's private secretary, but I have heard McNaughton boast of having killed the Prime Minister and of being the only man in the hospital to have Rules named after him. Indeed his case made legal history – but I digress.

It was a scene that one might come across at midnight in any of the squalid Lambeth taverns around here, but in my hospital it spelled disaster. I strode into the ward and glared at Oxford and Dadd. They had never seen me in a rage before, and it had some effect. The insane are very sensitive – perhaps it is the cause of all their woes. Oxford put down his fiddle, and I looked straight into Dadd's large blue eyes.

'What disgrace is this? Have you already forgotten your privileges here? There is no privilege without responsibility, gentlemen.' At this word they all became calmer. 'All of you remember your previous lives.' I walked over to the window, drew the curtains and pointed to the Home Office block. 'There it is, gentlemen, dark both within and without, awaiting your return. Do you wish to go back there?'

I looked around at all forty of them, into eyes that were frightened and angry and hurt and lonely. They stood now in a semi-circle, gazing back at me in silence.

'I know what you suffered over there. For four years I watched you and petitioned great men to have you moved. My argument was that you should not be kept in such conditions, cheek by jowl with common criminals, louts and bullies and brutes. I wrote that you were educated men, restrained and refined, and deserved better treatment. I went to great trouble and expense on your behalf. I moved patients into other galleries to make room for you here. Look around you, gentlemen. Listen to the birds that are twittering in their cages, alarmed by your pandemonium. Look around you at the flowers, pictures, carpets and glazed windows.

'When you first came here, just a few months ago, I remember your wonder that prison could be so civilized. Well, this is not a prison; it is a hospital for men and women who have been ill but who, with the help of God, may yet recover. It is on the same staircase as the chapel, which you may visit at any time to refresh your spirits.' I glanced at Dadd. Our conversations about religion have not been satisfactory. He refuses to attend services and insists that Osiris, an Egyptian god, would not allow him to set foot in a Christian church.

'You all know that your life here is far better than it was in the old block where only the most brutal and depraved criminals remain. Behave like savages, and you will rejoin them. Behave like gentlemen, and you may stay here for the rest of your lives, with your billiard table and your library and wholesome food brought to you three times a day. Now go to bed and remember what will happen if you disturb our community at night again.'

I waited until they had all gone into their sleeping-cubicles, then turned and left M4. Outside the door I paused to listen for noise, but there was none.

'Will I go to check on the ladies' galleries now, Dr Hood, sir?'

'Thank you, Jim. I will follow.'

Jim is a poor broken-down old Irishman, toothless and mal-odorous, who lost a leg building the railway at Camden Town and has but one on which he hops around the hospital all night on his melancholy task. He is rough but kind, and quite a few tragedies have been averted by his presence.

The insane are often tempted by the crime of self-murder, and I am proud that I have reduced the number of suicides in the hospital. Under the old Monro regime there were far too many. The terrible ingenuity of those who would destroy themselves – using braces, shoe strings, shirts torn into strips – requires our constant vigilance. We must watch over the patients always. It is one of the reasons why I prowl around my hospital at night. Sadly, this sense of being watched appears to increase the urge to self-destruction. Women are particularly vulnerable in this respect, for self-sacrifice comes naturally to one who spends her life yielding to the will and consulting the pleasures of another.

If I thought there was no afterlife I would have more sympathy for those who have not the willpower to continue with life. But I think of Dante's 'The Wood of Suicides'. Since they have destroyed their own bodies these poor creatures are denied a human body. Instead they must take on the form of trees, their leaves for ever picked at and eaten by harpies. Bleeding, the lost ones speak of their misery. When they eventually heal their leaves are destroyed again.

> . . . for what a man
> Takes from himself it is not just he have.
> Here we perforce shall drag them; and throughout
> The dismal glade our bodies shall be hung,
> Each on the wild thorn of his wretched shade.

No Christian could fail to be shocked by such an image of eternal damnation. Yet my Jane is not of my opinion. She comes to chapel with us every Sunday and appears to be devout, but last week she suddenly said, 'Billy, if I was God I would not punish suicides. They have been punished enough.'

'You are my goddess, my love, and must be content with a small "g".'

'No, I'm serious. We no longer bury suicides at crossroads, but why should it be a crime or a sin? My body belongs to myself – not to the Queen or the Almighty. If I am so desperate as to want to do away with it, if I find life unbearable, should I not be pitied?'

We were having one of our late suppers together after the children had gone to bed. I crossed to the other side of the table and took her in my arms. 'You must not speak of such things. We will have many contented years, working and loving together.'

'Oh, Billy, you always take things so literally.' It is true that she has more stomach than I do for abstract argument. A most remarkable woman.

On the top floor I entered the ward for incurable females. Here, above all, the risk of self-destruction is great. I passionately believe that when we understand more about diseases of the brain there will be no more incurables' wards here. We are only at the dawn of this new science.

Mrs Sanderson came to us four years ago, and at first it seemed she would soon return to her comfortable life as the wife of a Harley Street doctor. She suffered from the delusion that she had visited the future and spoke most eloquently of London a hundred and fifty years hence, the apotheosis of progress. Her drawings of this happy hereafter were so extraordinary that I showed them to Richard Dadd, who agreed that they were interesting. In every other respect Mrs Sanderson is a sensible and amiable person, of charming appearance. But this delusion has now invaded every aspect of her life. A few months after she came to us her little son died at his boarding-school. Her delusion had begun soon after her other child, a little girl, died of a fever.

Poor lady, she sits all day and much of the night gazing out of the window as if waiting for someone. I hope she is not expecting her husband, for he is very unlikely to come. My friend George, who has a practice in Cavendish Square, tells me that Dr Sanderson has had several undesirable liaisons and has made a great deal of money as a quack. Last time George came to dinner with us he whispered, over brandy and a cigar after Jane and his wife had left the room, that Charles Sanderson has built his fortune on selling an aphrodisiac called The Elysium, which is advertised in the more vulgar newspapers. This charlatan is building a museum of medical curiosities and, apart from a generous annual cheque for her upkeep, appears to take no interest in his poor wife. I would insist on her transferral to a private asylum, but we have all grown fond of her, and she seems, in her absent-minded way, to be contented among us. We allow her the freedom to be her own strange self, and a private institution might not be so tolerant.

I nodded to her as she sat in the shadowy corner, but Mrs Sanderson, although her wide blue eyes were open, made no sign of having seen me.

'Be careful, doctor. You will break me if you come so close.'

Startled, I swung around to see Miss Protheroe, who is convinced that she is made of glass. Despite her corpulence she persists in believing she is a kind of ornament, in constant danger of being dropped or smashed. She has expressed a wish to be kept on a mantelpiece, and in a sense it has been her destiny. Unmarried when her father died intestate and insolvent, she had to go out to be a governess. I think this class of women suffer more than any other in England. Educated enough to be sensible of their position as neither a servant nor a friend, many of them must live among children who taunt them in families where the sons or fathers take advantage of them. Again I thought of my Jane.

I apologized, but Miss Protheroe, who like me rarely sleeps, took two steps away as if I were a bull menacing her personal china shop and cried out peevishly, 'You none of you understand in the least! I am not coarse like the rest of you but made of a finer substance. I must be cherished and dusted with a feather every Wednesday.'

Again I murmured my apologies and turned to the sleeping-cubicles. Looking back at the two of them, Mrs Sanderson and Miss Protheroe, sitting a few yards away from one another at their lonely vigil, I reflected on the sadness of their isolation. In my experience the mad rarely communicate together much, preferring to confide in doctors, nurses and attendants. They are like children who compete with one another for the attention of their parents.

Every Monday at four, just after friends and relatives of patients have visited, I am 'at home' in the Physician's Parlour to all who have questions about my hospital; and then I meet my staff to discuss the patients. I interview all the attendants, who are well educated, gentle and humane, unlike the crude, harsh creatures of the old regime. They bring me sad tales, and I am struck by the way the seeds of madness are sown in childhood. I worry about my own children and fear for their future – but, as Jane tells me, I worry about everything.

Of all our attendants, gentle Neville is the most gifted in drawing out confidences. He has the knack of kindly silence, and from him I have learned much about my charges. Our attendants are so arranged as to be able to entertain a constant unobserved surveillance of the patients. They do not necessarily interfere but permit the indulgence of many innocent vagaries. Others, not so harmless, they control without any use of force. Yesterday I discharged Miss Bartlett, a young female who, when she first came to us, had a propensity to eat her faeces and strip off her clothes. She was prevented from doing either by the vigilant care of an attendant without the use of any restraint.

Outside the sleeping-cubicles I held my breath and listened for the tell-tale gasps and moans of that most pernicious and debasing vice. It is my duty to prevent masturbation and to help women to govern themselves. Otherwise hysteria, mania, idiocy and even death may result. Self-abuse lays the foundation for consumption, paralysis and heart disease. It weakens the memory, makes a boy or girl careless, negligent and listless. Many lose their minds, and others, when grown, commit suicide. Indulgent parents may think it does no harm to their children because they do not suffer now, but the effects of this vice come on slowly and inexorably.

Self-abuse was at the root of poor Dadd's troubles. At the early age of nine this motherless boy, under the evil influence of a worthless maidservant, contracted vicious habits of self-indulgence. An operation was performed but without any apparent benefit. We must all heed Lallemand's inflammatory warnings about the dangers of spermatorrhoea. Truly, the loss of sperm is dangerous to the health, and circumcision is the only advisable treatment.

Roaming these dark empty corridors, I often think of earlier generations of doctors. All those Monros who for a hundred and twenty-five years regarded this hospital and their private empire of madhouses as a family business. Genial, cultivated men, they lived a gentlemanly life and visited the wards here for a few hours a week, reluctantly, abandoning the inmates to squalor and cruelty. Dr John Monro, of the second generation of the dynasty, replied to criticism of his regime with a treatise that began: 'Madness is a distemper of such a nature, that very little of real use can be said concerning it.' A consequence of this blithe indifference was the lack of records I found when I arrived here.

A century of oblivion – although Sir Alexander Morison, my immediate predecessor, did keep meticulous records. The case histories he wrote during his seventeen years as a consultant here make fascinating reading, and I hope my own will be as full. A disciple of Esquirol, Morison was a fine and conscientious doctor, although rather elderly. He was over seventy when I first met him and somewhat grim, as can be seen in Dadd's portrait of him. I would feel guilty about ousting Morison were it not that I know his wife is a very rich woman and he has retired in some splendour to their estate in Balerno, the same that appears in Dadd's picture.

I am only acquainted with the last of the Monro dynasty, Edward. He acts as my locum when I am away, and I think he is adequate, although he is far too charming to want to spend much time in the company of lunatics. Well, I am not a charmer and have no hereditary fortune. My father was a hard-working doctor here in the slums of Lambeth, and I must work night and day. Yet I do feel them behind me, those other doctors. I hear their footsteps and wince at the screams and groans of their long-dead patients. For Bedlam is a lady with a notorious past; this is her third hospital and, I like to think, her best.

Our new kitchen and offices are spotless, and chains, lancet and straw have been replaced by kindness. Our ballroom and billiard room are miniature crystal palaces with sides all of glass and iron, and in our workshops the male patients can make useful items such as mats, paper bags and felt slippers. The three 'Ws' – worry, want and wickedness – can be cured by the three 'Ms' – method, meat and morality.

There is so much more to do. Every day I am humbled by my failure to understand the connections between body and mind. Goethe had a notion that in the secret archives of the vegetable kingdom there may exist a specific remedy for every human disease; I am convinced that this is also true of mental disease, if we could only read those secrets. First, we have to change attitudes to the insane, and that is why I scribble away at my pamphlets and my letters to the powerful. Political wisdom must be brought to bear upon and redress every social wrong. What are the civil rights of the insane? At the moment they have none, and this is yet another injustice I must address.

I cannot do it all alone and have been trying to attract more medical students from St Bartholomew's and St Thomas's. But young men feel that twenty guineas a year is too much to pay, since insanity is not one of the subjects required to qualify for a medical degree. I must lower the fees, for if I had a group of keen young fellows around me I could accomplish so much more. Together we could study each patient in more depth and, when they die, open up each corpse to see in what respects the brain of a lunatic differs from that of an ordinary person.

Jane calls me her Puffing Billy, a train rushing to unknown stations. These nocturnal ramblings are my escape valve when the steam of my doubt escapes into the lonely night. I worry about the future and pray that a time will come when lunacy no longer exists. The lease of our hospital expires in 2673, far beyond that Utopian year poor Mrs Sanderson claims to have flown to. Well, the mad experience hallucinations of sight and hearing not patent to the rest of us. As my daytime mind pooh-poohs her story, my nocturnal mind would like to believe that a time really will come when we have abolished poverty and suffering and can heal diseases of the mind with a scientific abracadabra.

3
SILVER MEDALS

As Neville leads me away from Powell the voice of Osiris is so loud that I think my head will split open. He fills the ward, the hospital, the whole city with his cruel demands. *Kill him! Kill the braggart! Kill the keeper, too! He is only a sheep. You must slaughter him and escape from here. Take your rightful place as a king among artists!*

I glance at Neville, afraid that he must have heard, but his face is as mild as usual. Doubtless he experiences himself as a single nature. Well, the double nature of human beings was known to the ancient Greeks, who believed the two natures were always contending for mastery. Only two?

'Now then, Mr Dadd, you have a nice peaceful lie-down in your cubicle, and I'll keep your supper hot for you over the flame in my room. It's boiled mutton today with cabbage and boiled potatoes. You're very fond of that, aren't you? And here's a little something to calm you down.'

I take the glass he hands me and drink the liquid greedily. Were it arsenic I would still gulp it down. There have been times when I have longed for poison, for an end to it. Perhaps my voices would follow me to the grave, as my father's voice has followed me beyond his. I cannot speak.

'Now you just take off those shoes and lie down peaceful-like. Have a little rest, and when you wake up I'll have your supper kept ready for you. There's the parcel Mr Frith left for you. I'll draw the curtains, and we'll just pretend it's evening, shall we, Mr Dadd?'

Peaceful-like. Alone in my darkened cubicle there is a moment of silence when I lie with my eyes tight shut and stroke my forehead to make sure it is really uninhabited. I sink gratefully into the mattress, the soft mattress of M4 so unlike the straw-stuffed, lice-infested one in my old dungeon.

Of course, they are listening for this. The hot air holds its breath.

There is a fizzing, whispering, giggling explosion of spite above my head. I pretend not to hear and keep my mouth and eyes shut, but they dance a vicious saraband behind my eyes.

They have grown up with me, my fairies. When I was a child they lived sweetly among the Kentish wild flowers and grasses, but now they have learned wicked London ways. They copulate in the air, climb on to each other like dogs, male on male, male on female, female on female, indiscriminately. Powell said they are all female, but he has never seen them except in a pantomime or a children's book where they are on their best behaviour. Left to their own devices, to their own vices, there is nothing they will not attempt. One old fairy, unable to find a partner, lowers his breeches and shamelessly pleasures himself. Another buggers a little boy fairy on a toadstool while a dainty female fairy sucks his tiny cock.

I long to touch myself; I am crucified with desire. I think of beautiful George. I cannot help it, although at this moment any body, male or female, would satisfy me. Well, there are no women here, they are in another wing, as inaccessible as in an Egyptian harem. The fairies want to seduce me, but as soon as my hand touches the burning rod between my legs the others will come to stop me.

They spy on me, Neville and Hood and the others. They censor me. They are happy for me to paint but only the right subjects. The fairies I am painting for Hood are not allowed to be their debauched little selves. He wants them prettified and mawkish. I paint them smaller and smaller, use a magnifying glass to give them their microscopic freedom. In my master-stroke, the one I am painting for George, there is a satyr fairy looking under the skirt of one of the lady's maids. A lecherous old fairy, the same one that masturbated in the air just now. He has escaped from my painting, and I wish him joy of the secrets of the flesh.

> Such secrets surely some must know.
> All are not saints on earth below.
> Or if they are they know the same.
> Or are shut out from nature's game.

Banished from nature's book of life . . . I have no talent as a poet, but at least my rhymes send me to sleep. Dreams of youth, mine and Powell's and Egg's and Phillip's. When we were students, new to London, drunk on beer and each other and ambition and promise. I cannot remember many particulars of my dreams; I think we danced with the skeleton in the room at the Academy we called the pepper-box and groped a couple of ballet girls from Covent Garden. The atmosphere of those years, the aura of wild hope that surrounded me, pursues me into the ruined present.

I wake up in tears. John McDonald, the attendant in charge of our distinguished ward, comes in with a plate of tepid boiled mutton and watches solicitously as I cram the food into my mouth. No wife could be more devoted. I weep and slobber and guzzle, but McDonald does not turn away. The tyranny of goodness. My punishment is never to be alone. Finally I shout at poor McDonald to get out, and he leaves meekly.

Much later I hear Oxford's voice outside my door. 'You were weeping, Apollo.'

'Go back to sleep, Hercules.'

'I cannot sleep when my comrade grieves. Would you like me to fight a duel on your behalf?'

'No.'

'With pistols or swords?'

'Neither.'

'Who was that fellow who came this afternoon? Did he insult you?'

'He made me remember too much.'

'Is he a man of distinction? Will he write about us in the illustrated papers?'

'Be quiet, Hercules.' But it is too late. Our voices have woken the others, and I hear a great shuffling and whispering outside my door.

When we first moved up here a few months ago I was astonished that the doors of our sleeping-cubicles were not locked at night. After thirteen years of captivity the shock of an open door is considerable. Sometimes, when we cannot sleep, I play a quiet game of chess with

Oxford, or Hercules, as he prefers to be called. He persists in believing that he is the commander-in-chief of a secret society called Young England, the members of which are pledged to go on patriotic missions. His first, and last, was when he was sent to assassinate the Queen – a false Queen, according to his heavenly messengers; the real Queen is a barmaid in a public house in Birmingham where Oxford once worked as a potboy. Although we are neither young nor in England, being citizens of the republic of the mind, we hold meetings of Young England once a month at which Oxford takes the minutes, all in praise of himself and his beautiful speaking.

I open my door and find quite a congregation of insomniacs. The night attendant must be sound asleep. Jonson hands around a large flask of rum he obtained in the old criminal block where keepers and attendants were easily bribed.

'Drink up, lads. This is the last grog you'll ever taste, for the saintly doctor won't give us anything but watery beer to drink.'

I take a great swig. The sweet liquor burns my throat and ignites me. Spirits raise our tamed spirits, and we act like free men. Oxford fetches his fiddle and plays the Tartini piece I taught him, 'The Devil's Trill', plays it so badly that the Devil, if he is listening, must have a headache. Jonson folds his arms and performs some kind of nautical dance, and McNaughton bursts into a Highland fling. He is, in a manner of speaking, our saviour and a great favourite among us, for we all know that without him most of us would have swung or been transported.

Tonight we laugh and cheer and applaud the musical entertainment. The rum and the noise defeat my voices, and I feel almost young again, almost a man. For months on end we hardly speak to one another, but tonight we are a fraternity. It reminds me of our old weekly meetings of The Clique, the same mood of exaltation seizes me, and I start to talk wildly about Blake and Titian, arguing their virtues although nobody is listening. I swagger and shout that I am not beaten; I have yet great work inside me; I will make mincemeat of Frith . . .

When Hood appears I try, for a few seconds, to stay up there. The doctor is proud of his abolition of restraints here and constantly reminds us that leather muffs, wrist-straps, iron handcuffs, manacles and hobbles for legs are no longer permitted. Hood does not realize that when he enters our ward he himself restrains and chills us with the cold shower of his reason. We are afraid. His power is cloaked in good sense and kindness, but it is absolute: he owns our lives and can make them a misery or a tolerable burden. When he points out of the window to our former dungeon we remember all too well what it would mean to be sent back there.

In silence we crawl back to our sleeping-cubicles. Alone again, my head on fire, I collapse upon my bed and try to escape into sleep.

Moonlight streams through my curtains and makes my nerves tingle. Osiris, my true father, is out there with the moon god Thoth. My fairies also like to drink the moonlight and will be back to torment me. I reach down to touch the parcel Neville left under my bed. Fear The Clique bearing gifts.

The brown paper crackles with mockery as I tear it open. *Twenty years are nothing to a rock*, says my father in his scientific voice. I am not a rock. I feel more like a jelly.

'London, my boy, that's the place.' My father's beautiful second wife, Sophia, has died at the age of twenty-eight, worn out by us all (as my father frequently tells us), and he is restless, anxious to secure our future. His ambition for both himself and me sells the little shop in Chatham High Street, makes new friends who may be useful to me and buys the business of a bronzer, carver and gilder. The shop at number 15 Suffolk Street is a grand affair recently built by Nash, just around the corner from the Royal Academy Schools in the National Gallery. Stephen becomes my father's partner, Robert is to become a chemist, and I am to bring them all glory. Above the elegant shop our family rooms are just as squalid and overcrowded as the ones above the shop in Chatham. The children romp and shout and are screamed at by my martyr sister Mary Ann.

I am seventeen, angry and proud and ashamed of my family. All my father's little store of capital has gone into buying the new business; there is none left with which to send me to the Henry Sass

School and prepare me for entrance to the Royal Academy Schools. 'Never mind,' says my father. 'I know you are a genius, and you must be your own master. Go to the British Museum and teach yourself to draw.'

For the first week I never reach the museum at all but lie to my father about the hours I spend there drawing ancient history. It is the present life of the streets around me that I long to make pictures about. In Chatham, when I walked out of our shop at the sign of the Golden Mortar, I could not go five paces without meeting someone I knew, but in huge, noisy, boisterous London neighbours have no curiosity about each other. Here I am free, a nobody, lost and invisible, a pair of eyes on skinny legs.

I have never seen so many people, such fast carriages and opulent shops: drapers, confectioners, pastry cooks, silversmiths, booksellers and print-sellers. Each shop window is a feast of dreams where I stand and tell myself stories of the silver-topped stick I will swagger out with, the ivory shaving brush that will make me irresistible, the cake in the shape of Nelson with which I will placate my sister Mary Ann.

The only paintings I have seen so far are the ones by Rubens, Reynolds, Salvatore Rosa, Titian and Tintoretto at Cobham Park. Now, in the print shops, I perceive a new visual universe and stand for hours in front of brilliant grotesques by Gillray, Rowlandson and Daumier. I discover Hogarth's *Marriage à la Mode*, Durer's apocalyptic visions, Fuseli's *Nightmare* and Daumier's clever satire on it with the pear-shaped Louis-Philippe sitting on the stomach of Lafayette. In the window of one shop I find prints and engravings of works by Turner, Constable and Gainsborough. As I stand within shouting distance of these great names, fancy propels me to join them, and I conveniently forget the years of hard work between us.

I walk slowly, a moon calf gawping at the people of the sun, each face a new planet. In the crowd I glimpse the most beautiful women's faces and the most hideous crones; enviable swaggering dandies and pitiful ragged gangs of thieving homeless boys who sleep every night under sheds and baskets in Covent Garden market. Longing to draw them all I have no desire to exchange them for fusty old stones in a museum. The vast crowds moving in different directions astonish me. Those first days, as I watch the constant successions of people throng this way and that, I constantly think that something momentous must have happened.

On Thursday evening it does. I've been truanting from my duties at the museum all day, wandering the streets. Now, cold and hungry, I reluctantly make my way home to my family supper table. In the Haymarket there is great commotion, people shouting and pointing, faces intoxicated with sensation. Over to the west the sky is red, blocking out the moon and illuminating the silhouettes of the rooftops with an apocalyptic glow. It is a beautiful effect that begs to be painted, so I take out my sketchpad. The heads of the rushing, pushing multitude obscure my view, and I allow myself to be swept along on their tide to Westminster.

The air is even dirtier than usual, and as we flow down Whitehall there is a horrid stench of burnt wood. From fragments of conversation I hear it was the Chartists . . . the chimneys overheated . . . the papists did it. I run, thrilled to be part of such a vast crowd, excited by the smell of destruction and hellfire and proud to find myself at a historic scene. When we reach Parliament the ashes are still smouldering. People throng the surrounding streets and the bridges, eyes shining with excitement.

'Any MPs roasted?' A ragged man in front of me asks his companion.

'None, more's the pity.'

My heart soars with perverse satisfaction at the sight of disaster. The old, corrupt order my father complains of has been annihilated like the Cities of the Plain, and I stand at the beginning of a new world that will belong to me.

My mood of exhilaration lasts until Sunday luncheon when my father says, 'Let me see some of your drawings, Richard.'

'They're not finished. There's nothing to show. Next week perhaps.'

We are all gathered at the table where my father carves the enormous joint of beef that must last until Tuesday, and Mary Ann brings in vegetables boiled to death. Her Yorkshire pudding has not risen; it never rises but flops over the dish in a puddle of flabby yellow batter. The little ones squabble and giggle and kick each other under the table, and Robert and Stephen look alarmingly sober and honest.

'Tell us how you have spent your week. What have you seen in the British Museum?'

The curator of the Chatham and Rochester Literary and Philosophical Institution's Museum is a thorough man. I try to take refuge in my well-known dreaminess. 'I hardly noticed other objects. I was absorbed in my work.'

'What did you draw?'

A drunken whore in Covent Garden, a red velvet jacket I longed to buy, two dogs mounting each other in an alley off the Strand. Inspired by Hogarth, I long to chronicle every scrap of London life. 'Egyptian bones, pyramids, that sort of thing.'

He looks at me sharply; he always knows when I lie. 'We are all counting on you, Richard,' he says quietly.

My father is not a cruel man. He does not delight in humiliating his children but punishes us by his disappointment. He has no imagination and often tells me that I get mine from my mother, as if it were a plague. His intelligence is cool, rational and precise. Already he has taught himself the new skills he needs as a bronzer and gilder, and he expects his children to be equally efficient and hungry for learning. He has left the Church of England and joined the Unitarians because, he says, they are more liberal and he can't be doing with all that hocus-pocus about holy ghosts. He is a Freemason only because it is a useful club to belong to and may bring trade. Papa is a man of the Enlightenment, in love with reason, yet he has enormous respect for art and talks about genius as if it were a very expensive jewel in which he has invested. I am his investment.

On Monday morning he escorts me to the British Museum. We walk briskly past the wondrous shops and do not stare at the fascinating crowds. The museum is a Brobdingnagian building site full of dust and old men. Gripping my arm firmly, Papa introduces me to one of the attendants, Mr Horne, who he has met at a geology lecture.

Papa has only been in London a month, but already, it seems, he knows everybody. Mr Horne, my father whispers, was wounded at Waterloo. To me he looks so ancient that it might have been Thermopylae. My father asks him to keep an eye on me and explains I am to go to the Greek and Egyptian sculpture galleries between nine and five every weekday to teach myself to draw.

Already I have lost my glorious anonymity. I am my father's son again, and it is like a return to school only without the flogging. Mr Horne will be sent to spy on me.

At first I dread my daily incarceration in the museum. It does not feel like a building at all but like a ruin, as if the age of the objects it contains is a disease which I am afraid will infect me: one afternoon I will emerge with grey hair and a stoop. As Sir Robert Smirke's vast neo-classical building slowly rises, scaffolding and rubble and grime surround this place where I am supposed to become a genius. Mr Horne supplies me with a folding canvas stool; my father buys me a drawing board and charcoal and chalks.

Sitting in front of the colossal bust of Rameses II I feel absolutely nothing. At home in Chatham my drawings were always made with passion. I loved the Kentish countryside and the busy harbour; ships and flowers and meadows flowed naturally from my eyes to my hand. It is quite impossible to love Rameses II. These gloomy new Egyptian sculpture galleries sap my energy, and I envy the visitors who come and go and chatter freely. Day after day I see only stone and hear only my father's voice. 'You must get on, Richard. I cannot support you all for ever. Nine children! There are important people at the museum. You must befriend them and show them your drawings. Perhaps you will meet some young gentlemen of good family there.'

I meet nobody. Ashamed of my provincial voice and clothes and my laziness I stare and stare at Rameses and the Rosetta Stone and the marbles from the Acropolis, and they stare back. All my attempts to draw them are unsatisfactory. I am furious with my weak hand and feeble brain. My father is in my head, smothering my imagination – or perhaps this is his head, this dry cold anteroom to death where I am condemned to sit day after day.

One dark November afternoon my hand comes back to life. It happens when I am feeling homesick for Chatham, for a time when I could draw whatever I liked and visit the heavenly pictures at Cobham Hall. It had its hellish side, of course, its resident demon, but I loved the house and wandered happily in the grounds. Beyond the Jacobean splendours of architecture there was a more recent folly, an unused mausoleum in the form of a Greek temple topped by a pyramid where I used to sit for hours pretending I lived there, telling myself that I was Lord Darnley's hermit and this was my real home – not the sordid overcrowded rooms above the sign of the golden mortar.

Suddenly I remember my first meeting with Osiris. I was four-teen. I did not know his name or what it was that descended from the heavy black triangle of the roof of the mausoleum to comfort me as I sat, alone and sobbing with humiliation because he had used me again and my mouth was full of the vile taste of him. I heard a voice and looked around. There was no body, only the booming voice. I could not tell if it came from inside my head or from the outside.

Richard, you will be a great artist. I will enter you and guide your hand, for you are my son and the power of the old gods will live again in you.

I felt chosen, flattered, invigorated. It was like a Bible story, but I was the hero instead of the child being droned at in our family pew.

Three years later, as I struggle to bring life to dead statues in the dark museum, I feel surrounded by warmth and light. Looking up, I see a long white pillar detach itself from the wall and step towards me.

I am Osiris, and you are my catspaw, Richard. Obey me, and I will teach you how to draw.

I feel a surge of energy. Osiris shows me the vitality locked in the ancient stones and marbles. The charcoal that has been so brittle and obstinately black softens in my fingers so that I am able to blend its crumbliness and make the transition from light to dark. My drawings gain the subtlety of chiaroscuro. I learn to concentrate. That afternoon I am so absorbed in my work that Mr Horne almost locks me in the gallery. The next morning I look forward to my solitary work and hurry through the streets to the museum. When I pass the great Smirke, the architect of the magnificent new building, I want to salute him as a fellow artist. At last I know who I am and what I must do with my life.

Curious that I found my vocation inside one Smirke building and must rot for the rest of my days beneath his brother's smirking dome.

That Christmas I make my family presents of my drawings and know that their pleasure is genuine. I have something valuable to give, and when my father shows my work to his friends in the art world they are impressed. Clarkson Stanfield says he will recommend me as a student to the Royal Academy, and whenever I pass the splendid façade of Somerset House I stare up at it, imagining the wonders inside. It must be full of men who have far more talent than me; they are my rivals, and I hear them criticize my drawings, which are never good enough.

All that year I labour in the museum, alone and silent like one of the slaves who built the pyramids that squat mysteriously around me. But I love my slavery, although there are many days when I fight with the charcoal and produce smudged failures. I feel I am at the beginning of a long journey; my stomach churns with excitement each morning as I carry my canvas stool in front of my chosen sculpture and try to possess it with my eye and hand. There is nothing like that daily battle with the blank sheet of paper.

Two years later my drawing of an antique plaster cast is accepted, and I am admitted to the august Royal Academy Schools.

That first January morning I walk around the corner from our house to the new National Gallery the schools have just moved to, shaking so much that I dare not go in. My little brothers and sisters will tease me if I go straight home, and I have no money to go to a coffee house or a tavern. Terrified of the superior beings who are already there, I am sure they will laugh at my Kentish vowels and smudged drawings.

At last I become more afraid of getting into trouble for my late arrival than I am of entering and drag my cold feet up the steps.

The National Gallery is another grand building site, a monument waiting to happen. The school has just moved from Somerset House, and there is a pleasant chaos in the air. I am not the only student who is confused. I imagine that now I have proved my ability to draw sculptures I will be unleashed and allowed to draw all the beautiful women and fairies and demons that nest in my head, but our training still rigidly follows the 'Rules of Art' laid down by Sir Joshua Reynolds. Although my tuition is free, much to my father's relief, we are not free spirits but soldiers who have to march in obedience to Sir Joshua's ghost. Art must be elevated and must not deal with the everyday. So I go home and destroy almost all my boyhood work because it is not elevated enough.

Our life classes are in the pepper-box, a small round room at the top of the East Wing, but there is not much life in them. Our subjects are skeletons, dead birds and yet more antique sculptures, which we have to draw again and again. That winter we draw lots to be near the coal stove and my fingers have chill-blains on them, but I keep on drawing. When I finally produce something that is good enough I will be allowed to paint copies of old masters borrowed from Dulwich College and the National Gallery. Those of us who are over twenty or married will also earn permission to draw naked models.

Left alone in the pepper-box, we boys argue and laugh and throw the pieces of bread we are supposed to use for rubbing out mistakes. I can't remember my first meeting with Powell and Egg and the others. It doesn't take them long to pierce the cocoon of loneliness in which I have sheltered for so long. To my amazement I discover there are other boys who are shy and ambitious and provincial. Only Egg is prosperous; the others all have to make their own way like me. Egg is small and kind and gentle, mortified by the laughter and puns his name provokes, and so I do not resent his good fortune. His family house in Bayswater seems palatial to us and becomes our social centre.

From the beginning Powell is my particular friend. His father is a butler-turned-innkeeper in Harrogate, and his mother is a cook. I am grateful to him for having a family even more ridiculous than my own, although his people have the decency to remain in Harrogate while mine are breathing down my neck.

My father interrogates me about my studies. 'Have you won any prizes?' 'What do the professors say of your work?' 'Are you making friends with young gentlemen who will help you to get on? Invite them back here, my boy, I would love to meet them.' 'This is my son the artist . . .' – boastfully, to any customers who happen to be in the shop – 'He is a student at the Royal Academy Schools, you know, and they say he will do great things.'

When I escape upstairs Mary Ann glares at me with hatred because I have no domestic duties and she is enslaved by hers. The children break my chalks and scribble on my drawings and burst into the room I still share with Robert and Stephen when I am attempting to work there. My older brothers are infuriatingly condescending, making it clear that they are to do real work while I am merely to play. Yet somehow my foolish games are to bring glory to us all.

I spend more and more time away from the house. Unable to work or think or breathe beneath my father's roof I dream of a space that is my own. Desperate for money, I turn to my teachers at the Academy for commissions. But most of my fellow students are even poorer than I am, and Frith and the others, who must pay for every crust they eat, think me mad to reject a free billet. It is impossible to explain to them that life with my family is not free. Too much has happened between us; too many memories shackle us to one another.

Most of my teachers at the Academy appear to me to be pompous bags of lard mouthing Sir Sloshua's platitudes. When I'm alone with Frith and Phillip and O'Neil and Egg we delight in mocking him. As we sit in the enviable room at the top of his family house in Bayswater that Egg is allowed to use as his studio, one of us, usually Powell, pretends to be Sir Joshua while the others heckle him.

'And now,' John Phillip blows an imaginary trumpet voluntary, 'you are to be honoured by an address from our late President, the greatest ornament of British art.'

Sir Powell Frith, wearing Egg's red tartan dressing-gown as a cloak and a white dishcloth as a wig, stands on a chair to pontificate.

'I have returned from the grave, dear acolytes, to remind you of your sacred duty –'

We boo and hiss and throw cushions at him. I yell, 'Of Reynolds what good shall be said? – or what harm? / His temper too frigid; his pencil too warm.'

Sir Joshua Frith frowns and glares at me. 'Boy! I would chiefly recommend that an implicit obedience to the Rules of Art, as established by the great masters, should be exacted from the *young* students.'

'You were never young, you old fart,' O'Neil yells.

'You show your vulgar taste by interrupting my discourse. It is that those models, which have passed through the approbation of ages, that should be considered by them as perfect and infallible guides as subjects for their imitation, not their criticism. Michelangelo and Raffaelle! Such is the Great Style as it appears in those who possessed it at its height. In this, search after novelty in conception or in treating the subject has no place –'

'I will do new things! I won't be stifled by you! Inspiration and enthusiasm, those are my masters!' I shout, as angry as if he really was my father.

'As our art is not a divine gift, so neither is it a mechanical trade. Its foundations are laid in solid science.'

'You have no imagination! I will live for my imagination!' I sob.

'Richard, it's only a jest, you fool!' Egg poured us more beer.

'When we read the lives of the most eminent painters every page informs us that no part of their time was spent in dissipation,' Sir Joshua Frith reproves us, reaching down from his pulpit for another glass.

'The painters who have applied themselves more particularly to low and vulgar characters and who express with precision the various shades of passion as they are exhibited by vulgar minds – such as we see in the works of Hogarth – deserve great praise, but as their genius has been employed on low and confined subjects the praise that we give must be as limited as its object.'

'Rubbish! Hogarth had more life in his little finger than you ever had. His London makes us laugh!' Phillip passionately defends his hero.

'But his work is devoid of the Great Style. His subjects are not noble. Alexander is said to have been of a low stature: a painter ought not so to represent him.'

'Would you have us flatter and falsify as you did? Portray Sir Flatulent Fitzarse who can't write his name as a handsome scholar?' Phillip shouts.

Powell's grandiloquence is all too convincing. The rest of us combine to pull him off his chair, and we collapse on the floor, weak with laughter. Egg's kind mother and sisters come up to see what all the noise is about and stand giggling in the doorway. It is all great fun, and we are full of belief in our youth and power. We have a new little Queen hardly older than my sister Maria, and England is getting younger.

But as soon as I leave Egg's house I am penniless again and must walk home.

That winter we become a group, The Clique, a name we take because the other students complain that we exclude them – and I suppose we do. We form a sketching club with weekly meetings and competitions, which I usually win. Fun and frolic mix with a big grain of folly as we drink beer and talk into the night, arguing and criticizing each other's work and competing for the few badly paid hack jobs that come our way, yet always united by our youth and ambition and talent. They are the brothers I should have had.

I am fascinated to hear that Turner is the son of a barber and a butcher's daughter and grew up in Maiden Lane, although, Frith and I agree, he seems to have learned no manners since. We are to be charming and elegant in our glorious future. Turner, to our ignorant eyes, is a decayed old sailor, coarse and stout with a red face and a hook nose. We call him Captain Crumble, and, as a teacher, he is disconcerting.

He shuffles into the pepper-box, grumbling, accompanied by our stifled giggles. Frith's mimicry will have us all in hysterics as soon as he leaves. There is a stench of beer and linseed oil as Turner looks over my shoulder at my drawing of the skeleton. He points to the ribcage, makes a scratch on the paper at the side, says nothing and moves on to John Phillip who is sitting beside me. I can see now what he means, yes, the shading on the ribcage is all wrong and the bones look like drumsticks. I alter it.

The next week when Turner comes he points to the skeleton's ribs, smiles and nods. After that he gives me hint after hint in almost total silence. We have heard that he used to give lectures but had to stop because he mispronounced words and muttered and mumbled incoherently. In vain I try to persuade him to talk by telling him how much I love his paintings, particularly one I have seen of Venice showing Canaletto at his easel. He grunts.

Anxious to ingratiate myself with him I smile and add, 'I admire your defiance of public disapproval when you painted Juliet in Venice instead of Verona. Artistic vision is not to be dictated to. Isn't that right, sir?'

But he is not to be flattered. He glares at me, blows his nose on an enormous handkerchief, mutters 'Rubbish!' and shuffles out of the room.

Henry Howard, our Professor of Painting, is the only teacher who stimulates me. He is so old that he knew Blake and Fuseli; I feel he carries their baton of enchantment and can pass it on to me. Like Turner Howard is shabby and broken-looking, but he is eloquent, and at his first lecture he ignites the flame of imagination that has been smouldering in my heart.

'The genius of the painter, like that of the poet, may ever call forth new species of beings – an Ariel, a Caliban or the *Midsummer* fairies . . . may lift us out of this visible diurnal sphere and lap us in Elysium.' This is unfashionable stuff. My fellow students titter, throw darts at each other and yawn. Howard's only disciple, I stay behind in the gloomy lecture hall and shyly introduce myself.

After that he takes an interest in my work and helps me to get an award and a few commissions. He invites me to his studio where I see his *Fairies on the Sea Shore*, *The Contention of Oberon and Titania* and a scene from Byron's *Manfred*. If I shut my eyes I can see them still, those dreamy, luminous canvases, and I know that Howard's spirit is invading the painting of Titania and Oberon I am doing now, twenty years later, for Hood.

My enthusiasm is sincere, both for Howard's paintings and for his studio. To us, poor boys from nowhere, the life of an artist seems as wondrous as the life of Titania. To have a studio, to evade the drudgery and tedium of my father's life, that is the yearning that wakes me up at five each morning to listen to the snores of my complacent brothers.

Among my father's friends David Roberts is my hero. In my father's workshop I listen, enthralled, to his romantic stories. Roberts grew up in Edinburgh in desperate poverty and, at the age of twelve, was apprenticed to a house painter. Quick-witted and ambitious, he soon taught himself to do marble wood-graining and *trompe-l'œil*. He became a fashionable decorator then worked as a scene painter in a travelling circus and later in the theatre. When he brings his paintings of Spain to be framed he tells us marvellous tales of the tantrums and jealousies of the theatrical world.

Once a rival scene painter destroyed his set for Mozart's *Il Seraglio*. 'So I decided to come down to London and become a real painter, a topographical artist,' he says airily, as if it were an easy thing to climb that greasy pole. My father has told me in confidence that Roberts's wife drinks like a fish and has had to be packed off back to Edinburgh.

Roberts has recently returned from an adventurous year sketching in Egypt and Palestine, and his work is hugely successful. He is on the committee at the Royal Academy and knows everybody I long to meet. He, far more than Turner, conforms to my idea of a great artist, and I am thrilled to be invited to visit him.

With his new money he has built himself a house and studio in Fitzroy Street. As I knock on the door I feel dizzy with adoration. In fact, it is not love but a kind of cannibalism, a hunger to devour him, to be him.

His studio is a vast bare space lit by huge windows. On a shelf that runs around the walls there are plaster casts, and all over the floor there are finished paintings, dummies, rocks, skulls, skeletons, richly coloured costumes hanging on a rail, scraps of exotic material, unframed canvases and empty frames. It reminds me of the backstage area of the Theatre Royal – where I sometimes earn a few extra shillings painting the sets – but twice as thrilling because this is the stage on which I mean to perform . The wonderful smells of paint, dust and charcoal go to my head as I stumble around, gawping at the mysterious ancient sculptures he has brought back from his travels, at the brilliant hangings and his elegant friends.

I am able to work only when I am alone in a silent room and envy Roberts his ability to dart from one painting to another while holding court. He is about the same age as my father but does not look old to me. His brisk Edinburgh voice sounds cool and intelligent as he welcomes me and introduces me – 'And this is Richard Dadd, a student of promise' – to half a dozen men. I have no idea who they are, but they look rich and important. Although I long to be charming and witty shyness asphyxiates me, and I hardly open my mouth.

My idol has unlocked the mysteries of Egypt and the Bible, and his pictures are both historical and modern. The dark stones of my long incarceration in the British Museum become, in his paintings, lambent visions of red, green and blue. I laugh and hang on his words as he tells us of his adventures.

'Of course, travel painting is a great humbug. People want to travel from the comfort of their parlour. They want it all sentimentalized and prettified. As a matter of fact I've never seen such filth and squalor, and my origins were a good deal more humble than anyone else in this room.' He sweeps his blue eyes over his audience, and I admire his frankness. Most men who rise in the world keep quiet about the place fromm which they rose, but Roberts boasts of it. I imagine how handsome he must have looked, tanned by the desert sun in his long white robes.

'Why, my very first day in Egypt the felucca we hired was so full of rats and bugs we had to submerge it in the Nile to drown them. Never having learned to swim myself I almost drowned with them!' He roars with laughter.

'When we reached Petra, for instance,' he points to the glowing pink rocks in another painting, ' I had a fever and could hardly hold my brush – but I went out and worked all day in the sun, for when could I ever hope to return? In our inn the fleas were so big you could hardly see what colour the sheets were, and the mosquitoes were so heavy with our blood they could hardly fly. The stew the landlord in Petra brewed for us was disgusting – I couldn't eat a spoonful, although I was faint with hunger. We joked that it was cooked up from the bones of dead travellers, and perhaps we were not wrong.'

He shows us another painting, of the dazzling interior of a mosque. 'My friend the pasha allowed me to paint the mosques of Cairo on the condition that I wore Arab dress – so practical in that heat – shaved off my whiskers and got rid of my hog's hair brushes . . .'

His stories fascinate me, and I long to visit those exotic places, to draw and paint them and come home like him to wild success. In his studio I inhale fame like oxygen and feel quite sure that in a few years I will preside over my own studio, dazzling my patrons.

I cannot go on.

At last I kneel in front of Frith's parcel and open it. I touch the three silver medals I won at the Academy, the letters I wrote to Powell when I eventually followed in Roberts's footsteps on my grand tour and the sketches I made in Egypt and Palestine. I must have given those sketchbooks to Powell when I returned, when we were still great friends. Before. Now they are all that remains of those years, and I cannot look at them. My grave goods.

4
NINA

Today would have been your ninth birthday. Bella would have been eleven, too old to romp with you, not that you ever did play together. If Henrietta was right, you are all angels now and my sister's piety should have earned her an officer's commission in the heavenly army. General Henrietta, blowing her bugle and ruthlessly officiating at the Last Judgement. You two are little angels dressed in white, playing in golden meadows and looking down on their sad mama whom they will never meet again for she will be blackballed out of the Angel Club.

I don't believe any of that. You are not above me, Tommy, but in a deep gulf I have never looked down before. Not Hell, for there are no flames nor any light or colour. All is grey. Silently you stare up at me, and behind you I can see the shadows of Bella and Henrietta and Mama and Papa, my beloved dead stretching back into nothingness. Just a small step towards you to join you all. What use is it to love when loved ones are taken away? Better not to feel at all.

But I do. I am sick and sorry like a wounded beast. I miss you as you were, Tommy, a lively, grubby, noisy little boy, much nicer than an angel, although I had no patience with you. I remember all the times I was angry with you. Charles said you were too much of a milk-sop and would suffer at school if you were not toughened, so I allowed him to be harsh with you and to beat you sometimes. You were never cuddled and petted like Bella, not in public. You used to come to me as I lay in bed, shut your eyes and push yourself into my arms. Then I would hug you when nobody was looking, as if it were a shameful thing to love a little boy. Once you said, 'I wish I could be Bella and be fussed over all the time.'

And then when she died you did become her. You dressed up in her nightgown and gave me such a fright that time stood still and began to play those dreadful tricks on me.

When I returned from those wonderful terrible days with Jonathan and had to lie in a darkened room you were my confidant. I wanted to tell you about the glorious future I had seen, for I was sure that you would live to see it.

One morning you came to me and said, 'I have seen it, Mama! I saw your shining towers and ladies in bloomers, and there was a talking box that showed me pictures that moved, and I travelled in a carriage that had no horses. Let's go and live there, Mama! It's much more jollier than smelly old London! Look, I did a drawing.' Before I could question you to see if you had only dreamed it or had really travelled in time Charles came in and tore up your drawing and told me not to fill your head with bosh.

If I had played with you more and snapped at you less, if I had loved you as much as Bella and kept you at home and stayed at home myself and defended you from Charles's anger, if I had done all those things, would you come back to me?

'Your luncheon, Mrs Sanderson. You have a visitor, a Mrs Jenkins. She says she will wait in the waiting-room for you.'

I do not know anybody of that name. I never speak to the attendants here. They are not unpleasant – indeed, they allow me to write and draw as much as I please, unlike Charles who confiscated my diary and sketchpad. But since I was promoted to the incurables' ward I have found it convenient not to speak or hear. The ladies are not congenial. They scream and blaspheme and quarrel and bite and slobber and appear to have no control over their bodily functions. So I turn my back on them, step into my diving bell and descend into the ocean of memory. Each time I go deeper and deeper, and perhaps one day I will not return. It does not matter.

The attendant takes me to see the mysterious Mrs Jenkins. The waiting-room is empty apart from a large black crinoline and bonnet, decent but a little rusty, which turns out to be Emmie. My old nurse embraces me, and I feel the surprising warmth and softness of her body.

'What have they been doing to you here? You're so thin and pale you look like your sister!'

That is not a compliment. Henrietta may have been good, but she was certainly not beautiful. I used to be considered a beauty – well, perhaps I was, but it did not keep my children alive or preserve my husband's love for me.

'Miss Nina! Don't you recognize me?'

I will have to speak. She has known me since I was an infant, and however much I have changed she is the same old Emmie. Something in her voice makes me a little girl again. I want to chatter and laugh and be petted as I used to be, but I am frozen. Then she starts to cry. Her kind brown eyes and button nose go red, and her chins wobble above the vast expanse of black. I have been hoping to cry for years, but I cannot, so I watch enviously as Emmie sits on a hard wooden bench, takes a green handkerchief from her sleeve and bawls. The uniformed attendant glares at her. Visitors are not supposed to be more bothersome than inmates.

In between sobs Emmie gasps, 'I had to see you. The funeral was more than I could bear. I asked Mr Jenkins to come with me, but he says funerals give him the pip, so it was only me, and it was Kensal Rise, same as poor little Bella. They sent the coffin from the school; such a small one, hardly big enough for a fiddle. That husband of yours what should of stepped into that grave himself if there was any justice pretended not to see me. There was a crowd of his posh friends – that nasty Dr Porter was there – and there was a slap-up funeral tea back at the house later only I wasn't invited.'

My voice comes out at last, it seems a long way from my head. 'Who is Mr Jenkins?'

Emmie stares at me in horror. Then she takes something out of her pocket and presses it into my hand. It is soft and dark. I stroke it and sniff it, but it does not smell as if it would be good to eat.

'Can't you see what it is? It's your own son's hair. They had to shave his head because of the scarlet fever. Lucy found it in his coffin-bed when she was laying him out. I'll put it in a locket and bring it next time I come.'

'We are not allowed jewellery because it might harm us.'

At this she starts to cry again. It is a very watery conversation, and I wish she would go away. A long time ago, I remember, I was the one who cried and Emmie was my comforter. As if through a half-open door in my mind I glimpse little Nina and Henrietta and Bella and Tommy, all the children who must die. It hardly seems worth the nuisance of giving birth to them.

'I shouldn't of come. You're not yourself, Miss Nina.'

I wait for her to tell me who I am. But she goes away, and this time she does not hug me. Perhaps Emmie heard my thoughts; perhaps my body felt as cold and stiff to her as it does to me.

Now that I have started to talk again there is no escape from words. When I return to the ward the voices that have been muffled for so long assault me.

'Bitch!'

'Whore!'

'Lying cow!'

'Now, ladies, you will have to go to the basement if you cannot restrain yourselves.'

'I don't understand why I am here. My husband is expecting me. He will wonder where his supper is. Let me pass.'

'No, Mrs Worth, you cannot leave.'

'Why not? Why are you keeping me here?'

'You are not well.'

'There is nothing the matter with me. I shall call a policeman!'

'Stop screaming, Mrs Worth. You will disturb the other patients.'

I don't wish to hear them, so I return to my chair by the window and look down at the gardens. The sun reflects my face on to the glass, and I try to look away. I used to gaze at myself in the mirror for hours, for I was vain, as Henrietta frequently told me. Charles used to say I was sweetly pretty and delighted in buying me new clothes until the dressmaker's bills got too high.

Now I would rather see anything other than my face. I look away, but my reflection pursues me with its huge sad eyes and sharp nose. I close my eyes. The heat makes me sleepy, but I don't want to give into it because I may dream of Jonathan. The dreams are very pleasant, but the waking up from them is dreadful.

'Dr Hood says we may have a day's pleasure to go to visit the dinosaurs!' Shrieks, whoops, giggles, clapping, stamping.

'If you are very good. I am to choose a group of six to go to the Crystal Palace next Wednesday. Only the best-behaved ladies will be selected.' This from the attendant in exactly the tone of voice I used with Tommy when bribing him with some treat.

Silence, which is the desired effect. We are good when we do not talk; we shall be extremely good when we are dead.

A great whispering breaks out about the dinosaurs and monsters and other wonders of the Crystal Palace, but I have no wish to see them for I am surrounded by monsters and am myself a monster, having outlived my children and my marriage and my youth. Were I built of brick and iron like the dinosaurs I could not feel any heavier.

Six years ago I was still made of flesh. Bella and Tommy were in a frenzy of excitement about our visit to the Great Exhibition. All the servants had been already and had brought back marvellous tales and pictures from the illustrated newspapers of the great cornucopia. Emmie was forever singing a popular song:

> If I sell the pig and donkey, the frying pan and the bed,
> I will see the Exhibition while it is a bob a head.

The children picked it up from her, and the house rang with anticipation. Charles was very critical at first. He said it was all a great folly dreamed up by that bossyboots of a German prince and that Paxton's Crystal Palace was only a cucumber frame between two chimneys and would blow away in the first storm. The mingling of so many races would bring about an outbreak of the plague, Charles feared, and feeding the multitudes attracted to London would lead to food shortages. But he has always loved museums and could not resist the greatest museum the world has ever assembled, so he agreed to see a few patients in the early morning and then take an entire day of liberty to accompany us.

We did not quite have to sell the frying pan, but we never had any money to spare, as Charles's patients paid late or not at all and we could not afford to go to Ramsgate that summer. The two guineas we put aside for our day out represented new summer clothes for the children and a new rug for Charles's waiting-room. We were to go in a 'handsome' cab, as Tommy called it, and not on a shilling day but on a Friday when the entrance fee was two and sixpence.

The cab was ordered for half past eight, and we were all dressed in our best – the children somewhat leggy, for they had grown so much that year. That remote epoch when I wore bright colours – the dress and bonnet I wore that day were pale blue – before perpetual mourning shrouded me.

London shone that warm June morning, as if the fog and gloom and dirt had been scrubbed away by the vigorous hands of Progress. How proud I was of my good-looking children and clever husband. My family seemed to me then as safe and beautiful as the enormous building glittering on the other side of the Serpentine, with all the flags of the world flying from its magnificent roof.

While Charles was paying the cabbie, arguing about the fare as usual, Bella and Tommy skipped over to the vast crowd waiting outside the South Entrance for admission at ten. I followed, nervous that my children would be lost or swallowed up by some monstrous invention. When Charles turned around he was alarmed to find us gone and looked red and cross when he joined us in the queue, but in those days he was never snappish for long.

I took Tommy's wriggly hand in mine and tucked my arm firmly into Charles's while Bella held his other hand. We had been warned of the danger from pickpockets and were determined to stay together in the largest crowd we had ever seen. Like a four-headed siege engine we moved forward into the entrance hall and gazed at the statue of the Queen and the wonderful crystal fountain, which Tommy wanted to bathe in. Although we bought a paper plan we did not really know where we were going. We thought ourselves very astute to devote eight hours to the exhibition, but one would need several hundred hours to do it justice.

Tommy and Bella were intoxicated by the fairground atmosphere and the great halls that brought geography lessons to life. We went first to the gorgeous Indian Court where there was a magnificent howdah on a stuffed elephant. Tommy wanted to take it home; he sat on the floor and cried when we told him we could not buy it, and Charles and I were mortified, for all the other children were so well behaved. Bella said, 'Tommy always spoils everything.' He was only three. How I wish we had bought him that stuffed elephant.

The rest of our visit passed in a daze. We teased lazybones Tommy with the machine that tipped people out of bed at a certain hour, and Bella said she would not marry unless her suitor gave her the Koh-i-Noor diamond in her engagement ring.

There were so many marvels that I became quite exhausted and soon had a sore throat from shrieking my laughter and astonishment. The sun beating down on the glass made it very hot; we were all parched and had to walk miles to the Refreshment Court which was so vast that there were two elm trees growing in the middle of it. 'Like the park in a cage,' Bella said. So many people were waiting there that she added it should be called Queue Gardens.

When at last we found a table a grubby waitress showed us an outrageously expensive menu. I pretended not to be hungry, but the children were more frank and poor Charles had to spend five shillings on tepid coffee, two miniature ices, Mr Schweppes's carbonated drinks and a plate of very dry sandwiches. I said that we would bring a picnic next time, and he said he did not know if there would be a next time, for our money was disappearing so rapidly. Then we had a delicate problem and were delighted to find that Bella and I had only to pay a penny to use a luxuriously equipped retiring-room. Charles and Tommy used other facilities, but I did not enquire into their details.

The exhibition itself made a powerful impression on me, and now I see that it was my first glimpse of Jonathan's world. This was the future we were all rushing towards, and I was thrilled when Charles explained to the children that they would live to see these wonderful inventions, and many more, in everyday use.

There were so many objects to fall in love with: Charles was enchanted by a doctor's walking-stick containing an enema and by a machine that turned out a hundred cigarettes a minute; Tommy adored the tableaux of stuffed animals made by some German gentleman, which Bella and I thought rather horrid. He stood for fifteen minutes in front of Mrs Partington's Tea Party, where stuffed ermine sat around a table drinking tea and another played the harmonium.

'That one playing the hymns looks exactly like Aunt Henrietta.'

'I think it looks like you, with its mean little eyes,' Bella said.

'No it doesn't. How do you stuff an animal, anyway? Let's stuff Archibald!'

At this Bella burst into tears, for Archibald was our cat.

My little girl's heart was conquered by the Stained Glass Gallery. She gazed up at the rich colours, reflected in their beautiful light as she imagined herself a little saint or angel in one of the stories they told.

And I? I believe I saw it all through the eyes of my husband and children, for they were my world then and I wanted no other.

At the end of the long afternoon we were exhausted but happy and decided to walk home to save the cab fare. We spent our last few shillings on a souvenir fan for Bella and a plaster model of a stuffed frog carrying an umbrella for Tommy.

That day is still vivid in my memory when so many others have quite faded. It was almost the last time we enjoyed an excursion as a family, for there was never enough time or money to do half the things the children demanded, and Charles had to work so hard to earn so little. Now it seems a greater marvel than the carriage drawn by kites (which Tommy longed to fly home in) that the four of us once lived under the same roof, squabbling and complaining but still united by some kind of love.

To see the Crystal Palace again now would be a cruel joke. Like me, it has been demolished and moved to a strange place. I have no wish to go anywhere. Once a month Dr Hood asks if I would like to return home for a few days and seems disappointed when I refuse. Perhaps they want to be rid of me. I am not mad enough for them.

I never liked our house in Harley Street with its dark, barred windows and shrivelled garden that smelled of fog and smoke. The big gloomy rooms were so dark that we had to burn gas even during the day. It was always a sad house, and without the children it would be unbearable. Every inch would remind me of them – and I believe I would even miss Henrietta, although I often wished her dead.

I could not live with Charles now, not even for a few days, could not even talk to him. He sent me away not knowing that I would be treated more kindly here than in our home, and he sent Tommy away when he might have sheltered him. Charles is a medical man. He had already lost one child to scarlet fever and might have preserved our little boy from the dangers of boarding-school life. Such a pang of bitterness comes over me when I think I shall never see my merry little children running to meet me again. I could not bear the nevermoreness of that house.

Three years and three deaths have divorced us more absolutely than the law which, as Charles complained, was too expensive. He came to see everything in terms of money, and I hope he finds it cheap to be alone. Perhaps he is not alone. He may have found companionship, some loose woman – no, he is too frightened of disease. A young lady with social accomplishments and hours of small talk and a large dowry he cannot get his hands on because he is still tied to me.

Charles stares at her tenderly as he once stared at me. He waltzes with her and goes into raptures when she plays the piano and tells her she is far too good for him. I hope she is not a bit good; I hope she is a heartless flirt with a squint and carroty hair. How odd that I should still be jealous of a man I no longer love. I will encumber him no more.

I stare out of this window and hours pass while I see nothing but the scenes of my past. It is dead, my present is even deader, and I have no future. There is but one person I want to see, one place I want to visit, and I can see Jonathan only in fantasy and dreams.

Every night I ask the attendant for a sleeping draught before I retire to my cubicle. Nights in the incurables' ward are a foretaste of that Hell I do not believe in. Henrietta, who is more vivid to me now than when she was alive, would say that we have sinned and are being punished by constant noise: groans, wails, sobs, moans, shouts, screams, grunts and maniacal laughter. Dr Hood is proud of his benign regime, but in the hours of darkness it seems that we choose to torture ourselves and wallow in our suffering, so the attendants here are always happy to tranquillize us that we may not be troublesome.

I am no trouble to anyone but myself. Greedily I swallow the contents of the little glass. I do not know what it is, but it tastes of oblivion. Perhaps I will store and hide the little glasses and one night swallow enough to forget everything for ever.

Last night Jonathan came to me in a dream. My dreary mourning shadows burst into colour as we walked together in a green park. He held my hand, and I felt as joyous as a swan that flies with its lifelong mate. My sad black crinoline fell away, and beneath it I was not naked but clothed in tight blue bloomers and a red 'tea-shirt'. Then we travelled on a vast red horseless omnibus like a house on wheels and from an upstairs window looked down on his prodigious city. Always Jonathan was with me, beside me, a warm and loving presence so that I did not feel like a stranger in his foreign time but as if I were at home there and then. Together we passed through streets where people rode hobby horses on wheels or glided effortlessly in metal boxes. High towers like great cliffs rose on either side, and crowds walked on spotless pavements. Not our ragged and dejected multitude: these people were free and prosperous and liberated from all care. I was so proud to be a citizen among them and felt quite sure I would be allowed to stay in their city.

When we became tired Jonathan instructed the omnibus to stop outside his house in Harley Street. We skimmed downstairs on dreamers' wings and stood together in the street where once I lived with my family. For a moment I felt giddy and confused, but then he took my hand again and led me up to his curious garret. As soon as we were alone Jonathan took me in his arms and we fell upon his couch in frenzied, almost convulsive transports and Said Goodnight.

To wake from such happiness is to sleepwalk, and to lose such companionship is to condemn my soul to imprisonment. I would like to draw or paint this wonderful dream, but I cannot work any more. My hands are useless – they have no power – and my eye is blinded by tears I cannot shed.

From the window I can see a group of male patients working in the garden. Mr Dadd is among them. An attendant pointed him out to me. A tall man with a beard, quite heavy-set and slow in his movements as he weeds a flower-bed.

Dr Hood moved him from the dreadful Home Office block, and now he is just a few wards away, although he might as well be in Timbuktu, for we are not allowed to talk to the male patients. We shall never meet and yet we are friends, for Dr Hood has often shown him my feeble drawings, and Mr Dadd has written back with kind words of encouragement and approval. He raises his head. I press my nose against the window-pane and will him to see me. If he did I think I would believe I still existed. Perhaps I would be able to make pictures for him. But he turns back to his work, and I return to my inner desert.

5
TWO CHAMBER POTS

This morning I was up at five and hard at work on my *Fairy Feller*. I watched the dawn break over the city and felt elated by the golden light that blessed my painting with a Mediterranean glow. From my easel I stared out over the gardens to the wall and the road beyond it. Up here in M4 I feel almost part of the world again. I could see the milkmaids with their pails and the first shabby clerks walking into London. It is enough to watch them from up here; perhaps I never wanted to join the workaday city. Brush in hand, my breakfast set beside me, I felt something very like contentment. For so many years I could not see the trees or grass at all, only a tiny patch of sky crushed behind bars. They say a man can get used to anything, and I marvel that I did get used to my imprisonment. Well, now I have got used to air and light and a generous horizon. This morning my voices were silent, and I could feel a thousand paintings germinating in the sunlight I am allowed to see again.

The peace was soon shattered. I recognized the voices of Oxford and Jonson, old enemies. When we were all in the criminal department together they were always quarrelling, and many's the time I've had to growl at Jonson to stop his bullying. I don't like to fight but can if needs must.

Edward Oxford is the only one among us who has not killed a man, and beneath his Young England bluster he's soft as curds. He retreats into his chess and fiddle playing (which I taught him) and his passion for learning languages. Jonson hates his gentlemanly pursuits as he hates my painting. Not daring to attack me he picks on Oxford, who is a great favourite with the attendants on account of his sweet nature. For years Edward longed to paint and followed me around like a sick lamb begging me to teach him. I let him play with paper and chalks, but the scribbles he produced were no better than a five-year-old's. Last month Haydon, seeing his own gentleness mirrored in Oxford, allowed him to train as a house-painter. Now he bustles around in his white overalls, beaming, his paintbrush a magic wand that has transformed his life.

Of course George Jonson cannot bear that. He's a brute, although an educated one. None of us has ever been able to understand how he managed to murder his entire crew. I long to ask the doctors and attendants, but they are not supposed to discuss the details of our crimes. Even if he was the captain of a small ship Jonson must have butchered at least half a dozen men. Poison? Or perhaps he slit their throats while they were all sleeping? Or made them all walk the plank?

Captain Bligh's fate on the *Bounty* is easier to comprehend than Jonson's. After all these years of being compelled to live with him I am quite sure he is capable of another massacre. There is danger in the air whenever he is near by, and I don't like to sit with my back to him, for I know he would destroy me and my paintings if he could. He is a man who hates what he does not understand.

I leaned forward and embraced the window of my vision. I was in the woods with them, hidden by wild grasses, safe in that rapt moment when my fairy feller – who cannot show his face (which is my own) – raises his axe. The birds are silent. I can smell the damp leaves under my feet and the rotten breath of the watching daisies. It is a trick I learned many years ago from Signor Leppardi, to concentrate so hard on one thing that you do not see or hear your surroundings. At first I only pretended to be deaf and blind, but with practice the useful loss of my faculties has become a screen I can put up at any time. More than anything, that trick has preserved me.

Shouting, crashing, yelling, manic laughter, screams of pain from Oxford. Reluctantly, I lay down my brush. I am a bad Samaritan and would find almost any excuse to ignore the troubles of others, feeling that I have enough of my own. But Edward is my friend, and I cannot spare him, for I have no others.

Turning away from my easel I find a scene more pantomime than tragedy. Edward sprawls on the floor in his painting overalls, beside his head a chamber pot which drips with its contents. A pale brown turd adorns his hair and piss drips from his nose to his mouth. Edward looks both concussed and disgusted, and Jonson stands over him triumphantly. It is like one of Benjamin West's paintings only with the heroism taken out. We are not easily shocked in M4, but ten of my fellow inmates stand around Edward in a circle, gawping in horrified silence.

'Lily-livered fucking grass!' Jonson glares defiance at us all.

Neville has been summoned. While McDonald takes Edward away to be mopped up Neville takes Jonson's arm. I expect a savage attack and get ready to assist Neville, but to my amazement Jonson allows himself to be led away.

I eat my breakfast before it is stolen by one of the others and turn back to my painting. Working on the beard of the grumpy old elf I stole from Fuseli my hand goes to my head and I feel the cold weight of another chamber pot there.

How memory insinuates itself into my fortress. I cannot get out, but the past can always get in. I have not thought of Leppardi for years, and now he returns twice in a morning.

I first met him in a pub where I sat arguing with Arthur. I had at last earned enough money from commissions to move away from home and had rented a studio and a tiny bedroom in Arthur's apartments. He was a solicitor's clerk, a dull man with a romantic streak which led him to fall wildly in love with Fanny, a ballet girl at the Theatre Royal, where I sometimes painted the scenery. Fanny was a trollop but a charming one. I comforted Arthur through his heart-break, and in return he offered me a cheap rent in Great Queen Street. Spending most of his life in the dust and tedium of Lincoln's Inn he thought it would be amusing to share rooms with an artist. Instead of amusing him I irritated him constantly with my untidiness, my late hours and my rowdy friends. It was worse than being at home, yet I did have a studio, a tiny attic all to myself to which I could invite my friends.

That evening we sat over a couple of beers in the Lamb and Flag, otherwise known as the Bucket of Blood.

'Really, Richard, why must you choose such disreputable places?'

'I'd rather listen to rogues than priggish lawyers.'

'I never saw such a bunch of cut-throats in my life. Well, I can't stay. I have a meeting.'

'At your lodge, I suppose?' He pretended not to hear. 'You needn't be so secretive. I know all about masons. My father is one and my uncle, too. Dressing up in silly clothes and reciting a lot of mumbo-jumbo.'

Arthur flushed and told me to keep my voice down. A few minutes later he left and I prepared myself for an all-night painting session. To my surprise another man, old and shabbily dressed, slid on to the bench beside me and offered to buy me a drink.

I accepted, of course, and glanced at him when he came back with two flagons of beer, a loaf of bread and a pot of Stilton he invited me to share. We exchanged names, and I busied myself with supper, which did not always come my way since I had decided to be independent.

Then I studied his face. It was so full of character that he might have come straight off the stage of the opera house around the corner. Dark and narrow beneath white hair that grew upwards as if to defy gravity, his face seemed too thin to contain his beaky nose and large mouth set in a crooked smile. Under thick white eyebrows his long golden eyes, flecked with dark green, stared back at me. Not a hand-some face but such an interesting one that I reached for my sketchpad as I asked, 'Are you an actor?'

'No. And I do not wish to be drawn.' His voice was not English but very cultivated. 'So you are an artist?'

'A student still.' I put my sketching things back in my leather satchel.

'And hungry for fame?'

'Most of the time just hungry. But, yes, I am ambitious.'

'I could not help overhearing your scorn of the Brotherhood.'

'In such a noisy tavern you must have made some effort to listen to our conversation. I can hardly hear you now above the noise.'

'You interested me. You have such an intelligent face, and you are at the beginning, full of hope and promise, while I am at the end.'

Unfortunately I succumbed to his flattery and leaned across the table towards him. For the next two hours we talked while quarrels and fights broke out around us.

Even now I can understand why he fascinated me so much. In his sonorous voice, still inflected with Italian, he told me he had been born in Rome and then, as a young man, had gone to Paris just before the revolution. I calculated he must be at least eighty, although his eyes were clear and on his frequent visits to the bar to buy us more drinks I noticed he moved swiftly and held himself straight. Every name that I mentioned was picked up by him and dropped into his anecdotes.

'David? Oh yes, a very great painter. I met him first in one of Anton Mesmer's baquets, or tubs. Twenty of us would sit there together, listening to the soothing glass armonica and imbibing the mysterious fluid of animal magnetism.'

'And was Mesmer a charlatan as they say now?'

'Who knows? People call a man a charlatan when he does not deliver everything for the nothing they are willing to risk. Before the revolution Paris was full of extraordinary people, idealists – people for whom ideas are more real than objects. Imagination is a higher mode of perception than the senses.'

That, of course, was music to my ears, and I listened even more intently. Leppardi paid me the compliment of assuming I knew all about the exotic personages in his stories. In fact, I had never heard of any of them except the French King and Napoleon.

'I was fortunate enough to meet the great Cagliostro after one of his seances. He was already a great favourite at the French court and held magic suppers at Versailles. Then the king discovered his involvement in the Affair of the Necklace, which, of course, was one of the major events that led to the French Revolution.

'Poor Cagliostro spent six months in the Bastille and was then banished from France. He went to Rome, my own beloved city, with his wife, the beautiful Comptesse Seraphina. They flourished for a few years, selling elixirs and holding seances once more. But then the

Inquisition arrested him, tortured the poor man and imprisoned him in the Castel Sant'Angelo, accusing him of heresy, magic, conjury and Freemasonry. Some say he died in prison, but I think he may have escaped and still be wandering around Europe.

'People wondered where Cagliostro's powers came from. He was, as you will know, a pupil of the Comte de St Germain, an even more mysterious man. I met him once in Paris at a reception given for Haydn. He was small and dark and always wore black velvet with the most amazing diamonds which he claimed to make himself. That evening he told me at once, with an easy, assured manner, that he was three hundred years old and knew the secret of the Universal Medicine.'

'And did he tell you what it was?'

'That must wait for another meeting. Napoleon was another pupil of St Germain's, of course. After the conquest of Egypt they spent a night talking inside the Great Pyramid. The Comte was familiar with the rites of the ancient Egyptian gods, and all who knew Napoleon said that when he emerged the next morning he was more god than man.'

'Egyptian gods?' At the thought that Leppardi was a messenger from Osiris my head whirled.

'Did you not know that all magic began in Egypt? Yes, St Germain, some say, was the reincarnation of Christian Rosencreutz, he of the Rosy Cross. And it is possible that Rosencreutz was really Hiram Abiff, the great architect who was murdered at the Temple of Solomon. But I forgot, you despise Freemasonry. Are you a free-thinker, young man?'

'I don't know what I think,' I gasped. I felt doors creaking open in my mind, dazzling light illuminating my glorious future. The beer in the Bucket of Blood was very strong.

That night I staggered home and painted all night, fizzing with excitement. Leppardi had asked if I would meet him again with my friends from the Academy, as he said he had mystical knowledge that was particularly valuable to young artists, but I had no intention of sharing him. Afraid that my friends would either laugh at me or be preferred by him or both, I kept our meetings secret. His words boomed in my head, and he dominated my dreams. I was not in love with the shrivelled old fellow, not physically, but he had power over me.

I never knew where he lived or how. Over the next few months he appeared suddenly, sliding out from behind a tree in St James's Park or out of a bookshop in Covent Garden. Each meeting made me feel closer to the great secrets with which he tantalized me.

Leppardi spoke eloquently of the cosmic mind and the third eye. He made me swear not to tell anyone that he was a member of the Ancient Order of Osiris. Apparently Mozart, Napoleon, Blake, Casanova, Goethe, Hogarth, Swift, Haydn, Voltaire and the Duke of Wellington had all been initiates. This Ancient Order had secret cells all over Europe, and Leppardi had been sent to London to search for suitable candidates, young men who were exceptionally talented, intelligent and sensitive. With every meeting he became more convinced that I was worthy of being initiated.

One afternoon, as we sat in a coffee house in Drury Lane, Leppardi explained that my scepticism about Freemasons was the first sign that I was meant for higher things. 'Lodges are for men of common clay – lawyers, soldiers, apothecaries and so on.' I thought of my father with enjoyable contempt. 'They can dress up and play foolish games and do business. But extraordinary men need to go deeper, to travel further. Love-feasts can be dangerous.'

I shivered with excitement. Since my amorous disasters in Chatham and Cobham I knew not what to do with my poor sugar stick. When I pleasured myself in my new solitary room at Great Queen Street I heard my father's voice telling me I would go blind or mad. Every day I saw beautiful men or women I thought I could love but had no idea how to set about it. I told myself I loved sweet Elizabeth Langley back in Chatham, but although we exchanged letters I had not seen her for two years, and engagement or marriage were out of the question, for I had no money and she came from a respectable family. With Powell and the others I joked about whores and the beautiful rich women who might help us in our careers; the other possibility – that the object of love should be another man – was not mentioned between us. They laughed at Laurence, one of our fellow students who was known to be a Miss Molly, and mimicked his soft voice and swaying walk. I was terrified that they would laugh at me.

Leppardi explained that the ancient Egyptian rites and the Eleusinian Mysteries had all been about pursuing wisdom and truth through what he called the arts of love. I craved more detail. We were sitting on a bench in St James's Park at the time. As always when I was with him I was oblivious to my surroundings. The only reality was his seductive voice and the judgement of his strange eyes.

'I am not speaking of smutty schoolboy japes but of serious matters. When men and women forget the teachings of those grim black crows who call themselves priests and give themselves freely to one another, the power hidden within is awakened. Perhaps you are not ready yet. Have you done your exercises?'

He had instructed me in various mental exercises involving deep breathing and meditation, which I practised diligently every day and still do. They, oddly enough, were genuine.

'Yes. I would like to attend a love-feast.'

'Ah, but it is so difficult to arrange. And expensive. Magicians and illuminati must be summoned from Bavaria, Venice and Paris. Suitable rooms must be found, safe from prying eyes, for our rites are often misunderstood by vulgar dolts –'

'How much?' I asked nervously.

'I would have to be quite sure that you are spiritually mature enough for such a profound experience.' He put both hands to his forehead and inhaled deeply. 'My angel tells me you are an old soul who has been reincarnated many times since you first walked with Osiris and Isis five thousand years ago.'

Osiris again! 'Please tell me how much,' I stammered, weak with desire.

'Twenty guineas. Does it seem a lot to you? But, remember, the illuminati must gather from all over Europe, the best food and wine must be provided, someone must be paid to stand at the door to guard our mysteries – I am asking you only to pay a fraction of the real cost.'

'I will get the money. When must I pay?'

'You must not think that money is important. These things are beyond price. One should not haggle over them. Let me see. We are in June – in six weeks I should be able to make the necessary arrangements.'

'August the 1st is my birthday.' I have always clutched desperately at birthday treats. Mama died a few days before my seventh birthday, and every year I feel the void is nearer at that time of year than at any other.

'Indeed? Then I must consult my astrologer to see if it is auspicious. Payment is in advance. Half one week before your initiation and half at the door. Do you wish to proceed?'

'Oh yes! Oh, thank you!'

I rushed off to the Theatre Royal to book more work as a scene painter and, staying up night after night, churned out revoltingly sentimental pictures of flowers, butterflies and fairies for a shop in Regent Street. Although I would have been ashamed to show them to any of my friends I had listened many times to my sisters and their friends chatting and knew what sent them into ecstasies of cooing.

I called myself Lucilla Langley, thinking of Elizabeth perhaps, and told the ladies who owned the shop that my sister made the pictures but was too shy to sell them. L.L.'s pictures were put in the window together with silk flowers, boxes of chocolates and china figurines of milkmaids and sold like aphrodisiacs in a convent to rich young ladies who put them in their bedrooms and gave them to each other as presents.

At the end of the month I was half dead from exhaustion, for I still had to attend classes at the Academy. I told my friends I had decided to spend my birthday with my family and told my family I wanted to celebrate with my friends. Everyone was offended except Arthur, who was delighted I had become such a quiet tenant.

My twenty guineas were hidden in a wooden chest under my bed. Each night I took it out, locked my door, counted the coins like some old miser and arranged them in neat piles on the floor; towers of silver and gold in the palace of the senses I was soon to inhabit.

On July the 25th I met Leppardi in a dark tavern near Lincoln's Inn Fields and handed over ten guineas in a heavy purse. As he snatched my hard-earned money it struck me that he might disappear with it, but, as if he read my thought, he smiled and bought me lunch and looked so distinguished I felt quite sure he must be trustworthy. Over our spotted dick Leppardi murmured the arrangements for the night of my rebirth, as he called it, and I became so excited I could not eat or drink but only gaze at him, hungry for sensation.

My birthday was hot and dry, as I saw when I drew my white curtains and looked out at the small patch of blue sky trapped between dirty rooftops and gasping elms. I longed for the summery Kent meadows, but London was where I was going to make my fortune. Mozart, Hogarth, Goethe . . . I felt their breath on the back of my neck, heard their voices whispering my name.

Arthur was at work. I told the landlady I was not at home and watched the pavement from the window of my attic studio. One by one I saw Powell, my father and my sister Maria call and retreat. I could not have talked to any of them that day for fear of making them suspicious. Too restless to work, I sat at my easel in delicious antici-pation of my love-feast.

At seven I washed, doused myself in expensive cologne and carefully dressed in a white silk shirt, tight green trousers and a green frock-coat I had carefully brushed. I had bought a Chinese golden-silk shawl-collar waistcoat of which I was very proud and took my new black-silk top hat out of its splendid box. Then I bobbed around, trying to see myself in the scrap of mirror above my washbowl and jug. Fragmented like a mosaic, my image pleased me, although, of course, I was only dressing so that my unknown lovers would tear my clothes off me.

At seven thirty, too nervous to eat, I waited for Arthur to come in from his long day at work and close his door, then tiptoed past it (so that he would not sneer at my finery and ask questions) and down the street.

A group of men in full Masonic regalia were going into the Grand Lodge, and I pitied them. They were only scratching the surface of arcane knowledge, whereas I was about to be initiated into its ancient depths.

For an hour and a half I walked around Covent Garden, the Strand and Fleet Street, trying to stay cool and elegant in the warm evening air. It seemed that the whole city was on the streets: hundreds of men and women as perfumed and well dressed as I were going out to dine or drink or dance, to the opera or the theatre or to meet friends; thousands of ragged others were selling flowers or fruit or cakes or pies, begging or pimping or soliciting. Outside Somerset House the torches were lit and carriages were driving up to some grand reception. Voices and laughter and music came from every house – even the horses seemed to be enjoying themselves – and I felt safely ensconced in the great panorama of London pleasure. For once I was carrying enough money to indulge in any of them.

At nine I stood outside the pub in an alley off Fleet Street. Leppardi was not there, but a man standing in a doorway sidled up to me. 'Mr Dadd? Where's the money?'

Surprised by his shabbiness and furtive air I handed over the ten guineas.

'You're to follow me.' He took me to a side door where I was grabbed and blindfolded. Unseen hands gripped my arms, and for the first time I felt suspicious.

Then Leppardi's noble baritone enriched my darkness. 'Dear Richard, we are so delighted that you have decided to join us tonight. Forgive the secrecy, but we have many enemies, from the Pope to the bobbies, and I am besieged by young men wanting to be initiated into our order. Now, come inside.'

I sensed I was in a large room and heard a door being locked behind me. The blindfold was so tight that I could see nothing through it but imagined figures in robes and gorgeous dresses standing around a table out of a Caravaggio painting, laden with candelabra, fruit, goblets and flagons of wine.

'First, let us all stand and join hands, dear brothers, to toast our newest and youngest adept. To Richard Dadd and his great future!'

As a chorus of male and female voices toasted me, a glass was put into my hand, and I drank. It was not wine but some sweet heavy liquid that burned my throat. 'To Richard Dadd!'

I was the hero of a theatrical scene. Beneath my blindfold I smiled and reached out my arms to my new friends. Leppardi's voice continued, warm and musical, but I cannot remember all that he said. The rest of that long night is confused, a half-remembered dream.

Leppardi said I had to be naked before I could be reborn. I was stripped and gagged and bound with ropes that cut into my skin. There was more to drink, then I was led inside a magic circle where I was told I would experience the long dark night of the soul. What about the love-feast? I wanted to ask, but my tongue was thick and the gag smothered my words.

'Repeat after me. If I ever speak to anyone about this ceremony my throat will be cut and my tongue will be torn out by its roots . . .' Leppardi's voice, terrifying but also familiar, so that I believed all he said. 'Soon, dear brother Richard, you will be carried in vision to the light where Osiris will greet you. But, first, you must descend into the bowels of the earth to be laid in your grave. Take seven solemn steps.'

I stumbled down some steps. 'Now you must halt and make obeisance for Osiris.'

I bowed low, and at that moment I felt the god's presence glowing all around me. He whispered in my ear, *You have come to me at last, my son. Remember my words in* The Book of the Dead: *I shall not decay. I shall not rot. Join my order and I will help you to greatness.*

Leppardi's voice continued, 'Now you must crawl. Remember how Osiris, when King of Thebes, was dismembered by his brother Seth. All night you must lie as a corpse in the grave in remembrance of his murder. Bury him, brothers.'

I smelled the damp earth and felt the metal coffin chill my bones. Leppardi was silent, but I felt Osiris beside me and was not afraid. Time stopped, I forgot the room above me and even the love-feast.

If I could only remember all the visions I had that night I could make the most beautiful paintings in the world. But they come back to me in fragments: Osiris took my hand, and we flew together across the night sky to the planets; Napoleon smiled on me; Blake and

Hogarth embraced me and told me I would be their brother in eternity; Osiris whispered great truths and prophecies, and my will dissolved as he dismembered the old Richard and helped me give birth to the new one.

As I lay there I felt the dawn chill on my skin and knew I was at the beginning of a new life. Now that Osiris had touched me I had courage enough to accomplish anything.

Leppardi's voice startled me. 'Brother Richard, you have survived the ordeals of the long dark night of the soul. Osiris has accepted you, and now you can join our revels.'

I imagined them in the great hall above me, men with animal masks and beautiful women, all waiting for me. Hands pulled me out of my coffin and back up the steps.

'Now I am placing the crown on your head.' I felt it, cold and heavy, and heard the joyous laughter of my brethren. 'When your blindfold is removed you will see the light of Osiris. First you must feel our daggers at your throat, reminding you that you must never reveal the secrets you have learned this night.'

I could feel them, sharp points on my skin. Hands untied me and removed the gag and blindfold. My eyes were blinded by the hours of darkness, and I had a headache from the burden of my crown.

'Now look up at the glorious morning star, beautiful Alba, whose rising brings peace and salvation, and take your reward from Osiris.'

There was a dazzling star that turned into a lovely naked woman who caressed me and fed me grapes and sweet cakes and wine. Then she led me to a soft couch where she gave herself to me and we delighted in each other.

I must have fallen asleep. As I drifted off I thought I heard Leppardi's voice. 'Do you want to know the ultimate secret, Richard? There is no secret.'

'Well? Where is it?' Her voice was harsh and grating, not a bit poetic. I kept my eyes tightly shut and hoped to return to my dreams.

'You look a right looby with that thing on your head. Take it off. I need a piss.' My crown was removed, and there was nothing angelic about the sounds she made. I still could not bear to open my eyes.

'Well? Where's my money?' It was painful to be dragged back to this world. I muttered, 'What money? I have no money.'

'Two quid he promised me, that foreign braggadocio. If you don't give it to me quick I'll get my cock bawd to give you a good bastonading, you fumbler.'

At this point, very reluctantly, I opened my eyes. The odious voice came from a gimblet-eyed woman old enough to be my mother, or possibly grandmother, who squatted beside me on a chamber pot. I sat up and looked for the beautiful maiden of the morning star.

'Well? I'm not hanging round here all morning. Two quid or I scream the house down.'

We were alone in a long low room with straw on the floor. I lay on a dirty mattress covered by a coarse grey blanket full of holes. The great hall, the soft couch, the candles, the banqueting table, the goblets and the flagons of wine had all disappeared. 'Whatcha looking for, you great booby?'

I had a raging headache and could hardly speak. 'My clothes. Signor Leppardi and the illuminati –'

'I'll give you loonybloodynati.' The termagant stood up, scratched her privates and advanced on me menacingly.

'My dear Alba, I will find the money.' I had no idea where but smiled and bowed exactly as my father used to do when the tradesmen came to our door in Chatham with their unpaid bills.

'Who are you calling Alba? My name's Jem. I want my money now, you shitsack.' I had backed away from her to a window from where I could look down on Fleet Street in all its morning bustle and anonymity.

Suddenly I snatched the grey blanket, wrapped it around me like a toga and ran to the door at the other end of the room, which opened. I leaped downstairs, past men already boozing in the pub below, pushed out into the alley and bolted down Fleet Street. I didn't look behind me to see if she was pursuing me. I'm sure she did. A half-naked man chased by a shrieking woman is hardly a sight to turn heads in London. I dived down a few more alleyways I knew and was home in fifteen minutes.

It was not a noble entrance. My landlady, who was cleaning the hallway and the stairs, roared with laughter when she saw me. Unfortunately Arthur was just leaving for work and winced with disgust.

A few days later I left my lodgings in Great Queen Street and joined Powell in Charlotte Street. I never told anybody about my initiation and never saw Signor Leppardi – or my fine clothes – again. For months I was afraid to go out at night in case Jem found me, and each morning I examined my thingambobs for fear she had been a fire ship.

Yet I believe I would have died of misery in the cages of the old criminal block without the exercises in meditation Leppardi taught me. And I did see Osiris that night. I will paint it. I will show Hood and Haydon what visions can be.

6
THE HUMBLE SERVANT
OF THE ARTS

This morning Haydon invited himself to breakfast, as he often does.

'Are you moving in with us, George?' I asked.

Jane looked up from her coffee in alarm. Haydon is our dearest friend in the hospital, lively-minded and sociable and immensely knowledgeable about art, but he has learned free-and-easy ways among the Australian sheep farmers and aborigines, and Jane is somewhat formal. Haydon was carrying an enormous box, a tripod and what appeared to be a black tent.

'Be back in a minute. That bacon smells good.' He disappeared and came back five minutes later carrying more enormous boxes, which filled our little dining-room. Donald and Chas, who had been playing outside, came running in and hurled themselves at him with screams of delight. As Jane and I are rather deficient in relations, Haydon is their honorary uncle, a delightful one.

Louisa, who had been reading in her room as usual, came in and stared at him shyly, being too old for hugs and giggles. Poor child, I wish I could speed her down the rocky coast to the harbour of womanhood. Her enormous dark eyes are trapped in her sullen face, and she has forgotten how to smile.

'Is Clarissa joining us?' Jane asked

'Walton gave her a hard time last night teething. She needs to sleep in.'

While Haydon wolfed down a plate of bacon, eggs and mushrooms, Chas and Donald shrieked the questions I had been too polite to ask.

'What's in all those boxes?'

'Is it presents for us?'

'Are you going to hunt lions in Africa?'

'Can we come?'

Laughing, eating toast and marmalade and unpacking one of the boxes, Haydon said, 'Your father and I are going on a kind of safari, boys. We are to tour the hospital, recording images of the patients, and if you wish you can come with us and help. We need Sherpas to carry our equipment.'

'But, George, I cannot spare the time today. I know we spoke of this and of Diamond's experiments at the Surrey Asylum, but it is an enormous project and must be planned –'

'Nonsense. Your planning will kill all the fun. We'll entertain ourselves as well as the children and the patients.'

'Are you going to sketch them, Uncle George?' Donald asked.

Haydon's cartoons and clever birthday cards adorn our mantelpiece. 'It would take months to do portraits of them all. I have discovered a way to cheat the exacting muses and produce an image instantaneously that requires no knowledge of drawing.'

When Louisa spoke it was a shock. We all looked at her as if we had forgotten she was in the room. 'Daguerreotypes,' she said in her low, toneless voice. She knows a great deal from all her reading but has not yet learned to converse with charm, as a young lady must.

'No, that would be too slow.' Haydon contradicted her without malice, but I saw Louisa flinch as if from a blow. 'Collodion, that is the process of the future, far quicker and cheaper. Each image is exposed in a few seconds and costs but a shilling instead of a guinea –'

'A shilling? How many shillings do you think I have to waste on frivolities? I don't think my governors would be amused.' I constantly have to play the ballast that tugs my friend's wild enthusiasms back to earth.

'They will be my shillings. I'm sure I'll be able to sell them, and I borrowed the equipment from my friend Hering, who is coming over in a minute to assist us, so my new mania won't cost you a penny. Our subjects will be able to keep their portraits, for we can print from the wet glass on to paper and make as many copies as we wish. The only problem I foresee is that we will have to carry our darkroom with us' – he pointed to the black tent – 'as the glass plates must be developed while they are still wet. Ah, here's Hering.'

The porter showed in a small, thin man. 'Let me introduce Henry Hering, who has a famous studio in Regent Street. And this is the great Dr Hood and his enchanting wife and children. You two should meet, for you are both changing the world.' He beamed so warmly that Hering and I could only bask together in his charm.

Hering shook my hand vigorously. 'I've just read Morley's article about your reforms in *Household Words*. I've been longing to meet you.'

Haydon is always bringing people together, for he is one of those rare men who spontaneously likes others. Jane and I have to learn kindness, but he seems to feel it quite naturally, and his *joie de vivre* has won him many friends in the art world, including the wild young Rossettis, who are, he tells me, anxious to visit our hospital. Mr Dickens's interest in our hospital and the generous article about us in his tuppenny weekly are most gratifying. However, I do not want our hospital to become a playground for the Bohemian classes, for we have serious work to do.

'Come, boys! Help me carry these boxes, and later I'll tell you about my kangaroo hunt.' Haydon charged off, followed by Hering and my whooping sons, and I saw that my carefully planned day was going to be disrupted.

Jane said, 'I'll call on Clarissa later and see if she wants any help with Walton. Such a ridiculous name for a baby!'

'He is to be a great angler like his father and namesake.' I kissed her brow, knowing her reluctance to follow me into the hospital, which brings back agonizing memories of her own incarceration.

I turned to say goodbye to Louisa, but she gripped my arm and said firmly, 'I want to come.' Although I did not think it suitable there was no time to argue, for I was worried that the noise and excitement would upset my fragile patients and feared for my boys' safety.

We found the experimental group at the top of the building, in the female incurables' ward, surrounded by a crowd of patients and attendants. It was a great novelty to have five males present, even if two of them were under the age of eleven, and I reflected that feminine vanity outlives its function: there was such a flurry of combs and paper flowers and ribbons, such a pinching of cheeks and tightening of stays and crimping of hair, that we might have been backstage at the Opera Comique. I had intended to record only a few patients, those who best illustrated the different types of madness, but soon saw that this would cause a riot. Haydon's new toy was a mirror in which everyone wished to see their reflection – except poor Mrs Sanderson, who sat apart gazing out of the window.

When she first arrived here, three years ago, she was a vivacious and intelligent lady, and I had great hopes of her swift recovery. But something has broken in her – her heart, for want of a more scientific term. She gazes vacantly out of the window, day and night, still beautiful but the very picture of melancholia. Mrs Sanderson ignored the tempest of excitement, marooned in her own doldrums. Miss Protheroe flinched from the metal equipment and cried out that we would shatter her into a thousand pieces, and Mrs Garston, who is excessively religious, shouted at Haydon, 'You blaspheme! God created us, and you are trying to steal our soul from him to print it on your stinking paper!'

The other ladies, however, watched eagerly as Haydon and the attendants arranged each one for her portrait. He and Hering organized Louisa and the boys into a remarkably efficient manu-factory, showing them how to clean the glass plate and pour the collodion mixture on to it. Then they had to immerse the glass plate in a solution of silver nitrate and water and hand him the wet plate to expose in his photographic machine. Haydon and Hering developed each image in a solution of iron sulphate, acetic acid and water in the portable darkroom they had erected in the middle of the ward and transferred what they called the negative on to albumen paper. Hering explained every stage of this process, and the children were delighted by their science lesson.

For me the true discovery was the effect our surprise visit had upon the patients. Had I engaged a circus to come and entertain them there could not have been more squeals and shrieks than when Hering emerged from his black tent with each new paper portrait as soon as it was dry. This was not merely a conjuring trick but a profound compliment: each lady stared at her image with relief and gratitude, as if her idea of herself had been returned to her after a long absence. Haydon had intended merely to show each lady her portrait before keeping it for the hospital records. Instead, he and Hering had to make two copies of each and allow the patient to hug her treasure. To tear it away would have done great harm to a creature already damaged.

For years I have tried to establish a routine here that is both soothing and interesting. My patients are encouraged to talk to one another, to sew and help in the laundry and bakery and in the garden and to dance at our regular balls. All of these ladies have been reluctantly kept on beyond the usual year because they need to remain secluded from the busier, but scarcely happier, world beyond our walls. Yet Haydon's novel disruption of their routine had cheered them immensely.

I whispered to Haydon that I wanted an image of Mrs Sanderson's melancholy madness. He agreed and directed his mechanical eye at her from behind to catch her in profile. The poor lady was so absorbed in her own misery that she did not even notice us, and the resulting collodiotype – if that is the correct word – may be instructive to my students. It shows a woman still young, with the delicate bone structure of a Leonardo saint. Her dark hair is unkempt, and her tragic eyes are full of shadows above her black dress.

We started to dismantle the black tent to move it on to the next ward, but Chas burst into tears. 'It isn't fair! I want my picture, too!'

It is always mortifying when my children's behaviour is worse than that of my patients. Louisa, who has no time for other people's tantrums, said from the pinnacle of fourteen, 'You're such a big baby, Chas. Nobody would think you were seven.'

Then Donald pulled her hair, and Louisa slapped him, and Haydon said, 'Very well, you shall have your picture. Go and stand over by the window, all three of you.'

'But, George, all these shillings . . .'

Haydon said in his amiable way, 'Your children make a charming picture. I shall sell it with ease.'

The patients greeted this little scene with beams of affection, as if they did not mind seeing their superintendent reduced to an anxious paterfamilias.

After a hurried picnic lunch of bread and cheese and ham in Haydon's cosy room we were all, children and adults alike, in a hurry to continue. I now understand the daguerreomania that swept across Europe a few years ago. My excitement was mingled with guilt, almost as if Mrs Garston, whose knees are raw and red from all her praying, was right. Is it ethical to copy nature mechanically?

When I raised the point with Haydon he retorted in his boisterous way, 'There's no right or wrong about it, Billy. This is a splendid instrument for a dunce like me, for I am cursed with the artistic temperament without having either the talent or the patience to dedicate my life to art.' He helped himself to another glass of ale and more bread and Stilton. 'Chaps who do go in for it in a serious way come to such a sticky end. My brother Sam has a terrible time selling his sculpture. One month he's flush, the next I have to send him money. I fear for his future.'

'Yes, much better to have a safe profession like us.'

'Yet I will always envy the artistic life. Did I ever tell you about our visit as boys to Benjamin Haydon? We could never decide if we were related or not, but Sam was anxious to meet him, and Ben was kind to him when Sam first came to London and introduced him to everyone. Ben was a brilliant historical painter and when he was young, before I was born, had great success. All London flocked to the Egyptian Hall to see his paintings, and he was a friend of Keats and Wordsworth and even the Duke of Wellington. Nobody could have been more serious about his art – why, he used to pray in front of his vast canvases before he started work each day. He despised English painting and was all for the Grand Manner, for great historical and religious subjects. Nothing else would do. I never dared to show him my silly little cartoons.

'I used to stand in his studio and lose myself in *The Raising of Lazarus* and *The Execution of Charles I*. I'd tell him, "Ben," I'd say, "when I'm rich and have a big house I'll buy them all." Only I never did, and neither did anybody else. He got into debt and was imprisoned for it and quarrelled with all his friends and tried to kill himself. More than once. Did I ever tell you how it ended?'

'I remember there was some tragedy. Perhaps the children should not –'

'They are busy playing and squabbling. Sam was devastated, Billy. It was about ten years back. Sam called on Ben one afternoon and found his servant in tears. Ben had cut his throat, the blood splashed all over *Alfred and the First British Jury*. He left a note: "Tom Thumb had 12,000 people last week; B.R. Haydon 133? (the half a little girl). Exquisite taste of the English people! O God! Bless me through the evils of this day."'

'Terrible.'

'Such a fate is not for me, Billy. I want to enjoy life. And we have another example, nearer at hand, of the vengeance the muses wreak on their most devoted servants.'

'Strange that you should mention Dadd. All morning he has been on my mind. What would he think of our mechanical eye?'

'Let's go downstairs and ask him. If he is in a sociable mood he'll tell us, and if he is morose and silent we'll leave him alone.'

I stared out of the window at the gloomy bulk of the Home Office buildings, dark even on this sunny day. If I achieve nothing else I will die contented that I have rescued Dadd and the others from that horrible place. I had no power to repair the damp, stinking building or reform the prison regimen. For my first four years here I had nightmares about it in which the suffering eyes of the prisoners wept tears of blood and their voices beseeched me to help them.

Now I have been able to. Dadd and the others, all of unsound but educated mind, live in our hospital. None of them will ever be able to leave it, but at least they are humanely treated here and no longer have to fear the brutality of their fellow prisoners, many of whom feigned madness to escape the scaffold or transportation. A few weeks back disaster struck in the shape of a chamber pot: Jonson hurled it at Oxford's head, injuring him, and has had to be sent back to the criminal block.

Following my gaze, Haydon said, 'Poor Jonson. Is there nothing we can do?'

'He might have killed Oxford as he killed all his crew. We cannot have murder in M4 or the governors will revolt against my reforms, the newspapers will get hold of the story, and I could even lose my job. There are plenty of hostile eyes on our hospital.' Haydon is too kind-hearted to grasp the complexities of political intrigue.

I have quite a collection of Dadd's work now and admire his talent, although I wish he would confine himself to charming fairy paintings and landscapes. I have commissioned a series of sketches to illustrate the passions, as I feel this may help him to control his own. The money I pay him goes to buy more canvas and paints, and I am proud to be the patron of so talented an artist.

Haydon and Hering set up their temporary darkroom again outside M4, and the children helped to mix the collodion mixture and clean the instruments.

'I want to see Mr Dadd!' Donald said from inside the black tent.

'So do I!' said Chas. 'Is he really dangerous? Like the lions we saw?'

'He will probably murder you both – and I shall help him.' Jane and I still pray that Louisa will grow up to be more womanly and tender.

I hushed them, for I have tried to teach them that lunatics are just like the rest of us only more unfortunate. I dislike that facetious way of talking about mental suffering. But, in fact, I did not want my children to enter M4. Some instinct warned me against it. Naturally, we have extra security at the door. I have chosen these men because they belong to the better class of criminal lunatics, but I am only too aware that they are all capable of violence. They are allowed in the gardens only at times when the other patients are not around.

When we opened the door we found that most of the men were out working in the gardens. They do this with zeal, for until a few months ago they were confined to a tiny exercise yard. Oxford sat at his studies and Dadd at his easel. He was working on 'my' painting of Oberon and Titania, and as we opened the door he turned to look up at us with surprise and power in his fine blue eyes. They are eyes that have, like Keats, 'travelled in the realms of gold, and many goodly states and pilgrims seen', and it took them a while to travel back to us. He did not look pleased to see me or the giggling children behind me, but when he saw Haydon pointing his machine at him his eyes softened and something like a blush spread over his cheeks.

I saw that he was not in one of his rages, and so I asked Charles Neville, my chief attendant, who has been with me since we both worked at Colney Hatch and is utterly trustworthy, to take the children down to play in the gardens. Haydon and I went to sit with Dadd, and Oxford joined us.

The four of us sat so companionably that we might have been old friends dropped in for a teatime chat. I know I do most good when I forget that I am a doctor.

I began by admiring the completed section of his circular canvas. Dadd promptly turned it around so that we could not see it, but I sensed that he was flattered.

'You will have it soon enough. There is another painting I have to work on. It is for you.' He looked directly at Haydon, who had his pipe out and sat beaming at us over his beard. He has the gift of looking relaxed under all circumstances. I never knew a saner man, yet he is a great favourite among the lunatics.

'How kind,' Haydon said benignly.

I did not ask which painting Dadd meant but hoped it was a sweetly pretty fairy scene. As he does so often, Dadd seemed to catch my thought and said sharply, 'You cannot buy my mind.'

'My dear fellow, why would I want to do that?'

'It is your job. I saw you just now recording my brain. You were the ringleader,' he looked at Haydon reproachfully.

'Do you mean our experiment with collodion images?' I spoke gently 'It is a project we are engaged on, to make pictures of our patients. For our own interest, for science and, we hope, for the amusement of the patients.'

'Why are there no pictures of me?' Oxford is very vain. He has a scrapbook of cuttings from newspapers and illustrated magazines about his trial and considers himself the most interesting person in the hospital, if not the world.

'I will make one.' Haydon jumped up and went to prepare his mechanical eye.

Dadd glared at me. 'You have been duped by this machine. Do you really believe it is possible to plagiarize nature, that a picture produced by such a trick can possess any depth? When I draw or paint I enter an imaginary, spiritual realm. I select my subjects, arrange them and open myself to them. I do not crudely reproduce the objects in front of my eyes.'

'You should not feel threatened by our steward's new toy. It is only the humble servant of true artists like you. I value your genius – we all do.' Dadd shivered and looked away.

Haydon came back into the ward and pointed his machine at Oxford, who stared into it hungrily. 'Will my picture be famous? Will I be in the newspapers again?'

'It is all nonsense. This frivolous toy will destroy art and make fools of us. You should keep your soul to yourself,' Dadd rebuked him.

I could not resist an argument. 'These words you use – spiritual, soul – they are the essence of Christianity. Yet you say you do not believe in religion.'

'Not yours. I have my own.'

'Will you not sample mine?'

'I have done so and do not like the taste.'

'Every Sunday we worship in the chapel above you. You must hear our joyful singing and the rich voice of our organ.'

'I block my ears.'

'I should so much like to welcome you among us. Will you not join us?'

'Dr Hood, I have no wish to join anything. I know you are a good man, and I am grateful to you.' He looked around M4. 'You have given me back my life. As a matter of fact, I have an idea for what you would call a religious painting.'

'How wonderful! What is it?'

'The story of the Good Samaritan. It was always my favourite when

I was a child and my father sent us to Sunday school. But I conceive of it as a vast subject. There is no space here for such an ambitious canvas . . .'

'I will find the space! My governors would be delighted to supply the materials for a religious painting. Perhaps we could exhibit it in the public space of the hospital, in the hallway or on the staircase. Yes, that would be best. At Bart's they have Hogarth's *Samaritan*, so why should we not have one of our own?'

'You are the Good Samaritan. I know what you have done for me.' He looked at me then with such fire and sadness in his eyes that I was dazzled.

Haydon returned with paper prints of his portraits of Dadd and Oxford, who had very different ways of responding. Oxford took his eagerly, gazed at it with delight and said, 'I thought I was even more handsome. Are you sure your machine is accurate?'

'Quite sure,' Haydon said with a smile. 'Would you like to keep it?'

'Thank you so much. I shall lock it away with my treasures.' He ran into his sleeping-cubicle where, Neville has told me, he has all the cuttings about his trial inside an old biscuit tin. He is immensely proud to be the hero, as he sees it, of such a story and to have been associated with royalty, even though he lost his liberty because of his bungled assassination attempt.

Some institutions do not allow patients to keep their own possessions. I believe that these personal collections reveal much about the men and women here and permit them on condition that the attendants discreetly search their hoards once a month to check that there are no poisons or knives or other weapons. I know that Dadd stores some of the money I have paid him for his work and keeps it with a strange collection of mementoes from his travels.

When Haydon gave him his portrait Dadd flinched and made as if to tear it up.

'No! It is a good likeness. Haydon gives it to you as a present, but if you do not want it I will keep it and put it on our mantelpiece to remind me of the charming painting that will be mine some day.'

Something had angered Dadd and he retreated into hostile silence. It is how most of our meetings end. I longed to reach out to this tragic, gifted man. 'We are taking our equipment upstairs, to the male incurables' ward, where your brother sits day after day with his copy of *The Old Curiosity Shop*. Next week, if you like, I will arrange for you to meet. Perhaps it will help both of you to speak of the past.'

Dadd had turned away and was crouched at his easel, stabbing his brush at the undergrowth of Oberon and Titania's magical wood.

I glanced at a most unhealthy canvas showing a heathen rite. Inside a great pillared hall with a black-and-white floor like a chessboard, men and women in ancient Egyptian robes couple obscenely. Most unfortunately this painting makes use of Masonic images: the sun, moon and morning star are all in the sky above a pyramid and what appear to be the Tower of Babel and the Temple of Solomon. A god-like creature in Egyptian robes holds a dagger to the throat of a naked man bound with ropes, blindfolded and gagged.

This painting has a strange power and beauty, but if it were ever seen in public it might bring our craft into disrepute, so I have agreed with Haydon that I will buy it from Dadd when it is completed and secretly destroy it.

Dadd told me Osiris showed him this scene in a beautiful vision, but if my governors saw his beautiful vision he would be sent back to the Home Office block like Jonson to rot there for the rest of his days.

7
TEA WITH THE GEORGES

Elizabeth has sent me another parcel. A jar of herrings, a box of the imperial peppermints we used to buy in the sweet-shop on the corner of Chatham High Street and a tartan tin of home-made gingerbread. How well she knows me. Yet we haven't met for more than twenty years.

When I saw my name and doomed address written on the brown paper in her clear childish hand and unwrapped her carefully chosen offerings I could smell her hair and hear her soft voice. Hers was the first face I looked at as a painter, with eyes that bored through her delicate pink skin to the bones and character beneath. I had done many sketches of my family but could hardly bear to look at them closely, for they would not let me breathe. My girl in a white dress, my Columbine. Now her face must have reddened and coarsened and she has grown fat, I suppose, giving birth to daughters who are older than she was when first I knew her. Married to Joel Carter who has built many ships and is a local hero as I am a local monster. Both famous in our own way. Elizabeth's hair no longer smells of grass but of tar and flour and responsibility.

By the same post Robert sent more brushes and ten fine tubes of watercolour paint. They do not want to see me, but I still exist for them: an ogre who likes to suck peppermints and paint eccentric pictures. My sensible eldest brother is her brother-in-law; they meet at Christmas and birthdays and sigh together when my name is mentioned.

My fairies were angry with me this morning because I have been neglecting them. I have to finish *Contradiction: Oberon and Titania* for the doctor; the Fairy Feller in beautiful George's picture is jealous of his king and queen who have invaded his painting and look down on him, he says. On the canvas I lay bare my soul and then hide it again with leaves and grass. At the top are the cherry-stone people: tinker, tailor, soldier, sailor, rich man, poor man, beggar man, thief. The futures that seemed so wondrous to us as children and which came crashing down all too fast. My father has insinuated himself there, smirking above his apothecary's pestle and mortar. I am glad to imprison him in my painting. I've pinned him down like the specimens he used to collect for his museum, and now that he is only a few inches tall he cannot harm me. Poor little fart, he has been banished for ever to my private realm.

Memories of Chatham took me back to the river and the meadows, the masts of ships and cranes in the distance, and I worked on my landscape for half an hour. Empty, for it is people who cause all the trouble. All morning I sat at my easel and flitted from one work to another, alone in the vast room. They had all had gone down to the sunny gardens. I am excused from domestic labours. The cleaners flit around me and leave me undisturbed. On such days as this I forget time and my voices are silenced. I am perhaps more fortunate than Frith, who has a dozen children to support and patrons and dealers banging on the door of his studio.

Sometimes I imagine what my life would have been if I had married Elizabeth, if the early success I confidently expected had come to me – for otherwise her papa would never have accepted such an erratic suitor. She was very much a country girl, natural and a little wild, who loved to walk and run in the meadows and listen to my stories of fairies and elves, although she was always ready to drag me back to earth – 'But, Richard, we're only pretending, aren't we?'

Elizabeth was no boarding-school miss; she would have despised the London art world with its salons and gossip and courtship of the rich. She would have pined for Chatham; and I would have watched miserably as the convolvulus I sketched in her hair withered and her fresh spirit with it. She is better off with a man who builds ships like her father. Even when I portrayed her as Columbine I knew that and wove a lead line among the flowers and blue ribbons in her hair. I will preserve Elizabeth's youth and beauty in my Egyptian harem and enjoy her there, in the aspic of her youth, in that locked chamber where nothing is forbidden.

A few years back, when I was still in that dungeon surrounded by rogues and brutes and in such despair that I could not paint or draw, Hood arrived among us. One afternoon I looked up and saw him silhouetted in the opening of the tunnel that led to the main hospital. He blinked in our darkness and gazed at us with wonder and horror like an archaeologist who had just excavated a tomb in Pompeii.

Soon we heard rumours that Hood was turning the hospital upside down. Our worst attendants disappeared, several sham lunatics were transferred to prison and our food and conditions improved. He has always treated me with great kindness, given me paper and paints and brushes and crayons and encouraged me to work again. At first he asked me to illustrate my passions.

'I can't remember the last time I felt any,' I replied from my living tomb.

The next time he came to visit he gave me a list of subjects: anger, grief, self-contempt, deceit, disappointment. I do not think he has ever experienced such horrible emotions, for he is a man of science and reason, a good husband and father. I would have been neither. He must have intended a didactic purpose for such a commission, a tidy moral to be drawn. People of no imagination think of artists as haberdashers, measuring life and emotion by the yard and always in control of their scissors. If I have a patron it is Dr Hood, and so I do try to give him what he wants. He does not want my deviant, complex passions.

To illustrate self-contempt my fingers traced the figure of the man I might have become if I had married Elizabeth and had stayed in Chatham. Mr Crayon the hack drawing-master, shuffling back to his furnished apartments for a single gentleman. I found to my surprise that I had given Mr Crayon old Turner's face. When I was an ambitious student, confident that the world was just about to fall at my feet, I despised his awkwardness. How often do my hand and eye and heart fight one another. I can never tell what features will appear in my work, for I have no models here. All ugly fellows or idiots or both. So I must work from memory – and what tricks she plays on me.

The Good Samaritan demands to be painted. I will give him Hood's face, with dark handsome features and a long beard, and the traveller lying half dead by the roadside will resemble me. A younger, idealized Richard, still young enough to be saved. Since he brought me up here to the light my brain seethes with ideas, and if I live to be a hundred there will not be time to execute them all.

'We must tidy you up for your tea party, Mr Dadd. Have you finished making a mess for today?' Neville is always dapper and clean. A boring face but very amiable.

'I don't want to go.'

'Of course you must go. It will be a pleasure to see your brother again, and the doctor and the steward are sparing you their valuable time.'

'Go away. I don't want their valuable time.'

I went on working all morning and refused luncheon, for my stomach was a tempest of nerves. My voices sensed my weakness and rushed to fill my head. Whenever I put down my paintbrush they sniggered. Osiris told me to slit the throats of George and Hood with the butter knife, while my father reminded me that the operation hurt him more than it hurt me. *I am doing this for your own good, Richard. Later you will thank me for it. Be kind to your little brother, and remember he has not your natural gifts.*

George was born to play the victim and follow me around. Why, he has even followed me here. By three o'clock I had a raging head-ache and longed to barricade myself in my sleeping-cubicle. But I cannot afford to offend Dr Hood and the steward. Hood has the power to send me back to the criminal dungeons as he has sent Jonson, and, whatever I do to beautiful George in my Egyptian harem he is also an official person. It is gargoyle George I fear more, the whining brat dripping with snot and tears.

Neville sent McDonald to shave, wash and comb me. He made me change my paint-stained suit, and I remembered how, when I was seven, my sister Mary Ann used to perform my toilette that I may not disgrace the family at children's parties to which we were invited. Although I was shy I was often called on to perform my party pieces, to recite Puck's speech or play the violin or sketch my hostess. But in the end I managed to disgrace the family anyway.

By the time I had been led to the steward's room I was faint with dread, for two hours of polite conversation are a worse punishment than solitary confinement. The door opened upon a scene of conviviality. By Frans Hals, perhaps, commissioned by Mr Pickwick. Hood and Haydon are great friends; their laughter hung in the air with the fragrance of hot tea and crumpets. Cakes and sandwiches encrusted the green cloth on the dining-table and pots of jam and honey overlooked plates of bread and butter.

My brother sat between them, an enormous small boy taken out for a treat. His eyes, like mine, were on the food, for all the Dadds are greedy-guts. At home there was never enough on the table, and so we fought over the food, racing to cram it into our mouths before the others could tear it from us.

Hood and Haydon both stood up and shook my hand vigorously. I could look at the doctor but found myself unable to meet the twinkling eyes of the steward. It is not tolerable that anyone should look as comfortable in his own skin as he does. His warmth and charm blazed out at me; I longed to touch him, and my fingers twitched to draw him, although I have never dared to ask him to sit for me. Nerves made me shiver in the warm afternoon. He was smoking his pipe, and his smile was adorable.

'So glad you could come,' Haydon said as if I had a busy social diary. 'We thought it would be delightful for you two brothers to meet again.'

I turned reluctantly from beautiful George to gargoyle George. He still has that squashed, undercooked, helpless look. My brother and I stared at one another. I could remember very clearly all the things I used to do to him, and I saw that he remembered, too. There was nothing to say. He fell upon the muffins and I fell upon the sandwiches, and for ten minutes we guzzled, watched with interest by Haydon and Hood who continued to chat benevolently.

'When may I expect my charming fairy painting, Mr Dadd?' Haydon asked as I spread apricot jam on my sixth muffin and whipped the last watercress sandwich from under my brother's nose with my other hand.

'He has higher matters than art to think of just now,' the doctor said, and they laughed, not maliciously. I attempted to laugh with them while eating and thinking of a witty reply, but it was not a success. My brother belched, and I farted. My father said, *Boys, you must not eat like animals or you will not be invited to the best houses. Play nicely with your little brother, Richard.*

When my mouth was empty I said, 'I am hard at work on fairy paintings for you both. I hope to finish them by the end of the year.'

Both men looked pleased and complimented me on my work, but my fairies were offended and drowned out their kind words with petulant buzzing. Titania whipped my nose with a thistle, and Oberon settled on Haydon's lap and performed lascivious gestures. They do not like it when I speak as if I owned them.

George, who has an unfortunate habit of eating with his mouth open, pointed to the mantelpiece and giggled. There was an unframed picture of a man seated at an easel painting an unfinished oval canvas. I recognized Oberon's legs before I could make sense of my own face. How old I look, and hairy and mad. I felt betrayed, as if my face had been stolen, and then a wild gust of hope: if he keeps my picture on his mantelpiece perhaps he loves me. Loves me just as much as I love him but dares not speak of it. At night when I lie awake and feverishly desire him he also longs for me, just a few yards away. All this passed through my head as I started on the Madeira cake, my eyes on my plate, still unable to look at him. Of course, he cannot let the doctor suspect his secret passion for me. He would lose his job. That is why he is so distant with me.

Then, beside my picture on the mantelpiece, a wedding scene. My beloved with his beloved. I had known Haydon was married, but the evidence was a painful blow. And a baby picture, a bundle of long clothes, the most fortunate child in the world. How I wish I could be reincarnated as that baby. My eyes filled with tears I must not shed as I contemplated the love from which I am excluded.

On the other side of the table I saw my brother's hand, still clutching *The Old Curiosity Shop*. He has been reading it for sixteen years. Soon we will have finished all the food and then we will have to talk, I thought, as the doctor conversed with my beloved. Last week, when they came to make my chemical picture, they talked with me almost as friends – if I had any friends. But just now at tea they were two scientists observing curious specimens. 'More tea, Mr Dadd?'

When all the food was gone the nerves at the end of my fingers craved a pencil to wrap themselves around. I know that Haydon draws, so I asked to borrow a sketchpad, and he generously gave me one with a box of excellent crayons. I sat and drew the handsome doctor, since I could not bear to look directly at either of the Georges. Although my hands were busy they were still restless, and my voices were clamorous.

Osiris shouted above the others. *He is Seth. Beneath that feeble-minded mask, beneath that shabby suit of clothes he is a raging hippopotamus, the Lord of Chaos. Our brother, yes, but wicked. You must pick up that poker and kill him before he kills you and scatters your dismembered body all over Egypt.*

'How many years is it since you two met?' the doctor asked benignly.

'About five thousand,' I said. Hood and Haydon took this as a joke and laughed.

George spoke for the first time. 'Two and a half years ago you kindly invited us to this very room, Dr Hood.' He still has the puffy, wheezy voice of an asthmatic, although he looks strong, taller than me with huge hands red from labouring. Lord Seth. Our lord was a carpenter.

The doctor's face was impassive, and I wondered how much of that other disastrous meeting he remembered. One afternoon he bundled me out of my dungeon, down the secret tunnel that connects the criminal block with the main part of the hospital. I thought I was going to be set free, and my heart sang as I smelled polish and fresh air and saw clear windows overlooking sky and trees and grass. But instead of freedom there was my brother's stupid face. We glared at each other. Had the doctor and the steward not been there we might have had a fight.

I heard my father's voice tell us to play, and so we did. We sat at the steward's table and played chess as we always used to do. I was red and George was white, and his pawns sneered at me, and my knight was unfairly captured by his bishop. When I realized he was cheating, just as he always did, I stood up and threw the board at him. It entangled itself with the tablecloth, and some ornaments smashed, and my brother's hand was bleeding, and I was returned to my dungeon in disgrace.

This second meeting between us was cooked up by the doctors here to do us good. These two men are immensely kind, but they cannot understand what they have not experienced themselves. I wanted to please them but my spirit voices intervened. I dropped the sketchpad and at once my father and Osiris were able to enter through my fingertips and take me over again.

You two motherless boys must learn to be friends, my father said, and I tried to think of something kind to say to George. But then Osiris commanded me to throw the honey pot at Seth. *You must destroy your evil brother. Do it now. The doctor will understand. You may never get another chance.*

I clutched my head, their battleground, and moaned and could not speak.

My beloved and the doctor went on in a tea-party sort of way, pouring each other more tea (George and I having finished all the food) and talking quietly.

I decided to ignore my voices. I neither spoke to my brother nor assaulted him, but Osiris was furious at my disobedience and roared so loudly that I thought the entire hospital must hear. *Insect! Puppet! Go now to the window and throw yourself from it. Your worthless bones will break on the paving stones, and you will come to live with me, where you belong. Go on! Get up! The window is open, and we are all in the underworld waiting for you.*

'Tell us another fascinating anecdote about your years in Australia. I am sure these two gentlemen would enjoy your yarns.' The doctor's voice had a note of desperation as these two gentlemen sat in gloomy silence, not even looking at one another.

Haydon's voice is clear and light. He never seems to falter and charming expressions mobilize his face as witty sentences pour from his mouth. If I could be with him always, if I could be him, there would be no more mental suffering.

'Shall I tell you about the presumptuous missionaries and their failed attempts to civilize the savages? How the aborigines tear the kidneys from their living victims, for they attribute supernatural powers to a man's kidneys? Rather alarming when one considers breakfast . . .' The doctor coughed meaningfully. 'Perhaps not. Well, let me sing you an aboriginal chant. More soothing.'

The most extraordinary sounds issued from the mouth of beautiful George. It was not quite singing, not quite music, a wild yet peaceful nasal humming that enchanted us all. He held our attention, and my voices were silenced. I wanted him to go on for ever. I shut my eyes and gave myself to his liquid chant. Then opened them again to drink in every detail of his face. His skin is still reddish from years of exposure to a sun hotter than our own, and he has many wrinkles for a man in his thirties. His grey eyes shine with humour and intelligence, and his mouth was made to smile.

Too soon his magical chanting ceased and his mouth returned to the English tongue. 'Perhaps Mr Dadd would like to see my aboriginal paintings?'

He looked at me so gently, with respect, and my heart was flooded with gratitude. 'Yes,' I said stupidly.

Haydon went to the cupboard under his sideboard and took out a large parcel. He removed the empty plates from the table and spread out six pictures unlike any I have ever seen. They were not portraits or landscapes or religious scenes or even ancient rituals, like the ones I saw when I was in Egypt. These were images of a world before houses and clothes and towns, a time when people lived in caves or forests in harmony with nature.

'Are they very old?' I asked.

'I watched the artist at work on them about six years back. He did not resemble our artists here, for he wore no smock or beret. He wore a loincloth, his face had bloodstains from the kangaroo he had just slaughtered, and his studio was a clearing in the bush. Do you like them?'

I nodded. I could not speak, for his strange music and paintings had taken my breath away.

Oxford, who insists that he will escape from here some day, intends to go to Australia. In a new country, he says, populated only by natives and Penton-villains, Young England will flourish, although he admits that it may be necessary to change the name of his secret society. Tomorrow I will tell him of these new revelations of Australian culture. Oxford wants me to accompany him; he says we will stow away and sail across the world together. But I shall not go, for I know that I carry my hell with me and there is no escape. Besides, I have had quite enough of uncomfortable travel.

The doctor made one last attempt to revive his tea party. He realized that general conversation was not going to be forthcoming, for my brother had turned away from us and buried his nose in *The Old Curiosity Shop*. 'Mr Dadd, I know you are an accomplished violinist. Will you play for us?'

'I have not brought my fiddle.'

But there was no escape, for Haydon produced an old violin from his inexhaustible sideboard and sat down at a piano I had not observed, which was covered with books and sheet music and old newspapers. I was a mass of nerves at the prospect of performing with my beloved. My hands shook so that I could hardly hold the instrument.

'My brother plays the flute,' I said resentfully, for I did not see why I should suffer alone. They looked at him with polite interest, but all that happened was that the back of George's neck became very red and the book was raised so that he appeared to be eating it.

'Come and look at my music, Mr Dadd. Let us choose something we both know.'

He sat on the piano stool, and I stood over him just a few inches away. I could feel the heat of his body and see the adorable curly brown hairs on his neck where they met his collar. He has slightly pointed ears, like a goblin, and his skin is quite coarse and reddened. Our hands almost touched as we fumbled through the music. His are large and reddish-brown with fingertips yellow from tobacco. My hands are as small and white as a young lady's, and for a second I told myself that I was his fiancée and we were about to play a romantic duet together.

'Mendelssohn, Schubert – these have violin parts. Do you see anything you like?'

I was engrossed in a volume of Shakespeare songs bound in red velvet. I paused at "Full Fathom Five Thy Father Lies", but Haydon turned the page on nervously.

As we are so many, let us form a family orchestra. It will amuse us in the evenings and be instructive. Richard, you and I will play the violin, and Robert will play the piano. Stephen, the cymbals, for you have no ear at all but can be counted on to make a noise. Mary Ann, you can sing for us, but please try to smile –

My beloved was still hunting for an appropriate song. He interrupted my father's voice. '"Where the Bee Sucks". This has always been a great favourite of mine, and it will remind us all of your charming fairy paintings. Shall we attempt it, Mr Dadd?'

'If you wish.'

Of course, my fairies thought we were mocking them, and they flew at me, spitting with pique. Titania wrestled my bow from me, and I dropped it with a clatter.

'Are you ready, Mr Dadd? Shall I begin?'

'In a minute.' I picked up my bow and tried to control my shaking. I knew how the song ought to sound, but the notes danced out of their parallel lines and turned into wicked little elves who urinated on the piano and pulled the hair of my beloved. He did not appear to notice but began to play, singing in a pleasant tenor voice.

When I was to come in Haydon signalled, but I could not take up my cue. Dr Hood smiled encouragingly as the music stopped. 'Come now, you are among friends and need not be nervous.'

He could not hear my enemies' voices:

My father, angrily, *You must practise every day, Richard, or you will never amount to anything.*

Osiris snarled at me, *You are a weak and foolish slave. Why do you love him more than you love me? Break the violin over his head, now, while he is sitting there.*

My father said, *I am glad to see that George keeps up with his reading. He is a little slow, but one day he will surprise us all.*

Haydon turned around and smiled at me with such tenderness that I thought he must love me. 'Shall we try again?'

I took a step towards him. My heart opened to him, it was like an earthquake inside me. The room was flooded with light, and I could not see his lovely face for it was hidden by the dazzle as I fell on my knees and reached out to him, to my saviour.

A high-pitched giggle from my brother. The steward stopped playing and looked down at me, puzzled.

The doctor's voice: 'Perhaps the excitement has been too much for you, Mr Dadd.'

Osiris said, *He is only a mortal. You must worship me instead.*

I could not see for tears. I dropped the violin and ran from the room and down the corridor. A passing attendant stared at me and tried to take my arm, but I shook him off and ran on. I heard an alarm bell and footsteps pursuing me. Perhaps they thought I was attempting to escape, but I only wanted the safety of my cubicle. As I ran I heard my father say, *They are talking about you back there. They are saying you are daft as a brush, mad as a hatter, not the full shilling windmills in the head, but I know there is nothing the matter with you, for you are my son and you will do great things.*

Charles Neville blocked my way. I collapsed into his arms, exhausted by my inner clamour. He led me to my sleeping-cubicle where I lay down and he gave me peace to drink.

Much later, when it was dark, I awoke. Terrified of what would come out of the night, I groped my way to my easel in the main gallery. The night attendants did not bother me for they know I often paint at strange hours. One of them fetched me a candle and a bowl of cold stew.

All night I worked. Not wanting to enrage my fairies, I left their paintings alone and started on a new fancy sketch. I must have been dreaming of Cobham Hall for Sir Harley's face jumped from my pencil in all its hideousness. His enormous nose hung over his selfish mouth as he lay back in his chair, sated. That ridiculous head-dress he wore to keep out the draughts that caused his incessant toothaches and headaches and neuralgia. It gave him the look of a crazed nun, and ever since I have detested both nuns and aristocrats. I meant to show us playing chess, but my hand would not seat the thirteen-year-old boy at the table. Instead, his head grew out of the floor, near the old man's robes. I could hear him snore and felt sick at the stench that came out of him when he was unbuttoned.

8
THE CHILD'S PROBLEM

Charles Neville came at first light and stood behind me. 'What is the subject of that one, Mr Dadd?'

'A game of chess.'

'But they are not playing chess.'

'The game is over.'

The morning showed up the weaknesses and confusion in my drawing, so I tore it up and started again on a new sheet of paper. This time I saw where I was going, although I did not want to go back there.

The others shuffled out of their sleeping-cubicles and were served with tea, bread and butter. I told myself I was not allowed to eat or sleep until I had finished drawing and concentrated with my whole self. It is only since I came up here that I have been able to do this, for in the old dungeon I had always to keep an ear and an eye open for Ben Masters who hated me. Once he tore away the canvas I was working on and defecated on it, and he would often steal my paints and brushes. The attendants were afraid of him, for he had killed a turnkey in Newgate.

As it was a fine day most of the men went down to work in the gardens. Fletcher and Grant stayed behind to play billiards, and the pleasant click of the balls merged with the birds singing in their cages to make a kind of music. I worked on peacefully while the ward was cleaned and the sun came through the high windows. M4 is the best studio I have ever had, and if they discharged me now I would chain myself to my easel and refuse to leave.

I meant to add some pale pink and grey and yellow and white from the watercolours Robert sent me. The midday sun must have overcome me, for I fell asleep on my chair and woke, stiff and with an aching head, to find Neville beside me again.

'The poor little boy! What has happened to him?'

'He has been enslaved, as we all are.'

'And that blackamoor behind him, on his knees with his hands tied together. Is he a slave? "Am I not a man and a brother?" – what does that mean?'

'You ask too many foolish questions! My work is what it is. I don't have to explain it to idiots like you!' I snatched my drawing and ran to my cubicle where I slammed the door. There are no locks on our doors, no true privacy, but they have the tact to know when I must be alone.

I hoped that sleep would come to me at last, but instead the past came flooding in and drowned me.

Before George killed our mother, my house, my brothers and sisters, my father, my garden and, most of all, my mother were perfect and did not have to be thought about. I was like the child in Words-worth's poem, rooted in 'this individual spot . . . / Made for itself, and happy in itself'. My brothers and I made boats out of walnut shells until we saved up enough pocket money to buy a toy yacht, and we longed to run away to sea

In my garden I explored a forest of apple trees, daisies gave me themselves as necklaces, and sunflowers beamed at me like comical aunts. Mary Ann took me by the hand, and we ran in the meadows until my legs refused to carry me any further and I fell down in the long grass, helpless with laughter. That was when my fairies stood around me in a great circle. When they saw I would not hurt them they swarmed all over me, friendly, like children but smaller and nicer. I held my breath and let them tickle my nose, dance on my stomach and swing on my hair.

'Get up, Richard! It's teatime.' I looked up at my sister and knew she could not see them. Then I whispered to my fairies that I would come back soon and took Mary Ann's sensible hand.

Mama knew all about fairies. When she was well she lay on the sofa in the living-room and told us stories. I was her best listener; the other children fidgeted or kept asking if it had really happened, but I curled up beside her and fitted myself into her warm lacy softness where wolves and goblins and witches couldn't get me. She vibrated against my ear as her voice promised me excitement and magic. My mother was slender, with pale translucent skin and deep-blue eyes; she seemed to belong more to the buttercup family than to our own. Her stories didn't come out of books but out of her own wild heart and mind.

'You are filling the child's head with poppycock. Come and do your Latin homework, Richard.'

It hurt when he dragged me away from her, and I could feel her loneliness springing up like grass around her as I left. Then I was in my father's study with his smells: tobacco and leather and sour wine. He was interesting, too, but you couldn't cuddle him or float away on his voice, which demanded answers and arguments. I had to be clever for him so that I could go to the King's School like Robert and make my way in the world.

When I passed from her to him I could hear a click inside my head like the sound of the hands of a clock when you move them. Mama and Papa lived on different islands, and I could not always swim between them. There were months when my mother's smell was all wrong, like medicine and dirty linen. Then she lay on her sofa day and night and would not tell me stories or speak, and my father was cross, and we tried not to hear when he shouted at her and called her a lazy slut.

We children escaped into the garden where Robert had started the Chatham and Rochester Philosophical Society behind the washing-line. At first I was not allowed to join because I was too young and Mary Ann and Maria and Rebecca were not allowed because they were only girls, but that summer when I was six and started Latin lessons with our papa Robert changed the constitution. He said he had become a radical and believed in universal suffrage. So all six of us sat on the bench against the wall, and Mary Ann held Rebecca on her knee and rocked Maria to sleep. Robert was chairman and Stephen was secretary and had to write it all down in an enormous brown book he had saved up his Christmas money to buy.

A choir of insects sang against Robert's voice, and on the sun-baked wall peaches and roses breathed their heavy perfume. Although I felt honoured to be allowed to attend the meeting I fell asleep and woke up to find Rebecca was wailing and Maria was wearing a white lace tablecloth draped like a Roman toga and six pairs of white drawers on her head. Robert's voice droned on until he became offended by our laughter and stopped, blinking indignantly.

'We're not laughing at you, only at Maria's antics,' Mary Ann said in a conciliatory voice.

'Why is Mama fat?' Maria was delighted to have attracted so much attention. She rubbed raspberry juice on her nose and cheeks and stuck out her tongue.

'All grown-ups are fat,' Stephen said wearily. 'Should I be writing this down?'

'Just put that the chairman was interrupted from the floor.'

'There isn't any floor. We're in the garden.'

'Ladies get fatter before there's a baby,' Mary Ann said.

'Papa says he won't order any more babies; he says there have been quite enough.'

'Go on, Robert, we are listening, really.' Mary Ann was a peace-maker in those days before she became a sourpuss.

Robert stood up straight, put his arm inside his short blue jacket to look like Napoleon or Nelson (I couldn't remember which) and read from his paper again. 'The French Revolution convulsed the nations of Europe, and opinion is still divided as to whether it was good or bad for Mankind. Some philosophers are of the opinion –'

This time he was interrupted by horrible screams, and we all went running towards the house. I thought Papa had killed Mama and heard more screams, which came from my own throat. Then Papa told us to stay in the garden, and we forgot about being philosophers and all cried except Mary Ann who tried to comfort us and Robert who said he was never going to let women into his society again and ran off to the river.

The next morning they told us we had a new baby brother called George. Mama was very ill, and the baby looked odd, red and bald and squashy. None of us wanted to cuddle him, and our mother did not want to touch him either.

Day after day she sat on the sofa and wept. We were not allowed in the parlour any more, and there was a jagged hole inside me that could only be filled by her arms and voice. I stood outside the parlour door and waited for her to come back. In the stone-flagged hall our maid, Susie, bustled past with washing, and Cissy, the wet nurse, carried screaming George upstairs followed by Maria, who could barely walk. Robert and Stephen went off to school, my father went to his shop, and Mary Ann helped in the kitchen. Becky wanted me to play with her in the garden.

'I am waiting for Mama.'

That winter she was moved upstairs and Papa slept on the sofa in the parlour. He was cross, and we all blamed the baby who had come to the wrong house and made everything go wrong.

'Can you send babies back?' I asked Robert, who knew a lot.

We three boys shared a room on the top floor overlooking the meadows at the back of our house. Stephen and I shared the big bed, and Robert had the truckle bed under the window. We used to tell each other ghost stories before we fell asleep. I was good at making them up, although I gave myself nightmares, but that year Stephen and Robert said stories were babyish, and they tested each other on French verbs and Latin declensions.

'Nominative?'

'*Rex.*'

'Accusative?'

'*Regem.*'

'You should listen, Richard. You will have to go to school soon.'

'But I want to talk about Mama.'

'I heard Grandpa Martin say she has no backbone,' Stephen said.

'Like a snake, you mean? Is that why she has to lie down all the time?'

'Anyway, you can't send them back. You do have to keep them,' Robert said with his air of authority. 'You were just as ugly when you were a baby.'

'No I wasn't!'

'Yes you were. You puked and pissed and bawled, and just when you were beginning to be less disgusting they went out and bought Rebecca. I don't know why they do it. I am not going to have any babies, ever,' said Robert, who has now fathered countless children I will never meet.

'Is Mama going to die?' They didn't answer, so I asked again.

'We are all going to die,' Robert said in his most philosophical voice. Then it was silent and cold and I fell asleep weeping.

On Christmas day we were allowed into her room. She was so white that the pillow seemed to be growing out of her shoulders and her hair was greenish seaweed, the shadows under her eyes like crushed bluebells.

We stood around her like in the painting I had just seen in church of all the people adoring Baby Jesus – except that we hated our baby. George was not in a manger but screaming in the next room as usual.

The next year various Dadd and Martin aunts came to look after us, and we became used to having a mother who was always in bed. She was ill, but we all knew that the illness was her fault and instead of sympathy there was anger and shame. Sometimes I heard my father in her room shouting at her.

One night I woke to find moonlight pouring over my face. Stephen and Robert were still in shadow. I knew the moon was telling me something, so I went to the window. Down on the lawn my fairies were dancing in a ring. I wanted to run downstairs to join them, but I knew I would frighten them away, so I stood and watched, shivering, barefoot in my nightgown. Then I saw a movement at the window beneath mine and knew my mother was there. They were dancing for her. She was a lost fairy princess and they wanted her back, and I was afraid she would let them take her away. I heard an owl cry and knew that would alarm the fairies, for they are cruel when they ride insects and birds, who hate them in return. I was terrified of losing this magical night, so I went down to make her stay with us.

I had so often woken up wanting Mama and planned this secret journey to her. I dreamed my way to her door and opened it to see her standing at the window in her long white nightgown with her back to me. When I touched her she would know me for a fairy prince, and we would stand together in our white robes. If she ran away to fairyland I would go with her, and if she stayed I would get into bed with her and go back to sleep in her embrace.

As I ran towards her a floorboard must have creaked. She turned, and I saw that she was furious with me. Her mouth was a spiteful gash. She had bruises and red scars at her pale throat and on her wrists. Then I heard my father's clip-clop footsteps, and he thundered into the room, and they shouted and screamed at each other, and someone carried me back to bed.

When my mother died there was not sadness in the house so much as rage and guilt, for she had done something wicked that must never be mentioned. Robert said the vicar would not allow her to be buried in the churchyard, and I have no memory of any funeral.

For a few months I could not see my fairies, and I knew that this was also George's fault. I often went into her room and stood with my eyes shut, begging her to come back and tell me stories. But nothing happened. Her room was empty and lonely and smelled of carbolic soap, and the one story I needed, why my mother died, was never told.

Robert and Stephen said that life was nasty, brutal and short and nobody was to blame for that. Becky and Maria were more open to persuasion when I explained that George had killed our mother and must be punished. He was slow to talk and tottered around on spindly legs following us. His face was always red from crying, and he had a slight squint and a hare lip. We called him the gargoyle because he looked like one of the carvings in Rochester Cathedral, and whenever he wanted to play with us we would run away screaming and giggling.

I told the girls that George was a changeling and that the fairies wanted him back. 'They'll give us another baby instead, a proper one.'

'I don't want any more,' said Becky, who was always having to look after Maria. 'Why can't boys look after babies?'

'We're too clever,' I explained and was surprised when she flounced off.

Generally I got on well with my little sisters. One wintry afternoon, when the gargoyle was being particularly annoying and kept following us into the parlour where Becky and I were trying to read and Maria was dressing her doll, I told them about changelings.

'The fairies want him back. He'll be happier, too; he won't cry so much. I expect he misses his own people.'

'Robert says there aren't any fairies and they're just stories for silly children.' Becky had never questioned me before, and I was furious.

'But we saw them last summer, you know we did, dancing in the meadows.'

'Robert says that was just our fancy, and Papa says he was right.'

'All right then, I'll prove it. Mama said –'

'We are not to speak of her.' Becky, who used to be my ally, was going over to the other side, turning into a little adult like Mary Ann.

Maria was still clutching my hand and gazing at me with adoring eyes, so I spoke to her. 'We must take him down to the river. Come on!'

George was delighted that we wanted to play with him. Maria and I pulled him between us over the meadows, where he staggered on his duck legs, and Becky followed reluctantly. When we stood on the bank, near the ford where the water was high and rushed towards the sea, I hesitated. My brother was very small and looked up at me with trust in his crooked face.

'We must bathe him three times to put the fairy out. When the fairies see him they will rescue him, for they know he belongs to them, and then they will bring back our proper brother.'

'I don't want any more brothers,' Becky said rebelliously. She knelt and put her hand in the river. 'But it's freezing cold, Richard. He'll catch an ague and we'll get into trouble.'

Maria and I ignored her and pushed George into the river. He fell in with a splash and looked at me with such surprise and horror that I could not bear to see him. I held his head under the water with one hand and grasped his arm with the other. The current was very fast, eager to carry him off. When his face bobbed up again it was blue, and I pushed it back again under the water. I could see fairies down there, pulling at his legs and shouting at me to give them back their baby. Maria was crouched beside me on the river bank crying, and Becky had disappeared.

'Three times,' I muttered and pushed him under again. I saw my mother's face under the water and knew that she had left us and gone back to her fairy kingdom. In grief and rage that she wanted George instead of me I pressed his head down with both hands and almost toppled over into the river.

Then I was seized from behind, and there was a great bellowing and confusion; no fairies but a crowd of people shouting at me and making a great fuss of the gargoyle.

Later that afternoon my father called me into his study where he made me take down my breeches and caned my backside until I bled. He had never been really angry with me before. I roared with pain and surprise.

'Your brother could have drowned. It is only thanks to Rebecca's good sense that he did not. She ran straight to my shop to fetch me, and Dr Warden happened to be there. George will be very ill, and if he does not recover it will be your fault.'

I was in disgrace for weeks. My sisters refused to talk to me, Maria burst into tears whenever she saw me, and when George got up from his sickbed he looked at me in terror. If I entered a room he was in he ran away from me and clutched the nearest petticoat. All the women in our household made a fuss of him, although after his illness I thought him uglier than ever, with his small eyes squinting down at his red button nose. Stephen and Robert called me a bully and a ruffian, and although I still shared a room with them they left me out of the conversation. The only person who showed me any tenderness was Susie, our maid, who sometimes gave me a smile and an extra helping of pudding.

In the spring my father called me into his study again, and I went in fear, expecting another beating.

'Don't look at me like that, Richard. I only want the best for my children, although Heaven knows there are so many of you and it's very hard to bring you all up alone. However, I have decided you are to start lessons with the Reverend Clutterbuck and his curate, who will prepare you and Stephen to join Robert at the King's School. I don't know how I shall manage to pay for it, but your grandfather Martin has kindly agreed to help. Let us hope you have reached the age of reason, for it is a terrible thing to be at the mercy of the irrational. You cannot yet know how terrible. It is bad for you to hang around the house doing nothing all day surrounded by females, and I have no time to educate you.'

Stephen was but a year older than me, a nervous boy who stammered. He had always admired our eldest brother and tried to please him, but now that Robert was at the famous grammar school he despised us younger ones. Stephen tried to lord it over me, but I soon outstripped him in Latin, Greek, French, algebra and theology, for I had decided that if I could not be good I would at least be clever.

The Reverend Buttercup, as we called him, was an insipid man, very pink with a few remaining strands of yellow hair which he arranged very carefully to disguise his bald pate. Stephen and I would bet conkers and marbles on where he would comb it each morning. His teaching consisted of setting us long passages to learn by heart while he disappeared to write his sermon and returned stinking of sherry.

His curate, James Masters, was a skeletal young man with pustules all over his face. He was in love with the daughter of a farmer near Gillingham and could usually be persuaded to walk in that direction when he was supposed to be improving our minds. Stephen and I used to fall about giggling when we walked past the gate of his beloved's farm and James decided to give us a botany lesson. Glancing anxiously at the muddy drive he would dawdle and tell us the names of all the flowers and trees, which we already knew being country lads. Sometimes his bucolic angel, a fat girl called Annie who later married a farmer, would appear, and James would blush and simper. When she did not he would hide notes in the hollow of a tree near the gatepost, pretending that he was tying his shoelace there. Stephen and I used to retrieve them later and scream with laughter at his bad poetry.

When I was nine Stephen was admitted to the grammar school and moved back into Robert's orbit, so I had to go to lessons alone and had nobody to snigger with. At home Maria, who was five and already the liveliest of my sisters, became my companion. I told her the stories our mother used to tell me and made up more. All my early pictures were for Maria. I drew fairies, caricatures of our family, a map of the volcanic eruptions on the curate's face and my illustrious tutor, with a red nose and a buttercup growing out of his head. Maria roared with lovely clear childish laughter; she was my first and best audience and always ready to sympathize with me, whether we were knocking on the earth to summon fairies or running away from the gargoyle.

Maria went to bed at six, and the evenings were long. We had a stepmother, Sophia, whom my father had married with indecent speed. Stephen and I had spied on their courtship, which took place in our parlour either from want of money or want of imagination. We watched our widowed papa go down on his knees and assure Sophia of his undying love for her.

If she expected romance she must have been quickly dis-illusioned for all she got was seven children and a husband who was rarely at home. Sophia resented the trick that had been played on her, and within six months had been transformed from a shy nymph into a bad-tempered harridan. Mealtimes were a battleground at which we charged to the table laden with burnt meat and overcooked vegetables and fought like savages. Sophia, whose upbringing had been rather prim, would try to make us say grace, but she was out-numbered and ignored.

My father appeared after supper to find his wife screaming at us to go upstairs and leave her in peace. Having drunk a good deal of wine at a Masonic or philosophical evening, my father only wanted his food and his bed.

'Your children are monsters!' Sophia sobbed as she slammed his cold supper down on the table.

'They are good children,' my father insisted as Becky turned somersaults over the sofa and Stephen held George's legs and made him walk on his hands like a wheelbarrow. 'They only want a little affection – like all of us.' Becky ran to him and caressed him, much to his delight and Sophia's annoyance. 'Now, it is late. Let us all go to bed, my dears.'

Papa lay with Sophia in the room in which my mother died, and this struck me as disgraceful, although I never spoke of it. Not that we boys envied him his nights with our stepmother, who was no exiled fairy queen but a very earthy woman with a coarse red face and hands like a butcher's. Yet I could not sleep for thinking of them in the room below, doing whatever it was men and women did to make babies. They had just made Arthur. I knew they had not bought him, for who would part with good money for such a squealer? Sophia walked around with him all day tucked under her arm like a parcel, but at night Arthur's cradle was in their room. In the middle of the night his yells would wake me, and then I would hear the voice of a different Sophia crooning a lullaby.

I now shared the big bed with George, who snorted and farted and whimpered and sometimes pissed in his sleep, while Stephen had moved into the truckle bed under the window with Robert. There was no space between our beds, and I felt suffocated by my brothers' regular breathing. It was like the rhythmic hoofbeats of a carriage that swept them off – Queen Mab's perhaps. She rode through their minds and brought them dreams I could not see while I was left behind, alone with my feverish mind where scraps of poetry, memories of my mother, Latin verbs and fear of the dark all jangled.

One night my whole body twitched with loneliness. The house creaked with secrets. I could hear rats and pigeons whispering about me. I climbed out of bed and tiptoed up to the attic where Susie slept. She had forgiven me for trying to drown George and was always ready with a cuddle or a slice of bread and dripping. I suppose Susie was about fifteen, but she was scarcely taller than me with greasy dark hair and a round white face. Not pretty exactly but sweet-natured and cheerful despite being my stepmother's skivvy.

Susie was fast asleep after her long day in the kitchen. I stood in the cold doorway and envied her deep slumber. I thought I might catch it like an illness if I lay with her, so I climbed into her narrow bed and fitted myself into the curve of her buttocks and knees. Her cotton nightgown rubbed against my nightshirt. I could smell cinnamon and cloves in her hair and feel her soft warmth. A chasm that had opened up in me when my mother died was filled. Susie's steady breathing stopped, but she did not speak or scream. We lay there, silent and happy, and fell asleep together.

I woke at first light to find she was already up and dressed in her skivvy's apron. She took my hand and led me downstairs to the door of the room I shared with my brothers, kissed the top of my head and went down to make the fires and boil the kettle and stir the porridge. She was smiling and so was I as I slid back into bed beside the snorting gargoyle.

All that winter Susie and I comforted each other. Most nights I tiptoed up to her garret, and she silently welcomed me. We slept in each other's arms, sometimes waking to fumble gently the moist tender places beneath our nightgowns. She was able to give me a sweet and astonishing pleasure, and I found that I could make her moan with delight when I tickled her bum in a certain way.

I found that I could regain that blissful sensation when I returned to my own bed and frequently did, entering the gates of paradise with the gargoyle snorting and farting beside me. I thought my games with Susie were secret because they happened in the dark, in silence. However, Robert, who was a great prig, had reported my nightly absences to our father.

One bright spring morning I was summoned into his study where Susie stood sobbing by the fire, looking so young and small and miserable that tears came to my eyes before my father said a word.

'Your brother has informed me of your corruption by this trollop in her school of Venus in the attic. What have you to say, Richard?'

I had nothing to say. I was so innocent that I had no idea what he was talking about, but my father's tone told me I was guilty.

Susie was sent away in disgrace, and my father said I would have to have an operation. Terrified that I was going to die I submitted.

What I had done was so terrible, my father said, that he was ashamed to speak of it to another doctor. Like most apothecaries he often performed operations, and so he appointed himself surgeon or executioner. The gates of paradise clanged shut behind me, and when I pissed or sat at stool I looked at the root of my troubles with disgust and fear.

The morning I had been dreading arrived. The other children were sent off to school or to spend the day with relations, and Minnie, the new maid, was told to scrub the kitchen table and then leave the house. My father looked very serious. He wore his bloodstained leather apron and was sharpening a large knife when my stepmother led me into our kitchen. This room was the heart of our house, where I had always come for warmth and titbits of food. It reminded me of Susie and my mother and made me feel even more wobbly. I could hardly walk to the table where my father blindfolded me and my stepmother – with some enjoyment, I sensed – helped him strap me to the table.

My father's voice said, 'I must hurt you now, Richard. When you are older you will understand why I am doing this. These vicious habits you have contracted will destroy you, my boy. This blindfold deprives you of sight for an hour, but imagine how it would be to be blind for ever. Even that is not the worst that may befall you. Onanists often go mad and have to be locked up for the rest of their lives. You are so young. There is yet time to divert the stream of dangerous sensuality and passion that will otherwise sweep you away from us.'

I felt him unbutton me and take out my tiny prick. Then there was blinding pain, I screamed and struggled and must have lost consciousness.

My next memory is of waking alone in my own bed to find my father sitting beside me. He looked pale and anxious, and I sensed that I had some new power over him.

'Are you all right, Richard? There was so much blood . . .' He kissed my hands and forehead. It was most unusual for him to demonstrate his affection.

'I don't know. What happened?'

It was my father's boast that he always answered his children's questions because, he said, he wanted us to become rational citizens. In fact, this wasn't true, for we had never received a satisfactory explanation for our mother's death.

He sighed and frowned and said, 'I have circumcised you, Richard. I have cut away enough skin to put your penis on the stretch when erections come. There must be no play in the skin after the wound has thoroughly healed, it must fit tightly over the penis to discourage you from resuming your vicious practice. I may not be sure that we have done away with the possibility of all masturbation, but I am confident that we have limited it to within the danger lines.'

I did not understand most of this but only knew that my doodle and nutmegs hurt. Later, when I needed to piss, I screamed with agony. My father held me over the chamber pot, and I felt his heart beat against mine.

'Oh, my son, my dearest son! I had to do this. You are clever, you have a great future and must be protected against your lower instincts.'

For some months afterwards my father treated me with particular tenderness, and I wondered if I really was his dearest son. I continued to be in pain and slept badly, waking from nightmares of flames and knives and torment. That Hell which old Buttercup mumbled about became a real place to me – not a subterranean threat but a nightly vision. My fairies also changed. On my long solitary walks in the meadows I often met gangs of them armed with axes and hammers and sharp nails, but I ran away from them and did not believe them when they cried after me that they were my friends.

I drew apart from my brothers and sisters, for I was sure that Robert and Stephen had spied on me and betrayed me to our father. Mary Ann and Rebecca belonged to the tedious kitchen world now; they seemed always to be cooking or looking after baby Arthur. My stepmother tried to keep me away from Maria as if I was a wild scapegrace instead of a confused small boy, and my little sister was disappointed that I no longer amused her with caricatures and romps.

When I tried to draw it was the minute details of the Kentish countryside that came flowing from my hand: lords and ladies, cowslips, nonesuch, bird's foot, sweet briar, goat's beard, marsh marigolds, creeping jenny and scurvy grass; periwinkles with their surprising blue eyes, hops in their bright-green frilly cases and filberts in their neat green houses. Violets, harebells, convolvulus, fat toadstool tables, honeysuckle – the landscape around me had not abandoned me. I looked at it carefully and with gratitude. Even now, thirty years later, when I shut my eyes I can see every plant in those fields and meadows I shall never revisit.

Those lonely walks restored me. I always took a book with me and sat down under a tree, whatever the weather, to read Shakespeare or Wordsworth or Scott. Silence became my friend, and in the evenings I found it a great strain to be with my noisy family. I felt they were all staring at me, whispering about my vicious habits, and I could not join in their games.

Only music soothed me, and when my father suggested that we each learn an instrument so that we could make music together in the evenings I chose to learn the violin. Papa, who knew everyone in Chatham, found an Italian exile called Signor Pinelli who was an excellent teacher. I suppose our family musical evenings were as painful to listen to as most amateur music, but we were our own audience, and we enjoyed them.

That September I had to walk into Rochester with my brothers to go to the King's School. Rochester's ancient cathedral and castle were stately, not like our cottagey Chatham with its brawling soldiers and sailors. Seeing that I was nervous, Robert and Stephen teased me with my ignorance and told me bloodcurdling tales of the initiations new boys had to pass through. When we approached the old stone building I begged them to stay with me and show me where to go, but they laughed and ran away to their own superior friends. I was left in the vast hall, feeling very small and alone, until an usher came and led me down corridors and upstairs to a door I hoped would never open.

It did, of course, and I was pushed into an enormous room full of desks and boys. I supposed they were the same species as myself, but they did not seem to be, for they ranged in age from ten to fourteen and some looked as old as my father while others seemed as young as Maria. I was told to sit next to one of these strange creatures, who kicked me vigorously under the desk and told me I was an idiot when I could not find the right page in Virgil.

There was a stink of chalk and custard and vomit, and angry masters strode around in black gowns like great crows armed with canes. Sofas and cushions and music, carpets and fresh linen and soft voices had all been withdrawn. If my father imagined it would be a civilizing influence on me he should have visited the madhouse he sent his sons to – although I have lived among lunatics for many years now I do not find them any worse than schoolboys.

The headmaster was Old Bumbrusher, a renowned flaybottomist who would have been in Newgate if it were not that boys' bums were considered fair game, like pheasants or grouse. When he was in a rage he would stride around the school, brandishing his cane and shouting, 'I have not time to flog all these boys. Make them draw lots, and I'll punish one.' Latin and Greek were thrashed into us, and our other teachers were scarcely less brutal.

I can see Brandyface, the clergyman who taught us Latin, with his savage red face like the mask of a Tibetan demon. When I was out in my lesson he turned upon me with round staring eyes and roared that I was a numbskull, spitting to give his insults added emphasis. Brandyface once knocked out one of my teeth with the back of a Homer, and he had a spiteful trick of pinching boys under the chin and pulling them up by the lobes of the ears.

Had I not already loved Ovid, Homer, Demosthenes, Juvenal and Virgil my education would have made me detest them. We had to learn passages by heart before we understood them and recite them the next morning. If we were not word perfect we were savagely punished. My Latin was quite good, thanks to Buttercup's lessons, but my Greek was feeble.

Although my father was not rich (all the teachers were servile to the sons of wealthy families) I was clever and had a good memory. I survived without too many floggings, but in this atmosphere of terror boys soon learned to be as brutal and mean-spirited as their masters. Their cruel chants still fill my ears. At Easter: 'He is risen, he is risen, / All the Jews must go to prison.' This would be followed by the beating of any boy suspected of having Jewish blood. Catholicism was also suspect, and John O'Hara, whose mother was said to be Catholic, was taunted by bigger boys who forced him down on his knees in the playground and made him crawl to the stinking privy they called his altar.

My father said we were scholars and gentlemen now and made us wear our school caps and ruffs even during the holidays to distinguish us from the Chatham urchins, who called us snobs. I loved my ruff, for it made me feel like Hamlet or King Richard, an honorary Elizabethan when we acted out Shakespeare plays in the garden.

I spent most of those four years at the King's School in a state of mental alienation. All my forays into schoolboy friendships ended in disaster, for frank emotion was despised and ridiculed. I fell in love with an older boy called Cuthbert Harrison, one of those golden youths who invariably spend too long gazing at their own reflections and suffer the same fate as Narcissus. The hounds that tore him apart, I heard later, were gambling and drink. However, at fourteen he was dazzlingly beautiful with golden hair and dark-blue eyes that stirred the battered remnants of my poor cock. He was a splendid athlete, heroic in his cricket whites, and also a good scholar. I found myself pursuing him, begging to be allowed to clean his shoes and blushing whenever he was near. I imagined my love to be a well-kept secret, but, of course, my brothers and schoolfellows noticed and teased me, a punishment worse than flogging, for Narcissus began to roar with laughter whenever he saw me approach.

Rumours of Bumbrusher's flaybottomy reached my father. Even Robert, who was a model of conformity, was flogged several times on some pretext or other. One morning I was called out of my classroom to find my father and brothers standing in the great stone hallway. Papa was shouting at Bumbrusher, who looked like an emperor whose minions had revolted. We followed with incredulous delight as our father simply led us out of the front door to freedom. A few years later I heard that Old Bumbrusher had flogged away all but one boy – and that was his own son.

My father loathed corporal punishment and campaigned vigorously against slavery. He truly believed the operation he had perpetrated upon me had been 'for my own good' and frequently apologized, embracing me weepily and urging me on to my great future.

At that time he was vulnerable, for Sophia had died leaving him with two little sons, Arthur and John. A widower with nine children, he had not had much luck with matrimony. I did not miss my stepmother and have never understood why men marry and get children. I agree with Malthus that we will never reach Utopia while our population is allowed to grow unchecked. Whatever the delights of tupping a woman (and I can hardly remember what they are), babies are the unpleasant result. Better to love a man and take your pleasure without domestic servitude. Better not to love at all.

Mary Ann took over our household at sixteen, and if she found any pleasure in it she did not let on. Robert and Stephen were apprenticed as chemists that they might join my father's business, which left but seven mouths to feed. At thirteen I was too young to be apprenticed and was relieved, for I knew I did not want to be a chemist or a clerk, which seemed to be the only choices available.

Then there were a few months of glorious freedom when I wandered through the meadows alone and opened myself once more to that landscape of hop fields and cornfields, with the Medway running through it and the towers of Rochester Cathedral and Castle in the distance. I walked it and drew it so many times that it burns in my memory still.

My drawings were admired, and my father sent me to study miniature painting and drawing at the academy in our high street run by his friend William Dadson, who gave him special rates. I loved my studies, and indeed it did not seem to be work at all to amuse myself all day with paints and crayons and charcoal. I learned to use a magnifying glass and loved to work secret details into a tiny canvas.

It was fairy work, an entrance into a world more subtle and delicate than my oafish family.

My father came home late, drunk as a wheelbarrow, complaining of his ruined life and the villainous inhabitants of Cheat'em, as he called our town, who did not pay their bills. Mary Ann was an even worse cook than Sophia, and many an evening we went to bed on bread and dripping or hasty pudding. We children ran wild and fought over whatever food appeared on the table. To my alarm, Papa decided that I was the hope of our family and wept over me a great deal when he was in his cups, sobbing that I would become a great man and raise them all.

In order to become a great artist it was necessary to see great art. One of my father's friends, John, was a servant at Cobham Park, Lord Darnley's great house. There was a famous collection of paintings by Titian, Tintoretto, Rubens, Salvator Rosa, Reynolds and Guido Reni. My teacher had shown me prints of them, but I longed to see them in the flesh.

John was to ask the Darnleys for permission for me to visit the hall. Where the child's problems really began. And now I am weary and cannot stomach any more of this picking at ancient scabs.

This evening, when at last I returned to the present, I found beside my bed the food that Neville left for me. He always forgives my outbursts of temper. He is the best of men although not the cleverest. I will give him my *Child's Problem* as a peace offering. Whatever has happened to the poor little boy? Well, he must figure that out for himself.

9
MORAL
MANAGEMENT

Haydon and I watched sadly as our mercurial guest rushed out of the room. I rang the bell for Neville and knew that he would accompany Dadd back to the safety of M4. George Dadd sat on for a while in silence. Naturally we did not discuss his brother in front of him.

'Will there be any more muffins?' The other patients call him Tiger because of his voracious appetite.

'I'm afraid not,' Haydon replied with his usual courtesy.

At this sorrowful news the younger Dadd stood up, and I rang the bell for Atwood, who gently took his arm and walked him back to the incurables' ward.

When they had both gone I felt a wave of helplessness. My well-intentioned attempt to bring the two brothers together and understand more about their afflictions had been a failure. Haydon sensed my disappointment and poured me a glass of sherry.

'How I wish I knew why he burst into tears and ran away. Was it our fault?' I asked Haydon.

'You look for reason where it does not exist.'

'Yet he is such a sensitive, gifted, cultivated man, a poet as well as an artist.'

Haydon replies, '"The lunatic, the lover and then poet, / Are of imagination all compact."'

'Again and again I return to Shakespeare. I often fancy that he visited our hospital when it was in Bishopsgate – after all, he lived near by. Sometimes when I walk these corridors at night I wish I could meet him and ask him for advice. He and Dryden and the other great poets understood more of the workings of the mind than we alienists do.'

'When our poor friend is at his best he reminds me of Puck or Ariel. Such a quick mind, so witty and full of mischief he makes me feel quite slow.'

'Yes, it would not surprise me if he had fairy blood and his pictures of Titania and Oberon were ancestral portraits.'

'His brother is all earth. Caliban perhaps. The attendants on the incurables' ward tell me that he can work for hours chopping and stacking wood. He labours in silence, then suddenly falls into a rage and attacks a fellow patient. Yet he can recite whole plays of Shakespeare by heart. How long has he been here now, Billy?'

'Three days after his brother murdered their father George Dadd became convinced that his bed was on fire and ran naked into the street. He was committed to the Kensington Asylum, and then, his family being unable to bear the double burden of grief and private fees, he came here like his brother. But his family seldom or never visit him'

'And what is the significance of that copy of *The Old Curiosity Shop* he always carries?'

'How I wish I knew.'

'I'm only the steward, my duties limited to clean sheets and red tape. I wish I shared your passion for statistics. I leave the mysteries of the brain to you.'

'Mysteries that I feel no closer to solving than I was ten years ago. Is madness produced by the imagination? Perhaps it is not a disease of the soul, not a punishment from God as we used to think but an incorrect association of ideas.'

'Well, you're the scientist. I understand nothing of these matters.'

'On the contrary, George, you understand kindness, which is everything. Pinel believed in *douceur*, gentleness, and I had rather treat our patients with your warmth and humanity than write a hundred treatises.'

'You look puzzled, Billy.'

'I am. In Richard Dadd and in his strange paintings I catch glimpses of the great sages. I often think that Jesus or Mohammed or the Buddha might have lived and died in our hospital.'

'Well, if the Buddha had murdered his papa –'

'I wish I could dive into that mental sea and understand why the mystics float and the madmen drown. For it is the same sea, George.'

'I thought Richard Dadd detested religion.'

'Ours. But he has his own, as you know. Religion is disastrous to unbalanced minds. In the cellars of the human house lie many strange tenants, and when they hear the bugle call of religion or politics they rush to the upper storeys of the mind where they smash up the furniture and set fire to their own fragile habitation.'

'I wish I had his talent. Do you think he is a great artist?'

'You are a better judge of art than I. But I believe his work is spoiled by an excess of fantasy. Art must improve us, and only an artist who is decent and self-controlled and reasonable can produce truly great work – Charles Eastlake, for example, who gives us such charming and educational scenes and also played a practical role as Keeper of the National Gallery. Yet there is interest in Dadd's work, Morison has just sent me five pounds for some drawings. I had to return the money, for his work must stay inside our hospital.'

'Poor Dadd.' Haydon lit up his pipe and sat twinkling and sipping sherry, the picture of sanity. 'Did he come here immediately after the murder?'

'No. He fled to France. While travelling in a diligence through the forest of Valence he started to play with the cravat of the passenger sitting opposite him and then lunged at his throat with a knife, being convinced the unfortunate man was the Emperor of Austria whom he had orders to assassinate.'

'Orders?'

'From his master, the Egyptian god Osiris. When Dadd was arrested he declared himself the son and envoy of his god, sent to exterminate the men most possessed with the Demon. He immediately confessed to his father's murder and handed over money to pay for the medical expenses of the chap he had attacked. Dadd was committed to Clermont, where his family would have liked him to stay. They sent him parcels of special food and paints and brushes and canvas, but – you must remember all the publicity, George.'

'I do not, for I was in Australia then.'

'The Governor of Clermont said Dadd was silent and did nothing but only stood in the courtyard gazing up at the sun, which he called his father. After about a year he was extradited and appeared before magistrates in Rochester, but there was no trial because his behaviour was so obviously insane. In court he laughed and exclaimed and called out to people in the audience, who roared with laughter, and to others who were not there. So he was sent here and had already been in the criminal block for six years when I arrived.'

'Poor fellow, with his Egyptian god and his Greek tragedy.' Haydon sighed but soon bounced back. 'Well, I must throw you out now. Clarissa has accepted an invitation to a smart dinner party in Kensington, and I must dress. To tell you the truth I rather dread our excursions into London society. In Australia I forgot all my small talk and etiquette, and perhaps that's why I enjoy the company of artists and lunatics: no hypocrisy.'

I laughed and hurried back to our little house under the portico. Jane and I live here like two barnacles encrusted in the carcass of a great whale. The whale sails on, bloated with all its accretions of history and tragedy, and we are snug together in our fragile shells.

Jane was delighted to see me at home so early, although she was somewhat frazzled by the children's bedtime. Louisa glowered at us all with the disagreeable air that has cloaked her since her fourteenth birthday. As I was particularly anxious to be alone with Jane I resorted to bribery, telling Chas and Donald that we would go to the Crystal Palace on Sunday if they went straight to bed and promising Louisa that she could read herself to sleep with any book she chose from my library. She disappeared, beaming, with a treatise on anatomy under her arm and a candle in her hand.

I took my wife in my arms and felt the glorious reality of her. She is my dearest friend as well as my lover and assistant. When I hear other men boast of their wives' dowries and accomplishments I know that no princess could have brought me more treasure. She has taught me the true meaning of my work, and every day she helps me with a mountain of administration. When my governors compliment me on my achievements and marvel that one man can do so much I wish I could acknowledge my invisible helpmeet. Jane's eyes were red from the hours she had spent tabulating statistics for our next report, but to me she is always beautiful.

We had a quiet supper and then looked over some work together.

'Don't leave me tonight, Billy,' she said and took my hand.

'You know I would never leave you. I only walk around the hospital at night because I feel responsible for all those pitiful ones –'

'Let go of them, Billy. Just for a few hours. Hold me instead.'

I did, and we lay together in love and peace.

Jane fell asleep with her head on my chest, and I stroked her hair, which had come loose from its moorings. Afraid to disturb her by a movement I lay half-naked in our bed and closed my eyes. Sleep would not come, but the tide of memory swept me back to our first meeting at Fiddington House.

It was my first appointment after my long training. I was grubby after an exhausting journey by train and cart, and my Londoner's heart sank at the sight of so much mud and grey sky. Although I had tried to find an appointment in London or Dublin, where I spent my riotous student years, or even in Brighton, where I went to school, there were few openings for physicians specializing in alienism, and my lack of experience made me an unattractive candidate.

The proprietor, a Mr Ashcroft, was an elegant gentleman who owned a string of madhouses and lived in Berkeley Square. It was there, in his drawing-room, overlooked by a fine portrait by Gainsborough, that my interview took place. His prosperity reassured me instead of alarming me, and as it was almost my first interview I was relieved that he asked me so few questions. Did I hunt? Had I known the Honourable Somebody or other at Trinity? When I replied in the negative to both he yawned and seemed quite uninterested in my medical qualifications. I never saw him again.

I had applied to Fiddington because the latest report by the Metropolitan Commissioners described it as among the best asylums outside London. There was a farm, the report said, and a good diet was provided for pauper patients. Still naïve enough to believe that such a report was truthful (instead of a confection whipped up from bribes and deception), I paid the carter and stood beside my trunk in front of the house full of hope.

That first November afternoon I merely observed that the house was very large and dark and echoed with cries and howls like the bird-house in the zoological gardens. A servant showed me up to my room on the second floor. He carried a vast bunch of keys and opened and locked so many doors on our journey through the house that I wondered if I was to be a prisoner rather than a resident physician. A prophetic gloom settled on me as I followed the stiff back of Abel, whose muttering interwove with the unseen voices in an ominous chorus.

In fact, the room he showed me to was spacious and well furnished with a cheerful fire in the grate. There was warm water to wash in and a bed with clean sheets and soft pillows on which I longed to throw myself.

A few hours later Abel returned and led me back through the echoing maze of locked doors and alarming voices down to a comfortable dining-room where dinner for two was served. My companion was Worthy Dunford, a young man of my own age who introduced himself as Mr Ashcroft's assistant. When I asked where he had trained he was evasive, and all my direct questions met with unsatisfactory answers, viz. 'You will understand me better tomorrow.' Wishing to understand today I grew chilly and impatient. We dined on soup, excellent fresh trout and grouse served by the most eccentric servants I had ever seen.

Hannah, who was at least seventy, had a mouth fixed in a toothless grin. Her limbs were distorted by some nervous disease, and when she spilled our soup and gravy Dunford, a heavily built young man with coarse features, roared at her although it was quite clear the old lady had no control over her movements. Abel returned in the guise of a butler in a dirty frock-coat and muttered to himself as he shuffled around the table, pouring our claret with a shaky hand and sniffing each dish before he put it on the table.

This topsy-turvydom of the generations made me very uneasy. Dunford's manner towards me was furtive, as if there was a dark secret he was waiting to communicate, and this, combined with his bullying manner towards Hannah and Abel, made me feel so guilty that by the end of the meal I had become silent. All my questions had been dodged, and Dunford was visibly drunk on the good claret and port. I had drunk a glass of each but wanted to remain sober.

'Since you refuse to illuminate me I had better go to bed and wait for the morning to shed light upon my situation here.'

He was so far away, at the other end of the mahogany table, that I could not see his expression. Another glass of port disappeared down his throat and loosened his tongue. He spoke with a strong local accent, and I never saw any evidence that he had more than an elementary education. Dunford's qualifications were an abacus for a brain and a stone for a heart.

'Dr Hood, I'm pleased to see you among us and hope as you'll last longer than the last physician chappie we had here. Mr Ashcroft says as you knows all about medicine and suchlike, so I'll leave that side of things to you and be contented if you'll leave the disciplining of the poor lunatics and the money side of things to me. That way we'll work well together and not go poking our noses into each other's business, that being a thing I can't abide.

'We're a tight little community here – about a hundred and fifty souls all told, although I can always find room for more. We've a hundred and thirty-five pauper patients and nine privates at the present time. It'll be part of your job to count them morning and evening before lock-up, as they are inclined to go missing and cause us all a deal of bother. If you could find me some more private ladies or gentlemen I'd be much obliged, and there'll be two guineas on this table for you,' he thumped it emphatically, 'for each one as stays more than three months.' Dunford belched and grinned with the air of a man who had discharged his duty.

A hundred questions rose to my lips. The horrible suspicion that I should not have come here, that I had just dined off blood and sweat and misery, made me so nauseous that I rose abruptly, said a brusque goodnight and rushed from the dining-room.

In the dark hall Abel hovered with a candle, as if he had been expecting me to flee from the table. The old house creaked and groaned, and the very walls seemed to cry out to me in grief. I followed the flickering light up the stairs and through doors the decrepit servant opened with his fist of keys.

When at last I reached my bed I was too nervous to sleep. All night I heard screams, howls, running footsteps and angry shouts. A dozen times I jerked out of fitful dreams and started to get out of bed to rescue unseen people from unknown terrors. But I was too cowardly. I sank back, ashamed, into my small island of warmth and safety.

In the morning I was a wreck. There was a knock on my door, and I found a tray with a jug of warm water, tea, toast, butter and marmalade outside my door. Relieved that I did not have to join Dunford for breakfast, I shaved and, studying my face in the mirror, thought that I had aged ten years already.

At eight I peered out of my window at the grey dawn and the sea of mud. A door opened and a crowd of people emerged. They were dressed in rags, and many were barefoot despite the chill of the November morning. Men and women alike were chained two by two, and three hulking young fellows with whips herded them through a gate.

Dunford appeared in the yard below, well dressed in a green coat and brown leather boots. He glared up at my window and waved his arms at me, mouthing that I was to count his human livestock. I did. There were one hundred and thirty-five. Fiddington House was not well run, whatever the commissioners said, but the mathematics were impeccable. One hundred and thirty-five times eight times the cost of feeding the community added up to a healthy profit for the gentlemanly Mr Ashcroft.

Later I discovered these were the pauper patients, being sent to work on the farm next door. In addition to the eight shillings a week their relations had to pay for their keep, the poor wretches had to slave every day in the dairy, barns and fields, producing food, most of which ended up on Dunford's table. Moral treatment and occupation he called it when I challenged him, explaining that 'Them as has lost their wits can only find 'em again if they're kept busy. It's a case of being cruel to be kind.'

Cruel they certainly were, those sturdy, thoughtless young men Dunford employed. Devoid of the finer feelings themselves, having grown up among pigs and cows and been set to work from the age of ten, they were content to be 'keepers' at Fiddington House, where they were paid more to dominate their own species. It was not so much a house as a manufactory for suffering where the sane were made miserable and the mad were destroyed. The servants and keepers were local people with no special training who treated the patients like so many troublesome cattle and turnips. Private madhouses were ruled by the need for profit – and still are, for all I know. If Fiddington House really was one of the best I hate to imagine conditions in the worse.

The nine private patients, who paid a guinea a week and had relations who were sufficiently interested in their welfare to visit them, did not have to work on the farm. They had individual rooms on the first floor, whereas the paupers slept in dormitories upstairs. At that time the private patients at Fiddington House included a clergyman who was convinced he was Noah and was sent away because he kept flooding his church and forcing his parishioners up to the gallery which he called his ark. There was also a solicitor who had embezzled his clients' money and insisted that Satan had commanded him. (This, I thought, was rather the proof of his talent for argument than of madness, but he was certainly more comfortable in his private room at Fiddington than he would have been in New-gate.) A young man fresh down from Oxford had been committed by his own father over money matters. He told me he was but a pawn in some argument between lawyers over a large inheritance, and since the young man's wits were sharp enough for him to converse and play chess with me I saw no reason to disbelieve him. These private patients were treated with some consideration, were fed well and kept in clean rooms, if only that the friends and relatives who paid for their keep should not take their business away. They were rich enough to be able to afford a soul.

But the pauper patients! I still see them in my dreams and believe the sights I saw at Fiddington House were the cause of my lifelong insomnia and my drive – Jane sometimes calls it a mania – to reform. Many of them were not mad at all but only excessively emotional or deformed in some way, backward in their understanding or otherwise unfavoured by God. Many of them had been admitted because they were accused of excitement, violence, incoherent speech, delusions or melancholia.

My unhappiness drove me out on long walks around the surrounding villages, where I saw many an elderly child with lolling tongue and rolling eyes being taken for a walk by a devoted mother. But our pauper patients had committed the sin of embarrassing their families, and so they were condemned to be locked away on Dunford's slave farm.

On the first occasions I saw keepers ill-treating patients I rushed to Dunford and quoted his own rules at him. I have them still, those admirable principles by which Fiddington House was to be run. Every keeper and patient is expected to rise at six . . . The keepers will then wash and comb their patients and examine the stools and urine . . . The keepers will clean out the rooms . . . No place will be considered *clean* which can be made *cleaner* . . . Any keeper striking or ill-treating a patient will for the first offence be admonished, and be dismissed for the second. Nor are the keepers to use any harsh or intemperate language . . . Any keeper found making a perquisite of any kind or selling anything to a patient will be admonished for the first offence and dismissed for the second . . . any keeper, nurse or servant from whose custody a patient escapes through negligence shall pay the expense of retaking the patient . . . any keeper or male servant who shall be found in any female patient's room without being directed to go there for some specific purpose shall be dismissed.

And the reality? I was on a remote farm where one group of human beings had absolute power over another group. As resident physician I was employed as a fig leaf to impress the Metropolitan Commissioners, whose visit in February was being anxiously prepared for in November. Dunford was to direct us all in a loathsome farce, and my discoveries were to be ignored. Again and again I told Worthless Dunford that I had found irregularities in admission documents and dangerous overcrowding in the paupers' dormitories. I pointed out his failure to hold religious services and even offered to organize them myself.

Most intolerable of all were the instances I had witnessed of keepers forcibly plunging patients into freezing-cold water – known as the bath of surprise – as a punishment for fouling their clothes or quarrelling. When I enquired about the causes of bruises and sores on the pauper patients' faces and bodies I was told they had had 'accidents' – although, as I roared at Dunford, they had, in fact, been injured by fetters and chains and blows with the fists or with straps or keys.

Incontinent patients were mopped down under an outside pump in the freezing yard. There were not enough keepers, and those few were mostly ignorant and idle. I observed the punitive use of solitary confinement without clothing or bedding for pauper patients who refused to work on the farm or eat. After biting Dunford's arm, one pauper was forced into a straitjacket, flogged and secluded. Later Dunford asked me to remove the man's two incisor teeth, but I refused.

Truly, the advocates for the extinction of foreign slavery would do well to look at home. My complaints were ignored or sneered at, and by the end of the first month I had decided to leave. That would mean an ignominious return to my father's house in Lambeth, for I had no money and Dunford and Ashcroft were far too crafty to pay me if I broke a single clause of my two-year contract. My mother was an invalid, and my father's own health had been broken by overwork; my glorious career as an alienist would end in carrying bedpans to my mother and assisting my poor old father in the slums.

As a student I had been inspired by a lecture by John Conolly about the treatment of mental patients without the use of physical restraint. At Hanwell he had a Chamber of Horrors where he exhibited the cruel implements that had been used: leglocks, iron handcuffs and fetters from wrist to ankle. Some of the other students thought that Conolly himself was mad, for he spoke like a man obsessed, not like a scientist. However, I had been deeply impressed by his criticisms of the treatment of the insane. 'In a madhouse,' he said, 'social bonds are broken, friendship ceases, self-confidence is destroyed and habits are changed. People act without decency, obey through fear and hurt others without even hating them. Each lives for himself alone and egotism isolates all.'

I had never met Conolly, but I could still hear his passionate voice as he stood in the dusty lecture theatre, haranguing us about the evils of asylums such as Fiddington House and trying to persuade us to join his campaign to take mental illness as seriously as physical sickness. More than anyone he had influenced my choice of alienism as an unfashionable area in which to specialize.

Late one night, in despair at the cruelties I had witnessed that day, I sat down and wrote a letter to Conolly. I intended to write as one scientist to another, to stick to the facts since there was no need to embroider. However, my emotions spilled out over eleven pages in what he described later as a howl of protest. I did not know if anyone would ever read my report from Inferno. Afraid that if I handed my letter to Abel to be posted it would be shown to Dunford and destroyed, I walked all the way to the post office in Devizes.

Some men meet their wives at balls. I first glimpsed Jane in a dark cupboard where she had been locked for refusing to eat or work and 'abusing her keeper'. I was told by Dunford to attend to her because he was afraid she would take her own life.

'I'd not miss her, but them blasted commissioners'll be here after Christmas, and they do take on so about dead patients.'

We were sitting over a late supper one Sunday. His mask and gloves were off now, and he spoke to me with grim frankness. My presence at his table made me feel that I was colluding in his crimes, and I was too young to know how to behave. For three days I had asked Abel to leave a tray outside my door at night, that I should not have to sup with a man I hated. But my trays held meagre rations – probably, I reflected, the pauper patients' own rations of gruel and bread and fatty bacon – and so hunger had driven me downstairs. I tucked into stuffed roast chicken with gusto while trying to scowl ferociously at Dunford.

'Who is this lady?'

'She's no lady! She was a governess over at Courtenay Hall. Very grand folks there, the Varzeys, friends of Mr Ashcroft. She got herself in the family way by one of the servants there and then accused the eldest son, Frederick Varzey. Said as how he was the father of her baby. Ran into the drawing-room when they was having some great bash and waved her baby under her ladyship's nose! Screamed and bawled like a fishwife, she did. Quite ruined their elegant sworry.

'Fortunately Mr Ashcroft was there. So he pronounced her mad and sent for a couple of keepers and the black van. Just in time they bundled her out. There was a grand hairess there – biscuits, I think, it was her dad made his money in – as the Honourable Frederick was a-going to marry. She was most upset by it all, and so was his lordship, watching all them biscuit millions a-going into issterics.'

'The name of the lady you have locked in the cupboard?'

'Jane Gowing. Prickly old maid with ideas above her station. It's her own fault if she can't get along here. For a few months the Varzeys paid for her to be a private patient, being kind folks and with that much money as a guinea a week to them is like a farthing to the likes of us. Only then they grew tired of the nasty threatening letters she contrived to send them and refused to pay any more.'

'Then who pays for her keep now?'

'I think there's a sister somewhere as stumps up the eight shillings a week. Wouldn't be surprised if her family's glad to see the back of her. She's a vixen and a scold is Miss Jane – aye, and a whore to spawn a baby as has no father.'

'Where is her baby now?'

'You do ask a lot of daft questions! Go and ask her yourself if you're so bothered. And make sure she don't top herself, for Mr Ashcroft'll not stand for that kind of nonsense.'

The next morning, after I had counted the pauper patients on their way to work on the farm, I asked Abel to take me to Jane Gowing. He snorted with contempt at the idea that anybody would want to see her as he led me down corridors and up some back stairs. Abel stopped outside a door, jerked his thumb at it, spat, handed me a key and shuffled off. I knocked on the door. Silence. I knocked again. A longer silence.

'Miss Gowing? My name is Dr Hood. Mr Dunford has sent me to examine you. May I come in?'

There was no sound from the other side of the door. A mental image came to me of a woman's body hanging from the ceiling, past examination. My hand trembled as I put the key in the lock, for I had not yet seen many dead bodies outside the dissecting-room.

As I opened the door something attacked me, claws scratched my face and I was pushed backwards. I fell on to the stone-flagged hall of the corridor and found I was gripping the wrists of a young woman who was sprawled on top of me.

'Let me go! How dare you touch me!'

The wild curtain of black hair that hung down over my face hid her features.

I held on to her wrists, for I could feel the heat of her rage and knew she would harm me if she could. 'Miss Gowing, you attacked me and I defended myself. Mr Dunford feared that you would harm yourself –'

'Mr Dunford is a vile knave who would sell his own mother for horsemeat. And you must be a quack and a charlatan if you work here.'

'I am a qualified alienist . . .' I tried to sound professional and experienced. 'Miss Gowing, your elbow is gouging my rib, and I cannot hold your wrists for ever. If I let go of you will you come to my consulting-room and permit me to examine you?'

'Oh, a gentleman! It makes no difference whether you hold me or not, for there is nowhere to run to.'

I stopped holding her wrists. She rolled off me, sat up and stared at me, pushing her hair back so that I could see her sad dark eyes in her pale face.

'Did I do that?' she asked suddenly, putting out her hand and touching the scratches I could feel stinging my cheeks. The hand was dirty but quite gentle.

'You have the longest fingernails I have ever seen. Are you planning to apply for a job as a Mandarin?'

'If only I could go to China! I must rot here for ever.'

'Miss Gowing, I sincerely want to help you.'

'And I sincerely want to put some iodine on those scratches.'

We sat on the cold stone floor, staring at each other. To my surprise I saw humour and intelligence in her face.

'Will you come now to my room on the first floor where we can talk like sensible people?' On chairs, several feet apart, without the dangerous warmth of your young body on top of mine.

'How can I do that when I am mad?'

In fact, she seemed calmer than I felt as we made our way down the back stairs and I unlocked the door of my consulting-room next to my bedroom on the first floor. When I drew back the curtains watery December sunshine poured in and illuminated the dust, for this room was rarely used, being but a sop with which to impress the commissioners and enable Mr Ashcroft to renew his licence. Most of the patients' illnesses and injuries met with a shrug from Dunford and the sympathetic advice to put a sock in it and stop swinging the lead.

Formality returned to our situation, and I felt like a doctor again. 'Please sit down, Miss Gowing. Shall I call for some refreshments?'

'I have had nothing to eat for three days. Bring me a roast goose with stuffing and gravy, roast potatoes and peas. With mint. And a blackberry-and-apple pie with cream.'

'Coffee and a slice of lard cake were all I had in mind. You make me feel quite inadequate.'

'Good. I would rather starve than eat the food here, prepared and served by slaves.'

'Are the servants patients as well then?'

'Sometimes Dunford makes them work in the kitchens. Not I, for he knows I would slip arsenic into his food and laugh as he died in agony.'

I believed her. Jane Gowing was unwashed and half starved, but, even so, a determined spirit shone out of her. I was already calling her Jane Glowering to myself. She sat on the other side of my desk with her arms crossed and glared at me as if I were a particularly repulsive turd she had condescended to step on. I wondered if she might spontaneously combust, for I could feel her rage smouldering deep inside her.

'Miss Gowing, please tell me how you come to be at Fiddington House.'

'I'm sure Dunford has already told you.'

'I would like to hear your version. Where were you born?'

She spoke slowly and hesitantly as if her voice was an instrument that had been too long in the attic of her mind. 'I grew up in Exeter.'

'What did you father do?'

'He was a solicitor.'

Silence.

Abel came in with a tray of coffee and cake and winked at me obnoxiously. I saw his coarse thought and moved my chair further away from Jane, who pretended she was not hungry. I saw her eyes devour the simnel cake I was eating, and when I passed her the plate she grabbed a slice and crammed it into her mouth. Then she choked and spluttered and I had to offer her water.

'My throat is sore where they have fed me by force.'

'Miss Gowing, there will be no force used against you while I am here.'

In the course of that long morning I coaxed her story from her. As she began to trust me and trust her own voice again it became an expressive instrument, a rich contralto.

When Jane was eighteen her father was accused of embezzling funds and committed suicide, leaving his wife and two daughters destitute. Within months his widow followed him to the grave, and Jane's older sister married an elderly undertaker who was very conscious of the honour he did her and wanted nothing more to do with her relations.

'One day I was safe and loved, invited to balls and evening parties. I thought only of my next new dress and the man I would dance with and, eventually, marry.

'But when my father blew his brains out he destroyed all of our lives. Within three months I became an orphan, exiled from my former comforts. My oldest friends turned away in embarrassment when they saw me in the street, and even my sister, who had always petted me, did not want to annoy her death's head of a husband by reminding him of our disgrace. The day the auctioneers came to sell our house and all our possessions I fled and went to an employment agency.

'My dame school had taught me to embroider, speak French, read maps, play the piano and draw. I was too genteel to be a domestic servant and too selfish to be a missionary, so of course I had to become a governess. According to the gorgon at the agency, I was very fortunate to be chosen by the Varzey family.'

'What were they like?'

'Rich, proud and charming. It was their charm that was fatal to me. There were six children aged between seven and twenty. The three pretty little girls vied for my affections and easily won them. Their house was magnificent, and as I ran around their beautiful gardens playing with my sweet little charges I imagined I had a family and a home again – even a better one than I had lost. I was not immune to the lure of wealth and splendour.'

'None of us is, Miss Gowing. You should not reproach yourself for that.'

'When I saw the older children, the ones near my own age, elegantly dressed ready to catch the London train, I longed to go with them. At night, when I sat alone over my supper in the night nursery – for I was too educated to eat with the servants but not grand enough to eat with the family – I would stride out in my own pathetic dreams of a social whirl.

'One evening the eldest son, Frederick, knocked on the door. He pretended he was looking for an old cricket bat and wanted to romp with his little sisters, but later he admitted that . . .' She faltered and looked ashamed.

'That you were the one he wanted to romp with? Describe him.'

'He was tall and fair with a dazzling smile and easy manners. He was in his second year at Oxford, and I loved to hear his stories of punts and wild parties and climbing into his college late at night. We became friends, I thought, although we had always to meet in secret, for Frederick said his parents were great snobs and thought too much of social distinctions – which, he assured me, he despised and, indeed, had had his jolliest times with the lower orders.'

As she spoke of her lover Jane's face became beautifully animated and then reddened as her eyes filled with tears. I saw how passionate she was beneath her crust of misery and felt distinctly jealous of Frederick Varzey.

'How long did you live in the Varzey household?'

'Eighteen months. At first I was happier than I have ever been. It sounds dreadful, but I quite forgot the tragedy of my own family in the lively currents of this new one. I fell in love with all of them, with the house itself, and woke each morning full of joyful anticipation. When Frederick returned to Oxford he sent me letters and books which I collected from a secret address in Salisbury. The tone of our letters became more intimate, and when he returned for the Easter vacation . . . we . . .'

Her voice broke again, and this time I did not prompt her. Such an old story, yet new for each poor girl who is seduced. Our asylums are full of governesses.

'If you would rather not tell me any more I shall understand.'

She shut her eyes as if to keep out unbearable memories, and when she opened them again her face was hard and bitter again and her dark eyes and voice were full of anger. I saw that she had an indomitable spirit, that hardship had not broken her but had only made her more heroic. I think I began to fall in love with her.

'I've been silent long enough. Everyone thinks the worst of me as it is. You are only a doctor and can have no feelings about the matter. Like most girls who have been treated like Dresden china for their first eighteen years I was quite ignorant. Frederick said he was careful during our embraces, and I thought babies only came when you were married. When I began to get fat, as the little girls observed, I thought it was on account of the good food from the Varzey table – passed on to me as scraps, like everything else. When my . . . monthly visits – you are a doctor so you know about such things – failed to arrive I was pleased, for they had always made me feel poorly and were a great nuisance. My mistake – my unforgivably stupid mistake – was to trust Frederick. I believed him when he said he loved me and would marry me as soon as he came down from Oxford. Can you believe that I was such a fool?'

'You are no fool, Miss Gowing. It is not a sin to love but it is always wrong to lie and selfishly follow your desires.' If Frederick Varzey had been in the room I would have thoroughly enjoyed throwing him out of the window.

'The housekeeper, Mrs Bartlett, who thought I was stuck up, went to Lady Varzey and denounced me just before Christmas. Of course, her ladyship had hysterics and gave me a week's notice and said her son could not possibly have been so foolish. However, she searched my room and found his letters, so she knew the truth but chose to disregard it. I was not allowed to see the little girls, whom I adored, for fear that I would contaminate them.

'For three days I lay in my room and wept. I had nowhere to go and I was about to lose my second beloved family. Even then I could not prevent wild imps of hope from persuading me that Frederick would come and rescue me, would come galloping up on his milk-white charger and carry me off. You will laugh . . .'

'I'm not laughing, Miss Gowing.'

'Well, anyway, I expected him to arrive at any minute. Instead, my baby arrived. Perhaps her birth was brought on early by my storm of emotion. I didn't even know what was happening to me. I was in agony and fell down screaming upon the bed. One of the house-maids, Minnie, rushed in to help. Although she was younger than me she had grown up in a cottage with ten younger brothers and sisters and knew what to do. She brought towels and hot water and stoically helped me through that terrible night. Later, of course, she was dismissed for showing me such kindness.

'The next night, Saturday, there was a grand reception. Nobody had dared to tell me it was to celebrate Frederick's engagement to a great heiress. All day I slept fitfully and woke up to see my baby's exquisite face and perfect little body, which I covered with kisses.

Louisa stared back at me with solemn, intelligent eyes, and I promised her I would always . . .' She could not go on but shook with dry sobs. 'That first day, that only day with my child, I knew that nothing mattered except her. I had not been told that Frederick was in the house, but I sensed his presence. I was convinced that if he could only see me with our child he would go away with us and we would all be happy together. If I ever have been mad it was then.

'That evening I heard carriages arriving and music and voices downstairs. I prepared our entrance, putting on my one good blue silk dress and wrapping Louisa in a piece of antique Brussels lace Lady Varzey had given me before my fall from grace. I slipped down the back stairs and entered the drawing-room by a side door before anybody could stop me. Frederick stood in front of the fire, bending over the hand of a beautiful young woman, as blonde as I was dark. Even then I did not hesitate but ran to him, holding out our baby, quite sure that he would be indifferent to worldly considerations, as he had always assured me he was.'

She fell into a silence so heartbroken that I longed to take her in my arms. I wanted to know what had happened to little Louisa but thought it cruel to press her. Even then, after three years in Hell, Jane was dignified and self-contained. When she spoke again she was angry, and I was relieved for her, seeing how she needed to nurse her rage in place of the child she had lost.

'Of course, you know what happened next. The whole county knows. Dunford will have entertained you over the port with his tales of Crazy Jane.'

'Miss Gowing, I will do anything I can to help you.'

'Then get me out of Fiddington House.'

'I will.'

She stood up and glared at me. 'Dr Hood, if you do not I shall kill myself. They watch me night and day – not because they would care about my death but because it would be an embarrassing statistic. But I will find a way.'

'Miss Gowing, I give you my word.' I rang for Abel and told him Miss Gowing was to have a private room and wholesome food for which I would pay. He chuckled and leered, and I knew what kind of stories he would circulate in the village and the servants' hall. Then I wrote a note to Dunford telling him what I was about to do.

Alone in my consulting-room I felt the horror and pathos of her story. I had never been in love before and had no professional experience to warn me that the head is a better diagnostic instrument than the heart. Yet there is nothing in my career that makes me prouder than my impulsive actions over the following weeks. Jane Gowing was a rare and delicate plant, withering beneath the influence of poisonous breath. Had I not liberated her from her Bastille I am quite sure that she would have died, either by her own hand or from starvation and misery.

Fortunately I knew my law. That afternoon I wrote to John Perceval, who had recently founded the Alleged Lunatics' Friend Society. He was the son of Spencer Perceval, the Prime Minister who was assassinated in 1812. As a young man he had suffered from religious mania and delusions of persecution, and his rich family confined him to an asylum near Bristol for three years. Since his return to the world he has become an eloquent defender of the rights of soi-disant lunatics.

I also knew that the Act of 1845 empowered Visitors to discharge any patient who appeared, on two distinct and separate visits, to be detained without cause. According to the Metropolitan Commissioners it was illegal to detain someone in an asylum 'wherever a man of ordinary intellect is able so to conduct himself, that he is not likely to do injury, in person or property, to himself or others'. Jane Gowing was extremely likely to do herself an injury if she remained at Fiddington, but I was convinced that she would blossom if she was given her freedom.

That first month at Fiddington I had seen enough to know that Dunford and Ashcroft had powerful local influence. Visitors were magistrates, noblemen, gentry and clergy, Ashcroft's neighbours who hunted and dined with him and would not readily believe that such a respectable fellow would be capable of brutality. Visiting was unpaid, an unpleasant duty, and the Visitors' Book was sent for in advance, thus warning Dunford to prepare. The angriest patients, like Jane, would be locked in their rooms into which few Visitors ventured even to look, retreating as soon as they possibly could from the unpleasant scene, which they regarded as inevitable.

I had more faith in the Metropolitan Commissioners, whose inspection was due soon. They had to visit licensed madhouses all over the country at least twice a year, which resulted in more uniform standards. They had no local connections to inhibit their judgement and, indeed, often found themselves in conflict with Visiting Magistrates. With the support both of Conolly and Perceval's Alleged Lunatics' Friends I thought I could persuade the commissioners that their previous good report of Fiddington had been mistaken. But they might choose to believe Dunford and Ashcroft – I spent several nights of insomnia fearing that I would fail both as a doctor and a human being. I would lose my job, and Miss Gowing would take her life.

On Saturday morning, after I had counted the poor souls going to slave on the farm, I walked into Devizes and found a letter from Conolly. I was enormously cheered by this, for despite his heavy workload at Hanwell he had taken the trouble to contact the Metropolitan Commissioners and arranged for them to put forward their visit to Fiddington by a month. They were to visit the following Wednesday, without warning, and so Dunford would have no time to cover up his villainy. Best of all, Conolly acknowledged that it would be impossible for me to continue at Fiddington and offered me a post as Joint Superintendent at Colney Hatch.

That afternoon I rushed up the stairs two at a time and knocked on the door of Jane Gowing's room. Her voice was fearful as she cried out, 'Who is it?'

'Dr Hood.' I realized she did not even know my first name. 'May I come in?'

I did not use the key until she assented and felt ashamed of my power over her. She crouched on her chair by the window, lonely and tense.

I could not use the bland language of a physician. I rushed up to her, then stopped before the invisible wall of her unhappiness. Jane looked up at me with dark, mistrustful eyes. The passionate embrace that had occurred a hundred times in the theatre of my mind could not yet be enacted. A lover is close to a lunatic, they say, and sometimes when I am attempting to understand my patients' delusions I think back to those days of our unusual courtship. Because I could not find adequate words I silently handed her Conolly's letter and watched her face as she read it.

'He is a man of his word. He will help us, Miss Gowing.'

'And you will go away to work for him, and I will never see you again.'

'But you will be free, Miss Gowing. If you wish to see me again . . .'

'I think I do.'

Her words gave me so much joy that I could only smile at her and gently put my hand on her thin white one, which was cold, with blue veins and red lines on the tips of her fingers where she had bitten her nails. 'My first duty is to set you free. Then you will have time and leisure to decide what you want to do with the rest of your life.'

'Shall I really have a life?' she asked in wonder.

I did not dare spend long with her that afternoon for fear of gossip and spite from the rest of the household. Of course, I knew that physicians in madhouses often abuse and exploit their female patients, and if Dunford could accuse me of having lascivious designs on Miss Gowing it would weaken my legal argument.

I sit beside my wife and watch her sleeping peacefully. All the years that Jane and I have spent working together to change this hospital and attitudes to lunacy in general came out of Fiddington House. Worthy Dunford should be congratulated, if the scoundrel is still alive, for turning an insipid young doctor into a passionate reformer. I do not think Jane will ever be healed of the mental scars left by those terrible years. She still trembles whenever we pass into the main hospital and tries to avoid direct contact with my patients. But here in our little house, behind the painful scenes of the great drama that is played out in every hospital, and perhaps most touchingly among the mind-sick, she dedicates herself. Jane is the driving force behind the arrows I shoot out at the indifferent public, behind all my letters, articles, reports and tables of statistics. Without her I would lose my engine and even the few hours of sleep I permit myself .

When she is not working to improve the world that once treated her so harshly Jane is a devoted mother. Chas and Donald are merry little fellows, and I hope they will become useful men. Louisa is a more difficult case, and I often fear that the upheavals of her early years have left indelible marks on her.

The Varzeys had placed her in an orphanage in Salisbury, and when we found her there she was as stiff and restrained as a wooden doll in her dark uniform. Jane ran to her with sobs and hugs which the little girl could not return, having had all feelings crushed out of her. She submitted to the stranger's kisses as if they were blows and asked coldly, 'Are you my mama?'

Jane and I looked at each other. We had been married a week and knew only too well the universal contempt for children born out of wedlock.

'I am your sister, darling. Our parents died and you were – lost. But now you will come to live with us, and we will love you always. Shall you like that?'

'I don't know.'

Three-year-old Louisa was the oldest child I have ever met. She showed no emotion until Donald was born a year later, when Jane found her standing over his cradle with my cut-throat razor in her hand. Tantrums and rages followed and again when Chas was born seven years ago. I try to love her as much as my own children but often fail. The cold little girl is becoming a ferocious young woman who rants absurdly that she wants to be a doctor.

10
COBHAM HALL

'It is a beautiful morning, sir.'

McDonald can be relied on to make the most banal remarks. I lost myself again in painting the nipples of my fairy ballet girl . . . the lovely young creatures I used to grope backstage in the theatres where I painted scenery, happy to risk a dose of Covent Garden ague. One night with Venus and a lifetime with Mercury.

'We might take a walk in the gardens, sir.'

McDonald does not usually persist in his botheration when I am working. I ignored him. The window behind me was open, and the perfume of grass and leaves and juicy buds distracted me as McDonald's words could not. Summer assaulted my nostrils and made me turn around to see the rival picture framed in the window. Since I last gazed out of myself grey has put on green, birds have nested, leaden clouds have been fluffed and whitewashed.

This time last year I could see only one small patch of sky through the bars. Seasons were reduced to a handkerchief waved mockingly by a world that had forgotten me. Staring at that tiny square of white or blue or grey I used to force myself to remember the meadows and fields and lawns and flowers I was struggling to paint.

'I thought you might like to see the flowers. For your picture, sir.'

How well he knows me. I could not permit myself to leave my easel for mere pleasure. Osiris and my father and my fairies would punish me, and my paintbrush would also have its revenge by refusing to obey me for the rest of the day. But if I go out to study flowers and draw them I will be working, and that is allowed.

Slowly McDonald leads me down the stairs, past the space where I must hang my Good Samaritan when I have finished him. So much work to do. As we approach the door I panic and clutch McDonald's arm.

'Are you all right, sir?'

No. The air is a cold gasp of emptiness. Too much space, green shouts at me, the shifting dome above makes me giddy. My fairies push past me and rush out into the gardens, giggling and turning cartwheels. I walk very slowly, supported by my attendant. I have become like one of the elderly bloodsucking Darnley relations I used to see in the grounds of Cobham Park, toad-eaters as they used to call them in the servants' hall. How I despised them for tottering around on the arms of their maids when I could run from the house to the pyramid in three minutes.

Cautiously I move forward into the void. Out here the past has more room in which to lurk. I am diminished by the vast gardens and the wall beyond. Not that I have any desire to climb over it. I turn and count the windows of the hospital that has suddenly become an architectural reality looming over me. McDonald confirms that it really is M4, that tiny rectangle of glass up there. Then I turn back to the threatening gardens, for you never know what will pounce on you from trees or bushes.

A woman appears and walks towards us. Like me she is leaning on the arm of an attendant and carries a sketchbook. Her face is so near that I can see the fine black hairs of her eyebrows, her thick eyelashes, the delicate blue veins on her lids above huge dark-blue eyes that stare back at me. She has the face of an Italian madonna; a Leonardo woman is in front of me, the first beautiful woman (almost the first woman of any kind) I have seen in the flesh for fourteen years. She is quite young, pale but internally very alive. I can see that she has been through a great ordeal and has lost the identity she once believed to be solid. All of us here are lost, but she is one of the few who have gained in strength.

We stare at each other for twenty seconds or twenty years. She has been touched by death; she is still grieving and has been much alone. The language behind our eyes is so rich that it smothers the words of polite introduction rising to my lips. How can I introduce myself to someone I already know so well?

Her attendant pulls her away, and I ask McDonald who she is. He is not supposed to gossip but can sometimes be persuaded.

'She is the wife of a doctor.'

'A doctor who works here? Then she is not a patient?'

'She is, sadly. She has been here for four years and is now in the female incurables' ward.'

'What is her name?'

'Mrs Sanderson –'

'Mrs Sanderson! The lady who sent me her remarkable drawings a few years back?'

'Yes. She suffers from the delusion that she has travelled to a future time. Returning to our own she found herself unable to attend to her domestic and wifely duties and had to be sent here.'

We continue to walk, and McDonald steers me away from other patients. I remember that I am dangerous, a murderer, a tiger among lambs and kittens. The wild beast has been allowed out of its cage for exercise, but already I am exhausted and long to be incarcerated again. Indeed I could not bear to meet anybody else, for my encounter with Mrs Sanderson has set my heart and mind thundering.

I remember the original purpose of my walk. Lambeth flowers have not the happy freedom of Kentish ones, but I sit on a bench near a patch of passable bluebells and begin to sketch them.

'Would you like me to pick some for you, sir? Then you can sketch them at your leisure when we get back to the ward.'

'No! You must never destroy a living plant. It is a wicked, wicked thing to do!'

Poor McDonald looks shocked and probably remembers the circumstances that brought me here, although he is too tactful to refer to them. He cannot see or hear them, the fairies that swarm up the green stalks and peer out of their fragile petal houses. They are shouting at me to leave them alone and whispering to each other about me.

'He is our enemy now and means to destroy us.'

'Get into his dreams and torment him!'

'Hold open his eyelids that he might not sleep at all!'

'He has pretended to be our friend all these years!'

'Tell Oberon he is only a mortal lump and has no right to exploit us in his paintings.'

'Excommunicate him from fairyland!'

I am forced to defend myself and kneel beside the clump of bluebells in supplication. To be cursed by fairies is a terrible fate. 'Please forgive me if I have offended you. I would never hurt you and paint you out of deep love and admiration.'

Neville looks embarrassed and pulls me to my feet. 'Shall we return now, sir?'

I do not argue but silently allow McDonald to steer me back inside the hospital. If he let go of my arm now I would not run away but would follow him meekly home. Home is M4.

When I sat again in front of my easel I was too tired to paint. My unfinished painting of the Fairy Feller, my love gift to Haydon, looked confused and worthless. Perhaps I should destroy it. The fairies in it were spitting at me, and I could not bear their mockery, so I took it down from my easel and turned it to the wall. What is there more thankless, more hopelessly stupid, more desperately wicked than a parcel of slaves, like all of us here in Bedlam, and what more slavish than painting, what more hopeless? My work will never be good enough, and, even if it were, nobody who matters will ever see it.

I shut my eyes and saw the glowing colours of genius that first set me on my lonely path, the paintings at Cobham Park that obsessed me when I was thirteen. I used to stand in front of them for hours, soaking up their rich colours and light. They opened doors to a better, more exciting universe. All my life I have been trying to reach those heights, to make just one painting that will be worth looking at after I die. Of course, I have failed. My whole life has been a catastrophe, I have betrayed that original vision and often fear that the doctors here only humour me when they praise my work. How could great or even good art come out of Bedlam?

I must have groaned aloud. Neville asked if I was ill, and I assented, for heartache and headache and melancholy had devastated me. He brought me a cup of his Tranquillity Tea, which I drank thankfully then went to lie down in my cubicle.

Cobham came back to me in dreams. When I woke my father said, *They like you up at the hall, Richard. You must go there more often and learn how to behave with important folk. It would be a great feather in your cap to be taken up by the Darnleys. And when you are rich and famous I hope you will remember your poor old father and help your brothers and sisters to get on in the world.*

I have never been sure if my father knew what happened to me at Cobham Hall; I still argue with him about it. He was friendly with one of the servants, John, and arranged for me to study the paintings in the great picture gallery there. I was to be allowed in not only on public days but whenever I wanted to go.

That was a strange period. Although I was relieved to be free of the flogging and bullying of school I was alarmed by my freedom. Robert and Stephen were apprentices in my father's apothecary shop; they had no time for me, and I didn't want to be at home with the little children. Each morning quizzed me on my qualifications for genius and found me wanting. I buried myself under the blankets until Mary Ann's harsh voice ejected me.

'Richard! Lazybones! Pa says you're to go up to the hall today. Says you're to be our salvation – as if we haven't got troubles enough.'

When I couldn't get a lift on a cart I stuffed my sketching things and a hunk of bread and cheese into my old school satchel and gladly walked the five miles along the old Roman road. I was Dick Whittington, Odysseus or Oliver Twist, relishing every leaf and flower and sure of finding my fortune in the magnificent Jacobean mansion. All the servants knew me and were kind to me, bringing me Madeira cake or pork pie to eat as I stood or sat sketching in the long picture gallery.

At first my favourite was Rubens's *A Lion Hunt*, with its rearing horses and ferociously energetic riders. When I tried to copy it all the fizz went out of it and the lions looked like statues. His sketches swirled with life in their subtle greys and sepia, and I loved them, particularly the one he had done of his wife and two children. I sighed with envy of the little boy in the naval cap held safe on his mother's lap and wished I could climb up there.

All these remarkable works had been collected back in the last century by the Old Earl, who lay dying upstairs, when he was on his grand tour. Of course, I did not realize then how fortunate I was to be allowed to see these masterpieces and gobbled them up as carelessly as the titbits the maids brought me from the kitchen.

I know now that it was an unusual collection because there were few religious works. Guido Reni's *Salome with the Head of St John the Baptist*, his *Massacre of the Innocents* and Titian's *The Scourging of Christ* all confirmed my suspicion that religion was cruel, nasty and dark.

Titian's dark, witty face mocked me from his self-portrait. At home I sat for hours in front of a mirror trying to draw myself but only felt more discontented with the pink moon of my face. Did real artists get spots?

After several visits I felt able to confront the strange, explosive pictures of Salvator Rosa, which at first hurt my eyes. Then I became able to see their poetry and romance and loved them, especially Jason overcoming the dragon. He was an amiable monster, so overcome by Medea's magic potion that he lay on his side like a kitten waiting for you to tickle its belly. I knew the story of the Golden Fleece from Ovid and wanted to warn Jason that he had better not marry Medea, who would chop up and dismember her little brother and then kill the two children she had with Jason just to spite him.

Reynolds's bored gentlefolk seemed very dull compared with these wild Italians, and I longed to escape from England. The stiffly tailored doll called *Lady Frances Cole When a Child* did not look a bit like any little girl I had ever met, and the grown-ups in the family portraits did not resemble the real aristocrats I saw around me, who talked and laughed just like anyone else. However, they were above me. I only observed them from a shy distance and had strict instructions to leave the gallery if any Darnleys appeared.

Sir Harley emerged from the dark wooden panelling one afternoon, an old man in an ancient red brocade dressing-gown and shuffling black velvet slippers. I was trying to copy my favourite Rubens, *Queen Tomyris Plunging the Head of Cyrus into a Vessel of Blood*.

'You must be the apothecary's son. What horrid taste you have!'

I stared at him in terror, wondering if this oddly dressed, elderly gentleman was family and I should run away. He never introduced himself but insisted on looking at my drawings.

'Not bad. You need more strength of line and brio. You know the story? No? Herodotus tells it. Queen Tomyris was a beastly Amazon, and when King Cyrus of Persia wanted to marry her she turned him down. I suspect those Amazonian ladies preferred each other, don't you? Look at the size of her! So, of course, they went to war over it, and Cyrus tricked the section of Queen Tomyris's army led by her beloved son, who was taken prisoner and committed suicide. Then the queen's army defeated the Persians, killing King Cyrus, and she chopped off his head, plunged it in his blood, as you see, and later used it to drink out of. You're smiling. I know how little boys adore these gory stories!'

In fact, I was smiling with relief because the housekeeper had just come into the picture gallery with a plate of hot biscuits for me and had looked approvingly at us, so I knew I was not at fault in talking to the curious old fellow.

'Oh yes, I know how naughty little boys can be! How I wish I had a son of my own. Look at these wicked little fellows.' He stopped in front of Veronese's *Allegories of Love*, which I had always avoided looking at because they were embarrassing and confusing. 'Look how wonderfully inventive he was! I do adore Veronese. Those chubby-arsed little fellows are putti, or cherubs, but not so cherubic. Whatever do you think they're doing? You're blushing and giggling, you naughty little fellow. And look, here's another.' He stopped in front of Tintoretto's *Origin of the Milky Way*. 'Of course, you know the story?'

Again I shook my head, ashamed of my ignorance.

'Well, Jupiter wanted to make Hercules immortal, so he held the baby to the breasts of Juno while she was asleep. Have you any little brothers and sisters, boy?'

'Hundreds,' I said gloomily.

'Well, I expect you've seen your mama feed them in that disgusting way. Rather like milking a cow I've always thought.'

I didn't mention that I had no mama. He talked to me as if to an equal who happened to be younger, and I did not want him to know what an overcrowded hovel I lived in.

'The milk from great Juno's breasts spurted upwards to form the Milky Way, while a few drops fell down to earth and the first lilies sprang up. See? At the bottom there.'

I was impressed that he knew so much about art. That afternoon I asked him a thousand questions and was flattered by his interest in me. As I left the gallery, much later than usual, John said as he showed me out, 'I see you're moving up in the world, Richard. You be nice to Sir Harley, and he'll do great things for you.'

The next week when I visited Cobham Hall Sir Harley appeared again and admired my feeble drawings. 'Of course, you've been to Italy?'

I shook my head, unwilling to admit that I'd never even been to London.

'Oh, but you must go! I went for the first time when I was not much older than you, accompanying my old friend who is lying upstairs, desperately ill. But in those days we were young, and what a time we had! I advised him, you know. It was thanks to me that all these great works come to be here. Together we studied Poussin's *The Sacrament of Ordination*, and my cousin got the idea for the mausoleum. You see it there, up on its hill? He wanted there to be a wonder of the world in sleepy little Cobham. Do you know what the seven wonders were, Richard? No? Oh dear. What a lot you have to learn, and what fun you will have learning it all. Do you play chess?'

'Yes. Last night I beat my father.'

'Indeed? Shall we see if you can beat me? I expect you're hungry and thirsty. Boys always are.'

We walked along corridors, up and down stairs, until we came to a cosy room in the private heart of Cobham Hall where I had never been allowed before. Sir Harley was not family but a friend of the Old Earl's, a knight, a link with the glories of London and Paris and Rome. He spoke with ridiculous vowels and a languid manner, and even at fourteen I knew that aristocrats like him commissioned the art I longed to make.

When I went home and bragged of my new acquaintance my father was delighted, and Maria asked if *she* could go and have toasted muffins in his room.

'He says he only likes boys.'

One summer afternoon I walked the flowering lanes from Chatham to Cobham in a happy daze. My fairies were still benign; they smiled at me from trees and wild flowers and bushes. I was in love with the great Jacobean house and with every painting in it, even the stiff family portraits. At night, as I lay with George snoring beside me, I memorized every detail of the wonderful gallery, even the Latin tag on the stone fireplace: 'Every man makes his own shipwreck.' Perhaps I should have heeded it as I translated it.

The grounds spread out in front of me, the Elysian fields where the blessed lived. When the man at the lodge nodded and let me pass I really felt that St Peter had admitted me to Heaven while I was still very much alive. I wanted to run up the drive and had to restrain myself, very conscious of my new dignity. The house rose ahead of me, a quarry of daydreams: Lord Darnley would call me to meet him on his deathbed and be so impressed by my talent and intelligence that he would adopt me as his heir; I would be appointed his official hermit and live in the wonderful Greek temple topped with a pyramid that I could see through the trees on my right; my talent would so dazzle the Darnleys that they would send me off on a grand tour; I would be commissioned to paint frescoes in one of the magnificent reception rooms where glorious colours and poetic narratives would flow from my untutored genius.

My ecstasy in front of the paintings had become something of a pose by then. I wanted my admiration to be admired, my sensitivity to be recognized. For ten minutes I stood in front of *Queen Tomyris*, contemplating it but also perfectly aware that Sir Harley was contemplating me. It was exciting to be watched; it added a new dimension to my romantic solitude.

When Sir Harley invited me again to take tea in his room I assented gladly and was proud when he put his hand on my shoulder. A couple of housemaids dusting the paintings giggled as they saw us pass. His touch was delicate and subtle as he felt up and down my spine and rested just above my bum. He was very quiet, and I sensed a new intensity in him, a kind of greed, which gave me an enjoyable sense of power.

He rang the bell for a maid who brought a tray laden with tea and cakes and muffins. When we had eaten he proposed a game of chess and easily put me in checkmate. 'I have won. You must pay me a forfeit, my dear boy.'

'But I have no money.'

'I will accept payment in kind.' He leaned towards me and put his hand on my thigh. My doodle and nutmegs, which had been ashamed of themselves ever since my father's mutilation, sprang to attention. I was mortified, but Sir Harley smiled as he gently pulled down my breeches and fondled me so expertly that I gasped and shuddered with pleasure, ending up on my back on the floor in a kind of swoon.

When I opened my eyes again I felt that I had done something very wrong. And yet I had done nothing, all had been done unto me. Sir Harley sat on a chair above me and observed me with a smile as I put on my besmirched breeches and wondered how I would explain their state to Mary Ann.

'How shabby your clothes are. Come, choose yourself some more.'

He opened a wardrobe and showed me shelves of boys' clothes: shirts and breeches and jackets, pressed and washed and smelling of lavender. All were too small to fit his paunchy body and some were too small even for me. I chose myself a fine white linen shirt, a pair of soft dark-green breeches, white silk stockings and a green jacket with brass buttons. They were the first new clothes I had had for years, and I was thrilled as he dressed me, his hands running tenderly over my body, his thick lips kissing my hair and neck. His breath stank of the charnel house, yet he had a wonderfully light touch. His fingers played me as if I were a harpsichord. Small white hands, dimpled, with manicured nails, his little fingers crooked to hold an invisible teacup.

At home my smart new clothes were much admired, and nobody

asked how I had come by them. My friendship with Sir Harley was considered a fine achievement, and in his more snobbish moments my father would open up an old book and show me where my benefactor perched on his exotic family tree.

So began three years of knowing and not knowing, taking all I could get with both eyes tightly shut. I accepted the old man's presents of books and clothes, his expertise about art, his fascinating stories about London and Paris and Rome in the last century. And his caresses, which became more urgent and impatient as familiarity blunted his manners. Often he would thrust me into his room and tear off my clothes and his own, without waiting for the tea tray or the chessboard.

The Old Earl died, and his son inherited the title and the house. I was jealous of the children born beneath the sheltering wings of the Darnley griffin, who ran about the house and grounds exquisitely dressed with their toys and ponies and adoring servants. Wandering around the house with Sir Harley I glimpsed the heavenly rooms they inhabited, the Chinese silk wallpaper, four-poster beds, Adam ceilings and the great Gilt Hall with its organ and minstrels' gallery.

Sir Harley, now that his old friend had died, was moved to a smaller, darker room on the third floor near the servants' quarters. He seemed to shrink with his room, and his voice became a petulant squeak. That last winter he was often too ill to come downstairs and would summon me to his stuffy room, where I submitted to being fumbled at.

One afternoon he was well enough to walk in the grounds, and I had to accompany him, reluctantly holding the shaking arm. A couple of nursemaids came towards us with two little Darnleys in their arms, then swerved away. I heard one say to the other, 'Don't go near the horrid old creature.' I wished I could drop Sir Harley's arm and run away.

Ever since my stepmother died my father had muttered that we were going to move to London. He worked hard in his shop all day and then went to meetings of various scientific societies or Masonic dinners. Frequently he came home drunk, and we children thought him a ridiculous figure. I was his favourite, and as my drawings and watercolours were passed around Chatham and admired he would preen himself on my behalf and boast about his son the genius. At home I bossed my little sisters around and was rude to Mary Ann when she tried to assert her authority in our anarchic household. I felt more interesting and important than Stephen and Robert with their practical, narrow minds and enjoyed Maria's admiration. Each night in bed before I fell asleep I would savour my glorious future, when I was to rise above my humble origins (a phrase of Sir Harley's, which rankled) and soar away to shine in the international art world.

That bed was still shared with George. The butt of our family jokes, sturdy and dim-witted as a little donkey – the nickname we gave him – George still had the look of a changeling. He grew tall and blankly handsome with golden hair and blue eyes that had nothing behind them. In the middle of the night his body pressed against mine, and his doodle, like mine, stiffened with dreams. Under the cover of darkness and sleep I seduced my little brother, doing to him the things that Sir Harley did to me; if our older brothers heard the creaking bed they never said anything, and George and I never spoke of what happened between us.

The only member of my family I did not despise was Maria, whose vivacity and charm I encouraged. She grew up to look very much like our mother, whose face I saw and loved in the developing sketch of her daughter's. I was flattered when Maria allowed me to be present at musical evenings and sewing parties with her little friends, and I delighted in drawing and flirting with them, as I did not think of myself as a Miss Molly. Elizabeth Langley, her sister Catherine, who later married my brother Robert, and the Carters, we were all cousins and friends, and when I was with them I felt safe.

In the parlour that had seen painful scenes between my father and both his wives, the fresh young faces gathered. All were charming and sweet, although only Maria and Elizabeth were real beauties. I listened to their chatter about common acquaintances and music and samplers, and among them I became a different Richard, kinder and warmer, quite happy to adore Elizabeth. I would no more have touched her secret places than I would have ridden out as a highwayman on the road to Dover. I courted her as gravely as if I, like her, was a virgin, and aunts and uncles gossiped that there would be a double wedding in our family.

I began to dread exposure of the foul secrets of my liaisons with Sir Harley and George. Silence had been my shield, but I often woke up sweating from dreams of my friends and family laughing at me, pointing and sneering. Don't go near the horrid little creature. I was sure the young girls would shun me if they knew what I was really like.

Sir Harvey's flabby old body was repulsive, but I could not free myself from my need for his patronage. Although I came to dread my visits to Cobham Hall I did not dare to confide in anyone, for I knew Sir Harley could destroy me with a word as quickly as he had raised me with his languid praise.

One day George went to our father to complain of blood in his stool, and I was terrified he would incriminate me not out of malice but out of donkeyness. With Elizabeth I felt that he, the Richard who wooed her, was a silly china ornament, only fit to be smashed with a hammer and shattered into a thousand pieces.

So when my father's threats of London became a reality I was relieved. The apothecary's shop was sold, money was borrowed from some Carter connection, and the Suffolk Street establishment was bought. I never troubled myself about the financial details, although it was all for me this vast upheaval in our lives. I was the artist whose brilliant future career justified the sacrifice of the rest of my family. At seventeen I fled gladly from them all, from Sir Harley and Cobham Hall and Chatham and Carters and Langleys. A new life was all I wanted, and I hurled myself at the excitements of London, never imagining that those early years would turn out to be the oven that had baked me.

11
NINA

I have seen Mr Dadd! He was in the gardens just now when Letty made me go for a walk. She held my arm very tight as if walking was a punishment – had she not been so gaolerish I think I would have run to him and kissed him although he might not have wanted my kisses. Nobody does any more.

It was odd to see a man again, although he is not exactly a man, more of a large dwarf with extraordinary blue eyes full of sadness and magic and wisdom. He looked straight into my heart. I heard the crack as some of the ice melted. I wished my heart had more in it that is worth seeing, but it is very small now, pale and shrivelled and squashed like a dead fly.

His eyes held me as I stood quite still, wanting to be held in their strange blue light. I felt that he knew all about Bella and Jonathan and Tommy, that he had learned about me from my drawings and forgave me whatever sins I committed that landed me here. There was humour in his eyes, as if we were in the same joke, and fellowship because we are both artists. Looking down for a moment from his ferocious gaze I saw that he, like me, was carrying a sketchbook. His eyes have sucked up power from years of devouring the world, and behind them is a mind of great originality. The doctors here would like to dissect him and pickle his brain and bottle his talent and parse all the poetry out of him so that they can find out exactly why he killed his papa and make sure it never happens again. I think the joke, the secret Mr Dadd and I shared just now, is that the mind cannot be understood or imprisoned. He is quite free and has made me feel that I am free, too.

I have no idea how long we stood there. We exchanged pictures instead of words and our silly attendants could not even see them. I showed him the gloomy house in Harley Street, Charles huffing and puffing and quacking and Bella and Tommy in their little coffin beds.

Then I showed him the glorious future in Jonathan's London, hoping to inspire him and give him hope. For if I was able to find a bridge to carry me there why should he not also find a way? At this I grew sad, thinking how my bridge to Jonathan has been blocked for years now and perhaps I will never find him again.

Mr Dadd caught my sadness like a ball and tossed it back to me with a picture of his own. A very singular scene with fairies, not nice fairies but perfectly beastly ones, not at all the sort of fairies I would have let my children look at. I was quite shocked by the things they seemed to be doing to each other. Tactfully he wiped that picture out of the air and showed me another, a boy walking through meadows carpeted with wild flowers. I smiled at him so that he would know I recognized him. If time were more flexible I could join that bright-eyed handsome boy and become his sister or his mother, and I truly believe we could be happy together.

I saw that he was trying to show me a new picture, but jagged spikes obscured the image that flickered in the air between us. His face grew flushed with effort or shame and clouds of terror darkened his eyes as I saw two figures struggling on a path, the glint of a knife – then the spikes of lightning hid them again. Mr Dadd has a whole universe in his head where most of us have only a few rooms.

I wanted to comfort him, so I showed him the memory I have never shared with anybody: that wonderful private ball I shared with Bella and Henrietta and my dear mother when death allowed them a holiday and Jonathan and I waltzed through the night. Mr Dadd smiled gently and nodded as if he had often attended such balls. He made me feel accepted, and I sighed with relief because I was no longer quite alone. A giant dwarf who cavorts with fairies and who does not speak is not exactly a friend, but I knew there was a bond between us. He is a good man despite his tragical history and has suffered dreadfully.

All this I saw without exchanging a word with him.

Then Letty and Mr Dadd's male attendant remembered their duties and dragged us away like two dogs whose owners do not wish them to sniff each other.

As well as this silent friendship I think I have made a human friend. Miss Robinson appeared in the ward six months ago, but we had never spoken. She is a small, faded woman of thirty who does not blaspheme and stage tantrums like the other females here but instead sits in a corner reading and writing, ignoring us all. The doctors have constantly warned her that over-studying is dangerous for women, but she takes no notice.

When I came back from my encounter with Mr Dadd I was so excited that I at once began to draw. Kind Dr Hood will pass my feeble efforts to Mr Dadd again, and in that way we will communicate.

I had not touched my pencils for months, although I always carry my sketchpad, rather as Tommy used to clutch his favourite knitted rabbit with him everywhere. Once my little boy was in my head I could not send him back to Heaven, which must be rather like the nursery Charles and I were always banishing him to as a punishment for naughtiness. My pencil brought him back to life, a little boy with black curls and a grin that was stronger than all our efforts to make him behave. Even when he was three or four Tommy saw the absurdity of things. That grin defeated me. I made the lines between his nose and mouth too dark so that he looked like an elderly elf. I rubbed and smudged and frowned.

'Is that your child?' The question came from Miss Robinson, who stood behind me.

'My little son. He died six months ago.' It was the first time I had spoken of Tommy's death, and I was surprised to find my voice so factual. I did not brim up with tears but turned to look at the curious little person.

She is so short that her head only reaches the back of my chair, and her nose and chin are very long. Although she is not much older than me she has grey hair she combs into a smooth chignon and always wears a grey dress. The general impression is of a vole dressed in a woman's clothes, like the stuffed animals that so entranced Tommy at the Great Exhibition. Miss Robinson has sharp grey eyes that glitter with intelligence, and her remarks are as pointed as her nose.

'Far too many children die, and too many of their mamas die giving birth to them. After the revolution all will be given free medicine and will die in their beds at the age of seventy-nine.'

She spoke with such conviction that I could not but believe her. I turned my chair to face her, introduced myself and invited her to draw up a chair. 'Is it going to happen soon, your revolution?'

'It is not mine. The revolution belongs to all of us.'

'You make me feel quite ignorant. I am afraid that since I came here I have been too absorbed in myself and have not so much as looked at a newspaper for five years. My husband used to read to me from The Thunderer every day.'

'The Thunderer! The Liar! You will not learn anything from newspapers. They are controlled by capitalist lackeys.'

'Oh dear – I did not realize – my father once met the editor of *The Times* and said he was perfectly charming.'

'Charm is the poison they bait their traps with.'

'Poison? How dreadful! But please tell me more about this revolution. I do hope nobody will be hurt like in that horrid one they had in France.'

'There will be many deaths. The royal family, the aristocracy and all other useless people will be shot at dawn and their property redistributed among the rest of us.'

'Even those of us who are confined here?'

'All the prisons and asylums will be flung open.'

'But, won't that mean that some very unpleasant people will be at large?'

'There are more unpleasant people in the Houses of Parliament than in this building.'

Perhaps it is weak of me but I have quite fallen beneath her spell. She seems to know everything. 'Do not think me foolish, Miss Robinson, if I confide in you. This is something I stopped talking about years ago because nobody believed me – you see, I think I have seen what will happen to London after your – our – revolution.'

'Seen it? Bosh! You must be mad as a hatter!'

I sighed. It is quite common for the patients here to accuse one another of insanity. 'That is not helpful. Why are you here, Miss Robinson?'

'My family are reactionaries, *rentiers* who live off the sweat of the labouring masses.'

'I do not understand you.'

'My father owns a mill near Manchester. When I was a child I used to watch children younger than myself walk barefoot to slave in his mill and factories. I knew their labour paid for our grand mansion, for my food and my boarding-school, and I felt the injustice of it long before I read Shelley and Wordsworth.'

'You are a radical?'

'That's what my father and brother used to call me. "Blue stockings won't get you a husband! You're plain enough already without making your eyes red from reading! I grew up in the school of hard knocks, my girl, and you're heading for another beating if you lecture me again on blooming inequality! What do you know of work to be preaching to us about the working classes?"'

Her eyes shone, whether with tears or rage I could not tell. 'And was it your family who sent you here?'

'When I was seventeen I ran away and came to London. I had an aunt, my mother's unmarried sister, who lived in Highgate, and I was fond of her. Aunt Harriet gave me a room in her house and allowed me to study and read as much as I liked. She wrote to my father – for my mother had died when I was six, as mothers do, giving birth to my little sister who also died. When will women free themselves from the tyranny of their biology? Now where was I? Oh yes, my aunt told my father she would be responsible for me, and he was only too glad to be rid of me. He was just about to marry again, a silly chit of a girl not much older than me who only wanted new frocks and evening parties and men to flirt with.'

Miss Robinson has so much anger inside her, like a hot stream that bubbles up all the time. She spits and raises her voice and is what Charles would call a regular virago, but I must confess I enjoy her company.

'And were you happy in your aunt's house?'

'At first, very much so. I joined the Highgate Literary and Scientific Institution and even gave a paper on female suffrage.'

'And do they suffer very much? To which females do you refer?'

'Goodness, how ignorant you are! I suppose you went to a stupid dame school and learned only how to do embroidery and play the pianoforte! Did you say your name is Nina? I think you are a ninny, Nina! I mean, of course, that women should be allowed to vote.'

'Vote for what?'

'For themselves! For a government!'

'Tell me the rest of your story and then I will tell you something very surprising that I have seen. I am not mad or stupid,' I added, peeved by her contemptuous tone but eager to hear more.

'I met a young man, a schoolteacher, who was very learned and was kind to me. He lent me books and invited me to join a discussion group that met once a week in a house in Heath Street.' Her voice softened, and I longed to ask if there had been any tender passion between them but did not dare. Voles have sharp teeth.

'They were Chartists, fascinating men and women from all walks of life who read and thought and talked brilliantly. They taught me to see the world around me in a different way. It was as if they took a hammer to the comfortable life of regular meals and servants and polite society that was all I'd known and smashed it. There was a revolution in my head long before the events of 1848.'

And so your revolution and your poor shattered brain got you confined to a madhouse, I thought, remembering how my father and husband and all our neighbours feared the Chartists and barricaded their houses against them. Charles used to say that it was a charter for criminals and lunatics, and I remember how delighted he was when their great meeting on Kennington Common fizzled out.

'My aunt, who had always let me do as I pleased, did not like Edward my schoolmaster friend. She told her maid to follow me to the house in Heath Street, and when she discovered I'd been attending Chartist meetings she forbade me to go.

'There was a dreadful scene between us. Aunt Harriet screamed that they would ruin my life, that such people brought only destruction and misery and I was too young to understand the danger I was in. Of course, at twenty I thought myself fully grown and much cleverer than my aunt. I was enraged by her interference and shouted back at her. In her cosy little panelled drawing-room, where I had sat with her harmoniously reading and playing cards so many evenings, we came to blows. I was late for a meeting. I longed to see my friends and feel again the excitement of being part of a great movement that would change the world.'

Miss Robinson fell silent, and I saw her brush a few tears away. 'I can never forgive myself for what happened next. My aunt tried to bar my way to the door, I pushed her roughly aside, she clutched her heart and collapsed on to a chair. By the time I rang for a servant she was dead. My poor aunt had always had a fluttering heart, a gentle heart, and I had broken it.

'Nobody heard our angry words. The doctor said she died of natural causes, and in her will Aunt Harriet left me her house and all her money. Friends praised my devotion when I wept uncontrollably at her funeral and shrouded myself in mourning clothes and became pale and thin. I felt that I had murdered her and stolen her money. The house where I had once been so happy was full of her now; every room reminded me of her thousand kindnesses and my own ingratitude.

'I decided the only way I could absolve myself was to give away my inheritance. I told Edward and the other comrades of my plan to sell the house in Highgate and my aunt's investments and give the proceeds to our great cause. I would keep only a pittance for myself and spend the rest of my life working towards change. I longed for poverty, for hard work and the companionship of serious-minded, honest people. Edward said he was proud of me, he said I was his best pupil and even . . .'

Her quick, clear voice stumbled over some boulder of painful memory.

'One day my father, stepmother and brother appeared on the doorstep of the Highgate house. I had not seen them since Aunt Harriet's funeral when they were very distant with me. They must have got wind of my inheritance. I greeted them warmly, for I was racked with guilt at that time and blamed myself for the capricious way I quarrelled with them and bolted to London. When they asked if they could spend a few weeks with me I made no objection, for the house was large.

'How stupid I was! I spoke to them of my plans and hopes and even introduced them to dear Edward. I imagined I was independent of them, free to do whatever I wished. When I saw the looks they exchanged, their stifled laughter at my eulogies of Chartism, I did not worry. I was a few months short of my twenty-first birthday when I should come into my property.

'One afternoon my father invited a friend of his, a Dr Lowe, to tea. I ordered cakes and sandwiches in the drawing-room and tried to be cordial, although I found the man impudent. A great fat lout I should not have liked to find at my bedside, he interrogated me about my political ideals and plans for the future. I felt most uncomfortable and kept looking at my father to see if he also found it odd that a man I had never met before should ask such intimate questions. "Just tell him the truth, girl," he said, and I did. A few days later another doctor, a friend of my brother's, called.

'This time I was more suspicious for I had noticed a change in the atmosphere. Whenever I came into a room the conversation stopped, and even the servants had been treating me with less respect, going to my stepmother to take their orders for the day. I told my slyboots brother to show his friend out as I was not ill, but he only snorted and said that was a matter of opinion. There was no mistaking the aggressive way the two young men strode into my drawing-room. With no pretence of small talk the doctor asked me similar questions to Dr Lowe. He took notes and exchanged smirks with my brother as he fired at me the most insulting . . . the most humiliating . . .'

Miss Robinson could not continue. I leaned towards her and took her hand, for I knew the rest of her story. Painfully I relived my own entrapment by Charles and his medical friends. How easy it is to pronounce another person mad. Women must live within such a narrow frame, and if we take one step out of it we are denounced as whores, termagants or madwomen. It is men who make these judgements and women of spirit who are broken by them.

Mary puts me in mind of Henrietta. I feel much closer to my unloved sister in death than I did when she was alive. Both Henrietta and Miss Robinson have been the victims of their own intelligence. With too much energy and passion to be bread-and-butter misses and not enough beauty to attract men, they poured their zeal into ideas.

While I was listening to Miss Robinson's story the ward had grown dark around us and supper was served. We were led like infants to the table in the middle of the ward and ate in silence punctuated by slobbering, dribbling, muttering, humming and arbitrary laughter and singing. Not silence at all really, but there was, as usual, no conversation between us. We were given food, and we consumed it, except Mrs Brighouse, who is inclined to vomit, and Miss Parker, who did not like her rice pudding and spat it out into the dish of Mrs French who walloped her with her spoon.

It was the same ward where I have existed for the last three years, yet because of Miss Robinson it felt different. At the table we sat opposite each other, but I avoided her eyes from shyness. Her confidences are like valuable gifts. I feel I owe her some return, and as I chewed and swallowed I tried to put my own story into words. I never have talked frankly of my experiences in Jonathan's London in all these years in the hospital. Although Dr Hood is kind he is a man of reason and cannot stretch his excellent brain to accept the peculiarities of mine.

All night I lay awake in my cubicle and rehearsed my tale in my head. I used to be cross at Tommy for telling tales, but we all must tell them and cannot always be sure whether or not they are true. Past and future swirled together to form a misty creature who was Nina. By dawn she had grown clearer and I began to know myself again. I saw those towers and palaces and shining streets and heard the voice of Jonathan, who seemed to be helping me to find the right words.

This morning, as soon as we had been given breakfast, I sought

Miss Robinson out. She sat near one of the windows in the day ward, small and grey, trying to disappear into a book. I thought perhaps she regretted giving me her friendship and wished to snatch it back again.

'Good morning, Mary.' She made rather a show of being astonished to see me. Mary had rolled up the sleeves of her grey dress to feel more comfortable, and I saw that her arms were a mass of scars where she had cut herself. Many of the ladies here injure themselves. We are not allowed sharp objects, but perhaps she hid a fruit knife in her cubicle and punished herself with it. She caught my gaze and sullenly pulled her sleeves back down to her wrists.

'Would you prefer to read, Mary?'

'What alternative entertainment do you offer me?' she asked in her coolest voice.

I nearly fled, but I needed to talk. 'You most generously shared your history with me. Will you listen to mine?'

She pointed to the chair beside her, and I sat down.

'Yesterday afternoon you told me about the revolution you dream of.'

'I have done more than dream. I worked, studied, thought and planned until I was imprisoned here by my family. But I know there are others out there who are still working towards the revolution – and it will come, I know it will!' Her eyes flashed. Mary would be a Savonarola if it she were not a caged vole.

'I thought you would like to know that it does happen, your revolution.'

'When? Here in England? What are you talking about?'

I had to brave her ferocity to continue. 'I don't know exactly when. At some point in the next hundred and fifty years a great change will take place.'

'I have only to look out of my window to see change! The march of bricks and mortar, the spread of the railways. In the nine years of my confinement London has expanded, and it is quite obvious that in another century it will be transformed. That is hardly a prophecy, Mrs Sanderson.'

'That's not what I mean. Machines will fly and tunnel beneath the pavements and will think faster than the swiftest brain. Why, I've seen a machine called a teavee that shows moving pictures. People talk and laugh and cry inside it – I was quite offended because they would not answer me when I spoke to them. My companion explained that they were only mechanical pictures of people – like walking daguerreotypes. How I wish I could show you these things!

'There will be astonishing changes in men and women, too. People will be equal, there will be no more poverty or crime because all will have enough to live on. Women will be the equals of men in every way. They will be well educated and go to university and even study science and law and medicine. If they do not wish to marry they will be free to earn hard cash and live alone, and there will be no scandal if they entertain gentlemen. All will wear bloomers –'

Mary interrupted me with scornful laughter that made me blush and fall silent. 'Really, you are just like Mrs Winkworth in the nasty private madhouse my family sent me to. She thought she was Queen of the May and tried to force us all to dance around a maypole and wear garlands. She also rattled on about bloomers and told us to wear them on our heads.'

I turned away, very hurt by her contempt and went to sit in my old chair near the window that overlooks the gardens; where I saw Mr Dadd yesterday, where Jonathan stood so long ago and stared up at me with promises of a bright future in his eyes.

Behind me I could hear two ladies discussing the atrocities in India with relish. We are not allowed newspapers because they are too sensational and may overexcite us, but we do hear titbits of gossip from visitors and attendants.

'Did you hear about the massacre? Thousands of British women and children chopped up like so much meat.'

'Fancy! Yet I met an Indian once at the Bazaar in Oxford Street, and he was ever so polite.'

I wonder if the Indians will triumph over our soldiers and have a revolution. Perhaps there will be a general revolution all over the world. There must be some enormous change coming that will build the future I have seen.

I am living at the beginning of a book I have opened, a very unsatisfactory story so far. I have peeked at the end, I have lived the end, but I cannot return to it, nor can I know what happens in between. All these things will happen when I am dead, and I might as well be dead as imprisoned here on the incurables' ward. I don't want to be cured, for then I will forget or disbelieve what I saw with Jonathan.

As I sat on my lonely chair, longing for the impossible, I felt Jonathan's presence. Then I saw him, as if my grief and loneliness had summoned him. He stood in the gardens looking up at my window, I knew him by his strange clothes, beardless face and shorn hair. I stood up and pressed my face against the window-pane to show myself. We are not allowed to open the windows lest we throw ourselves out of them – and, indeed, I would willingly have jumped down into his arms. Jonathan looked perfectly solid and real as he stood there. Yet a gardener rolled a lawnmower through him.

Frantic with terror I picked up my chair and would have smashed it through the window to break the glass had Letty not gripped my arm. 'Whatever do you think you're doing, Mrs Sanderson?'

'I must go down. I must rescue him before he is hurt.'

'Who, Mrs Sanderson?'

'Please, Letty, take me down to the gardens.'

'I've all the sheets to change. They won't change themselves, you know.'

'Letty, I beg you. I must go now!'

'Stop pulling at my sleeve, Mrs Sanderson. We'll go down to the gardens tomorrow morning if you're a good girl.'

12
SIR T.

'You have a visitor, Mr Dadd.'

Not Frith again . . . *He has come here to laugh at you once more*, Osiris roars. *To mock and humiliate you. Strangle him! He has stolen your destiny.*

'Sir Thomas Phillips,' McDonald says with the deference a title brings to the voice. 'He is waiting to see you in the steward's room.'

I turn back to my *Contradiction* and try to lose myself in Oberon and Titania again, but my concentration has been destroyed. To meet the ridiculous with the sublime. How could I bear it?

'I am ill. I cannot go.' It is true; my stomach has wrapped itself around my throat and my legs have turned to water. McDonald looks concerned. He never questions the mind's power over the body. 'I think I should lie down in my cubicle.'

It would have ended there, but beautiful George suddenly appears, and I fling away my brush and bury my head in my hands. Like a child in a game he knows he will lose, I peer at him through the pink bars of my fingers.

Haydon radiates health as he bounds across the room and stands beside my easel, beaming down at me. Osiris snarls but cannot think of anything evil to say of him. My beloved is all sweetness and light, and the ancient gods recognize these things.

'Good news, my dear Dadd! Your old patron, Sir Thomas, has honoured us with a visit.'

'No!' I shout.

Really, Richard, you are far too old for tantrums, my father says. *You must not keep him waiting. Manners maketh man and punctuality is the politeness of –*

'Be quiet, you old fool!' I yell, banging my fists against my head where my father smirks.

'He does not mean to be offensive, sir,' McDonald says quietly to Haydon. 'He hears voices. It is part of his illness, and he cannot help it.'

'In earlier centuries they would have said that he is possessed.' Haydon stares down at me as if I were an interesting specimen he has collected on his travels.

Their tolerance is intolerable. I force myself to stand up and submit to being visited, following Haydon along the corridors to his room. My admiration of his arse is diluted by my dread of meeting the man who witnessed my excesses and humiliation.

Sir T. is fatter, redder, still the same old windbag. When I portrayed him in a turban and exotic robes lying on a divan, his hubble-bubble beside him, I chuckled to myself because his weak, undistinguished face could not live up to his fancy dress. He resembled a wet night in Pontypool far more than an Arabian one. Today he is wearing a suit of clothes so new that I would wager he bought it only yesterday from an expensive tailor, but his straggly moustache and long pimply nose still look hopelessly provincial.

'My dear old friend and travelling companion!' He embraces me, and I freeze with embarrassment. He stinks less than he did on our unwashed travels, but I can still smell his pomposity and furtive sexuality.

There is not much to say about my health, so he launches at once upon an indignant monologue against the English. The Blue Books have succeeded the Chartists as his hobbyhorse. If one of my fellow inmates were to speak like this the doctors would say he was a monomaniac, but in a lawyer such obsessions pay. Of course, his eloquence is wasted on me; I have never heard of the Blue Books and could hardly point to the Principality, as he calls it, on a map. He has prospered and lets us know that he is now the proprietor of a colliery.

Determined, as he always was, to educate me, Sir T. foists on me a heavy volume he has published with the irresistible title *Wales, the Language, Social Condition, Moral Character, and Religious Opinions of the People*. He is on his way to the House of Commons to bore them, and I cannot understand why he has made this detour to bore me.

I hardly say a word to him. Haydon behaves like an anxious duenna in charge of a young lady who will not encourage an eligible bachelor. He is simply too nice himself to understand why I am not pleased to see an old friend.

He is the devil, Osiris observes from the ceiling, where he swings from the corner of Haydon's bookcase. *You missed the opportunity to cut his throat fifteen years ago, so do it now. You will rid the world of a scurvy rat, and they cannot punish you more than you have been punished already. There is the breadknife! What are you waiting for?*

It is true that Haydon, trusting as a cherub, has left his breadknife on the table after slicing our bread and butter. We all see it at the same moment. My breathing quickens and cold sweat drenches my clothes – then McDonald whispers discreetly to Haydon, who quietly puts the knife in a drawer.

I stuff my mouth with delicious thin slices of bread and butter while Sir T. drones on. That whining, platitudinous chant of self-praise; how often on our travels I had to cover my ears to open myself to new impressions and smother his lectures, which reduced the glories of Venice, Egypt and Palestine to a geography textbook. I am relieved when Sir T. looks at his pocket watch and – wait for it . . . Yes, here it comes.

'This very splendid gold watch was presented to me by our beloved Queen in gracious recognition of my services to her when, as Mayor of Newport, I saved that town from the Chartist rabble. I still feel the pain of a Chartist musket ball in my arm – a wound I bear with pride.'

Haydon and McDonald look impressed and obligingly admire the inscription on the watch. I turn my back on the old pedant and start on the muffins, ignoring Phillips's effusive farewell and belching loudly when he puts his hand on my shoulder.

'He is quite, quite mad,' Sir T. whispers loudly to Haydon on his way out. 'Yet he was once such a promising young man.'

'Richard, you could have been more polite – or less rude. It was kind of him to visit you.'

For the first time in all these years I am angry with the Archangel George. He is one of them after all: conventional, grovelling to a title.

Osiris is delighted and urges me on. *At last you have seen through him. I am your only true friend. All these mortals are treacherous and deserve to be killed. What difference would it make? They live but for a few short years.*

Had I obeyed all his commands I would have murdered more people than Genghis Khan by now. I glare at Haydon, but although I do not strike him the violent conflict in my head makes it ache so that I think it must explode.

Neville sees my wretchedness and leads me back to my cubicle, where my past is waiting to ambush me. From under my bed I take out the painting I did some eight years back. In that dark prison I sought with my brush to illuminate my gloom. Then its colours glowed and comforted me in my darkness, but now it looks garish and wrong, and so I have exiled it to the dusty underworld beneath my bed.

'What is this?' Dr Morison asked when he first saw my desert crowd scene. 'Is it the flight out of Egypt?'

The doctors love it when I paint biblical scenes. I was silent, pleased that his mind did not leap like mine from this Bethlehem to that other one, that dusty little village. It is nothing, a few crumbling sandy hovels, yet how it rears up in our imagination and now I am trapped here in its London reflection. In my desert scene there are Roman soldiers and a holy family in whom I do not believe, because Mary and her improbable son would have argued like any other family. When we camped in the cold desert the stars were so close, deep and bright and plentiful, melting time. The sun eliminated shadows and made colours more intense, unbearably so, green skies and purple rocks and mirages shimmering in the time-less light.

I long to see those desert stars again and to be truly solitary. As I push my painting back under the bed the letters I wrote to Powell while I was abroad fall out of the parcel he left, and I allow myself to read them.

I had left the Academy and was floundering in London, desperate to make my name and enough money to stay away from my shameful family. I had a commission to paint decorative panels for the reception rooms of a house in Grosvenor Square owned by Lord Foley, a munificent patron who allowed me to choose my own subjects and to work on a grand scale.

I immersed myself in majestic images of Tasso's *Jerusalem Delivered* and Byron's *Manfred*, whose 'solitude is solitude no more but peopled with the Furies'. My own solitude was not yet peopled with Osiris and my father, but I already had my demons. The Grosvenor Square house was full of elegant young men of my age who did not need to work. Stupefied with boredom they drifted off to places I longed to visit and treated me as a tradesman. On their grand tours they ignored or sneered at art and returned to London with the clap and enough French and Italian to gamble and flirt with, arousing in me a savage hatred I learned to mask with charm. My fairies had learned bad habits. They tempted me to steal Lord Foley's collection of snuff-boxes and pick the pockets of an aristocratic booby who sprawled, dead drunk, beneath the scaffolding in Lord Foley's drawing-room where I was at work.

I adored Byron's poetry and muttered it to myself as I worked.

> When the moon is on the wave,
> And the glow-worm in the grass,
> And the meteor on the grave,
> And the wisp on the morass;
> When the falling stars are shooting,
> And the answer'd owls are hooting,
> And the silent leaves are still
> In the shadow of the hill,
> Shall my soul be upon thine,
> With a power and with a sign . . .

I was Manfred, but nobody noticed, and I was stranded in dreary London.

One night I lingered in David Roberts's studio after his other admirers had left and stared at his paintings of Venice and Karnak. Tears of frustration distorted the Grand Canal and the great temple at Karnak.

'What is it, Richard? Are you ill?'

'Sick with longing. If I did not love you I think I would have to kill you out of envy. All those wonderful places I shall never see, for I was born under a threepenny-halfpenny planet and shall never to be worth a groat.'

'What shite! You must make your own planet, as I have done. Once I was just like you, poor and talented and sick with envy. We must find you a benefactor.'

Sir T. already looked old when I met him the following week in David's studio. He must have been over forty, which to a young man of twenty-four seemed decrepit. I saw at once that he was my passport to travel and no more a gentleman than I was. He needed the kudos of a grand tour to go with his knighthood, and I was to be his pet artist, recording the sights I yearned to see. We were a pair of mongrels setting off on our travels, betraying our lowly birth by our enthusiasm and excitement. No English milord would have pursued culture so earnestly.

I felt sure that I stood on the threshold of a glorious future. The pictures I was to make abroad would be admired and sell like hot cakes. Like David I would be able to afford a large, fashionable studio where a salon would form. Those weeks of preparation were a fever of anticipated triumph. I was like a bride whose great marriage is about to raise her far beyond her humble roots – no, that is not a good analogy. I never felt like Sir Thomas Phillips's bride. His pocketbook made him attractive, but his person always repelled me.

How I condescended to my family, even my favourite sister Maria; how I explained to Frith and Egg and my other old friends that I would soon be soaring off into the heavens, leaving them to plod along on earth. I said my farewells without regret; my earliest memories were of watching the ships on the Medway sailing off to romance. I always wanted to swim out to them or leap from the bank to their thrilling otherness. Wherever they were going, I was certain it was better than where I was.

Now Dover, a town I had visited a hundred times on dull errands, was transformed. As I walked up the gangplank to the ship that was to take us to Ostend I felt the story of which I was to be the hero was beginning at last. I was grateful to Sir Thomas and hardly heard his voice. The vivid novelties around me took my breath away and made it hard to speak or even draw. London's wet July sprouted wings, sulky clouds became a triumphant blue arch, colours wrapped me in their revealed intensity, and I lived through my eyes.

All was wonderful, even the thunderstorm over Lake Maggiore as we crossed it in a rowing boat and the bumpy horseback ride over the Bernese Alps. I was too busy being Manfred and Byron and Rousseau, safe in my castle eyrie above the craggy peaks and the clouds, to allow my spirits to be dampened by the rain or Sir Thomas's persistent whine.

'I do hope, my dear boy, you will find the time to record our travels. I do not, of course, begrudge the expense I am being put to, but these flea-ridden inns do charge the earth for their maggoty pork. Your sketchbook is in the saddlebag.'

It stayed there. I had always drawn out of solitude and boredom. Art was to be my passport to a more interesting life and now I was living it. I wrote a few excited letters to Frith and, more formally, to David Roberts, missing their companionship. I took great care over those letters, confident that they would be cherished and valued and would one day be of use to the biographers who would flock to chronicle my brilliant career.

With Sir Thomas I felt constrained by the silken bonds of obligation and the charade that we were two great gentlemen. Venice floated towards us one dark night on a four-hour gondola ride from Mestre. Our gondolier was so handsome that at first I only had eyes for his sultry face and taut muscles, illuminated by the lantern that swayed beside him. He filled the small window of the box where Sir T. and I lay on soft cushions, weary and cross.

Shifting my position I saw a shimmering golden screen encrusted with lights reflected in the dark water. I had thought I knew Venice well from paintings and travel books, but it was like the difference between a Shakespeare play on the page and one brilliantly staged. She was the theatre for which my imagination had always yearned.

'But can you really admire this Byzantine monstrosity?' Sir T. asked incredulously next morning as we stood outside San Marco's curves and glories.

In pursuit of good taste and an artistic sensibility he could show off to his brother Benjamin, who held a salon in his Wimpole Street drawing-room, the brand-new baronet puffed after me. When I was hurling myself into Tintoretto's visions in the Scuola San Rocco he lay on the floor, which the guide book recommended, and wheezed, 'How remarkably large and dark they are. That Tim Toretty must have been a nimble fellow. Did he use scaffolding? Sixty-nine paintings, good gracious me! Let us hope, Richard, that you will be equally diligent.'

He enjoyed sitting in Florian's, trying to start conversations with English boobies. There were only five days to devour Venice, and I resented time wasted on sleeping and eating. When Sir T. insisted on long meals in grand restaurants in the hope of meeting English tourists whom he could bore with his anti-Chartist exploits, I could not hide my impatience. My city of wonders was faded and crumbling into the water; she might drown before I could embrace her. Horrid modernity, in the shape of gaslight and the ugly skeleton of a bridge being constructed from Mestre, threatened Venice's enchantment.

Each morning I got up at six, hoping to breakfast and be out before he could catch me. But Sir T. wanted to get his money's worth. Just as I was about to escape he came huffing into the breakfast room, his pink face shining with soap and self-love. 'Why, Richard, don't go without me! I shall lose my way in that stinking maze.'

Impatiently I watched him guzzle a steak, a basket of rolls and a pot of coffee while scratching his bites.

'I don't know if it is the bedbugs or the mosquitoes who afflict me most. Now where shall we go today, my dear boy? Let's see more of that Cannyletty chappie. You frown. Do you not admire his work? Now that is what I call painting.'

'He is very fine, but a daguerreotype could achieve as much.'

'It is an artist's job to copy nature, and he does it to perfection.'

'"Copies from Nature are incorrect while Copies of the Imagination are Correct,"' I quoted Blake's epigram without the least hope that Sir T. would understand.

'You are very paradoxical this morning. Well, let us compromise. I shall have my Cannylettys and then you can have your whatsisname.'

'Veronese.' Only to pronounce him was poetry. How I wished I had an Italianate name instead of a blunt Anglo-Saxon monosyllable.

'Verynicey. Well, let us hope he is.'

That afternoon in the Doge's Palace I learned more about light and colour from Veronese and Tintoretto in a few hours than in all my years at the Academy.

I stood for a long time in front of the strangest painting I had ever seen, *Visions of the Hereafter* or, in Italian, *Visioni dell'aldila*. I whispered the musical word to myself, transfixed by the beautifully painted figures flying up to Heaven and tumbling down to Hell. These were truly visions. I felt that the artist must have soared with angels and suffered infernal tortures to create such work, and three hundred years of grime and smoke could not dim his inspiration.

Sir T. adjusted his pince-nez to see what was detaining me so long. 'And what have we here?' No *aldila* for him; he tutted and pursed his lips. 'Very curious stuff. Is this your Verynicey?'

'These panels are by Hieronymus Bosch.'

'Bosh!' His hearty laughter destroyed any connection I had briefly felt with worlds beyond this one. 'The fellow should have been locked up.'

'He was.'

At dinner Sir T. quizzed me. 'And what are your plans, Richard?'

Thinking that he was offended by my coolness and had decided to abandon me in Venice, I stared at him in horror. 'Am I not to accompany you on the rest of your tour, sir?'

'Of course, but you must have ambitions beyond that. Why, when I was your age I had been hard at work for ten years and was well on my way to a partnership.'

'My ambition is to spend my life drawing and painting.'

'Yes, but what do you propose to live on?'

That night was our last in Venice. We were dining magnificently in a restaurant with a terrace overlooking the Grand Canal. I hardly noticed what I ate as the beauty of the floating pageant absorbed me: gondolas, barges, mysterious masked and veiled figures, all the more poetical in the shimmering candle and moonlight. I longed to spend the rest of my life in one of the torchlit Gothic palaces on the other side of the canal.

'Well, I've never starved yet. How I wish we could stay a few more weeks here, Sir Thomas. I should like to make a thousand pictures of this city in all her moods.'

'But the malaria! And the rumours of cholera we heard but this morning. Perhaps you will return some day.'

I never doubted it. Whenever I fell in love with a face or a landscape or a building on my grand tour I would mutter to myself, 'I will come back and know you better.'

Now I wish I had stayed in Venice. Useless, of course, like all regrets, but I can see that other Richard, flabby from too much pasta, sitting in a café in a secretive piazza sketching a church, a cat, a handsome gondolier or a strong young woman carrying water on her graceful head. Perhaps he has even married such a woman. His fairies have drowned in the filthy waters and no spirits possess him.

13
OSIRIS

After we sailed to Patras and Athens the voices began. In Italy my head and my heart blossomed, and I held those flowers in my resolute hands, but as the sun turned from gold to jagged flames and the landscape curiouser, strange plants grew within me.

Sailing from Ancona to Greece I began to feel the presence of the ancient gods. Why do they stuff the heads of English boys with classical studies if they do not want them to be transformed, to start to believe that the world of Homer and Virgil and Ovid is all around them? Debased but alive. In Delphi, where formerly the priestess screamed out the oracle of the deity, angry washerwomen screamed out an intolerable jargon of abuse at each other. The waters, once deemed full of inspiration, were full of frogs and watercresses, and I thought the goddess might be obliged to sell those watercresses for her living. My letters to Powell make light of all this, but in truth I felt torn between the nineteenth century and golden, lawless mythology.

My patron, whose weaknesses until now had seemed merely harmless and comical, began to assume monstrous proportions. We had complained about the flea-ridden inns in Italy, but in Greece and Turkey we had often to share a room not much better than a stable. Sir T. snored and farted all night, and our stomachs wreaked their revenge on the bad, oily food. I lay, exhausted by hours on the backs of half-starved horses or mules, waiting for the fetid, tepid air to release me into sleep. His voice droned on, shrinking all my dreams and visions to the exploits of the hero of Newport.

'Did I ever tell you, Richard my boy, about my visit to Windsor three years back?' So many times I could recite it with you as a duet were I not afraid of being dismissed as a travelling companion and presented with the bill for this vile inn.

'To my great astonishment Her Majesty invited me there to be knighted. I had never left the Principality before; I was quite nervous. The castle was so enormous and the Queen so small, just a slip of a girl, yet so gracious and dignified. I must confess it brought tears to my eyes when she tapped me on the shoulder and said I had done my duty and served my nation well. I thought that was quite honour enough and expected to take my leave. I was quite certain that etiquette would not permit one of my rank in life to be invited to the royal table. But you will never guess what happened next!' In the dark I silently mouthed the words as he spoke them.

'Lord Normanby invited me to dine! Yes indeed, I sat at table with Lord Melbourne and Charles Greville and all those great folk, and the Queen was most civil to me. I never saw so much splendour and crystal and gold plate, but I remembered it was vulgar to exclaim and gape. So I behaved as if my whole life had been spent at court, perfectly at my ease, quiet, unobtrusive but with complete self-possession. I do recommend, Richard, that you should model your behaviour on mine should you ever be so fortunate as to move among the great. Yes, since the hand of royalty anointed me, I have felt quite different.'

In just three years Sir T. had become a tremendous snob. Everywhere we went he insisted on meeting the right people – the best people as he called them – and bragging about his humble origins. The further we moved away from his beloved Principality, the more it dominated his conversation. I longed to forget my home and past and become a new man, absorbing all these new impressions with eyes and mouth wide open. With insatiable appetite I swallowed the succession of picturesque characters, that menagerie of pompous ruffians and splendid savages in their grubby finery and wild costumes. I never saw such an assemblage of deliciously villainous faces: they grinned, glowered and exhibited every variety of curiosity. Oh, such expression! Oh, such heads! Enough to turn the brain of an artist.

Although I would have liked to draw them all we were forever on the move, perched on the most intransigent mules, horses or camels. We travelled immensely fast and by such long stages that very little daylight was ever left to sketch. I could not understand how David

Roberts and the other artists had produced so much work. They must have had stomachs and wills of iron.

During the day I was worn out by the discomforts of our travels – bad food, mosquitoes, bedbugs, fleas, sleepless nights, the heat and the dearth of lavatories all diminished me, peeling away my top layer of skin until I often felt like a quivering mass of nerves and eyes. The horses and mules we had to ride all day were of a very sorry description, constantly tripping and lying down. Over the first painful weeks I acquired the art of riding, by dint of sundry falls and bruises and one or two plunges into rivers and streams.

Sir T., however, seemed to thrive on muleback and horseback. Perhaps his own obstinacy was equal to that of the beasts. He grew tougher each day and despised my physical weakness. However uncomfortable our lodgings, he was always shaved and dressed by seven, ready to 'do' the local antiquities while I still lay in my unsavoury bed, complaining and groaning. He was always immaculately dressed, whether in English or native costume, in anticipation of impressing the next important person.

I, however, looked very bizarre. My fez was secured to my head by two handkerchiefs, one white and one red. As there were no opportunities to shave comfortably I grew a beard and mustachios, which covered some of my angry-red mosquito bites. My trousers were tucked into long Russian leather boots, and my filthy white blouse was stuffed full of little things for the convenience of travelling, viz. a knife and fork, a corkscrew and my sketching things.

It was the people who fascinated me, as I dutifully sketched an endless succession of tombs, ruins and temples. Sir T., who had never married, was indifferent to people, unless they could be of use to him – or were boys. Early on in our travels I noticed the way his eyes followed the buttocks and faces of passing boys. Like Sir Harley he liked them at about twelve or thirteen. He told me proudly that he worked in Boys' Clubs in Newport, helping boys from the slums. In Greece and Turkey many boys sensed his attraction and flirted shamelessly with him, causing him to blush and become confused. I was too conscious of the damage Sir Harley had done to me to exploit those children, who would have performed the most depraved acts for a small coin. With amusement I watched Sir T.'s internal battles between respectability and lust. As far as I could see, respectability won. Perhaps he feared the dear little Queen, as he called her, might hear of this less altruistic side of his nature and withdraw her favour and his knighthood.

In Smyrna Sir T. received a letter from the Ambassador to Turkey, Sir Stratford Canning, asking him to begin secret negotiations to purchase from the Sultan marble fragments from the tomb of Mausolus in the Castle of St Peter in Bodrum, which was ancient Halicarnassus. My patron was thrilled by this combination of stealth and snobbery and boasted of our secret mission until I thought every spy in Turkey must know of it.

I sketched those fragments, which were to be shipped to the British Museum, for Canning. They were one of the Seven Wonders of the Ancient World, the finest works in bas-relief in marble that I had seen, second only to the marbles in the Parthenon. The subject of the frieze was the combat of the Athenians with the Amazons, and it had all the energy and spirit of Greek art in its highest perfection. As I gazed up at their subtle and delicate lines I reflected that those people who died two thousand years before I was born must have been greater than us, less selfish, their civilization superior.

Because I was employed by Canning, Sir T. did not dare to stand over me and demand that I should work faster, as he usually did, as if I were a drawing locomotive he had bought a ticket for. Left in peace for a few hours I lingered at the beautiful site, allowing myself to absorb the atmosphere. It was easy to see why the ancients (who were beginning to feel so modern to me) had chosen this lovely Mediterranean site to build their city and why, much later, the Knights of St John had built their castle there. Already the centuries were receding like Sir T.'s hair, and I felt at one with the artists who had carved the marbles I was admiring as we swam together in time's currents.

Then we were off again, jolting our bones and brains as we rode under the infernal heat over rocks and stones. I longed for the meadows and flowers of my native Kent but did not speak of my homesickness because I did not want to sound like Sir T., who mentally never left his beloved Wales. I yearned to grow beyond my self and the narrow life that I had known so far.

Often now, as I rode beneath the hot afternoon sun, I heard voices chanting to the rhythm of the hoofbeats of whichever cantankerous beast I was mounted on. Voices that reminded me I was to be a famous painter and would leave the ranks of the great unappreciated, no longer destined to sit philosophizing in the workhouse, as we used to joke bitterly when we were students together in The Clique. My voices told me it was my destiny to leave my comrades Frith and Egg far behind and become a much greater man than Sir T.

One night, after a long day of muleback tedium, we reached a poverty-stricken village where there was no inn. We were shown to the house of the local sheikh and told to wait in a large square room with a mud floor. I think it must have been the council chamber, courthouse and concert hall, and that evening we were the village's entertainment: a large crowd stood behind a railing and stared at us. Exhausted, I wanted only to lie down and rest. Inhibited by the watching eyes I felt some foolish obligation to remain vertical and pretend that, as Sir T. would say, Britons are made of sterner stuff than all the other nations of the earth.

My heart churned as smoke and light and shadow befuddled my eyes. What a painting it would make! The handsome men and women in their bright clothes, the old men like patriarchs and the young ones like beautiful girls; the bubbling pipes, the glow of the fire and the hallucinogenic smoke . . . I was quite overwhelmed. The sheikh sat on a splendid red carpet, very serious and dignified as he smoked his pipe.

Sir T. refused the pipes we were offered, muttering that no gentleman would put such a thing in his mouth. Once I induced him to try it and promptly drew him, capturing his awkwardness in his desert robes that always contrived to droop on him and make him look more sober and dull than ever. I had always enjoyed a smoke, and, oh, how I did luxuriate in the fug of peace that came to me after a few deep breaths of that bubbling liquid.

'It hisses and babbles and seethes like the waters of the Styx itself,' said Sir T. in disgust. I had rather give myself to its mysterious voices than to your babble, I replied, but not aloud. There was no need to speak once the smoke hit my brain and all the glorious colours and shapes and shadows grew more intense.

The picturesque audience were fascinated by our meal, nudging each other and giggling at our knives and forks – their sheikh, of course, used his hands to eat. Our dinner was a bowl of rice in chicken broth followed by the scraggy chickens themselves, and the flat bread was full of grit – but I was too hungry to care. We ate in silence as we did not speak a word of each other's languages, and I longed for their hospitality to end so that I could sleep.

Yet when at last I lay down on the mud floor, covered with my travelling cloak, excitement and colour blazed behind my eyes and kept me awake for hours. That night my poor weak brain started to fry and sizzle from the heat and wild beauty and confusion of it all. Strange fancies danced before me. I was ashamed and feared for my sanity.

In the morning, before we set off again, I wrote to Powell and tried to confide in him. As I said in my letter, my mind was opening, and not all that fell out of it was admirable. I could not admit to him that I burned with lust, not for the prim Welsh solicitor who too often lay beside me but for the effeminate men and powerful young women I had seen that day. Perhaps I always felt that the rigid demarcation of the sexes was artificial. I often felt like a woman in trousers, like one of Shakespeare's ambiguous heroines, and perceived masculine strength in the women to whom I was most attracted.

I remember how it aroused my senses to enter a new village every evening and see the women working away while the men lay back and smoked. The dresses of these handsome women were rolled up around their strong brown thighs – I could not take my eyes off them as they mixed mud and straw to make bricks. Then there were the water-carriers, lovely young women who wore a dress like a loose blue-belted shirt, silver bracelets and blue tattoos on their bare arms and hands and faces. They also fascinated me, I longed to seize one of them and ride off into the desert with her, tear off her dress . . . Such impulses frightened me. Most bewildering of all were the lascivious smiles of the handsome boys and men whose coquettishness made me feel like the belle of a perplexing ball.

All day I longed to paint these beautiful men and women, but at night they tantalized me. I drifted into feverish sleep, tormented by sensual images, my lullaby a chorus of voices calling me to Egypt. *Come home, my son; Osiris demands your presence; you belong here among the pyramids where your life began; come back to us and fulfil your destiny; leave your tedious old man and take your place among the gods.*

Even before I reached Egypt my adventures began to seem phantasmagoric. All those broken nights sapped my energies during the day; I did not accomplish nearly as much in the way of sketching as I hoped and Sir T. expected. I asked a servant to hold a sunshade over me while I tried to draw on a sketchpad supported by my knees and saddle, but it was acutely uncomfortable, and I think the beastly nag I had to ride resented it, too. Often it stumbled, and I tumbled off, sketchpad and all. By the time our journey ended for the day it was either too dark to see or a crowd of people gathered to gawp at me. All my life I have needed solitude when I draw or paint.

One day in Damascus, when I was trying to draw an elegant fountain, I looked up to find about a hundred people surrounding me. I could smell the sweat on their hot brown skin as those nearest to me turned the pages of my sketchpad to see what I had drawn. Angrily I struggled to snatch it from them and continue drawing, but they sensed my hostility and began to mutter and hiss. In the end I had to flee, pursued by a mob howling and throwing husks of corn and rotten fruit.

In Palestine we visited the Holy City and all its sights, and I thought of Signor Leppardi and his tales of the Temple of Solomon. A few days later, in Jericho, we found ourselves in real danger when we were surrounded by a group of wild Arab tribesmen on horseback, waving spears and pistols at us. Fortunately we had some naval officers with us and were rescued by a sheikh who came galloping up and kissed the leader of the tribesmen on both cheeks. I enjoyed writing home about such adventures, but I remember how scared I was at the time and how their shining, naked limbs overwhelmed my senses. I wanted to draw them but also to touch them, to . . . well, I only stared.

One man in particular, the patriarch I suppose, still blazes in my mind, his long hair blowing around his cruel face, his ancient boots tucked into shabby trousers, his stomach bursting out of his torn vest. The sheikh who had protected us was even more splendid, with his turban and shining black beard. I longed to pluck a few hairs from it to make a paintbrush as we followed him into his village. There we all sat in a courtyard while he demanded five hundred piastres of baksheesh (reduced by our servant's haggling to one hundred) for rescuing us.

That night we stopped beside the Dead Sea with guards we paid to keep watch over us. They were almost naked, their flesh glowing sensually in the firelight beneath the palm trees. I could not sleep but lay there, seething with excitement. Was it that night or another – I can't remember – we rode by moonlight through wild mountains where extinct volcanoes and strange rock formations made me feel I had reached the end of the world.

As I joked and punned in my letters to Frith, all this while my mind is opening – yes, I opened my mind – and, mind what I say, it is uncommon good soil. But there was so much that I could not write. I had cut the ropes that tethered me to The Clique and my old life one by one. I was floating alone and knew not where.

We sailed to Alexandria via Jaffa on the Hecate, a man-of-war steamer, which saved us from a long hot trek across the desert. The officers on board smiled and deferred to Sir T. – for all the world loves a title – but by this time my own smiles to him were so forced that they almost broke my face in two.

'How good it is to have Christians around us again and to hear the clear, manly tones of our compatriots.'

'I do not agree.' It was breakfast time and I had not yet smoked the pipe that drowned all words. 'I admire the people of these nations with their force and beauty.'

'But, Richard, they are so effete. Do you not pine for a jar of ale and a good red beefsteak and a game of cricket?'

'Not a bit.'

'Would you go native then? Become a lotus eater like Lewis, that painter chappie who lives in Cairo almost as one of them, the captain was telling me.'

'I can imagine a far worse fate.' It has befallen me, although I could not have imagined it then.

'You artists! You're quite a race apart. Perhaps that is why you can settle anywhere.'

'You solicitors! You carry your stool and desk and dry old tomes around the world with you.' Then, seeing a flicker of anger in his cold eyes, I added, 'A joke, of course, Sir Thomas. You know how grateful I am to you.'

Alexandria at the end of November was a dazzle of light and brilliant colour. As soon as we landed in Egypt the voices – above all his, my father's, Osiris – became much louder. *Richard, come to us, stay with us. At last you have come home. Why do you fritter away your life among foreign devils? Leave your old man and come to us!*

I felt helplessly foreign, bewildered and lost – and at the same time like a prodigal son. The pyramids looked visionary and dream-like from a distance, but as we approached them some young boys ruined my dream as they came running over and leaping up to us, trying to persuade us to hire them as guides and servants.

Then we saw the Sphinx, who has the head of a woman, the body of a lion, bird's wings and likes to dine on dimwits. I would gladly have fed Sir T. to the venerable monster. We found an encampment of Europeans in front of the Sphinx, which had been excavated in front in order that they might read the tablet between its paws. They consisted of Dr Lepsius, Bonomi, a Mr Wild – an architect from London – and some artists employed in copying the hieroglyphics in the tombs. These were the kind of men I had met at the British Museum. My father would have adored them for they had devoted years to the scholarly understanding of ancient history.

Yet my voices sneered at them. *It's all lies! They see nothing of what we really were, what we are. Only you are permitted to live among us and know us.*

And I did begin to see them, those figures striding up the sides of the pyramids and across the angry blue sky. The pyramids were only stone boxes that could not contain their wild spirits.

After staggering around the desert under the ruthless sun I needed a hubble-bubble pipe to cool my roasting brain. I walked about the streets of Cairo with my eyes and mouth wide open, swallowing with insatiable appetite the everlasting procession of picturesque characters. The cafés were very interesting on account of the assemblage of characters outside their doors; contentment was never better expressed than by a man lounging in listless idleness, the only noise accompanying his thoughts being that of the smoke bubbling through the water. After I stopped in a café to buy a pipe colours and shadows came to life again and the voice of Osiris communicated with me through the bubbling water. I felt the most unaccountable impulses that would not let me stop to sketch but were constantly prompting me on, to drink in, with greedy enjoyment, the stream of new sensations.

Sir T. reproached me one morning when I came back from one of my all-night smoking sessions. 'Really, Richard, you look more like a beggar than a gentleman's companion. I am surprised they allowed you to enter the hotel. Where is your hat?'

I could not remember. The smoke in my head stifled the words before they could rise to my mouth.

'And where is your sketchbook? You told me you were going into the bazaars to draw the picturesque scenes there, but it seems to me you are doing very little work. I shall have to write to your father, Richard.'

Which father? Old pisspot Dadd or the king of the ancient skies?

'I hope you will be more industrious when we are on the Nile. You appear to have no idea how expensive all this travelling is. I count on you to produce enough sellable pictures to pay for your expenses, which are considerable.'

Sir T. never missed an opportunity to remind me I was a nobody.

As a somebody he had to be seen to travel in style and hired a comfortable boat with a crew of sixteen from the British consul in Cairo for our cruise up the Nile. The thin veneer of Englishness that had protected him in Cairo and Alexandria wore off as we were rowed up the great river. Surrounded by twelve half-naked oarsmen who spoke no English, beneath vivid green-and-red skies in an alien landscape, Sir T. lost his moorings and I found mine.

The second morning I rose in time to watch the theatrical dawn and sat beneath an awning on deck to sketch the handsome crew, the strange birds and the peasants working in the meadows. I had always been happy near water, although my Medway childhood receded with every rhythmic gasp of the oars. I was becoming a new man, baptized in water that was old before Jesus Christ was born, pulled towards the magnetic personality of my master Osiris. As we floated past rural Egypt I was astonished to see the abject condition of the Arab fellah. The ruined villages and towns indicated the most rotten state in which men can live and call himself not a savage.

The sun was already high when Sir T. emerged from his cabin, pale green and cantankerous. 'I could not sleep. So much yelling last night, I thought they were about to mutiny and slit our throats.'

'They are well paid and perfectly contented to be here.'

'I do believe you speak their confounded language. Glad to see you're doing some work at last. What is that supposed to be?'

'A vulture hovering over the corpse of a donkey.'

'How very horrid. I wish you would choose subjects likely to appeal to civilized people.'

He asserted his own civilized nature each morning by shooting crocodiles and anything else that moved with a very poor-quality double-barrelled gun. Two pigeons he wounded but failed to kill became our pets and made to serve as a subject of conversation: the long voyage was so tedious that we clutched at any amusement. By the end of the second day Sir T. was bored and disagreeable, and I think we would have quarrelled but that I was very conscious of my need of him. I entered into his fatuous conversations, talking trash with the two domesticated pigeons, which he had christened Hengist and Horsa.

Christmas Day found us at Thebes, breakfasting off fresh eggs and a plum pudding bought at the English grocer's shop in Cairo.

'No bells,' Sir T. said mournfully. 'Shall we sing a few carols?'

'I would rather listen to their songs.'

As they rowed the men chanted, and one man, whom I might describe as an *improvisatore*, made up and sang rhymes on passing occurrences, the crew joining in a chorus at the end of each line and prolonging the same a little at the end of what might be called each verse. They wove their voices into a chain of quavering tremulous sound that drew me back to a time before time was measured. I drew them, and they smiled back at me, preferring my silent observation to Sir Bangbang Phillips.

At Thebes and, above all, at Karnak I was astonished by the pyramids, by the madness of the tyrants who ordered them to be built and the stupidity of those who obeyed them. That was my response as a tourist, in my letters home, but there were other feelings, too, as I opened myself joyfully to the ancient powers that called me.

At nightfall the crew used to moor our boat and sit around the fire to sing to the music of a pipe, which sounded rather like an Irish bagpipe, and a drum they beat with their hands. One of the crew used to stand up and dance to this monotonous music while his companions clapped, and I sat on deck and watched, sharing with the crew the fragrant cigarettes they passed around.

'But, Richard, how can you put your lips where those ruffians' mouths have been? Think of the diseases they must carry!'

More than my lips were involved. We dined at around five on diverse chickens roasted and made into soup, with rice or vermicelli, and we ate onions enough for an army of Spaniards. After Sir T. retired to his cabin each night I stayed on deck waiting for Ali. I had been drawing him since the first day of our cruise, hoping my pencil would find a blemish in his perfection. He had the face of a Pharaoh, with golden skin and huge eyes that slanted upwards. All day, as I sat sketching beneath the awning on deck, my eyes returned to the curve of his head and neck with its crown of black curls, to the muscles flowing beneath his skin as he rowed.

At night I sat beside Ali and we smoked together, sliding into a wordless intimacy and later, when the rest of the crew were asleep, into each other. I could not have voiced my desire for him, for words would have summoned guilt and shame and fear of rejection. But he did not reject me, and as far as I could tell the other members of the crew also accepted our silent passion. All art is a quest for beauty, and when you find it what can you do but love it? We were afloat, adrift from drawing-room conventions, and I felt free.

One moonlit night, about six weeks into our cruise, our boat moored near the temples of Luxor. All day I had suffered from a bad headache and had been unable to work or even lust after Ali. After a light supper I staggered down to my cabin and fell asleep. I was woken by a low, strange chanting, not the usual rowing songs but an incantation. It seemed to me as I lay there with the moon bright on my pillow that they were calling me, initiating me into their great religion: Richard! Prince of Osiris! Lord of the Sun and of the Nile!

So I pulled on my clothes and went up on deck, half afraid that I was dreaming. The ship was deserted, and when my eyes followed the mysterious chanting I saw the entire crew standing in the desert beside our boat. They held hands in a circle, writhing and singing while one of them wailed in Arabic. Several of the men were foaming at the mouth, and as my eyes adjusted to the silver light I recognized Ali among them, moaning and clutching his heart, gasping for breath as he sank on to the sand. My own heart vibrated in sympathy as I moved towards the gangplank to help him, to join their magical circle.

'Richard! Whatever do you think you're doing!'

Sir T. stood in his nightshirt and nightcap, clutching my arm, and all the wonder drained out of the night. 'You must lie down, my dear chap. You have sunstroke. You are sleepwalking. We must find you an English doctor when we return to Cairo. What the devil are those scoundrels up to?'

He had never laid hands on me before, but that night he marched me back down to my cabin and locked the door. I screamed and raged and rattled the door until at last I fell asleep.

The next morning it was all quite clear to me: Sir T., invoking the devil, had shown me his own true nature. He was the devil, resolved to rob me of my glorious destiny. 'Ariel's Song', which I had turned into a painting but a few months ago, danced in my head:

> Come unto these yellow sands,
>> And then take hands;
> Curtsied when you have and kiss'd,
>> The wild waves whist,
> Foot it featly here and there,
> And, sweet sprites, the burden bear.
>> Hark, hark!

I understood that they were all one, my childhood fairies and Shakespeare's sprites and the ancient gods who summoned me and still had enough power to make men whirl in the desert.

For the last week of our voyage Sir T. treated me like an invalid, like his prisoner, and I hated him. I never saw Ali again, for I was not allowed out of my stifling cabin. Food and water were left morning and night at my door, and through it I conversed with the diabolical solicitor. 'Richard? I hope you realize this is for your own good.'

'Go back to Hell.'

'I am really most concerned about you. You need medical attention. I will write to your father and dear Roberts for advice.'

If he imagined that gods could be incarcerated he was even more of a fool than I thought. Consumed with longing for Ali's sweet flesh and the fragrant smoke that had floated me upon enchanted clouds, alone in my cabin, deprived of my freedom and my love, I was visited by Osiris. He appeared to me as a shimmering ripple of light, a quivering slice of the moon, a shadow that filled the ceiling and loomed over me. All that week we conversed – naturally gods speak English – and he explained the true nature of the world to me.

I was his beloved son, stolen at birth by malicious fairies who disguised me as a human child and planted me in the lacklustre nursery of the Dadd family. All my life my divine father had watched over me. It was he who enticed me to the pyramid above the mausoleum at Cobham Hall, he who strengthened my will among the Egyptian antiquities in the British Museum and compelled Sir T. (who was really, of course, an evil spirit) to invite me on his grand tour in order that I should return to my royal origins in Egypt.

Now, Osiris told me, I was to voyage back to England, and it was my mission to destroy all the devils I would encounter on the way, viz. Sir T., the Pope, The Emperor of Austria, my impostor father and all those false friends of mine in London. When they had all been eliminated I would be permitted to return to Egypt and take my place among the gods, who had need of a great artist. They would be my patrons, something like Holbein at the court of Henry VIII with the distinction that we would live for ever.

At the end of these encounters, exhausted, I lay on my bunk in a swoon and felt Osiris enter me. Not as Ali had done a few nights before, up my arse, but in every part of me. From head to foot, from heart to brain, from eye to hand I was his creature.

I have no memory of our arrival in Alexandria. The next thing I remember is the ship to Malta, the grey February weather and the long misery of quarantine. My spirits sank as I left my true homeland, and for hours I wept alone in my cabin. Sir T. no longer locked my door, but I was afraid to join him now that I knew his true diabolical nature. At night he played gin rummy with the captain of the steamer (ominously called the *Medea*), and although I tried to warn the poor fellow that Sir T. would steal his soul he only laughed that I had fried my brains in the Egyptian sun. Perhaps the captain had already become one of them. I learned to be more secretive, for, as any sensible person knows, when you are surrounded by devils you can trust nobody.

When Sir T. told me he had written to Roberts and my father informing them of my illness I feared his satanic guiles and wrote to them myself to reassure them his tales of my madness were a pack of lies. I did not say so directly, of course, but wrote in my normal voice, mocking the vanity of the pyramids and the Arabs' fawning clamour for baksheesh. Naturally I could not allow Sir T. to destroy my reputation in London's artistic circles. It had already occurred to me that since my so-called father, Robert Dadd, was a devil, more demons might intercept my letters; it was even possible that David Roberts, my benefactor and hero, might be a particularly clever devil in disguise. At times I shook with terror, for I was to go alone among all these dangers with only the inner voice of Osiris to guide me and tell me what to do.

I anticipated much pleasure in Naples, Rome, Florence, Genoa, Lyons and Paris, but devils pursued me everywhere and distracted me. In the Vatican galleries I tried to give my whole concentration to a particularly fine sketch by Botticelli when I realized that the old lady beside me, pretending to examine a Michelangelo through her lorgnette, was really a devil sent to torment me, using her lorgnette to flash signals to her fellow demons. Naturally I defended myself. When she screamed and I was ejected from the galleries I found at my elbow a priest who appeared to be sympathetic and explained to him that I was being persecuted and wished only to enjoy the artistic riches of Rome. But he pretended not to understand English, a common trick among foreign devils.

Then, as the sunset painted St Peter's piazza with a celestial glow, I looked up at the Vicar of Rome's lodgings. The old devil stood there on a balcony, and suddenly I found myself among a huge crowd, kneeling and mumbling prayers and crossing themselves. I remembered how Signor Leppardi had told me that the papal Inquisition had imprisoned and tortured artists and illuminati. Then the infernal voice muttering Latin ceased and I heard only the command of Osiris: *He has stolen our glory and made it his own. He is a charlatan and a thief. Slit his throat, my son, and I shall be well pleased.*

'Richard? Why ever did you attack poor old Miss Allerdyce? She is seventy-three and likely to have a heart attack. Stop waving that knife! The Swiss guards will see it, and you will find yourself in the Vatican dungeons. You know, the sight of all this Romish excitement reminds me of the passion of the crowd in my native Newport when I appeared on the balcony to reason with them. Now come back to the hotel with me. Tomorrow we will visit Overbeck's studio. Perhaps that will calm you down.'

I had heard much of the Nazarenes and the wonderful clarity of their work, which was said to equal Raphael. Overbeck, who was German, had lived in Rome for thirty years and had the most beautiful studio I have ever seen, a vast space strewn with gigantic canvases and grovelling acolytes and servants. I found the paintings themselves anaemic with a repulsively didactic aura. Like many converts to Roman Catholicism he wore his religion on his sleeve and Osiris was furious. *That upstart Jesus again! You bungled your assassination of the Pope. Snatch that palette knife and slash his overpriced paintings!*

Exhausted by my efforts to keep my hands to myself, I clasped them in front of me and skulked in a dark corner while Sir T. went into raptures over the paintings.

'Such magnificent colours and a truly angelic light! I notice that he chooses only admirable subjects, Richard, unlike you with your taste for ragamuffins and beggars. He is indeed a great painter, and it is an honour to visit him. You could learn much from his example.'

I disguised my rage with a sickly smile.

There are few memories of the rest of our travels. Hardly eating for fear that Sir T. would poison me, I could not sleep either, for at night devils mocked and insulted me, pushing me into nightmares from which I woke screaming. Fears of meeting my family and friends again were an additional torture now that I knew they were all devils. Osiris reminded me that he had been killed and dismembered by his brother Seth. My brother George, the changeling, made a very plausible devil and had every reason to hate me.

And so all the great art of Italy passed me by. My responses to painting were muffled and foggy, for I was locked in my soul and had lost the key.

When we reached Paris, in early summer, Sir T. had dozens of important people to meet and was increasingly embarrassed to be seen with me. I tried to conceal my thoughts, aware that, in the world's fashion, I would be thought unreasonable or worse. Paris was the world, the skies as grey as London's and the people coldly fashionable. After the rich colours and intensity of Egypt Paris felt moribund, and I even missed the discomforts and smells of my native land.

Osiris was furious with me. *You have failed in your mission! You have not killed a single devil! Go now, stain these dreary stones with the blood of your victims!*

I did not, but I was terrified that Osiris would punish me or Sir T. would find a way of poisoning me. I hardly dared to leave my hotel room.

One Monday afternoon Sir T. asked me to accompany him. We drove in a carriage to a high wall with a door in it. He rang a bell, a servant came to let us in and, as we passed through a large and beautiful garden I thought we were about to meet one of his rich acquaintances. When I saw dozens of men and women in white uniforms tending the plants I became suspicious.

Inside the front door there was a vast expanse of polished floor smelling of carbolic soap and a silence that was suddenly broken by a woman's scream. Sounds of running footsteps and sobs. An old black crow of a man approached, and I turned to run, but Sir T. gripped one arm and a servant held the other as I was led firmly into a room that pretended to be a drawing-room but clearly had some ulterior motive. The old crow devil, Dr Lunn, spoke English, was English. 'Many of our compatriots suffer from the nervous stresses of travel and recover in our little community,' he said in an unctuous voice.

It was obvious that Sir T. had told Dr Lunn I was mad and had asked him to incarcerate me. Fear sharpened my brain, and I fenced nimbly in our duel of wits, speaking lucidly and looking perplexed when the doctor asked me if I had ever experienced any hallucinations. We discussed the work of Tintoretto, Caravaggio and Titian and agreed that poor Hieronymus Bosch was too crazed to be a great artist. We pontificated about the laziness of the Arabs and the wonders of the pyramids. I was as bland as a Baedeker, sane as a Stilton.

I enjoyed the puzzled looks the other two exchanged and smiled at Sir T. while Osiris thundered, *He has betrayed you! Knock him out with that paperweight and run for your life!*

Dr Lunn said, 'Mr Dadd, I would like you to meet my colleague, Dr Leveque. He is French but speaks excellent English and is interested in artists and their – special problems. I know he'd love to meet you, but unfortunately he can't be with us this afternoon.' I heard shouts and moans and screeches outside the door. 'Could you possibly return tomorrow? If you could bring the sketches you did abroad I know Dr Leveque would be fascinated by them – and so would I, for Sir Thomas has told me of your remarkable talent. I'm sure you have a magnificent future, young man.'

My manners were faultless as we shook hands, and I bowed out of the madhouse with earnest promises to return the following afternoon. I said nothing to Sir T. in the carriage and went straight up to my room in the hotel. I knew that he was going to the opera that evening.

Shaking all over, I packed and then sat on the edge of my bed. There is only London now, I remember thinking, I must get back before Sir T. imprisons me or poisons me or poisons all my friends and relatives against me.

I had been living off Sir T. for so long that I could not even find my purse, for I had not used it since I bought hubble-bubble pipes in the bazaars of Cairo. At the memory of those warm, peaceful, moonlit nights I sighed and wished I could go downstairs, buy a pipe and forget about my persecutors. But I had to go out into the harsh, starless northern night and could not travel alone without money, the curse of artists. When at last I found my purse it contained but a five-pound note and a few piastres, and I had no idea how much the journey back to London would cost. At eight I picked up two valises, one containing my clothes and the other my drawing and painting materials and sketchbooks. I was bitterly aware that I had not produced nearly as much work as Roberts did on his travels. And so I set out, leaving no note for Sir T. After almost a year together there was nothing more to say.

I fled the hotel.

14
ESCAPE

'What the devil is Louisa doing in my library in the middle of the night?' In my anger I held my candle over my wife's sleeping face, and Jane awoke with a start.

'I do wish you weren't such a night owl. It's one o'clock in the morning! I suppose Lou, like you, is a nocturnal creature. She spends most of her time in your library.'

'Jane! Why didn't you tell me?'

'I was afraid you'd be cross. Oh, Billy, she's such a help to me, to us. She researched all the information we needed for your speech at the governors' meeting tomorrow, and when Donald had the chicken pox she spotted the first signs before I did.'

'But that was months ago. You said nothing. Besides, she does not care a fig for Donald or Chas.'

'You are hard on her, darling. I know she's not your own child, but she is clever and quite determined to study medicine.'

'But think of the scandal! She will never get a husband! And even if she did it is a well-known fact that higher education would make it difficult for women to conceive and bear a child.'

'It's a little late to try to turn her into a drawing-room miss. She has just read in *The Times* that a doctoress, a lady called Elizabeth Blackshaw, has opened an infirmary for indigent women and children in New York.'

'The Yankees are quite mad and their women as brassy as fishwives. Perhaps she might study midwifery and help some gentlemanly *accoucheur* – but, no, she would only grow coarse and take to drink.'

'She says she doesn't want to slave for some man but to work on her own account. This morning she glared at me and said, "I will become a doctor even if I have to dress up in men's clothes and run away."'

'Jane! We have brought up a monster!'

'She's my daughter, Billy. I love her and want her to find more satisfying work than I was able to. If you oppose her she really will run away, and I couldn't bear that.'

'You say you love her. Have you no longer any tender feelings for me?'

'Oh, Billy!' Her caress reassured me that my womenfolk are not altogether in a state of mutiny.

Jane put on her dressing-gown, and we stood together in the doorway of my library where Louisa had fallen asleep over *Clinical Lectures on Pulmonary Consumption*, a candle guttering dangerously beside her.

'She might have set fire to the entire hospital!' I hissed furiously.

'Billy, she did not. Let's get her to bed and discuss this matter in the morning – if you are here, which you won't be. There is no mystery about her vocation. She has watched us devote our lives to medical work and wishes to do the same.'

We approached the sleeping virago, who looked touchingly young and very like a smaller edition of her mother as we carried her back to her room. She did not even wake up. I looked around the tiny bedroom which I had not seen for years. Louisa generally occupies it in a state of siege, having flounced away from us and slammed her door. To my surprise her room was extremely tidy and stacked with books I had assumed were in my library.

After three hours sleep I was summoned by Neville to help with a female patient who had tried to push another into an oven while 'helping' in the kitchens. I had no sooner arrived to soothe the hysterical ladies than I was told that a male patient had been found *in flagrante* with another in the gardens. As a result I was late for the governors' meeting and had to pretend to a calm and dignity I did not feel.

On days like this – every day is like this – I remember the indignation of Edward Monro, the last of the dynasty who ruled this hospital for over a century, when he was dismissed. He was required to visit the hospital only four times a week and protested that it was a monstrous supposition that he could supervise the minute details of over two hundred patients.

Monro was more interested in being a gentleman than a doctor. I, however, as a resident superintendent without any grand connections, have every one of these lost souls in my keeping. If any one of them is ill-treated or neglected, if they injure or murder one another or themselves, if, in short, they behave like lunatics and the attendants like normal people with a limited supply of patience – then it is my responsibility.

Tonight when I returned home Chas and Donald were already in bed, and Jane sat at our desk, Louisa beside her. They looked very beautiful, like a painting by Vermeer, as they sat with their dark heads together beneath the lamp. If I were more tender towards Jane I at least did not growl at Louisa, whose guilty look relaxed as I drew up a chair and joined them.

'Martha's gone to bed. I'll get your supper . . .' Louisa always pauses before my name, for she does not know what to call me.

'Louisa, before you go, let's talk.' I was relieved Jane was there, for the girl makes me feel awkward. 'Your sister has told me that you wish to study medicine. I don't know if you will ever be able to practise it, but I won't hinder you. Call me Billy, my dear, for we are to work together.'

Louisa looked astonished; then the first spontaneous smile I have seen on her face for years softened her sharp little face and she ran out of the room without (as usual) slamming the door.

'Thank you, Billy. Lou has helped me so much today. We're compiling tables of statistics for that letter to Lord Shaftesbury. Her eyes are better than mine, and she has very neat handwriting.'

Jane went to the window to draw the curtains, and I groaned. 'What's the matter?'

'That building!'

'It's not your responsibility.'

'No, but it sits upon my conscience like a tombstone.'

'Billy, you drive me to distraction. You never stop talking about that building. You've already helped so many of those poor creatures.'

'But I worry constantly about those who remain. Their misery reproaches me always. A few months ago I had to send Jonson back there, away from the comparative paradise of M4, because he struck Oxford and almost killed him. Did I do wrong?'

'We cannot have murder committed in our hospital, Billy.'

'Criminal lunatics should be treated as patients not as prisoners. Those callous officials at the Home Office won't spend a farthing on improving those dark monuments to outdated ideas. You've never seen them, Jane.'

'I couldn't bear it!'

'I know. It grieves me to think of those gloomy corridors with tiny barred windows where strong men are condemned to spend the rest of their lives. That dismal gallery must be a hundred feet long, and there they must eat, congregate and annoy one another. At night they retire to tiny sleeping-cubicles where they are locked in every night. Mouldering there without any real exercise or meaningful occupation –'

'Yet Mr Dadd succeeded in painting the delightful works we see around us, and Mr Oxford taught himself several languages there –'

'But they are extraordinary. Brilliant men are never bored. If you put Mr Dadd on the moon he would make pictures out of the moon rocks to entertain himself. But we should also respect the dignity of ordinary criminal lunatics. Of course, they must be confined to protect society, but if they never associate with anybody except each other, breathing only the contaminated air of insanity and hearing only foul language, they will never recover.'

'In a few years the Home Office is to demolish the Ogres' Castle, as the children call it.'

'Yes, but what will they replace it with? I detest this proposal to build a great dustbin and fling all the criminal lunatics in England into it. I'm afraid it will be another Newgate, with barred windows, encircled by high walls topped with spikes and glass. What use is it to be surrounded by acres of beautiful countryside if they are to be locked in their cells day and night? They will not recover from mental disease.'

'But they are murderers or men who have attempted murder.'

'Such men are not a proper subject for punishment. They are smitten of Heaven and not morally responsible for their acts.'

'Then where should they go?'

'I would like to classify our criminal lunatics and look after those who have committed murder, treason and sedition here in our Bethlehem Hospital.'

'But they must be isolated.'

'Yes, they would be confined here, securely and humanely. And insane persons guilty of minor offences might be confined to their local county asylums.'

'Darling, you can't take upon yourself the burden of curing every lunatic in the country. Think more about your children –'

'But they are all my children!'

'You say yourself that the inmates of the criminal block are a mixture of debased characters, hardened villains and impostors. What can we possibly do to change them?'

'We must believe that the present system can be improved and not made worse. What is the use of being alive at all if we do not believe in progress? I saw my father work himself to death in the slums of Lambeth, just outside our gates. When the cholera, the new disease as he called it, arrived twenty years ago my father was bewildered. He watched hundreds of his patients die, whole families wiped out, and had no idea what to do for them. I remember his despair when he returned from those fatal nights. I was about seven. I would wake up and go downstairs to him, and he would push me away for fear of passing on any infection. But now – have we had any cholera in our hospital?'

'Not yet. We have enough troubles here.'

My Jane looked sad, and I took her hand. 'Do you wish you had married a man who left his work at the office?'

'You forget what happened to me before we married. I'm sailing on the same ship as you, Billy, on a voyage that will consume all our lives. A ship of fools perhaps. I think you truly love the mad and poor.'

'I only wish I could love them more. It is so much easier to care about a Dadd or an Oxford, an educated man I can converse with and respect.'

'And the pauper insane? When I think of the treatment they received at Fiddington House.'

'Yes, it was horrible. And yet I believe the feelings of that class are not so acute or sensitive. Governesses and solicitors, in my opinion, suffer more when they lose their minds. The time has come to elevate the social status of our patients, and in order to attract a more educated and refined class I must offer wards that resemble their own homes.'

'You have already done that. Is it not enough to have reformed one hospital?'

'No! Are you losing your fire, Jane?'

'I'm so tired. The children need all my attention, and I have so little to give them and you are never here!'

'Without your support I don't think I could go on.'

We held each other, more like two drowning creatures than two lovers. I felt her warmth against my heart and believed in myself again.

Until this morning, when disaster struck our community.

At seven we were awoken by the sound of the alarm bells ringing. We thought it was a fire, so Jane and Martha hurried the children into their clothes and out on to the lawn while I rushed into the main building. In the main hall I found Haydon and a group of attendants all shouting and gesticulating.

'She can't have climbed over the walls!'

'The night porter would have seen her, yet he insists that nobody came or went through the gate during the night.'

'Then she must be hiding somewhere in the building. Search every cupboard!'

'But I saw her fast asleep in her cubicle at eleven last night when I looked through the peephole.'

This last from Agnes Duval, matron of the female incurables' ward, an excellent woman. I asked her the name of the missing patient.

'It's Mrs Sanderson, Dr Hood. Last night we had a social evening, and she played the piano for the dancing, played very nicely, in fact, and seemed perfectly happy. She went to bed, but when we came around this morning to get the patients up she was nowhere to be seen.'

'The hospital must be thoroughly searched. Tell them to stop ringing the alarm bell. It will only upset the other patients and bring the police.'

Even as I spoke, the local constable came puffing up the drive to stick his bulbous nose into our affairs.

'Morning, doctor. Constable Potts. One of them escaped, I suppose?'

'One of whom, constable?' I asked, irritated by his tone.

'Noddies, crackpots, whatever it is you call them nowadays. I was afraid this would happen.'

'Constable, in the five years since I became responsible for this hospital hardly any patients have escaped. Our security is excellent.'

'It's only to be expected. They need to know who's their master, just like dogs and horses. When the Monros was in charge everyone knew his place, but now . . . ! What with all the pictures and blooming birdcages and carpets and billiard tables and gooseberry pie – so I heard from my niece as works in the kitchens – all them loonies must think they've died and gone to Heaven.'

'Constable, allow me to organize my hospital, and I will not interfere with your police station.'

'It's no use coming the great Dr Panjandrum with me. One of your dangerous lunatics has escaped into my neighbourhood, so it is my business. Can't have the parish terrorized by maniacs on the run.' He brought out his notebook with an infuriating smirk. 'What's his name?'

'It is a lady.'

'O-ho. What was she in for then?'

'I strongly object to the tone of your questions. We are still searching the hospital for her.'

'I see. I shall wait here until you complete your search. Then I shall need a full description.' He stood there, planted on the stone floor like a navy-blue maypole, and I dreaded his curious gaze, for I am sure he will report his crass observations to journalists who will flock to abuse my liberal reforms.

I ran upstairs to the female incurables' ward, which was in uproar. Mrs Duval showed me Mrs Sanderson's cubicle where her few clothes were hung and folded neatly in a closet. Her painting and drawing things, together with some sheet music, were in the small chest of drawers beside her bed, which appeared to have been slept in.

'This ward is locked all night, as you know, Dr Hood. Mrs Sanderson was asleep here when I checked at eleven before finishing my shift, and the night nurses go around every hour to make sure the ladies are in bed – in their own beds, that is.'

'Quite.' Last year two of the ladies on the incurables' ward were possessed by an unnatural passion for one another, and one contrived to climb into the other's bed where they were discovered. Both had to be isolated in padded rooms.

'Mrs Duval, is it at all possible that you forgot to lock the door of the ward last night? If so, please tell me frankly. I shall not be cross, for I know how exhausting your work is.'

Mrs Duval rattled the bunch of keys at her waist. 'Quite sure.'

I went over to the window, which is glazed like all the windows since I had the bars removed soon after my arrival. It was shut. Up there at the top of the building there is a very long drop down to the gardens.

'She cannot have jumped.' Mrs Duval voiced my thoughts. 'She has simply disappeared.'

I growled impatiently. I am a rational man and do not like to be told that impossible things have happened. Belief in the impossible is very often the beginning of mental illness, as it was indeed with Mrs Sanderson, who was convinced that she had travelled through time to a future London where money has been abolished and ladies wear bloomers, carriages fly and all are free and equal. This nonsense would have been a harmless fantasy had she not insisted on talking about it constantly. Her husband, a doctor who has since confirmed my suspicion that he is a charlatan, was concerned or perhaps found his wife surplus to his requirements and had her confined here.

'Did you ever think that she might wish to leave us, Mrs Duval?'

'On the contrary. Whenever I asked her if she wanted to return home for a few days she grew tearful and begged me not to send her back. Both her children are dead, poor lady, and I don't think she cares for her husband. He has never visited her.'

'I have just remembered something. Dr Sanderson told me that on the occasion of her soi-disant journey to the future she disappeared for several days. I will write to him to see if he can shed any light on this. In any case, he is her next of kin and must be informed.'

'The other ladies are most upset, Dr Hood. What shall I tell them?'

'Tell them that . . . that we are fully in control of the situation.'

How am I to deal with her disappearance in our statistics? Discharged cured? What shall I say to the committee next week? The panic I wanted to suppress in my patients rose in my own breast as I rushed downstairs to face Constable Potts. Haydon was still in the main hall attempting to charm him, but as I came down the staircase George looked up at me and raised his eyebrows to signify hopelessness. My steward possesses far more charm than me, and I decided to conserve my limited supply as I faced Potts.

'Well, doctor? Has she flitted the cage?'

'Yes, Mrs Sanderson appears to have absconded.'

'So we have a dangerous lunatic charging around Lambeth? I must put up notices describing her.'

'Mrs Sanderson is no danger to anybody except herself.'

'Nevertheless I must publicize her disappearance.'

That dreadful word: journalists, newspapers, indignant governors, patrons tightening their purse strings, investigations by the Home Office.

'How old is she, doctor?'

'Thirty-two.' I went on to describe her, seeing her grace and beauty in my mind's eye as I made an inventory of her dark-blue eyes, wavy black hair and slim figure. I produced the image of her we made when Haydon and I went around the hospital with Hering and his new-fangled machine a few months back.

As my voice barked out the facts I wished I had spent more time talking to her. Of course, I would like to know all my patients better, but Mrs Sanderson is – was – exceptionally interesting; a talented artist whose drawings of a future London impressed even Mr Dadd. It may be that her drawings will explain the mystery.

When I finally got rid of Constable Potts I asked Mrs Duval to bring me all Mrs Sanderson's drawings. She returned with a large portfolio.

'I don't know how we're going to calm the patients down, Dr Hood. The ladies on my ward are all of a fidget, crying one minute and the next minute laughing hysterically. There's been a cup of tea flung at an attendant, and they won't settle to their raffia work.'

'Their attention must be diverted in every possible way, Mrs Duval. By occupying their minds with fresh ideas, impulses and scenes a new career of thoughts and actions will be provided which may erase any lingering delusions.'

'But it is not a delusion, Dr Hood. Mrs Sanderson really has disappeared.'

'I count on you to distract them. Try a strong dose of Tranquillity Tea at bedtime.'

'But what shall I tell them now?'

'Tell them Mrs Sanderson has been discharged.'

'But . . .' Mrs Duval closed her lips on her disapproval.

'Mrs Duval, we are medical folk not missionaries. Sometimes it is kinder and wiser to doctor the truth. Now I really must go.'

I could feel the change in atmosphere throughout the hospital. Somehow the news has spread, and all the attendants have reported unusual problems: tension, restlessness, conflict and tantrums. Insane people are exceptionally sensitive, and, although I objected to Constable Potts's comparison with horses and dogs, I have often observed a herd instinct. Our little community crackled with sparks awaiting the chance to burst out into flames. I wanted to protect them all, to keep out the world that has damaged them and which now threatens my reforms.

Having no time to examine Mrs Sanderson's drawings, I asked a servant to take the portfolio to Jane, together with a note explaining the crisis. I knew she would stay in our house for she rarely ventures here to the other side of the wall. Yet I needed her support and approval. Jane always makes me feel that my work is valuable and important. This morning I desperately needed to believe that.

I have failed with Mrs Sanderson. She was one of my secret favourites. Of course, all patients must be treated equally, but I am no saint and am not immune to the appeal of intelligence and beauty. For years now I have been proud that our little community has been her chosen refuge from an unhappy marriage. She has seemed thankful for a harbour of safety and anxious to escape the public gaze and the finger of scorn. Sometimes the severance of all family associations and social intercourse is beneficial, and I have long hoped that Mrs Sanderson would eventually return to her life outside our gates.

Our hospital is but a metaphor for that world outside. We go to chapel and celebrate Christmas, we teach cooking and gardening and other practical skills and encourage our patients to enjoy musical evenings, balls and theatricals. We assume that all our patients are curable, although it is always with mixed feelings that I watch each one take his or her first faltering steps beyond these gates, like a fond parent accompanying his child on its first day at school. How often have I wished I could go with them to watch over them.

Usually I do not hear any more news of them. On leaving us they return to their families, their social pride unabashed and their gratitude unalloyed. There is no cost for the treatment they receive here, only a bond to be returned on discharge. I have always been proud to display our hospital and have sent out tickets and invitations to our balls and concerts. Very few of our patients try to escape. Indeed, I have sometimes joked with Haydon and Jane that to do so would in itself be evidence of mental disease.

Since I came here a workhouse has been transformed into a club. Visitors are astonished by the comforts they see here: pianos and periodicals, decent food, singing classes and a glass-sided ballroom. Some, like Constable Potts, may consider us over-indulgent.

Escape is a cruel verb; our hospital is no prison. Why did she want to leave us? How can she have done so without opening a window or forcing a lock?

These questions distressed me all day, making me snappish and nervous. When I returned home this evening Jane saw at once that I was troubled and made me sit down in the drawing-room with a glass of wine before I shut myself in my study to do more work.

'Why are you here, Papa?' Donald asked from the table where he and Chas were doing their prep. They are a little too old now to be kissed, although I longed to feel their solid warmth near me.

'Am I not allowed in my own home?'

'But you don't usually come so early. Papa is working, children,' Chas said in a good imitation of his mama's voice. I reflected sadly that I spend more time with my patients than with my sons. 'I'm working, too. Beastly Latin. Why did those old Romans have to speak such a difficult language?'

'Greek's even worse,' Donald said from the wisdom of nine. 'School gets horrider and horrider.'

That expensive school the fees for which I struggle to pay each term. In a few years I must find enough money to send Donald to Rugby, although Jane does not want to lose her little boys.

'I expect the Romans invented school. They invented everything,' Chas sighed.

I stared at the two brown heads beneath the gaslight and wished I knew more of their contents.

'Martha says one of your lunatics escaped.' Donald stuck out his tongue, rolled his eyes and lolled his head on one side, provoking a fit of giggles from Chas. I wish the servants would not gossip, but they do.

Chas's giggles turned to petulance. 'The boys at school say I must be mad to live in a madhouse. But I'm not am I, Papa?'

'You are the sons of a doctor and need never be ashamed of that.' But they will be, once I have sent them both off to public school and made gentlemen of them.

Martha came to shoo them off to bed. I kissed their foreheads and promised them cricket on the lawn on Saturday afternoon. They have always played freely in the gardens here, and it pleases me to think of the patients looking down from their windows and seeing us here, a family, that mystery from which most happiness and mental illness emanate.

I longed to be alone with Jane, but Louisa hovered. She has a most irritating habit of following Jane about and demanding all her attention – which I have the greater need of, particularly this evening.

'Poor Billy! Mrs Sanderson will be a most unfortunate statistic in our next governors' report.'

'Who is she? How did she escape?' Louisa exhausts me with her endless questions.

'My dear, would you take this bundle of letters and file them in my study? Then you may take a book from my library and read it until your bedtime.'

When Louisa smiles she looks almost pretty. Although not nearly as pretty as her mother, who I could now embrace freely. I told Jane everything, and, as always, she gave me good advice.

'Billy, she has gone, and we must forget her. Remember instead the patients who are still here, who need you and are grateful to you, like those forty lost souls you resurrected in M4. You are inclined to dwell on your failures rather than your successes.'

'Did you look at her portfolio of drawings?'

'I attempted to, but they're too confusing. They gave me a headache. Only a diseased brain could have invented such a chaotic world. Those dreadful, savage people, half-naked, and those hideous buildings –'

'The future that she saw in her visions –'

'Never mind the future, Billy, you have more than enough to do in the present. Forget Mrs Sanderson.'

I cannot. All evening I worried that some ruffian had abducted her or that she had returned to her husband and was miserable. Jane's reference to M4 reminded me of Mr Dadd, whose artist's eye may perhaps make sense of her wild drawings and find clues that are invisible to the rest of us.

When Jane and the children were safely asleep I took the portfolio, left our little house under the portico and went upstairs to M4. As I expected, Dadd was hard at work at his easel. We allow him to paint at any time he wishes because, as Neville says, he do be special.

He sat in a circle of gaslight like an actor alone on a vast, empty stage. I have always thought that his work has a theatrical quality. I saw with pleasure that he was working on my *Contradiction*, which I long to add to my collection. He did not raise his head as I approached, for he has the concentration of a man who is deaf or blind. Tightly sealed in his private universe he acts out his lonely play.

Afraid to disturb him, I was about to put the portfolio on the floor beside him and tiptoe away when he spoke.

'So she got away, did she?'

'How do you know? Did Neville tell you?'

His brush filled the silence. It amazes me that such a sullen, unfeeling man can produce such delicate pictures. He was working on the undergrowth at the bottom of his – my – oval painting of Oberon and Titania quarrelling. The fairy couple are not a bit ethereal but are quite solid and even burly, of Mediterranean aspect. I have had to rebuke him before for indecent activities between the fairies. Having accepted that he was not in the mood to talk I decided to examine my picture to make sure it will be fit to hang in a decent family home.

'May I?' I picked up the magnifying glass that Dadd, who in his youth trained to be a miniaturist, often uses when he paints.

At once I was able to see that he has given a satyr fairy the face of a poor imbecile called Ronson, who is confined to the criminal block for dismembering a prostitute. Ronson constantly exposes his person and is addicted to disgusting behaviour, and fairy Ronson was masturbating against Helena's left foot.

'Really, Dadd, this will not do.'

'What sharp eyes you have.' He painted out the tiny penis with a stroke.

My eye travelled over the fascinating canvas. Dadd's minuteness of detail is characteristic of monomania. I remember a fellow who was here a few years back – a lawyer's clerk who threw all his employer's legal tomes out of the window and injured a passing lady – who spent his year in our hospital drawing tiny umbrellas. He had not the imagination or the skill to draw anything else. In Dadd's work, however, fancy and talent unite to embroider the undergrowth with demonic fairies who fight, threaten Titania with a bow, load a fir cone on to a snail and chase each other, inventively echoing the quarrel between their king and queen.

'This is magnificent, Dadd.' He said nothing, but I know that, like most of us, he adores compliments. 'Have you made any progress on *The Good Samaritan*?'

'Not this month. Will you really hang it on the main staircase?'

'Most certainly. Just like Hogarth's painting at Bart's. Every visitor to the hospital will be able to admire it.'

'It's not as big as Hogarth's.'

'I'm sure it will be a splendid painting.' His silence was less hostile. 'By the way, I would be most grateful if you would look at these drawings. They are the work of Mrs Sanderson, the lady who absconded last night. You may remember that you saw some of her work a few years back . . .'

'I remember her very well.'

'And were kind enough to comment on it. Perhaps you could look at her drawings again in the light of her disappearance and tell me if you can find in them any indication as to why she left us or where she might have gone.'

He barely nodded. It was obvious that he was not in the mood for conversation. Sometimes he remains sunk in gloom and silence for weeks; at other times we have long and interesting talks. I had been about to remind him of our service on Sunday. I considered making another attempt to persuade him to attend chapel this coming Sunday and abandon his bizarre faith in the ancient Egyptian gods, but I could see that my missionary efforts would fall on even stonier ground than usual, so I asked if he needed any more art materials. Without speaking, Dadd handed me a list.

'I will leave you in peace now.' He did not look up from his – my – canvas as I left M4.

15

THE BOOK
OF THE DEAD

At first when I heard those footsteps marching towards me down the dark corridor a wild hope seized me: Haydon has come for a secret tryst. My mind was already lingering on such matters, for I had been staring at my little painting of my nocturnal adventures with Susie, my first love, made respectable by the title *Cupid and Psyche*. I have added the elegant floor I admired a few years later at Cobham Hall, shrunk my nine-year-old self into a putto and given the saucy maid a classical dignity she never had – still, I know whom my brush caresses. Call it mythology or a fairy painting and you are free to portray the delights of nakedness forbidden in our killjoy England.

My brush stroked her nipples and hole, then gently replaced her on the floor and took up the *Contradiction*. If it was Haydon, I wanted him to see my best work and admire me as an artist not pity me as a lunatic. As is usual in the middle of the night I was in a state of unbearable excitement, for I had been visiting my secret *Hareme Egyptienne* where Susie, Elizabeth, Ali and beautiful George submit nightly to my insatiable desires. Of course, this leaves me tumescent and unable to gain any satisfaction as we are always watched. Occasionally, in my sleeping-cubicle, I manage to evade prying eyes. Even when I paint at night, alone in this vast room, I have no real privacy, for the night attendants and watchmen are paid to spy on us.

Each man has his own predestined fate, and mine, it seems, is to be frustrated. Again and again I relive my few sensual adventures and wish I had had more, wish I had out-tupped Don Juan the length and breadth of Europe.

It was not beautiful George but Hood, also a handsome young man but too serious to appeal to me. It is easier to imagine him in a pulpit than spreadeagled on the red velvet divan of my fancy. If I were

Hood I would spend my nights making love to my wife, not prowling the wards of his madhouse.

He pretends to be my friend but is always my master. I know I should be grateful to him for rescuing me from the degrading criminal block, and indeed I am, but he has the power to send me back there as he sent Jonson when he threw the chamber pot at Oxford. Hood tells me to illustrate the passions, but then he has so few. Cool men have no problems with conventional morality.

So the beautiful creature has flown. I should have put her in my harem for safekeeping. McDonald told me the news yesterday after the alarm sounded, and Oxford says it is the sign he has been waiting for that Young England is to triumph and take over the world. Last night he rushed around the ward packing up his belongings and appointing his ministers. I am to be Minister for the Arts.

It is a pleasure to look at Mrs Sanderson's drawings again, for she has a lucid eye, a lively imagination and a strong line. I remember how surprised I was the first time I saw them a few years back that a woman had produced such powerful work. Not a flower in sight. She has an inner world as strange as that of Hieronymus Bosch: a city populated with indecently dressed barbarians, too large and coarse to be fairies. There appears to be no distinction between male and female, an idea that attracts me very much. They have mastered bizarre machines with wings and wheels in which they move around their city, a seething labyrinth of geometric towers of Babel and vast monuments that hide the sky.

I lost myself in Mrs Sanderson's world – the mark of quality, I have always believed. If you can travel inside a drawing or painting and forget yourself for a few minutes, it has worked its spell.

I return to M4 and feel unaccountably nervous. When I try to return to my *Contradiction* my brush defies me; it is but a stick with bristles on the end wielded by a wooden arm. My beefy Titania has just trampled a flower fairy and a grotesque archer is trying to shoot his queen. They fight and quarrel. How cruel and spiteful my fairies have become. Capricious little devils. I will not paint them any more.

The hospital is too quiet – an odd observation for I have always loved the silent hours of the night. Then I realize that the silence is booming inside my own head: Osiris and my father are ignoring me, and my fairies are merely painted images cavorting on a canvas.

I look around, stricken with loneliness. Their voices have kept me company for so long. I call to them, at first mouthing the words then whispering them into the darkness. 'Osiris! Papa! Oberon! Titania!'

Nothing.

I begin to weep. If I am to live out the rest of my days here quite alone, unable to paint or draw, I could not bear it. My voices kept out the vile behaviour of the men in the criminal block, the violence, nightmares and obscenity. They illuminated my darkness and made music out of screams and oaths and belches. They gave my ship-wrecked life meaning and connected me with that younger Richard who was to have been a great artist.

I call them again, louder. 'Osiris! Papa! Oberon! Titania!'

I cannot come, Richard, for I am dead.

It is his voice exactly, reasonable and pedantic, his Kentish vowels overlaid with the smart London accent with which he hoped to impress his customers. My father's voice comes from behind me.

I whip around to see him lying at my feet in a dark puddle of blood. His throat has been slit. He has been stabbed and mutilated by some butcher. He is wearing the old moleskin jacket and breeches he kept for country walks, and his soft-leather walking shoes are maroon, dyed in his own blood. Marooned, he has died.

I kneel beside him. I want to touch him but am afraid of blood, and so I turn my back on my father again and walk thankfully into my past.

I bought the cheapest tickets for the diligence to Calais and the *Rob Roy* to Dover. Wrapped in my cloak on the deck of the boat, I felt the salt air clean my lungs as I watched the Dadd-infested coast of Kent approach and with it my magnificent future.

In Dover I was terrified of meeting acquaintances, so I wrapped my travelling cloak around my face, very conscious that the journey that had begun almost a year ago with such luxury and high hopes was ending in humiliation. Then Sir T. and I had travelled first class and eaten in the best restaurants. Now I spent my last shillings on coffee, brandy, bread and an outside seat on the stagecoach to London. By the time I arrived at the White Bear in Piccadilly my bones were rattled, my nerves were shaken, and I felt sick, hungry and exhausted.

I walked to Suffolk Street, seeing London through feverish eyes, foggy and overcrowded, peopled with bustling devils. Penniless as I was, there was nowhere to go but home.

It was a Wednesday afternoon. My father was in his workshop downstairs with a customer, but when he saw me he opened his arms and rushed to embrace me. He looked smaller, older and sadder.

'My dearest boy! What a wonderful surprise!' Then, turning to his customer, 'My son, you know, a talented young artist who has been on a most extensive grand tour with Sir Thomas Phillips . . .'

I could not speak. The children came downstairs and crowded around me, hoping for presents and entertaining stories. The greyness of London, the ghastly familiarity of my family and the shame of my moonlit flit from Sir T. all padlocked my mouth. I was like Pappageno in *The Magic Flute* but not so lovable; their hugs and kisses and prattle were hateful to me.

That day my silence was accepted as exhaustion. After Mary Ann grumblingly brought me some cold beef and potatoes – 'Come back for a bit of lowlife, have you? I suppose you're too good to eat with us now. Well, you'll just have to get used to us again!' – I was allowed to go to bed in the room I shared with George and Stephen. My step-brothers followed me up there and shouted the family news through the door as I undressed and got into bed: how Great Aunt Dadd had finally died and left our father a hundred pounds; how our brother Robert was to be married to a young lady so rich that she brought them sugarplums; and how Maria and Rebecca were to be brides-maids with beautiful pink frocks.

The next morning I woke early to find my brothers snoring beside me. Their breath seemed to drain my own. I dreaded the questions that would be asked as soon as they woke up. Maria, my favourite sister, would be sure to winkle out my confidences with her sharp perceptions. Realizing I could not spend another night beneath my father's roof I gathered my portfolio of oriental sketches and hurried around the corner to a dealer in the Haymarket to sell three of my Egyptian drawings. As Sir T. had constantly reminded me, they belonged by rights to him – and as a solicitor he knew his rights – so I did not dare to sell any more.

After an hour of haggling I raised enough money to live cheaply for a few weeks. My horror of being with my family, of being with anyone I knew, sharpened my wits as I rushed around London. By evening I had rented a tiny room in a tawdry house in Newman Street. By nine that night I was locked safely alone in my room and had told my landlady she was never to set foot in my rooms – not even to clean.

The demons who had been pursuing me abroad had followed me to London. Each day they multiplied and grew more subtle and clever in their disguises.

I don't remember the exact moment when Osiris, who had been visiting me for years, took up permanent residence in my head. It was just after I went to live in Newman Street. He was a demanding tenant who warned me against everybody and would allow me to drink only ale and eat only hard-boiled eggs. When I complained that it was a monotonous diet that made me fart constantly and gave me the stomach ache, my master replied that I was ungrateful for his loving care of me, for he wanted only to protect me from all the demons who were trying to poison me. *Ex ova omnia*. Out of the egg came insomnia and indigestion – but when I disobeyed him and ate some bread and cheese Osiris shouted at me.

Frith came to see me, bounding up the stairs and rapping on my door. How confident and buoyant his voice sounded. His knuckles assaulted my door with the certainty of a man who had never doubted himself.

'Richard! I only heard today that you're back in London! Are you there, Richard? Your landlady said you were at home.'

I stood on the other side of the door shaking. Frith was always at home, everywhere. *You must not open your door!* Osiris commanded. *He is the greatest trickster of all. He will steal your work and your ideas.*

'Dear Richard, have I disturbed you? Were you sleeping? I will go away and come back tomorrow. I long to see the work you did abroad.'

Only a year had passed since we had adjoining studios in Charlotte Street. Powell and I used to show each other every scrap of work; we criticized with passion and encouraged one another through many a gloom. He used to come to me for advice and said I had a better grasp of technique than any artist he knew.

If you must talk to this Frith devil, kill him. I ignored Osiris, removed the chest that was blocking the door and called out to Powell as he went sadly downstairs, 'Wait! I am here.'

He turned and galloped back, greeting me with a warmth that shamed me. Apart from an old bedstead, my room contained only two rickety cane chairs, so I offered him one and sat on the other.

Then I showed him my enormous cartoon of St George after the death of the dragon. It was almost as big as the room itself. I had been battling with it as if the paper was another dragon. I was racing to finish it for the competition to design a fresco for the new House of Lords. When I first came to London, a bumpkin of seventeen, I had watched the old Palace of Westminster burn down, and now I longed for my work to be embedded in the new building.

If I won the competition I would be established as one of the best young artists in London, and the prize money would allow me to live for a year independently. It would also be my defence against Sir T., the ringleader of all the devils. I feared he would arrive back in London at any minute, bearing tales of my strange behaviour, and turn everybody against me.

'Ah, the Palace of Westminster competition! I'm afraid we're all chasing after that. I delivered my attempt last week. I've heard they've had over a hundred entries already. You know the closing date is tomorrow?'

You see, hissed Osiris. *He is jealous and wants to destroy you.*

223

'I shall stay up all night to finish it. But what do you think of it, Powell?'

With difficulty we pinned it up against the window so that he could see it properly. 'What a pretty girl clinging to the conquering hero. Did you find her abroad?'

'I can't afford to pay a model just now, so I begged my sister Maria to come and sit for me. She was here all morning. Do you think it has a chance? I desperately need to win.'

'Don't we all. Who knows? What an eccentric dragon! He looks like a crocodile yawning with a tail as long as the Nile.'

'Don't tease me, Powell. Do you think I should tear it up and start again?'

'Why, Richard, whatever is the matter with you? You always used to have such confidence in your work. Quite rightly, for you have more talent in your little finger than most of us in our entire bodies. May I see the work you did abroad?'

I handed him the portfolio. 'These are wonderful, Richard. Just wait until you sell them. You'll be able to move from this hovel and rent the biggest studio in London. What marvels you've accomplished while I've been stuck here.'

I muttered that I could not sell them, for they belonged to Sir Thomas.

'And how did you find him as a travelling companion? Your letters hinted that it was not all paradise having such a patron.'

I longed to joke and mock and gossip as we used to do. But at that moment Osiris appeared behind Frith's shoulder: a long, elegant man in a white robe with a narrow green face and long green hands. He looked rather like my beloved Ali, and I took a step towards him, but his black kohl-lined eyes were cruel, and I watched in wonderment as he grew. His white head-dress touched my low ceiling, and he stretched until he was thin as a column. Then I saw that he was holding a large knife over my friend's head. 'No! Please! Let him live!'

'What's the matter, Richard? Who are you talking to?' Puzzled, Frith turned. It was obvious that he could not see the towering god.

'You cannot stay, Powell. Please go. It is dangerous for you here.'

'What are you afraid of? You're pale and shaking. Are you ill?'

'Please go, Powell. Now.' I shoved him to the door.

'But . . . when may I see you again? Egg and Phillip are longing for a reunion of our old Clique, a jolly evening together –'

'Just go! Please!'

Trembling, I locked the door behind him and replaced the chest of drawers. My room was empty and silent again. I checked under the bed and in my closet to make sure there were no stray Egyptian gods. It was about six of the evening, and I prepared to work all night on my cartoon. My sister had left me a tempting basket of bread and cheese and an apple pie and a bottle of ginger beer. The smell of fresh bread and sweet pastry drove me wild with hunger, but I was afraid it might be poisoned, so I boiled two more eggs and washed them down with a bottle of ale.

I worked in peace until about eleven when the house was quiet. The sound of horses in the street outside and the shouts and giggles of passing drunks with their girls made me feel safe. This was my city. I belonged here and would make a good life here. My charcoal met the friendly paper and enclosed me in my private world beyond thought.

Then, at about midnight I was attacked by a blinding headache and the crackle of his booming voice. It was rather like the muezzin, the call to prayer I had heard so often. Not on some distant minaret but in the reluctant temple of my own head.

You disobeyed me. You must be punished! You must wear the devil's mark on your forehead!

'But I don't want to!' I protested as Osiris forced a breadknife into my hand, pushed me to the mirror above my washbasin and held my hand in his tight grip as he carved my brow. Blood flowed from the deep cut down into my eyes, and I must have yelled with pain and fear for my new landlady, Mrs Hampton, used her own key to unlock my door, pushed aside the chest of drawers and rushed up to me.

'Why, Mr Dadd, whatever have you done to yourself?' She brought a jug of hot water and bandages and wiped my face. Her touch was gentle and kind, and I longed to rest on her enormous bosom.

Osiris was furious. *Fool! Can't you see she is a female demon? She will entrap you with her infernal tricks.*

'Shall I call the doctor, Mr Dadd? You young gentlemen don't know how to look after yourselves. You don't look well. Are you eating proper?' She looked around the room with maternal curiosity. 'All I can see is empty bottles and eggshells.'

'I – I need the eggs to make my paints with.' I clenched my buttocks to suppress more *ars musica*.

'Well, whatever are you eating then? You'd best join us downstairs for meals. If it's money you're worried about you can pay me at the end of the month. I'll have a word with your sister as was here this morning, such a sweet girl. Now I'll get you some ointment for that horrid cut.'

As soon as Mrs Hampton bustled out Osiris made me lock my door and push the chest of drawers back against it.

Simpleton! The devil can put on any disguise he wishes. How can you do battle with him when all his tricks take you in? I shall disown you as my son and heir if you do not display more caution. Show me the portraits you have done of your so-called friends.

Nervously I opened an old folder of drawings I had done of my family and members of The Clique.

Take out your brush. Red paint – no, too dark – crimson! You must wash their crimes in blood!

Osiris forced me to paint a red slash at each throat. I felt sick and dizzy as paint turned into blood.

All of them are false. You must not trust anybody. Now, take pen and paper. I will dictate a list of all the devils you must kill before I can anoint you as my divine son and we can return to our thrones in Egypt.

Then my master dictated a long list of names, beginning with the Emperor of Austria and my father.

All through that long summer I stayed in my stifling room and worked, for I have always been able to work. Without that comfort I would have killed myself that summer, which perhaps would have been the best solution.

When I heard that my St George had not won the competition I was furious and wanted to cut my wrists to punish my hands, which had not enough power in them. Osiris forced me to drop the breadknife. *Your life belongs to me now.*

Occasionally I ventured out to visit friends. But Osiris came with me, whispering in my ear that they were plotting to destroy me, that I must kill them before they killed me. Among people I saw only demons and hatred and returned, shaking and terrified, to the solitude of my room.

It was only when I was working that I felt I belonged to myself. The voice of Osiris became fainter and the contours of my painted world hid him from me. My mind and eye were still in the desert as I painted my group of water-carriers, men and camels at a spring on the sea shore at Fortuna, near Mount Carmel in Syria. My sketches came to life as I transferred them to oils, and when that painting was exhibited at the Liverpool Academy its acceptance restored some of my confidence. I also worked on several watercolours, including one of a dead camel I would love to see again. The intensity of the desert light and its colours – browns and yellows and corals – haunted me, and I wished I could return.

We will go back to Egypt and reign together, Osiris said. *We will leave this dull grey city and live in sun and freedom. But, first, you must kill all the devils.*

Once or twice I left the house to sell my work to the dealer in the Haymarket, for I needed money. I no longer accepted any invitations and left my room only to buy eggs and ale and art materials, scurrying to the shops with my head down, hoping not to meet anyone I knew.

Almost every day a friend or relation called at the house in Newman Street. Frith came several times, and I locked myself away from him in silence. Egg came once and knocked persistently until I waved a knife under the door at him. My sister Maria came often, leaving baskets of food outside my door. I could smell my favourite foods; pork pies, homemade cakes, pickled herrings and leek soup. *All poisoned*, Osiris said. *You are weak and cowardly, not worthy to be my son. You still have not killed a single person on the list.*

I heard Maria weep outside my door and went to open it, but my master said, *She is not your sister but a devil. How easily you are deceived. You must kill her with this knife.*

My brothers and father came, too. I would sit in my room listening to their whispered conversations on the stairs with Mrs Hampton and the little maid who brought me hot water and emptied my slops and who referred to me as the peculiar gent in the third-floor back. There was a strange pleasure in withholding myself from these people who loved me, whom I had once loved. It was like the perverse enjoyment I felt as a child when I hid in the undergrowth with my fairies and ignored the voices calling me for meals.

One hot July afternoon I heard my father's voice just outside my door. No anger, just the sweet reason I had not inherited.

'Richard? I know you are there. Open your door, please, my boy. I have a custard and a chocolate cake Mary Ann has baked specially. I've been thinking, you need a holiday. You're exhausted by your travels, my boy, and perhaps still suffering from sunstroke. Let us go to dear old Cobham together. This month I'm busy with a big order of frames, but next month I could spare a few days. Richard?'

I heard the rustling of paper and the clink of dishes as he put the basket down. The smell of baked custard with nutmeg and cinnamon and the rich moist cake were a torment as they wafted under my door.

'I saw Roberts yesterday, and he is anxious to see you. He has invited you to a soirée at his studio tonight. You must go, my boy. There will be people there who can help you get on. Sir Thomas came to see me yesterday and he is anxious about your health. We all are. Come home for a few days so that we can talk.'

I longed to see my father, to be again the promising son who was to save our family fortunes. Greed and loneliness compelled me to go to the door, but just as I was about to open it Osiris spoke. *He is the first on the list. Kill him now.*

During the following weeks my father came frequently, and we spoke through my door. He and Maria arranged a party in Suffolk Street for my twenty-sixth birthday on August the 1st. My dread of birthdays, which I had felt ever since my mother destroyed herself (as I have always believed) just before my seventh birthday, was uncontrollable. I wept and shivered and castigated myself for the failure of my life.

That evening they came to fetch me for my party, but at the last minute I panicked and could not leave my room. They called to me again and again, but I could not answer them. After an hour they went away.

That night I sat alone and brooded on my failure. No longer young, I was flinging away the ladder I had built so carefully. The ladder up which I was to have climbed to the clouds, the stars and the sun. My fate was to crawl alone beneath the lowest rung, in the stink of oil paint and eggs and ale and my own farts.

Yes, you have a strange destiny but a great one, Osiris said. *When you have killed these devils you will be raised far above the vulgar herd. We will go back to Egypt.*

The next day my father came to my door and spoke again of our trip to Cobham. 'We will be peaceful there, my boy. You know how you love the countryside. All the hedges and meadows will be in flower. We can revisit our old haunts and speak with old friends and walk for many a mile. It will do you good.'

I said nothing but shut my eyes on the other side of the door and longed to go with him. That night I painted a little watercolour of my childhood landscape, the meadows carpeted with wild flowers and the ships on the Medway beyond.

We must go with that impostor who says he is your father, Osiris said.

I had been hoping to escape from Osiris for a few days, but he always read my thoughts. *I will help you to kill him, for you are too weak to do it alone. Then we will cross to France and return to our kingdom in Egypt. You must prepare. Have you that papyrus they force you to show when you travel?*

'My passport? Yes. Shall we really go back to Egypt?' I often spoke aloud to him, for he was as real as I was.

Show me. Yes, we will go soon. But you must be armed, for you will meet many more devils. Where can you buy weapons?

'I have this knife.'

It is not sharp enough. Take me to the souk.

'But I want to work this afternoon –'

Go!

He pushed me out of the room and down the stairs. It was like being frog-marched by a great wind. I remembered a cutler's shop, Moseley's, in New Street and led him there or, rather, allowed myself to be propelled there. In the window there was a shining array of knives.

That one! And that one!

Osiris pointed, and I bought a razor and a spring knife, a beautiful little object that fitted in my pocket and, when a button was pressed, became a deadly weapon.

The next time my father came I spoke to him through my door. 'Yes, we will go to Cobham, Papa. Let's go this month while the nights are long. I will unburthen my mind to you.'

'Richard! How wonderful to hear your voice! Come home with me now. I know you are tired and sick and need to be cared for.'

He rattled my door, and I saw Osiris in his long white robe move swiftly towards it, raising a scimitar above his head.

'I can't come now, Papa. But we will go together to Cobham.'

'When?'

'Later this month.'

'I wish you would come home with me now.'

'I must stay here and work.'

As my father sadly descended the stairs I turned on Osiris in a rage. 'Why do you tyrannize me so? You will ruin my life.'

But I am offering you eternal life. The god sounded surprised.

'I'm tired and sick, as my father says.'

He is not your true father! You are my son!

'Don't start shouting at me again. I need to rest, to be with my family and friends, not to be always locked alone in this tomb of a room.'

If Jehovah, as the Bible tells us, was a jealous god, I think he was an ewe lamb compared with Osiris.

You are not alone. I am with you, in you, day and night. I am your

*real father, not this abject cur who sniffs at your door. I will protect
you from all these devils who pretend to be your friends until the time
comes to kill them.*

'All this talk of killing is madness. We're not in ancient Egypt but
in nineteenth-century London, and the police will come if we break
the law.'

Then let us return to my kingdom where I am the law.

'Leave me alone!'

In my distress I had been shouting, and I heard my landlady on
the other side of the door. 'Mr Dadd? What was that about the police?
This is a respectable house. I've never had no trouble, and I don't
want any now . . .'

'Calm down, Mrs Hampton. There is nothing to worry about.'

'So you say, Mr Dadd. I've had some strange coves in my lodgings,
but I've never had a ninnyhammer like you. Who are you shouting at
in there? Open this door, Mr Dadd!'

I let her in and showed her my empty room.

'Yelling away to yourself! Eggshells and empty bottles and smelly
paint all over my carpet! What's that supposed to be?'

'It's a dead camel.'

'I'll dead camel you! Gives me the creeps. I'm not having such
dicked-in-the-nob doings in my house. I want you out of here, or
you'll be out on your ear.'

Why do you allow your slaves to insult you? Osiris asked as Mrs
Hampton slammed the door. On the stairs I heard her complaining
loudly about me.

Suddenly I yearned to be at home, surrounded by people who
loved me. I had paid until the end of the week and should have asked
Mrs Hampton for a refund, but I had not enough courage to face her
again. Too upset to pack up everything, I gathered all the possessions
I could carry and left a note on my table that I would send someone
to collect the rest in a few days. I fled Mrs Hampton's, spending my
last shilling on a cab to Suffolk Street.

As I hugged my portfolio I stared out of the window at the crowds
in Oxford Street. On the hot August evening thousands of people

were on the streets. The very rich were in those gracious country houses to which I still longed to be invited, but the middling sort were there in pale, elegant clothes, shopping or beginning a sociable evening. On the pavements boys and girls were selling newspapers, flowers, strawberries, toys, buns, lavender and ices. Prostitutes were out hunting for customers, and pickpockets and beggars eagerly worked the crowds while slum children played among them in the alleys. The traffic lock gave me the opportunity to view the panorama of London, and I remember how the dirt, floating on the heat, coated all the colours with a varnish of golden brown. Had I known I was seeing it for the last time I would have devoured that pageant even more hungrily.

The shop in Suffolk Street was closed so I rang the bell, and Maria flew down to let me in. When I told her I had left my lodgings she pressed her warm, damp cheek against mine. 'Dear Richard! How wonderful that you've come home. We're just about to eat. Come and join us.'

I thought at first the tears were hers but realized they were my own. In the dining-room my father sat with all my brothers and sisters, who greeted me with hugs and smiles. A shepherd's pie was brought in, with peas and carrots and cabbage.

'Aren't you hungry, Richard?' Maria asked when I sat staring at the fragrant mounds of orange, green and creamy brown.

Then I picked up my knife and fork and ate so much, so fast that they all laughed at me. The talk was all of Robert's wedding, and for a while I felt quite safe. Osiris was silent and invisible, as a god ought to be, and the banality of family life was oddly comforting.

'Where's George?' I asked.

'He's not well.' Maria avoided my gaze. 'He's in his room. He needs rest. You will sleep with Robert and Stephen.'

Upstairs I undressed and lay down, exhausted, in the little bed I used to sleep in as a boy. When my brothers came up I pretended to be asleep, not wanting to have to make conversation with them, and listened to their own whispered conversation with some interest.

'The prodigal son,' Stephen remarked.

'The genius. Let us hope he's not dangerous.'

'George is even more cork-brained. When Maria knocked on his door to ask if he wanted any pudding he recited Ophelia's mad speech to her.'

'I only hope my wedding goes off without any embarrassing incidents. I've told our father he must take him to St Luke's tomorrow.'

'To which of our lunatic brothers do you refer?'

'To Richard, of course. George is less shaming because nobody knows him. Frith and Egg say that Richard is a danger both to himself and others and must be locked up.'

'What a family! I envy you, Robert. Soon you'll be free of this bedlam.'

'And I advise you to find a sensible little woman, as I have done, from a prodigiously sane family and marry her as soon as possible.'

After that I could not sleep. I stared at the moon through the curtains but feared that Isis might see me and join her brother in my head. She was, after all, my aunt. My earthly family was proving most unsatisfactory, and I wondered how I could avoid visiting the hospital. If I must go, I was determined to outwit the doctor as I had done in Paris.

All night I sailed on moonbeams into my tempestuous past and uncertain future. Waking from dreams of Chatham and Cobham, I longed to return. After my brothers rose to go to work I lay there alone, full of dread. Osiris would come, or my father or Maria or George would burst in to reproach me. If only I could return to the pure air of my childhood meadows all would be well. I would be well.

That afternoon I reluctantly agreed to go with my father to St Luke's Hospital in Old Street. He called a cab, an unusual extravagance, and kept up a nervous stream of chatter as we travelled northwards towards Clerkenwell. In the sticky gloom of the interior I noticed how shrunken and withered he looked.

'What is it, this place we're going to? Is it a madhouse like Bedlam?'

'When I was young there was a rhyme: "St Luke's is clean with tyranny, Bedlam's all filth with liberty." Don't be angry, dear Richard, I know you're no more mad than I am, but Alexander Sutherland is one of the best alienists in London and has kindly agreed to see us today. I promised your brothers we would go – and Sir Thomas – and Frith and Egg. I dare say it's only sunstroke, but your behaviour – we are all concerned about you. Then on Monday morning we will get the steamer and go to Cobham together. I remember how you always loved boats . . .'

It was the voice in which he used to promise me barley sugar after my bitter medicine, the tone he used when he explained that he was torturing my little nutmegs for my own good. Kind and obtuse.

St Luke's was a magnificent building, a palace of lunacy. The waiting-room was full of unhappy couples: a mother with her twitching son; a husband with his terrified wife; a middle-aged woman with her gibbering old mother. It was painfully obvious, in each case, who had made the appointment and who had submitted to becoming a patient. I noticed we were the only father and son there.

My father stayed in the waiting-room when I followed the nurse down a corridor into a large panelled room. Dr Sutherland, grim and craggy, sat behind a desk and pointed to a comfortable leather chair on the other side of it.

'Mr Dadd, please sit down. I believe you have recently returned from a grand tour?'

I spoke of my travels, name-dropping carefully and looking Dr Sutherland in the eye as an equal. We spoke of Venice and Jerusalem and the pyramids, all of which he had visited.

'While you were abroad, did you ever hallucinate?'

'What can you mean?' I smiled politely.

'I mean, did you ever see or hear things which your companions could not?'

'Things?'

'The Egyptian god Osiris, for example.'

'Certainly not!'

Perhaps I would have duplicated my triumph with Dr Lunn in

Paris if Osiris, who had been dormant since I left my lodgings, had not chosen that moment to erupt. I held my head, which felt as if it was splitting open.

Traitor! I have loved you as a son, and you deny my existence. Who is this poltroon?

Osiris materialized in his long white robe and head-dress, and I saw that he was holding a large paperweight over the doctor's head. I jumped up and tried to restrain him, but he turned on me and we wrestled together. My master expanded in that disconcerting way he has, and I was no match for a nine-foot god. He threw me to the carpet where I lay gasping, fending him off with my arm over my face. 'No! Don't hurt me, please. If you attack the doctor we will both be doomed.'

I did not know if I spoke aloud or to myself. The god slowly shrank and disappeared. When I had enough breath to sit up I found Dr Sutherland still sitting at his desk, observing me with interest.

'With whom were you conversing, Mr Dadd?'

I scrambled back on to my chair and attempted to regain my dignity.

'With whom were you fighting just now?'

I tried to smile, to suggest it had all been a joke.

Above his luxuriant beard the doctor's eyes condemned me without malice. He rang a bell and asked an attendant to summon my father, who entered obsequiously. I always hated the way he knew his place and estimated it so low and was sure he would obey the eminent doctor.

'Mr Dadd, you have done well to bring your son here. Sadly, he is no longer responsible for his actions and should be put under restraint.'

'Do you mean you want to keep him here?'

'I must. He is *non compos mentis* and may be dangerous. He will be well treated here, and you will be able to visit him.'

To my surprise my father showed some spirit. 'Dr Sutherland, I know you are a famous alienist, but you must respect my feelings as a father. I know my son. He is a dear, affectionate boy and could not possibly be dangerous. If he is ill and needs to be cured the best place for him is at home. I will care for him myself, and if you wish we will return next week to see you again.'

'I would not advise that. For your own safety and for his I beg you to leave him here this afternoon. I cannot force you, but my twenty years' experience tell me that your son is very ill.'

My father took my arm and bustled me out, very red and emotional. In the cab going home he and Osiris spoke in counterpoint:

'Dr Sutherland is used to dealing with ordinary folk. You are a great artist and at times your behaviour is eccentric . . .'

Kill him. He is a devil in disguise and a foolish one.

'We will go together to Cobham, Richard, and you will find peace there.'

Take your knife and gold and passport. After you have killed him we will escape together and return to Egypt.

'We will go on Monday, just the two of us. I will take a few days' holiday. Do you remember how you loved the meadows and the wild flowers when you were a child? We will sit together on the wall near our old house and watch the boats sail by. In your family you will be safe, my son.'

You are not his son. Stab him. Dismember him as my brother Seth dismembered me.

'Richard? Are you listening? You will come, won't you?'

'Yes, Father. We will go to Cobham together, and I will disburthen my mind to you.'

By the time we arrived at Suffolk Street my head was exploding with pain. I stumbled upstairs to bed and slept until late the following morning.

Robert and Stephen had already left, doubtless to go to church or some other respectable occupation. On the other side of the thin wall I could hear my brother George reading aloud to himself from *The Old Curiosity Shop*.

Osiris made me put my passport and spring knife in my jacket pocket. *Take gold*, he said, *for we must travel a long way.*

I had no money, and the obliging dealer around the corner was closed, for it was a Sunday.

Well? There is no freedom without gold. Do you want to stay here and be locked up?

I hunted through the drawers in my bedroom and found two guineas in a leather purse that must have belonged to one of my brothers. I took it, telling myself that I would pay him back when I was rich and famous.

Then I went downstairs and complained to Maria that I had urgent need of money. Without asking any questions she went to the room she shared with Mary Ann and came back with a five-pound note she pressed into my hand. I knew she had been saving for years, and I protested as I pocketed the money. She must have said something to our father, for later that day he smilingly gave me ten pounds he said was a late birthday present.

The money joined my knife and passport in my pocket where my fingers touched them again and again, together with the scarab Ali had given me. It was an amulet with a spell bound upon it from *The Book of the Dead*, and my lover had shown me the inscription: 'Do not stand as a witness against me.'

The day passed in a haze. My mind rushed ahead to the morrow, and I scarcely heard or saw the family hubbub around me. They all seemed far away, grey and small, their voices fainter than the Sunday bells.

We caught the steamer to Gravesend the following day. My father wanted to visit relations in Chatham and meet up with my brother Stephen, who was in Rochester to watch the military manœuvres that we boys used to get so excited about. But I could not face people and insisted that we should go straight to Cobham.

We found a carter to take us, and as we bumped along the country lanes my senses returned. I exalted in the subtle greens, each tree and blade of glass a different shade, in the intense blue of the August sky and the jewel colours and delicate perfumes of the wild flowers. Unfortunately my hearing returned with my other senses, and interwoven with the birds and the hum of insects I heard the drone of my father's voice. He appeared to think that looking after me meant repeating the obvious *ad nauseum*.

Then he began to tell me that he had been studying ancient Egyptian religion. As always his voice possessed his new subject, complacent as a stamp in an album. 'And, of course, Osiris and Christ have much in common. What is the cross but the tree of life where Osiris was imprisoned? Both were brutally murdered but rose again to judge the dead. How many similarities there are in all these myths: Dionysus, Adonis, Mithras, too. I mean to prepare a lecture on the universality of religion . . .'

I tried to warn him. Of course, Osiris was offended and roared at me, *Who is this idiot who pretends to be your father? He has blasphemed, and he must die. Chop him up into pieces, as my brother Seth hacked me to death. Then he will know the truth of religion.*

We arrived in Cobham at about six.

'And there is Cobham Hall where Sir Harley was so kind to you. Do you remember, Richard? I wonder if he's still alive. The dear old Ship! We will stay there tonight, and tomorrow morning we'll go for a long walk and perhaps call on Sir Harley. He's a considerable personage and may still be of use to you. As soon as you're better we must plan your future. I've always known you will be a great man.'

John at the Ship greeted us as old friends and found a tiny room my father and I could share, for the inn was crowded with summer visitors. Although John smiled and fussed over us I could not stop thinking that he been Sir Harley's pimp, introducing me like a fly to a spider. The humiliation of those years when I was Sir Harley's spittoon and George was mine came flowing back as I watched John's yellow teeth and thick lips mouth pleasantries.

'You was quite a favourite of his, wasn't you, Richard? Poor old gent. The New Earl didn't care for him, and I heard he died a pauper in a cottage over by Rochester.'

I suppressed my joy and glared suspiciously back at the beamish old man. Did he know what Sir Harley was doing to me? Did all the servants know, and did my father collude with them?

We were served supper – I don't remember what we ate – I had no appetite from dreading the night I must spend with my father.

'You are tired, Richard. We will go straight to bed.'

'No. I want to walk.'

'But it will soon be dark! In the morning we will walk for miles if you like.'

'No. I want to go now.' I stood up, gasping for breath.

The walls of the little parlour were dissolving and through them I could see Osiris, Isis and their priests preparing an altar for a great sacrifice. I rushed outside and stood in the lane, staring up at the darkening trees that creaked and swayed and rustled.

My father might have gone to bed then. How often have I thought that over the years. Instead, he followed me outside and insisted on accompanying me on my walk.

Apart from a few pisspots at the Ship and the Leather Bottle the country folk were all in bed and the road to Cobham Hall was silent.

'Where are we going? It's late to walk alone in the country, my boy.'

He could not see the procession that marched ahead of us. Fairies poured out of the hedgerows, giggling and singing in their high, sweet voices. They waved up at me and smiled, and some swarmed up my legs to my shoulders where they pulled my hair and whispered in my ear, *You've come back. Stay with us now. Put us in your pockets. We want to go to Egypt, too.*

'Richard, let's turn back now. It's so dark and we are both tired.' My father looked up at me with weak, tired eyes.

I walked on in silence, following the procession, and he followed me through the little side gate into Cobham Park. We came to a chalk pit called the Paddock Hole where we used to go blackberrying. Osiris and Isis told the priests to lay down their sacrificial altar in front of us. The priests chanted their incantation, and there was wild singing from the fairies as they all looked at me and waited.

'What a desolate spot. I want my bed, Richard.'

'You shall have it.'

'I need to piss.' My father's face was white and flabby as he looked up at me then turned away to unbutton himself. It reminded me of

Sir Harley getting ready to sodomize me. At that moment the setting sun flashed through the trees and the pyramid of the mausoleum I used to flee to shone like gold. *He is the first of your demons*, Osiris said. *You must kill them all.*

I touched the friendly weight in my pocket, pressed the button and brought out my beautiful knife. It kissed my father's throat as I put my other hand over his mouth and pushed him backwards on to the altar.

He looked at me in astonishment, and there was hot stickiness all over my hands. Osiris and my fairies disappeared with their altar, and I was alone, slashing wildly at the heavy lump that had been my father. The Radiant Ones had disappeared, and I did not feel like an avenging god but like an incompetent butcher.

There was enough light to see that I had only one father now. I fled over the stile to the road.

16
DANCING UPON
NOTHING

'Mr Dadd? Are you awake?'

I am not sure. Through my eyelashes I stare at McDonald, my cubicle and the rectangle framing trees and blue sky: the world. 'I've brought you some food, Mr Dadd. You've not eaten since I found you yesterday morning collapsed on the floor near your easel.'

As soon as he leaves I attack the mutton stew and hunk of bread on the tin tray. My jaws chomp and gobble, but when I have licked the last crumb from my fingers my ears are shocked by the silence. I am alone; my head is an empty stage. Osiris and my father no longer command me, and my fairies have also withdrawn. I hold my breath and wait for them to come back to me. Dispossessed, I am lonely.

From the window of my tiny cubicle I stare down at the gardens where Dr Hood's boys are playing, at the walls and the road beyond which London sprouts. I have not left this hospital for thirteen summers and may never leave it again. Mrs Sanderson is out there somewhere, my brothers and sisters are still alive, I have nieces and nephews I've never met. Frith and Egg have stolen my career. All these people are conversations I am waiting to have.

If the voices were my illness their silence is my cure. If I am not ill I should not be here. I am like a living man accidentally buried alive. The McNaughton Rule – he is always boasting about having a law named after him, but what does it mean exactly? I can hardly understand McNaughton's Glaswegian patois, and he himself seems none too sure of the law he has inspired. If I confess to Dr Hood that my voices have left me I may become responsible for my father's murder. All these years I have told them that I did not do it, that I do not remember. With memory comes guilt and responsibility.

To go from this hospital to prison is no progress, as the cunning bastards in the criminal wing used to tell me when the attendants weren't listening. Both Oxford and McNaughton were in Newgate until they were transferred here, to Dr Hood's golden bank. They've told me all about that hell-above-ground where the prisoners have to wear leg-irons and live in solitary confinement in unheated cells except when worshipping or working. They've told me about the coarse food, the dress of shame and the hard labour: beating hemp, pulling oakum, pounding bricks and the mindless treadwheel. Ten hours a day. Slavery was abolished twenty years back but not for criminals. No use for me to argue that I want to paint and don't want to worship the upstart Christian god. Oxford has told me how criminal lunatics become the sport of the idle and the depraved and how the authorities have no control over prisoners after locking-up time.

And if I do not save my neck? I watched a public execution once. Rolling home after a night drinking and swaggering with The Clique, I saw a crowd gathering outside Newgate. There was a carnival atmosphere. I was in a jolly mood and did not feel like sleep, so I stayed. They said a murderer was to swing, that he had strangled his wife and children and hidden their bodies in his cellar. It was the rats that betrayed him, swarming down to feed on dead flesh.

That night I never thought for a moment that he was a human being who was to be pitied. He was a monster, and we all felt better for hating him. I got out my sketchbook and began to draw the scene.

There were over a hundred callous gawping faces around me, come to enjoy the spectacle. 'S'help me, ain't it fine?' said a blowsa-bella in front of me as she clung to the arm of her bully boy. There were not many women in the crowd. Most of them were fast young men – labourers, card-sharpers, dock-workmen, gamblers and thieves who knew they were lucky to escape the gallows themselves; half drunk, laughing and quarrelling, they were the rakings of cheap singing halls and billiard rooms.

We all pushed to get a good view. Some West End aristocrats, young men in evening dress, drove up in fine carriages, drunk on wine rather than gin, and offered twenty-five pounds to rent a first-floor front opposite the gallows. Giggling, they rushed upstairs and stood at the window, squealing with excitement. There was a preacher in the crowd, droning on about brimstone and sin. Then he started to sing a hymn, 'The Promised Land': 'Oh, my! Think I've got to die.' A few people joined in and a rival group sang 'Over the Hills and Far Away'.

The summer dawn came early and with it rain. We did not go home but turned up our eager faces as if we were waiting for Grimaldi to entertain us. The crowd swelled. There must have been a thousand of us as women came around selling trays of hot gingerbread and spiced ale. When the hangman appeared the crowd heaved and struggled to get nearer.

At the moment of death we were all quiet for a moment. I was near enough to the gallows to see the last vibrations of the body as he danced upon nothing, and I drew it all calmly, thinking it would make a sellable picture, a cautionary tale.

I felt a child's hand in my pocket and slapped it away. Just ahead of me two men, drunk as emperors, were fighting, and as soon as the hangman left a crowd surrounded the corpse, laughing and swearing. A young woman jumped up on to the platform to kiss him passionately, rubbing herself against the still warm cadaver. Then her lover passed her a knife and she cut off the dead man's prick, waving it triumphantly at the guffawing mob. A gang of Resurrection men moved in to protect their corpse, for damaged goods are less sellable. They say public executions deter crime.

I'll make sure they bring me a slap-up last meal in my cell. Clear turtle soup, the real thing, not mock turtle. Then I'll have turbot with lobster sauce followed by a haunch of mutton cooked with rosemary. Roast potatoes, carrots and peas. A roast partridge with chestnut stuffing, the skin crisp and brown but not greasy. A Queen Mab pudding and a strawberry ice. I'll have it all served on white china, with a clean blue linen tablecloth and napkins, and I'll wash it down with a good claret and perhaps a sweet wine to go with my pudding.

I don't think I shall make a speech. There will be a huge crowd, for it's not every day they hang a parricide. They'll be jeering and howling and throwing rotten eggs and tomatoes at me. When I come out of the dark prison and step up on to the platform there'll be a dazzling moment when I see it all for the last time, all that beauty, for even the most brutal crowd has beauty in it. There'll be a girl with a pretty face staring up at me, some red geraniums in a window box, a sparrow flying against the dawn sky. The hangman will nod at me before he puts his hood on, quite genial, for he is only doing his job. I'll give him a sovereign to get it over with quickly.

Who will come to watch? The mob, of course, and my family, if they're not too ashamed: faithful Maria and stern Mary Ann who often said I'd come to a bad end; Robert, the sensible Dadd, and Stephen, who wanted to be like him but showed dangerous imaginative tendencies; George, if he is given a day's release, will not lift his head from *The Old Curiosity Shop*; and my two half-brothers will not come, for they have fled the family curse to set up shop in Milwaukee. Frith and Egg will sketch me, of course, and I will have an afterlife at the Royal Academy Summer Show. Dr Hood and Neville will have to be there, to certify my sanity as they have watched over my madness. I hope Haydon comes. I'd like his face to be the last I see.

As for those others who have lived in my head for so many years, I wonder where they will go when my neck breaks and their residence lolls on to my shoulder. Perhaps they will spew out of my mouth like painted medieval demons. If I'm sold for dissection Osiris will watch with interest as medical students do to me what his brother Seth did to him. My fairies, led by Oberon and Titania, will have to find a new imagination to colonize, and my father will look down on this last act of his son's brilliant career.

And afterwards? After his resurrection Osiris became King of the Underworld. How often have I dreaded his judgement. He will weigh my heart against the feather of truth. Pure souls pass onwards to immortality, but my heart is as heavy as lead, so I will be sent down to Amemit the Devourer, who has the head of a crocodile, the body of a hippopotamus and the hind legs of a lioness. I will be swallowed by him to be reborn in a different body.

17
LONDON

Oh my! Don't want to die.

Silence. My voices ignore me. I've come to depend on them as a prisoner may come to need fleas or lice for company. Time is behaving oddly now that I've lost my working routine.

It's dark again, the night punctuated by the noisy sleeping habits of my fellow inmates. Denied life, we live vigorously in our sleep, bellowing and snorting and screaming and gasping and howling, panting with love in passionate dreams, hoping to pump our sugar sticks in peace before we are spotted.

I want to get out of here. How did Mrs Sanderson escape?

I take out her portfolio of drawings from under my bed, lay them on the floor and make myself open my deepest eyes. There are so many ways of looking, and most of the time we are half blind.

When I was young and saw my first drawings and paintings by Rubens and Salvatore Rosa at Cobham Hall I entered them with my whole mind, body and soul. First, I lived the story, becoming a nymph, god or satyr. I could smell the perfume of a voluptuous woman and feel the spray of a waterfall, taste the food on the golden platters, feel my legs ache from climbing romantic mountains. Then I searched each figure and detail of the landscape to see how it was done, this magic of colour and form. I felt sick with excitement to think that I, alone with a brush, might learn how to conjure a blank canvas into a glowing world.

Later my eyes and mind closed as drawing and painting became a painful exercise, a daily battle I could never win. On my travels with Sir T. there were moments when I was able to pour myself into a painting, landscape or ruin. Perhaps it was at those moments that my illness began. There is an invisible frontier between intensity and madness, and I have never been sure when I was crossing it.

Now I sit on the floor of my cubicle and sharpen my eyes as I might sharpen a pencil. There is power in those drawings that I need to harness. Although they're not great art they do have energy and strangeness. Mrs Sanderson told Dr Hood that her drawings represent a future London she has visited, a city of glorious progress and heavenly visions. Hungrily I stare at them.

I concentrate on a drawing of high towers looming over small, almost naked people. Not fairies but earthy urban creatures walking with eyes downcast among curious machines and overgrown buildings. There are no horses or trees, and the sky is blotted out by the monstrous towers.

As I stare, I hear a roar and see expressions on the tiny faces. Anger, loneliness and worry are reflected there, and I think of Blake's poem: 'And mark in every face I meet, / Marks of weakness, marks of woe.' The roar becomes an ocean of sounds I cannot identify, and a face comes nearer, swells to life size as I stare into a pale mask, dark eyes with spiky eyelashes and a sullen red mouth. I am standing beside the mask, and it or she is angry with me.

'Sod off! Can't you see I'm trying to get to work?'

Backing away, I am nearly trampled by a marching army of men and women. They do not look at me or at each other but hurry to mysterious appointments. I envy their sense of purpose, for I have none and feel overwhelmed by the hard grey street and the wide road seething with horseless carriages. Ahead of me a brave man steps into the torrent and darts across to the pavement on the other side where another stream of people tramp forward with ruthless determination.

I skulk in a doorway and look inside the building. Through a kind of veil I can see the faint outline of M4, my cubicle, Neville coming towards me. For a confused moment I take a step towards him then remember I have chosen freedom.

I force myself back to the street, where a horrible mechanical scream bears down on me. As I leap out of its way the traffic stops and parts to allow the wailing vehicle to rush through. Too much speed, too much noise. I turn back to the familiar shape of M4, but it is no longer there.

People are rushing past me to enter a vast marble lobby full of plants and fountains and crystal boxes that move up and down. It is like a cross between a conservatory and a cathedral, but there is no peace in its angry geometry or in the hard faces of the people bustling here. The women balance on sharp daggers and wear very short skirts that expose their legs like ballet girls. Staring at the forest of limbs I try to comprehend the rhythm of their dance. The men wear grey suits; most of them are clean-shaven, and both men and women are enormously tall, a race of giants. They carry large bags, and I wonder if there are weapons in them to account for their military haste and brusqueness.

'Can I help you?'

The question is not helpful but barked at me by a young female sitting at a long marble desk. I stare at her enamelled face and down at the endless golden legs folded behind her desk. She sees my gaze and shifts her position angrily.

'Have you got an appointment?'

'For what?'

'There are ten companies in this building. Who do you want to see?'

'I only want to see – this place. All the people – the legs – such tall buildings, and all of you so tall. Very strange. Do your legs not feel cold?'

It's the wrong answer. She presses a bell and a huge man in dark uniform appears.

'Having problems, love?'

'He's a perv. Got a thing about legs. Creepy guy.'

'I'm going to have to escort you to the door, sir.'

'But there is no need. I can walk.'

He grips my arm painfully and almost lifts me to the glass door, which glides open as if unseen elves are conspiring with this uniformed bully.

On the crowded pavement I walk swiftly away, watched by the giant, and turn a corner. When I feel sure I am out of his sight I stop and lean against a lamp-post, tired and hungry and confused. It would be a great comfort to see Neville approach with a plate of bread and cheese and his kind smile.

If this is Mrs Sanderson's magnificent future I feel ashamed of my unhappiness here. To be miserable in Utopia is indeed a sign of lunacy. I stare into faces coming towards me in the hope of asking a friendly stranger if this really is London and, if so, when; but nobody is friendly, nobody even looks back at me – in fact, they avoid my gaze. I catch the eye of a thin young man in a suit so sharp that it looks as if it has been cut out of grey cardboard. He glances at me, then, as he looks away, presses a coin into my hand muttering, 'Get a job.'

Before I can reply he has disappeared, half running like the others. They are all hurrying to reach some magnificent party to which I have not been invited. It seems that I no longer exist. I have no memory of my death and can hope only that it was painless and not too sentimental. I might be said to have died already, at the age of twenty-six, so I have some experience of being a corpse. If this is my afterlife I have done nothing to earn a place in any heaven, pagan or Christian. So this must be the underworld, and since I am to spend eternity here I had better explore it well. This is, after all, my final grand tour.

They have done away with fiery pits, brimstone and pitchforks. The streets I wander down are clean, there is no mud or filth underfoot and the air is clear of fog. No children play on these streets. There are no horses or caterwauling pedlars or costermongers. I don't see any rookeries or squalid alleyways – life itself seems to have been washed away. There's no weather, I can't tell what season it is, for it is neither cold nor hot and I don't pass any trees or grass. Grey has swallowed up other colours. When I see a woman in a red jacket I smile at her gratefully, but she looks alarmed and crosses over to the opposite pavement.

If I dared to speak I would tell her I admire her bright-red jacket and tight black trousers, so much more attractive than a crinoline, which makes a woman look like an egg-timer and prevents her from moving freely. After so many years without seeing women at all it is strange to see so many. These women stride around and some even run, wearing their underwear. Or was that a boy? I have always found the gulf between the sexes confusing, and if it has been bridged I would like to talk about it.

But these people don't talk – or not to each other. They hold long conversations with themselves; almost every person I pass is speaking into a small box. One or two speak English, but I also hear snatches of French, Italian, Arabic and other languages. Dr Hood would consider this alarming behaviour, the social equivalent of onanism. When I try to catch their eye in the hope of starting a dialogue they glare at me or flee.

I recognize enough place-names to know that I am in London: Moorgate, Mansion House, Cheapside. When I was a boy all those names had an aura of romance. They were going to be part of my kingdom when I conquered London with my dazzling talent. The Old Lady of Threadneedle Street still stands, surrounded by a wall like a great fortress. Since I fell out of the world everything has changed. Looking up at the skyline of cliff-like towers I spot the maternal breast of St Paul's dome and walk towards it.

I have never been so pleased to see a church. I am exhausted, I must sit down, even if I have to endure a tedious religious service. Wren's cathedral was black last time I met her, but now she is pale grey, almost white, a whitened sepulchre. Puffing, I climb the steps and join a queue of exotic-looking people waiting to enter.

'Do you want to buy a ticket, sir?'

'I want to sit down to rest and think.'

'That will be fifteen pounds, sir.'

I hand him the coin the sharp young man gave me.

'You need another fourteen pounds. We accept credit cards.'

I gape at him.

'Do you speak English, sir?'

'Not any more.'

I stumble out and sit on the steps, which appear to be free of charge. Below me is traffic, more enormous buildings and then a shining river. It must be the Thames, and I am glad to see it. When I feel stronger I will follow it and see where it leads me. Water is always comforting.

There are other people sitting on these steps, foreigners – everyone is a foreigner now. In front of me two young men share a drink with a straw in it, exchanging caresses and kisses. I watch, fascinated, as one of them, who has skin as brown as Ali's, nuzzles and kisses the pink hand of his fair companion. They are beautiful, shameless, and nobody except me is staring at them. They eat something malodorous out of a paper bag and then jump up, leaving the bag and the drink they have shared on the steps. They walk off hand in hand. My heart soars as I watch them and will them to be happy together.

Then I pick up the remains of their strange meal and finish it. The drink is gassy and the contents of the paper bag are greasy and over-seasoned, but I am too hungry to be critical. Revived, I go down to the pavement and stand in front of the terrifying stream of vehicles. Each road is an ordeal, but I have discovered that if I attach myself to other people I can cross safely. So I find a group of school-children with a young woman playing sheepdog. She is far too lenient with her little charges, who are untidily dressed and who chatter and squawk and giggle.

The traffic stops, and the children cross the road. Just as I am about to follow a hideous wailing bears down on me. A vehicle swoops past, insanely fast, lights flashing. At the same time there is a clattering above my head, and I see a vast mechanical bird rattling in the sky. I feel assaulted and cover my ears with my hands, closing my eyes in terror.

Eventually I do cross the road, shadowing a group of men and women in garish clothes. Different languages, races and sexes mingle freely, and I begin to enjoy the strangeness of it. Perhaps the Indian Mutiny succeeded and has been followed by mutinies of Africans and women. I do hope so.

Shallow steps take me down to the Thames where a slender footbridge allows me a breathtaking view. I stand there for a long time until my eyes adjust to the shocking newness and I am able to see beauty.

The river has been tamed and narrowed; it slices through the city like a canal. The water no longer stinks; it has become clean and silvery, and although it is low tide there are no mudlarks on the beach. There are few ships, the forest of masts has disappeared and so has the coarse foul-mouthed drama of sailors, dockers and watermen I used to love to watch. On both sides of the river the city has shed its slums and black factories and sprouted enormous palaces. It is exciting to see so many powerful buildings fighting for space in the sky: a million windows dazzlingly reflect the watery sun, and I savour a banquet of unexpected shapes. Here and there a spire greets me from the older city, and just beyond the bridge there is a black-and-white Tudor building. Over to my left a vast, slender pyramid plunges up into the clouds, and on my right a huge wheel slowly turns.

I could stand here for hours, watching and drawing. Perhaps my coin is enough to buy a sketchpad and pencil – but I'm afraid of going into a shop, afraid of feeling a fool again. Silent as a ghost, I inhale the future until it goes to my head and changes my thoughts.

These are the soaring towers and bizarre monuments of Mrs Sanderson's drawings. Dr Hood told me she insisted she had seen a future London where poverty and suffering had been abolished. Now I wish I had found a way of speaking to her, secretly in the gardens or through the benign intervention of the doctors or Haydon – no, better not think of him and of my life in that hospital. I must not miss captivity. I must enjoy my freedom, else I am a slave.

The crowds on the bridge are brightly dressed and seem to be in a holiday mood. They sweep me over to the south side where there is a wide paved area in front of an enormous building that has great chimneys like a factory. People spew in and out of it. I long to join them and see what attracts such multitudes, but I stay outside. Always outside.

Cold and tired and hungry, I sit on a bench. I would like to sleep but am afraid of what might happen if I shut my eyes. Dreams, nightmares, conjuring tricks with time. There is music on the air. The singer is a young woman who accompanies herself on an accordion.

The words are in French. It is a melancholy song, and the young woman is attractive, painfully thin and half naked in a camisole and tight blue trousers. People throw coins into the hat in front of her, and she looks cheerful and happy. If I had a violin I could stand there and play a jig or a Kentish folk song to earn a meal. My eyes stay on the young woman, who looks like a boy and like herself.

Some revolution has occurred in relations between men and women. Couples drift past me, laughing, arm in arm and hand in hand. An elderly man and woman stop and kiss passionately just in front of me. The French song makes me think for a moment that I'm in Paris, which was always scandalously amorous. But, no, this is London, and prim young misses have gone the way of the dodo. Men with men, women with women, men with women; what a wonderful time I could have here if I existed.

A young woman sits beside me on the bench, and I study her furtively. She has short dark hair framing a sallow face and wears a tight black jacket with a short skirt. I try not to stare at her legs. She takes a large box out of a bag, opens it and starts playing it as if it was a piano. No noise comes out, but curious moving images appear on a glass shelf. When she sees me looking at it she edges away until she sits at the outer edge of the bench, frowning at her instrument.

'My dear young lady, please don't be afraid.'

She looks terrified, packs up her instrument in her bag and gets up to leave.

'No, please stay. May I ask you a question?'

'What?' she asks angrily.

'I would like to know the name of that strange instrument you were playing.'

'Do you mean my laptop?'

'Is that what it's called? Why does it make no sound?'

'Because I've turned the volume down, stupid. If you want noise I could press this,' She indicates a small object in her hand.

'Is it a penny whistle?'

'No, it's a rape alarm.'

She glares at me and strides off. Failed again. Condemned to loneliness, I reason that my clothes are odd – yet everybody here is strangely dressed. Perhaps I smell unpleasant and have not shaken off the noisome aura of Bedlam.

When a dark-skinned man sits on the bench beside me I do not dare to speak to him although I long to. He eats something out of a paper bag and produces a drink in a cardboard cup with a straw. Halfway through his hurried picnic he rushes away, leaving his half-eaten debris. A seagull hovers greedily, but I outwit the bird and gorge myself on soft bread and tepid meat with long, soggy, greasy objects washed down by a sugary drink. Osiris is not here to tell me it might be poisoned, and I feel better for the food, whatever it is. Manna from Hell. It is hard to be an outcast. I have known men who were driven mad by the silent system in our prisons.

Along the river I walk past glassy palaces and restaurants where people wallow in their fleshpots, eating and drinking on tables and chairs outside. There is no traffic here, only the surging multitude. The mocking cackle of seagulls and the rattle clatter of flying machines are almost the only sounds. I pass a few musicians playing for money, and there are many beggars. Although I'm too proud to join them I become adept at scrounging leftovers: a buttered roll and the dregs of a glass of wine on an abandoned restaurant table; a piece of cake on a bench by the river; a mouthful of beer and a packet of salty biscuits left outside a public house. A hungry ghost, I need fuel.

Far ahead, on the other side of the river, I can see elegant towers floating above the ruthless geometry of roofs. They must be medieval, but I can't place them. They become my goal as I cross another bridge and find myself in streets again, pushing through indifferent crowds towards my fairy citadel. The river is on my left now, and I pause frequently to stare at it as a child might hold his nurse's hand for reassurance – still my Thames, the one that flowed to Gravesend and carried me home long ago.

Westminster Bridge. Not a fairy castle at all but the reactionary sham cathedral that cost the nation two million and destroyed Barry and Pugin. How we used to argue over it when we were students. I was warm for classicism and the pure lines of revolution, while the others were all for Gothic conservatism and religion. Having seen Westminster burn down, I always felt possessive about the place and longed to have a hand in rebuilding it.

A policeman eyes me suspiciously as I stare up at the over-decorated walls and wonder what is inside. Not my dragon. My hundred-pound prize was won by that bounder Frost with *Una and the Satyrs*, an excuse for venal politicians to ogle naked women. My *St George* was far superior, and winning that competition would have saved my life – my father's life. I cross the road to avoid the policeman and stand by the remains of the Jewel Tower, still gazing upwards.

Haydon went to the opening of the new Palace of Westminster and told me all about it, in the days when I was still in the dungeons of the criminal block and had to be smuggled up to his room down the secret tunnel. Before he and Hood rescued me and elevated me to M4, I thought Haydon's room a sanctuary. All books and pictures and leather armchairs and muffins and firelight. His dear face alive with intelligence and humour as he described the scene.

'Such pageantry and grandiosity! Those pompous old men in their ermine and velvet, spouting their humbug patriotism. Crystal coaches and trumpets. Her Majesty was there, of course, having knighted Barry to make up for his twenty-five years of frustration. The poor fellow must be in his fifties now but looks a hundred, monosyllabic and gloomy, worn out by years of Select Committees, members' endless complaints, rows over hideous ventilating shafts, the masons' strike . . . his problems are still not over. There's a ludicrously tall clock tower with a useless cracked bell nobody can mend.

'Barry and I reminisced about Pugin. A papist fanatic, we agreed, but a brilliant man. Dead now at forty after a spell of our Bedlam hospitality. How English philistines detest artists and love to make them suffer.'

I hoped I was included in his compassion for artists. As usual I was reduced to silent idiocy in his presence, but I knew that I would think of witty and amusing things to say to him later when I returned to my oubliette. Yet, as it turned out, I was not forgotten there: a few years later Hood fought, argued, wrote letters and endured death by committee to raise me from inferno to the *purgatorio* of M4.

I gaze at the other side of the river – where Hood and my beloved are or were – and shake my head to clear the muddle. The clock in the tower strikes three, a deep, rich tone. It has been mended, but the crack in my head is still here.

I turn away from the Surrey side, for I must not think of beautiful George. Walking is the best medicine. I've walked further today than for the past fourteen years, and my legs feel like macaroni, but I force them westwards.

Barefoot children, fishing boats, swamps and barges have all been tidied away. The Thames flows tamely on my left beneath a dull wall, and to my right the monstrous traffic roars. I never knew this part of London well. I think I'm going towards Millbank Penitentiary. There are tall buildings on the other side of the road, too tall. I have a headache and will be glad to see the gardens and meadows of Chelsea.

A couple walk ahead of me, their happiness enclosing them like an embroidered tent. If I stink of Bedlam they stink of love. They are about thirty, I suppose, young enough to make me feel old. They walk with their arms around each other, pausing every few steps to talk or laugh or kiss. Such joy is indecent; they make me feel ugly and lonely and miserable. Yet I can't take my eyes off them, stopping whenever they stop. I don't want to overtake them because then I will lose sight of the terrible fact that such love is possible.

The man is quite tall, with brown hair and thin, ordinary features. The profile I glimpse gives no indication of why he should be so blessed. He wears a brown jacket and the usual tight blue trousers. At first all I can see of the young woman is a mass of dark wavy hair that looks as if it has a life of its own. Watery sunshine brings out black, blue and reddish lights. He strokes it during a particularly long kiss, and when he removes his hand the thick hair springs back like undergrowth. A few steps later she turns to him suddenly, and I see her nose and mouth, which make me gasp.

Uncertain, not trusting my senses on this day that has demanded so much of them, I pass the couple and sit on a bench just beyond them. As they approach I stare at them intently. It doesn't matter what I do, for they are tightly sealed in their private universe. I see her full face, and then I am quite sure, for I never forget a face I have studied, and during our one silent meeting I scorched her beauty into my eyes.

Mrs Sanderson and her lover cross the busy road, dart up wide steps and disappear inside an enormous building.

At once I feel abandoned and wish I had spoken to her. I must follow her. I wait for a gap in the monstrous vehicles. They move so fast and so ruthlessly, I know now how a rabbit feels when it strays into a town. An old, moth-eaten, nervous rabbit.

At last there is a clear space, and I charge across, arriving on the other side with beating heart. I have to sit on the steps to recover my strength. There are other people sitting there, I wonder if it's a cathedral like St Paul's and I will have to pay to enter. Dizziness sweeps over me as I grip the step beneath me. I need to lie down in my peaceful cubicle and be brought mutton stew and a glass of ale by Neville. From where I am sitting I can see across the grey river to the Surrey side, which has also been narrowed and cleaned and snubs me.

If I could talk to Mrs Sanderson she would understand; she is the only person in this harsh city I could tell my story to. My anxiety to find her drives me inside the building.

In front of me a young woman sits at a desk. Her legs are hidden, so I can't offend her by staring at them, and she is looking down. An absent-minded Cerberus. I walk towards her, fingering the coin in my pocket in case she demands payment. To my surprise she smiles at me courteously and allows me to go on.

I am in a palace devoted to art. It is much bigger than the old National Gallery where I studied, and there are more walls than pictures and sculptures; a very curious way of hanging which seems to me a great waste of space. Each painting rules over a large patch of wall in splendid isolation from its fellows. I pass many works which are neither beautiful nor useful but which are, presumably, considered to be art.

There are not many people here, and at first I am confident that I will find Mrs Sanderson and her companion, so I pay less attention to the exhibits than I ought, chasing after my fellow ghost. I pass a restaurant where a meal costs more than a labourer would earn in a month and an exhibition I am not allowed to see without paying the enormous sum of twelve pounds, surely enough to buy one of the exhibits.

After an hour I fear that Mrs Sanderson must have left the building. Devastated, I collapse on to a bench. I do not know what I expected of her, but to be robbed of the hope of meeting her is a terrible blow. Doubly lost, I sit for some time in despair. Perhaps I fall asleep; my life has become so dream-like that I cannot tell.

Then I sit up and remind myself that I am at least my own man, free to wander in a cultivated place which is warm and offers comfortable seats and free water to drink. It is the best of today's phantasmagorias, and I decide to explore.

The galleries are cold and white as if art has grown sick and needs to be kept in a hospital. Men and women are peering at canvases that are almost blank, they have been primed but are empty of meaning. Yet they stand and look interested, moved, amused. I am missing the point and feel very stupid. The labels tell me nothing, as if language itself has changed.

I charge through the rooms, searching for something, I know not what. On a wall I pass a plan of the building and see there is a Turner wing.

Is it possible that I will at last see that famous private gallery in the sinister house in Queen Ann Street, guarded by a filthy old hag of a housekeeper and a nuisance of tailless cats? Where you had to stand with an umbrella on wet days, watching the rain fall on his peeling, cracked paintings. I longed to visit his gallery but was too shy. They said he had a peep-hole in his painting-room so that he could see and hear what visitors were doing, and he didn't like visits from other artists.

Turner didn't live in his gallery. None of us knew where he lived. They said he kept a mistress and children somewhere. Once Powell, Egg, Phillip and I attempted to follow him home, but he managed to lose us by darting on to an omnibus.

I always thought there would be plenty of time to do everything, yet I have done so little. Haydon told me Turner left thousands of works on canvas and paper.

Suddenly I find myself in a maze of tempests and storms. Blustering winds and surging waves sting my cheeks as I hear old Captain Crumble laughing behind them. I can see him, bow-legged, shabby and grumpy, waving the umbrella that is almost as big as he is. Egg said it concealed a fishing rod, but Phillip said it was a bayonet.

How we all sniggered at his low birth, coarse manners and mis-pronunciation of words. If only Frith was here to be proved wrong in that argument we had when he visited me. Room after room asserts that the old fellow knew what he was doing in his strange, unfashionable paintings. In his leaky studio he carried on making a world that has outlived him and all his critics, and I would like to kiss his filthy hand.

Instead I stand in front of his work and feel connected again. In the presence of my crusty old friend I can breathe more freely. How prolific he was. He puts me to shame.

I turn right into a small room where I meet Blake and Fuseli; their small radiant canvasses confirm my faith in imaginative painting. They were right – I was right! I want to shout my euphoria at the people who sleepwalk into the room, give each painting a bored glance as if it was a cabbage and wander out again.

Then I meet myself.

The Fairy Feller's Master-Stroke . . . Richard Dadd painted this work in the Bethlem Hospital where he was sent after murdering his father and being declared insane . . . shows the 'fairy-feller' poised to split a large chestnut which will be used to construct Queen Mab's new fairy carriage . . .

It is mine and not mine. The painting I have been working on for the last two years as a gift for beautiful George has been finished, but the result is nothing like my original vision. As for the label some idiot has stuck on it, it is nonsense. I must tell them. I must take it away and finish it, for it is all wrong, and I meant it to be my masterwork. Only the best is good enough for him. My eyes are blinded by tears. I can hardly see as I step forward and stare anxiously at the familiar, alien figures. I touch the nipples of my ballet girls – why did I make them so hard? Like bullets. Oberon and Titania are ugly; I meant them to be seductive. I must work on it; it isn't good enough. I take my painting off the wall, but it resists me. A bell sounds.

Suddenly I am surrounded by people, bells, shouting, anger.

'Put that down, sir. Let me take it from you. Gently, now.'

'But it is mine. I am Dadd.'

'You're not allowed to touch the paintings, sir. Please take your hands off it.'

'But I am Dadd! I am Dadd!'

The man in uniform speaks into a box. 'Got a problem here, sir. Room 103. Chap trying to steal a painting . . . *The Fairy Feller's Master-Stroke* . . . Yes, I know, it's always a nutter magnet that one . . . Keeps saying he's my dad . . . Oh, I see . . . No, sir, not violent. Just seems very upset and confused.'

'It is mine!' I shout as he takes my painting away. 'You have stolen it, not I!'

'I'm afraid you're going to have to leave, sir. Don't want to have to call the police. Just come with me quietly now, and we won't press charges.'

I am weeping, shouting nonsense, I can't stop shouting. The man in uniform is unexpectedly strong. He grips my arm. The crowd that has gathered parts to let us through, and I hear insulting voices.

'Needs help, poor chap.'

'What a pong. Must be sleeping rough.'

'You get a lot of loonies in here. Last time I was here there was a bloke thought he was Stubbs, kept galloping around looking for his horses.'

'They should bring back museum charges, then these down-and-outs couldn't get in.'

I am out on the pavement, alone and weeping. Now it is dark, and the weather, which was absent all day, has returned with a vengeance. It is cold and raining hard, the streets are shiny and malevolent with harsh blinding lights and shadowy people running away from me. Wet and cold and hungry, I stumble on. I have no idea where I am going, and it does not matter.

My fingers touch the coin in the pocket of my old brown corduroy jacket. Behind an enormous sheet of glass people are eating and drinking in a brilliant red-and-yellow restaurant. They look poor, eyes downcast, shoulders hunched with failure. Perhaps they will allow me to sit among them.

The doors open as if I am expected, and a gust of warm salty air encloses me. Dizzy with hunger, I go to the counter and hold out my coin. 'What can I buy with this?'

He smiles, and I see that I have made myself ridiculous again. 'You could get a small fries.'

'Give it to me. And to drink?'

'Water's free.'

My banquet comes in cardboard and paper. I take it to a table in the corner and sit alone. The warm greasy stuff fills and comforts me, the water cleans my mouth and clarifies memories. A day of humiliations and disasters, I shut my eyes against them and my head drops to the table.

'We're closing now, guys. Open again at six.'

I am stiff but warm. Perhaps I really am invisible and they will let me sleep here all night.

'Closing time. You have to go now.' Before he throws me out I leave, the last person out of the door before it is locked for the night. The streets are deserted, and it is still raining.

There are figures slumped in doorways asleep under piles of bedding, I am tempted to join them, but it is so cold that I'm afraid I won't wake up again. I have no bedding, no friends, nothing to eat or drink. Nobody going nowhere with nothing. The longest night I've ever known and the loneliest. My clothes and shoes are so wet and heavy that they become a burden I drag around like the shell of a decrepit tortoise.

When a horseless carriage marked POLICE slows down I back away down an alley smelling of piss, sick with fear . . . A woman standing in a doorway asks if I want to come home with her. She has short green spiky hair, blue shadows around her eyes, crimson lips and hat pins embedded in her nose and eyebrows. If she were not so hideous perhaps I would go with her, for her room would be warm and dry and women are less dangerous than men. But she will ask questions, demand money, humiliate me. I flee . . . Three drunks stagger down a street towards me and ask if I want to come to a party. Loud music throbs from an illuminated open window opposite; inside the room up there I can see men and women dancing. There will be food and drink, but I will have to talk, and I couldn't bear that. I shake my head and cross the empty street to avoid them . . . a fox stands in the middle of the pavement, scoffing a parcel of food. It looks up and glares at me with yellow eyes, and I return its enmity for it has stolen my supper.

The city pierces the night with a hard glare that hides the stars, and the tall buildings are going to fall, I don't know when for I have mislaid time. Every clock I pass tells a different hour. The moon would be a comfort, but there is no comfort tonight.

Go home.

Astonished I look around. I can't see him but am pathetically relieved to hear him again. I realize he is the only person I can speak to here. On the deserted street, water dripping down my neck, I hold out my arms to an invisible Egyptian god.

'I don't know where to go.'

He pushes me. I feel his presence behind me like a warm wind. And I a scuttled sailing dinghy that has been nearly broken on the rocks. The rain stops, and the sky lightens over to my left. If that is east, the river must be straight ahead, my river. Water makes sense of things. At Chatham we children were afraid of the hulks silhouetted on the horizon, and I never thought I would live among thieves and murderers.

The sky is splashed with pink and yellow now, benign and hopeful. From Goya's nightmares to Rubens: soft pastel clouds waiting for putti and angels to sit on them. The towers of Westminster are straight ahead, and as I approach the clock tower that killed Barry strikes six. There is traffic already and people on the streets. I cannot tell if they are coming home late or going to work. My legs are so tired, the ache travels from my feet right up to my head.

Somehow I go on and as I cross Westminster Bridge the river resumes its natural shape, spreading out like a woman who has just removed her corset, oozing with black mud and crowded with rowing boats, barges, fishing boats, paddle steamers and schooners. I turn right, so exhausted now that I can no longer see the streets around me.

You must not be late for breakfast, Richard. Punctuality is the politeness of kings. It is my father's old chestnut but not his voice, and I know he will be silent now. Osiris senses victory. As he pushes me forward I feel a click in my aching head. He is adjusting his throne there and will not leave me again.

Fool! Freedom is wasted on you. You are a natural slave.

How glad I am to see Neville coming towards me with a smile. I am shivering and weeping, yet he is pleased to see me. I will finish my painting now, the gift for Haydon, and Hood can have all my other paintings if he will only allow me to stay. As Neville leads me home I hear words in my head, echoing above the voice of Osiris:

> But whether it be or be not so
> You can afford to let this go
> For nought as nothing it explains
> And nothing from nothing nothing gains.

AFTERWORD

The historian Roy Porter – best known for his work on the history of medicine – referred to Richard Dadd as one of the most notorious lunatics of the nineteenth century, and when I was writing this book the most common reaction was a knowing 'Ah, yes, and he murdered his dad!' He did, in August 1843, but this awful pun should not be the last word on his tragic life.

Patricia Allderidge's fascinating book *The Late Richard Dadd* (Tate Publishing, 1974) vividly describes his isolation and stoical determination to carry on working. I felt that curious twitching of my inner antennae that was the sign I wanted to write about him, but I was afraid the task was beyond me because I am not a biographer and because his life, incarcerated in Bedlam and later Broadmoor from the age of twenty-six until he died at sixty-nine, seemed unbearably sad. He was so interesting that I feared he would dominate my novel, and so I made him a minor character in *Nina in Utopia*.

Dadd's work and long imprisonment continued to haunt me. I read everything I could find about him and decided to give him a novel of his own. On one of my visits to the Bethlem Archives I discovered that in 1857 Dr Hood had succeeded in moving Dadd and other 'gentlemen criminal lunatics' from the overcrowded dungeon-like criminal wing to a spacious, airy ward in the main part of the hospital. This improvement in his conditions seems to have coincided with Dadd's best work, and I decided to focus on this.

A wonderful early photograph shows Dadd at this time, sitting in front of his easel where the unfinished oval of *Contradiction: Oberon and Titania* sits, waiting for the brush he holds to continue to bring it to life. He stares at the camera, at us, with recognition and warmth, looking more like an artist in his studio than a prisoner in his cell. Those clear eyes have not been incarcerated or institutionalized. He is a man of about forty with longish hair, a wide forehead and a greying beard. Instead of a uniform he wears a velvet or corduroy painting suit and a rather elegant shirt with a frill at the front. This photograph has helped me through many days when I found it difficult and painful to write about madness from his point of view. I have tried to dramatize his hallucinations without using psychological jargon, which, of course, did not exist at the time.

My admiration for Richard Dadd, working away year after year all alone, increased as he became more vividly alive for me. Although he was cut off from the art world he must have valued the encouragement of Dr Hood, the steward George Haydon and the head keeper Charles Neville because he entrusted them with his best work. This can be seen as a success story of art therapy *avant la lettre*.

In 21st-century terms, what was the mental illness from which Richard Dadd suffered? We do know quite a lot about his symptoms. It is clear that there was a hereditary predisposition: of seven siblings, Richard, George, Stephen and Maria were all considered mad at the time of their death. Richard's mother died a few days before his seventh birthday, and in the 1850s a doctor at Bedlam wrote that 'at the early age of nine, being under the evil influence of a worthless maidservant, he contracted vicious habits of self-indulgence. An operation was performed but without any apparent benefit.' At that time boys were often circumcised to prevent 'masturbatory insanity'.

When he was twenty-six, as a gifted and promising artist Dadd was employed as a draftsman to accompany the recently knighted solicitor Sir Thomas Phillips on a grand tour of Europe and the Middle East, and his hallucinations and delusions were thought at the time to have been triggered by the excitement, heat and confusion of these travels. Nicholas Tromans in *Richard Dadd: The Artist and the Asylum* (Tate Publishing, 2011) has suggested that another factor might have been 'poisoning from the mercury used in the water-gilding process that took place daily at Suffolk Street' in the framing business run by Richard's father Robert Dadd. On his return to London in 1843 his friends and family thought his behaviour was insane, but his father insisted that he was suffering only from overwork and heatstroke. He took his son to St Luke's Hospital for Lunatics where Dr Alexander Sutherland said Richard must be 'strictly attended to, not being allowed out of sight'. Robert Dadd insisted that he knew his son better than anybody else.

Richard's medical record contains more information. These notes were made by Dr Hood in 1854, by which time Dadd had been an inmate of Bedlam for nearly ten years – astonishingly, earlier doctors there did not believe in keeping records:

> For some years after his admission he was considered a violent and dangerous patient for he would jump up and strike a violent blow without any aggravation and then beg pardon for the deed. This arose from some vague idea that filled his mind, and still does so to a certain extent, that certain spirits have the power of possessing a man's body and compelling him to adopt a particular course whether he will or not . . . He is very eccentric and glories that he is not influenced by motives that other men pride themselves in possessing – thus he pays no sort of attention to decency in his acts or words . . . He will gorge himself with food till he actually vomits and then again return to the meal. With all these disgusting points in his conduct he can be a very sensible and agreeable companion, and shew in conversation, a mind once well. Educated and thoroughly informed in all the particulars of his profession in which he still shines . . . he was once in a public place in Rome with the Pope, felt a strong inclination to assault him, but that on second thoughts the Pope was so well protected that he should come off second best, and therefore he overcame the desire. After he killed his father, his rooms were searched and a portfolio was found containing likenesses of many of his friends all with their throats cut.

In his quarterly reports to the Home Office Dr Hood described Dadd as 'dangerous'. Tromans comments: 'So far as we know, the sum total of treatments given Dadd by any psychiatrist (other than, presumably, occasional sedatives) was a course of iced water baths administered at Clermont in 1843.'

In 1887 Dr Emile Kraepelin used the term *dementia praecox* for individuals who had symptoms that we now associate with schizophrenia – a word introduced in 1911 by the Swiss psychiatrist Eugen Bleuler, deriving from the Greek roots *schizo* (split) and *phrene* (mind) and used to describe the fragmented thinking of people with the disorder. I am not qualified to make a posthumous diagnosis of Richard Dadd, but John MacGregor, in *The Discovery of the Art of the Insane* (Princeton University Press, 1993), David Greysmith in *Richard Dadd: The Rock and Castle of Seclusion* (Studio Vista, 1973) and Nicholas Tromans have all concluded that Richard's illness would now be diagnosed as schizophrenia. Dadd probably smoked hashish while he was travelling in the Middle East, and some studies suggest that smoking cannabis can actually trigger schizophrenia earlier in individuals who are predisposed.

Richard Dadd's art, as Nicholas Tromans says, does not 'fit the model of the obsessive pattern – or model-making of so-called Outsider (untutored) art'. Until the murder Richard was an insider, with a sound classical training from the Royal Academy Schools. Much of the work he did during his long confinement is quite conventional and not particularly imaginative, although it is the strangeness of *The Fairy Feller's Master-Stroke* and his other fairy visions that interest us most now. Madness and art cannot really be explained. We are fortunate to have as much work as we do by this remarkable and ill-fated man.

Dr William Charles Hood was one of the great Victorian reformers and deserves to be more famous than he is. When he became Resident Physician and Superintendent of Bethlem in 1852 the Monro dynasty had ruled it, mainly *in absentia*, for 128 years. During that time there had been many allegations of neglect and ill-treatment. Dr Hood lived in the hospital with his wife and family, unlike earlier physicians who had only visited for a few hours a week, abandoning their patients to keepers, many of whom were corrupt and unkind.

Dr Hood made the hospital a far more comfortable place. He removed the bars from the windows, abolished restraint and allowed some patients to go on supervised day trips to Kew Gardens and Crystal Palace. He listened to his patients, sometimes believed their stories rather than the versions he was told by their relations and friends and personally selected the keepers. He observed that the criminal lunatics were kept in cages 'more like those which enclose the fiercer carnivores of the Zoological Gardens than anything we have elsewhere seen employed for the detention of afflicted humanity' and lobbied tirelessly to transfer Dadd, together with about twenty other male criminal lunatics, to the main part of the hospital

In 1857, the year when this novel is set and when, thanks to Hood, Richard Dadd was moved from the grim criminal block to a ward inside the hospital, an article entitled 'The Star of Bethlehem' by Henry Morley in Dickens's magazine *Household Words* describes Hood's transformation of the hospital:

> Within the entrance gates, as we went round the lawn towards the building, glancing aside, we saw several groups of patients quietly sunning themselves in the garden, some playing on a grass-plot with two or three happy little children. We found afterwards that these were the children of the Resident Physician and Superintendent, Dr Hood. They are trusted freely among the patients, and the patients take great pleasure in their presence among them. The sufferers feel that surely they are not cut off from fellowship with man, not objects of a harsh distrust, when even little children come to play with them, and prattle confidently in their ears. There are no chains nor strait waistcoats now in Bethlehem; yet, upon the staircase of a ward occupied by men the greater number of whom would, in the old time, have been beheld by strong-nerved adults with a shudder, there stood a noble little boy, another fragment of the Resident Physician's family, with a bright smile upon his face, who looked like an embodiment of the good spirit that had found its way into the hospital, and chased out all the gloom.

Morley concluded that 'thousands of middle-class homes contain nothing so pretty as a ward in Bedlam' and that 'as to all the small comforts of life, patients in Bethlehem are as much at liberty to make provision for themselves as they would be at home'.

Like another humane and compassionate man, his contemporary Henry Mayhew, Hood had a passion for statistics. He was a man of his time and class and had what we would consider a paternalistic attitude to his asylum and a condescending view of women and 'pauper lunatics'. Immensely hard-working and idealistic, he accomplished a great deal in his short life.

Richard Dadd (1817–1886) was transferred to Broadmoor, together with his fellow criminal lunatics from Bedlam, when it opened in 1864. Richard was in Block 2, which was for privileged patients. He continued to draw, paint and design theatre sets prolifically, but most of his work was lost or destroyed. In 1877 a journalist described him as a 'recluse doing the honour of his modest unpretending abode; a pleasant-visaged old man with a long and flowing snow-white beard, with mild blue eyes that beam benignly through spectacles when in conversation'. When he died of consumption Elizabeth Langley, who had stayed in touch with him all his life, was the only person to be informed of his death.

Charles Neville moved with the patients to Broadmoor as head attendant. His great-grandson gave Dadd's *The Child's Problem* to the Tate in 1955. *Contradiction: Oberon and Titania* was first exhibited in 1930 and *The Fairy Feller's Master-Stroke* in 1935. Robbie Ross, Oscar Wilde's friend and literary executor, was an early admirer of Dadd's work. Somehow *The Flight Out of Egypt* turned up in the picture-framing department of the Army and Navy stores. Sacheverell Sitwell bought it there, and it was purchased by the Tate in 1947. In 1974 the Tate Gallery put on the first exhibition of Dadd's work.

Most of the characters in the novel – including Dadd's relatives – are based on real people. Below is some information about their lives:

> **George Dadd** (1822–1868) remained in Bedlam as an incurable patient for the rest of his life. He died of consumption.

Maria Dadd (1821–1893) married the artist John Phillip, Richard's friend, but suffered a series of breakdowns. After she tried to strangle her youngest child in 1863 she was admitted to an asylum in Aberdeen where she spent the rest of her life. According to her case notes, 'she weaves anything she reads into a delusion, especially if it be anything connected with royalty'.

Mary Ann Dadd (1814–1903) emigrated to the United States at the age of sixty-five, spent ten years in Galveston, Texas, and then went to live with her half-brother John in Milwaukee. When Richard died she wrote: 'I am truly thankful to know him at rest, it is less grief to me than it was to think of him in the changed condition in which he has lived for many years past. His life has been for me a living death.' Neither Mary Ann nor her sister Rebecca ever married.

Robert Dadd (1813–1876) became a chemist and seems to have been remarkably stable. He had a large family, and his grandson, Stephen Gabriel, was a talented young sculptor who died in the First World War together with his brother Edmund. The third brother, Julian, who survived the war but later committed suicide, was a close friend of Siegfried Sassoon, who presented *The Fairy Feller's Master-Stroke* to Tate Britain in memory of Richard Dadd's three great-nephews.

Stephen Dadd (1816–1854) had a private attendant by 1853 and died insane in Manchester, leaving a wife and three children.

William Powell Frith, RA, (1819–1909) had an immensely successful career, although his paintings eventually went out of fashion. His *My Autobiography and Reminiscences* is very entertaining. First published in 1888, it was a great success and went into many editions. In Volume III there is a chapter on Richard Dadd. His best-known paintings are *Ramsgate Sands (Life at the Seaside)* (1854) and *The Derby Day* (1858). In the latter there is a portrait of Richard Dadd wearing a fez.

George Henry Haydon (1822–1891) stayed on as steward at Bedlam until his retirement in 1889. In the 1860s he contributed sketches to *Punch* and had many friends in the art world. In his obituary it was said that he 'made numerous friends and no enemies'.

Dr William Charles Hood (1824–1870) stayed on at Bedlam until 1862. In *Suggestions for the Future Provision of Criminal Lunatics* (1854) he argued against the establishment of Broadmoor to which Dadd and the other criminal lunatics were later transferred in 1864. Hood believed it was healthier to house criminal lunatics with other non-violent lunatics and that the new public institution would become the focus of public fear and hysteria. He was appointed Lord Chancellor's Visitor in Lunacy, advising on the estates of rich people who became mentally ill. In 1868 he was elected Treasurer of Bridewell and Bethlem and was knighted the same year. At the time of his death from pleurisy he owned thirty-three of Dadd's works.

Daniel McNaughton (sometimes spelled M'Naghten) (1813–1865) ran a successful woodturning business before becoming involved in radical politics. Intending to assassinate the Prime Minister, Robert Peel, he mistakenly shot his secretary, Edward Drummond, who later died of the wound. In court McNaughton said, 'The Tories in my native city [Glasgow] have compelled me to do this. They follow, persecute me wherever I go, and have entirely destroyed my peace of mind.' His trial in 1843 was a milestone because it established the McNaughton Rules, making a legal defence of insanity acceptable. Witnesses, including Dr Edward Monro and Sir Alexander Morison, testified that McNaughton's delusions had deprived him of 'all restraint over his actions'. Without this precedent it is possible that Richard Dadd would have been executed for the murder of his father later that same year. McNaughton died in Broadmoor of diabetes and heart problems.

Edward Oxford (1822–1900) was eighteen when he tried to shoot Queen Victoria. He was transferred to Broadmoor with Dadd and the other criminal lunatics in 1864. During his years in hospital he taught himself French, German, Italian, carpentry and house-painting as well as learning to play chess and the violin. He was released in 1878 and went to Australia, changing his name to John Freeman. Haydon paid his fare (£43 18s), an act of extraordinary generosity at a time when his salary was only £350 a year. Oxford married and wrote a book about Melbourne.

SOME AUTHORS WE HAVE PUBLISHED

James Agee • Bella Akhmadulina • Tariq Ali • Kenneth Allsop • Alfred Andersch
Guillaume Apollinaire • Machado de Assis • Miguel Angel Asturias • Duke of Bedford
Oliver Bernard • Thomas Blackburn • Jane Bowles • Paul Bowles • Richard Bradford
Ilse, Countess von Bredow • Lenny Bruce • Finn Carling • Blaise Cendrars • Marc Chagall
Giorgio de Chirico • Uno Chiyo • Hugo Claus • Jean Cocteau • Albert Cohen
Colette • Ithell Colquhoun • Richard Corson • Benedetto Croce • Margaret Crosland
e.e. cummings • Stig Dalager • Salvador Dalí • Osamu Dazai • Anita Desai
Charles Dickens • Bernard Diederich • Fabián Dobles • William Donaldson
Autran Dourado • Yuri Druzhnikov • Lawrence Durrell • Isabelle Eberhardt
Sergei Eisenstein • Shusaku Endo • Erté • Knut Faldbakken • Ida Fink
Wolfgang George Fischer • Nicholas Freeling • Philip Freund • Dennis Friedman
Carlo Emilio Gadda • Rhea Galanaki • Salvador Garmendia • Michel Gauquelin
André Gide • Natalia Ginzburg • Jean Giono • Geoffrey Gorer • William Goyen
Julien Gracq • Sue Grafton • Robert Graves • Angela Green • Julien Green
George Grosz • Barbara Hardy • H.D. • Rayner Heppenstall • David Herbert
Gustaw Herling • Hermann Hesse • Shere Hite • Stewart Home • Abdullah Hussein
King Hussein of Jordan • Ruth Inglis • Grace Ingoldby • Yasushi Inoue
Hans Henny Jahnn • Karl Jaspers • Takeshi Kaiko • Jaan Kaplinski • Anna Kavan
Yasunuri Kawabata • Nikos Kazantzakis • Orhan Kemal • Christer Kihlman
James Kirkup • Paul Klee • James Laughlin • Patricia Laurent • Violette Leduc
Lee Seung-U • Vernon Lee • József Lengyel • Robert Liddell • Francisco García Lorca
Moura Lympany • Dacia Maraini • Marcel Marceau • André Maurois
Henri Michaux • Henry Miller • Miranda Miller • Marga Minco • Yukio Mishima
Quim Monzó • Margaret Morris • Angus Wolfe Murray • Atle Næss • Gérard de Nerval
Anaïs Nin • Yoko Ono • Uri Orlev • Wendy Owen • Arto Paasilinna • Marco Pallis
Oscar Parland • Boris Pasternak • Cesare Pavese • Milorad Pavic • Octavio Paz
Mervyn Peake • Carlos Pedretti • Dame Margery Perham • Graciliano Ramos
Jeremy Reed • Rodrigo Rey Rosa • Joseph Roth • Ken Russell • Marquis de Sade
Cora Sandel • George Santayana • May Sarton • Jean-Paul Sartre
Ferdinand de Saussure • Gerald Scarfe • Albert Schweitzer • George Bernard Shaw
Isaac Bashevis Singer • Patwant Singh • Edith Sitwell • Suzanne St Albans • Stevie Smith
C.P. Snow • Bengt Söderbergh • Vladimir Soloukhin • Natsume Soseki • Muriel Spark
Gertrude Stein • Bram Stoker • August Strindberg • Rabindranath Tagore
Tambimuttu • Elisabeth Russell Taylor • Emma Tennant • Anne Tibble • Roland Topor
Miloš Urban • Anne Valery • Peter Vansittart • José J. Veiga • Tarjei Vesaas
Noel Virtue • Max Weber • Edith Wharton • William Carlos Williams • Phyllis Willmott
G. Peter Winnington • Monique Wittig • A.B. Yehoshua • Marguerite Young
Fakhar Zaman • Alexander Zinoviev • Emile Zola

Peter Owen Publishers
81 Ridge Road, London N8 9NP, UK
+44 (0)20 8350 1775
info@peterowen.com
www.peterowen.com